THE
betrayal

By the same author

The Brotherhood

THE
betrayal
Y. A. ERSKINE

BANTAM

SYDNEY • AUCKLAND • TORONTO • NEW YORK • LONDON

A Bantam book
Published by Random House Australia Pty Ltd
Level 3, 100 Pacific Highway, North Sydney NSW 2060
www.randomhouse.com.au

First published by Bantam in 2012

Addresses for companies within the Random House Group can be found
at www.randomhouse.com.au/offices

National Library of Australia
Cataloguing-in-Publication Entry

Erskine, Y. A.
The betrayal/Y. A. Erskine

ISBN 978 1 74275 018 7 (pbk.)

A823.4

Cover photograph (woman sitting on snowy pier at sunset)
© Jamie Kingham/cultura/Corbis
Cover design by Blue Cork
Internal design by Midland Typesetters, Australia
Typeset in Sabon 11/17 pt by Midland Typesetters, Australia
Printed in Australia by Griffin Press, an accredited ISO AS/NZS
14001:2004 Environmental Management System printer

Random House Australia uses papers that are natural, renewable and
recyclable products and made from wood grown in sustainable forests.
The logging and manufacturing processes are expected to conform to the
environmental regulations of the country of origin.

For Sam

Contents

Prologue
Hobart Police Station
6.37 am Wednesday 13 July

The muster room was oddly silent, devoid of the routine signs of early-morning life: an exhausted night shift crew rushing haphazardly through the last of the paperwork, a harassed day shift sergeant scribbling duties on the whiteboard, the gentle waft of toast, the clanking of teaspoons and a sprinkle of laughter filtering from the kitchen. Instead, there was nothing. The low, comforting hum of the central heating and fluorescent lights was magnified tenfold by the silence. Somewhere down the hall a phone rang out.

Behind her, the doors to the elevator clunked shut as it began the journey back down to the ground floor, the door to the outside world closing.

It will be all right.

1

Her fingers were a ghostly, bluish white from the pre-dawn walk in from where she'd parked her car up at Paternoster Row, but her palms itched with sweat. She wiped them up her trousers, removed the backpack from her aching shoulders and headed for the locker room chanting her well-rehearsed mantras the entire twenty-three steps.

Relax.

It's okay.

You'll be fine.

Stop being silly.

You've done nothing wrong.

You had every right.

She pushed against the swinging locker room door, stepped inside and heaved a sigh of relief. It might have been five degrees cooler and dimly lit with a dodgy, flickering fluoro, somewhat reminiscent of a basement in a horror movie, but it was a sanctuary from the open plains of the muster room, that fearful wilderness where the prospect of social encounters lingered. A minute or two to gather her thoughts. That's all she needed. The chance to take a few deep breaths and pull on her work mask before dealing with the real world.

The mantras continued.

Relax.

You've done nothing wrong.

Her still frozen fingers fumbled in the front pocket of the backpack for her locker keys.

You had every right.

She threw the bag on the floor and turned the lock.

It's going to be okay.

The door creaked open. She stifled a cry, jumped back in horror and stumbled over the backpack, throwing one hand out to stop herself from falling. A razor-sharp pain ripped through her thumb as it caught on the neighbouring locker. But the pain and the ooze of fresh blood were meaningless. For amid the usual jumble of notebook, Cup-a-Soups, muesli bars and folders was a rat. Her heart thundered in her temples.

It was dead.

But not just dead. Dead, she could cope with. Accidentally crawling into her locker and breathing its last shallow breaths among her few tired belongings was perfectly understandable. Gross, but manageable nonetheless. She'd screw up her nose, find a plastic bag, remove the stiff sad little body, scrape out the death throe droppings and perhaps even have a giggle about the whole thing somewhere down the track. *Remember that time I came to work and found a dead rat in my stuff . . . ?*

But not like this.

Ignoring the pain that sliced through the pad of her thumb, she took a cautious step forwards, examining the rat with an unparalleled level of horror. A single strand of red wool had been looped around its neck and pulled tight. The woollen noose had then been strung to a hook attached to the ceiling of the cold, grey locker that had become its coffin. It dangled in a weightless, macabre dance before swinging around to face her. She gasped.

Its eyes were ink black, beady and terrified; its mouth, revoltingly sewn shut, the neat, methodical red-wool stitches like some grotesque smile in the half-light. The fluoro above her flickered and buzzed and with shaky hands she slammed the door shut, took a step backwards and gagged as her throat closed over. A hot chill cascaded from her scalp to the soles of her cold, heavy feet.

The message was unmistakable.

Oh God.

What the hell have I got myself into?

The Complainant

Before she'd even opened her eyes, Lucy Howard knew that something was wrong. *Very* wrong. The split second they fluttered open, gritty and crusty with sleep, simply confirmed it, and she clamped them shut again. She regulated her breathing, willed herself to remain calm and attempted to pinpoint the root of the overwhelming feeling of dread.

Problem number one: the light was wrong. Even with the sunlight streaming through her west-facing window on a midsummer's afternoon, there was never *this* much light in her bedroom, courtesy of the newly installed blackout curtains she'd purchased after her first horrific night shift back in January.

Problem number two: the weighty doona cover was a far cry from her familiar pastel sheets. She didn't own a doona, full stop. Didn't need one. The cosy red-brick family home on

5

Warwick Street was always toasty from the central heating, courtesy of her perpetually freezing mother who had insisted on having the most expensive system installed for the long, icy Hobart winters. Hence, Lucy always slept warm. Even in the dead of winter, when Mount Wellington refused to shrug off her white blanket for weeks at a time, she slept warm under her sheets.

Which brought her to problem number three.

The coarse material of the doona wasn't just covering her. It was kissing her skin. Every centimetre of her skin. And no matter how warm she slept, she *never* slept in the nude. She'd done it once years before and had felt so vulnerable that she'd tossed and turned all night and vowed never to do it again. *Ever.* Even on the handful of occasions she'd slept over at her boyfriend's place she'd always thrown on her undies and one of his old T-shirts before nodding off beside him.

Problem number four: the bed didn't smell right. It wasn't her scent. Nor, for that matter, was it her boyfriend's, the only other bed she was familiar with.

Problem five: her entire body felt somehow wrong, almost like it was composed of concrete. She tried to move her right arm to her face and winced as it refused to budge. She hoped for a second that perhaps she'd just fallen asleep on it and it was nothing more than the weird, weightless yet heavy sensation that preceded the annoying tingle of pins and needles. But if that was the case, she rationalised, why then could she not feel her left arm, or both of her legs for that matter?

An accident perhaps?

She gulped, took another slow, deep breath. That brought her to her head – a huge immovable stone deposited on a pillow. Her temples throbbed and after running her tongue lightly across her dry lips, she swallowed, the action grating her throat.

Was she hung-over?

Had she been drinking?

Oh. She had been drinking.

But . . . enough to be hung-over?

Surely not.

For some reason, she couldn't seem to remember how many she'd had the night before. *Shit.*

Problem number six, and perhaps the worst of them all: with her eyes shut tight, and her breath held, there was the distinct, unmistakable sound of someone breathing beside her. Only one other person had done that in her twenty-two years of life. One lover. But two and a half weeks had passed since she'd woken to *his* breathing and had rolled over to watch his sleep-filled face, smiling to herself, knowing that everything was right with the world. But now . . . it couldn't be him. It wasn't physically possible. Not at the moment.

Oh, dear God . . . what is going on here?

No need to panic. A perfectly rational, logical explanation will present itself the second you open your eyes again and take stock of your surroundings.

Please, God.

Knowing she could no longer avoid the inevitable, she opened one eye first, then the other, searching for the familiar purple Chinese lantern in the middle of the ceiling and cringing at the single, alien bulb. Her familiar rose petal pink walls dotted with laminated, Blu-Tacked prints of her favourite Monets. But *Woman with a Parasol, The Bridge at Argenteuil* and *Water Lilies* had morphed overnight into stark white walls, one featuring a life-sized poster of a shiny, slick, 1970s Arnold Schwarzenegger pulling a bicep curl.

What the hell?

She turned her head slightly to the right, wincing at the effort it took to do so.

And the sight was mortifying.

Not ten centimetres from her face lay the square-jawed, five-o'clock-shadowed slumbering face of Nick Greaves. *Constable* Nick Greaves. Her new friend, the guy she'd met only two weeks earlier on the first day of the Detective Training Course at the Tasmania Police Academy. The course that was supposed to change her life. Make her into a detective. Advance her career prospects. The course she'd been headhunted for, despite her lack of general uniform experience. The one at which she'd felt totally out of her depth.

Until Nick came along.

Nick with his massive shoulders and even bigger laugh. He'd taken up residence at the desk beside her. Made it known that he was looking out for her, sheltering the class junior burger under his wing. Thoughtful, kind, understanding Nick who'd bothered to listen to her bleating on miserably in between lectures about her boyfriend and her anxieties about passing the course. Nick the class clown who'd made it his job to take her mind off her worries with his laughter, his jokes, his covert impressions of the instructors, his piss-taking, his silly antics, his own whispered insecurities and, last night, Friday night, the final night of the course . . . a DVD and a bottle of Bundy.

At his place.

I've just bought the place and I haven't had anyone over yet. Consider it a mini house-warming as well as an end-of-course celebration. I'm formally prescribing a night of frivolity to cheer you up. Come on.

His words echoed in her mind.

Oh no.

Oh no.

Oh, please, God, no.

She gulped, turned her head back and closed her eyes again, willing it to all go away. Perhaps it was just a dream and when she opened her eyes she'd be back in her own bedroom, snug under her own weightless sheets. *Please, God.* She held her breath and counted slowly to ten before opening her eyes once more.

Light bulb.

Schwarzenegger.

It was no dream.

Oh God. What have I done?

She waggled the fingers on her right hand, felt some movement creep back into them. Her wrist snapped back and forth, elbow unlocked. Fearfully, she ran her fingers lightly over her body, watching the shape of her hand under the doona cover as they touched first her naked breasts, next her naked stomach and then, horror of horror, her pubic hair. It was springy to her touch and she paused on it a moment before tentatively sliding her hand down a little further.

Please, God, don't let it be.

But it was. Her fingers connected with the sticky, wet patch between her thighs and a sob welled in her already constricted throat.

Oh no. No. No. No.

There was only one explanation. Only one person to blame. It was all frighteningly simple. She'd had way too much to drink and had fallen into bed with Nick Greaves.

A wave of panic crashed over her.

Oh God.

How could I have been so stupid?

And then, the worst thought of all. The last time she'd seen *him*. Soft blond hair, a smile tinged with sadness, haunted green eyes. His fingertips brushing her cheek. *I'll see you in a couple of months. Just go and nail the CIB course, throw yourself into work and before you know it I'll be back. Okay?*

She choked and closed her eyes again.

Oh my God. I've cheated on him . . .

Another sob rose in her throat but she swallowed it before it bubbled to the surface and threatened to wake the sleeping form beside her.

Deal with it later.

I have to get out of here.

Now.

Summoning as much strength as she could, she dragged her leaden body up, groaning inwardly at the effort it took. She rotated her wrists slowly under the covers in an attempt to get some more blood flowing through the veins. Beside her, Nick let out a light snore and rolled over onto his back, nestling his head deeper into the pillow. She paused and waited for him to settle before taking another deep breath and pulling her legs up to a sitting position.

A dull pain ricocheted through them and she took a sharp breath, barely managing to stop herself from crying out. She lifted the doona gingerly and examined her thighs, almost crying out again in surprise at the patchwork of ugly blue and purple splotches that ran from groin to knee. She bit her lip and swallowed back another sob. No wonder she ached. *But . . . how? Why?* This was getting weirder and weirder by the second.

What the hell has happened?

On second thoughts, she didn't want to think about it. Not now. She slid out from under the doona and planted her bare feet firmly on the carpet, shivering again at the dull aches that now turned into needles, jabbing and piercing every inch of her body. Her head swam and she took a minute to steady herself before going any further. Thankfully, her clothes were piled up neatly beside the bed and without hesitating she reached over to grab her undies. As she leaned forwards her vision blurred and she toppled, headfirst, onto the carpet with a loud thud.

She froze, her heart dipping as the bed creaked and the doona rustled above.

'Morning, Luce,' Nick said, peering over with a grin and rubbing the sleep out of his eyes. 'You all right?'

She couldn't speak. Had no idea what she was supposed to say.

Sorry?

It shouldn't have happened?

If I was sober, I would never have touched you in a million years?

Even if I didn't already have a boyfriend, I wouldn't have touched you in a million years.

She didn't want to hurt his feelings, but then again, there was no point in giving him the impression that it had been anything more than an awful mistake. But how to do it politely? *God, I wish I had more practice at this sort of thing.*

'Um, yeah, look . . . I've gotta go, Nick,' she murmured, sitting up and wrapping one hand self-consciously across her breasts while trying to pull on her undies with the other.

'You don't want to stay for breakfast?' he asked. 'I can do some bacon and eggs . . .'

'Uh . . . no. Thanks, though.'

'You sure? No offence, but you look a bit rough. We killed that bottle last night between us and . . . don't mean to brag, but I do a mean hangover fry-up, you know.'

She flushed, reaching for her bra and trying to clasp it with trembling fingers.

Could this possibly be any worse?

'Here, let me,' he said, leaning towards her.

'No! It's okay,' she said and turned quickly, unable to bear the thought of him touching her again. She already felt filthy and disgusting and just wanted to go home and wash his scent off her body. And, to make matters worse, she realised for the first time that her bladder was full, achingly full, but it'd have to wait. *Tell him and then get the hell out. You can go when you get home.* She threw her pink top over her head, pulled up her pants and faced him, determined to put a stop to whatever the hell it was that had started before she left.

'Um . . . look . . . Nick, you're really nice and everything, but this shouldn't have happened. I have a boyfriend . . . and . . . and . . .'

A hint of sadness crossed his face, just a glimmer and only for a split second, but he mustered half a smile and put up a hand to stop her. 'It's okay, Luce. You don't need to explain.

12

I guess it was just one of those things. We both had too much to drink, you were feeling lonely and . . . one thing led to another, yeah? It's my fault. I should've said no, or called you a taxi, or . . .'

'Oh Nick, it's not your fault. I'm the one who should be sorry. It's just . . .'

'I know. It's cool, Luce. You don't owe me any explanations. If you want to leave it at that, then that's fine, all right? I like you, but I understand the situation. It's not as if we haven't talked about it, eh? I know how much you like *him* and as much as I really like you, I don't want to get in the middle of things and be the . . . I dunno . . . the baddie in the scenario. Okay?'

She flushed again, not quite believing her luck. Thank God he hadn't dragged it out and made it even more awkward than it already was. 'Um . . . thanks, Nick. I appreciate that. I really do. Well . . . I'll be going then. But I'll see you round?'

'Sure thing,' he said casually, snuggling back down under the doona.

Her cheeks still burning with humiliation, her bladder bulging, she opened the bedroom door and fled into the darkened, unfamiliar hallway, momentarily confused about which direction to take. *Light. Look for light.* She orientated herself towards a sharp pinprick of daylight that crept along the floor. Bypassing a couple of other closed doors, her hand reached out and wrapped around a handle. She wrenched it down, overcome with relief to find herself standing in the blue and white kitchenette that was no bigger than a bathroom. *That's right.* Somewhere familiar at last. She hadn't been in it last night, but she knew where it led. The light grew stronger.

She paused, catching sight of the half-empty bottle of Bundy Red on the counter in the otherwise tidy room. She shuddered briefly and kept going, thankful he wasn't following her. Tile gave way to carpet and the lounge opened up before her, white walls, huge plasma, dark blue couches. *Oh yes. I remember this.* An empty blue chip bowl on the coffee table. *Barbecue. They were barbecue.* A memory of the taste danced briefly on her tongue. She shuddered again before grabbing her bag from the floor by the couch and pulling the front door open. She stepped out into the crisp, clear autumn morning, took a deep breath and commenced the long, painful walk of shame to the purple Hyundai parked just out front.

Nothing was far from anything in Hobart. Nick's Augusta Road flat, a mere blink away from the bungalow that nestled comfortably into the built-up hills of West Hobart. The one she called home. By the time the sun had peeked over Mount Rumney her key was in the lock. Before the old Greek deli owner on the corner had had the chance to switch the *Closed* sign to *Open* she'd scrubbed her skin in a scalding-hot shower until it was shiny, pink and raw, pulled on a fresh pair of pyjamas and curled up in her bed, silently thankful that her parents were spending the weekend at their beach house on the east coast, trying to track down some elusive sun.

She was alone, the comforting smell of her own sheets a soothing balm.

Get some sleep. It will all be better after some sleep.

But the harder she tried, the more elusive it was. Her thighs ached. Her pyjamas felt as though they were strangling her.

14

No matter how she tugged at the material around her neck, no matter what position she rolled or turned into, the sensation remained. Her skin burned. Her mind skipped fitfully from thought to would-be thought. Tears of sadness alternating with tears of fury and self-reproach.

If only I'd stopped being so bloody needy and had kept to myself during the course.

If only I hadn't gone to his place.

If only I hadn't drunk so much.

If only I'd had some self-control.

Oh God. What the hell have I done?

The red glow of the alarm clock by the bed bore witness to her tumbling and twisting.

9.27.

10.13.

11.48.

12.09.

At 1.58 pm she rolled over again and realised that her pillow was saturated with tears. She sat up, tugged at the cotton top around her neck again and stared blindly at the wall, the ceiling, the misty, rain-spattered window, before reaching for the teddy bear that lay nestled among the tangled sheets. The one *he'd* bought for her birthday only a month earlier. The one with the soft brown fur, the yellow ribbon around its neck and the adoring gaze. To touch it brought another tear.

If only I could turn back time.

She'd gladly do the past few weeks over again. Even the painful bits, the stressful bits, the boring bits. The debilitating five-day period she'd endured a few weeks back that had left her curled up on the bathroom floor, arms wrapped around her body, teeth clenched in agony. The CIB exams. The practical scenarios. The long silent evenings of picking over her dinner, disapproving parents staring on. The day she'd found out *he* was going away . . .

She'd do it all over, just to have *not* been with Nick. To have never befriended him, laughed at his jokes, let him take her mind off her misery and then accidentally . . . well . . . it didn't bear thinking about again. If only her mind was like a video tape, she could edit Nick out of the past two weeks, then simply fast-forward six weeks. To have her beloved here with her again, right here and now. The thought of his arms around her and the clean, fresh smell of his skin brought another rush of tears and she hugged the soft brown bear closer, its very presence an agonising reminder of what she now stood to lose.

All down to her own stupidity.

She closed her eyes, locked out the present and tried to rewind.

Change had drifted in on the summer air. It was January. The day their sergeant, John White, had died. Stabbed and gone before either she or Cameron Walsh could react. There'd been nothing to do except leave the scene, drive back to the station in stunned silence and spend the rest of the day wondering how they would pick up the pieces.

She'd always been there for Cam, had been in love with him since day one. Not that he'd noticed her. She was a colleague. A shift mate. Someone to make small talk with in the car for ten-hour stretches. From her nervous stream of chatter he knew more about her than anyone else in the world had ever bothered to find out.

He knew she was shy, adored pizza, freaked out at spiders and was finding policing a lot more confronting than she'd expected it to be. She had a uni degree and dreamed of working overseas. One day. Nothing specific, but it would hopefully involve a heritage home, antiques and a family library where you needed a ladder to reach the high, dust-caked shelves. It would involve inanimate objects as opposed to animate ones. For although policing challenged her and she felt some sort of mysterious desire to master it further, it was proving to her that bricks and shelves and books and gardens might be a whole lot easier to deal with than people.

He'd also discovered, after a particularly confronting mother–daughter domestic they'd attended in South Hobart, that Lucy, an only child, lived with the heavy and all-consuming burden of having disappointed her mother in every respect, beginning with her greatest crime: her failure at not having been born a son. Her immaculately made-up well-spoken, well-connected, prominent society mother. He knew that her mother's perpetual disappointment about every facet of Lucy's existence – her clothing choices, make-up choices, career choices, diet choices and 'antisocial' extracurricular activities – made Lucy despair to the point that she wondered if there'd ever come a time in her life when she'd be able to please her. If she'd ever feel worthy. Ever feel like anything more than an inconvenient stranger in her own family home.

His own conversation during work hours was more restrained. She knew he worshipped Sergeant John White, barracked for the Western Bulldogs, voted Green, existed on

Thai takeaway and lived alone. Somewhere on the eastern shore. From his phone calls and the odd ribbing he copped in the muster room she suspected he dated a string of glamorous women, but he was discreet enough never to go into details. Moreover, she suspected she never stood a chance and was quietly resigned to adoring him from afar, content to ride with him, work with him, listen to him and dream.

But then John died. Literally overnight, Cam, easygoing, dependable, smiling Cam, had fallen apart. After losing the plot and punching a guy in the pub, he'd been handcuffed and thrown into the Hobart cells, where he'd thrown a thousand crooks before. He'd been charged with assault the following morning, but despite the pleas from the police association rep, he'd been marched up to the commissioner's office and informed in no uncertain terms that he was officially suspended, pending the outcome of the court case. He was a 'loose cannon', a 'pathetic excuse for a copper', a 'coward' who'd been 'given chance after chance after chance'.

He'd called her in tears, distraught, desperate for a friendly, familiar ear.

'I was expecting to be made non-operational till the case comes up, but *suspended*? Is he kidding me? What the hell am I going to do, Lucy? It might take six months or a year before it gets to court.'

Her heart stung at the anguish in his voice. Work was everything to him. It wasn't just what he did, it was who he was.

When she turned up on his doorstep an hour later with a block of chocolate, a bag of DVDs and two of her favourite jigsaw puzzles he'd cried again, initially speechless at her kindness. But eventually he talked and once he started, there was no end to his outpouring of misery. He couldn't believe what he'd done to the guy in the pub, couldn't believe he'd lost his temper and was so utterly ashamed of his outburst, even more ashamed to wonder what John would have thought had he been alive.

She listened, not really knowing what else to do. And as the bright summer days faded into blustery autumn greys she watched on silently, helplessly, from the grey chair in his lounge, as he fell to pieces.

He sat around his flat, watched TV, ate junk and drank too much waiting for the court case. His hair, always a neat number two for work, had slipped past his collar and into his eyes, and his eyes themselves, those sparkling, vibrant green eyes that had mesmerised her from day one, had morphed into a dull, haunted grey.

She did what she could, letting him know that she was there for him every step of the way, happy to come over if he called, happy to sit with him while he offloaded, happy to make him coffees and, most of all, just happy to try to make him laugh if and when the occasion arose.

But the wait for court took its toll. Adjournment after adjournment. Formal appearance after formal appearance. A change in lawyers. Strategy meetings. Talks of deals, done then undone. Quibbles with the police association over bills. His agonising fear of being jailed. His unrelenting fear of being personally sued. And more. And still she remained in the large grey chair, legs folded beneath her, patiently waiting, listening and offering the odd skerrick of friendly unsolicited advice if there was a lull in the conversation. It was all she could do.

He wanted a friend. He'd always made that clear. She contented herself with being his official sounding-board. At the very least, she was pretty sure he wasn't seeing anyone and that was as much as she could hope for. So she was taken by surprise a few months down the track to turn up on his doorstep one rainy evening and find him with a clean shirt, hair pushed out of his eyes and a pot of rice, stock, wine, onion, garlic and bacon hissing and bubbling on the stove. Triple J flooded the room and a glass of red stood watch on the counter.

'My mother's risotto recipe,' he said with a shrug, taking her coat and shaking out the raindrops.

'I didn't know you cooked,' she laughed, running a hand through her cold wet hair. 'I thought you had shares in the local fish and chip shop.'

'Aha! There's a lot you don't know about me, Lucy Howard.'

She smiled, wishing she knew everything. 'Well, I'll go if you're about to eat . . .'

'No way. I told you to come around because I'm cooking for you, dummy.'

'Me?'

'Yes, you. You've been looking after me for so long now,' he said with an embarrassed smile. 'Putting up with my whinge-ing, bitching and moaning, so . . . I thought I should return the favour. Especially seeing as it's your birthday.'

'H-how did you know?' she mumbled, certain she'd never mentioned it.

He tapped his nose. 'I have my sources.'

As he led her by the hand through to the tiny lounge room that had become their sanctuary from the world over the past few stormy months, her jaw dropped. The sparse white-brick walls were decorated with brightly coloured bunches of balloons and rainbows of streamers. The dinner table with the wobbly leg had also had a makeover: candles, a crimson tablecloth, wineglasses and his best matching crockery.

'Well, well, well. I *am* impressed,' she said, throwing her bag on the couch and kicking off her shoes.

'You should be. It's taken me all bloody day. But wait . . . there's more,' he said and raced off down the hall like an excited four-year-old.

She giggled when he returned with a large white box, complete with pink ribbon, and pushed it into her hands.

'Cam, you didn't need to . . .'

'Just shut up and open it.'

She tore off the layers of ribbon, paper and cardboard before pulling out the cutest, softest brown teddy bear in the whole world. Her hands shook as she held it up and gazed into its little brown eyes. He watched on, looking delighted at the expression on her face.

'I know it seems a bit silly, but we've been talking a lot lately. And I figured you might need someone else to yak to if things go badly in court and I'm not around for a . . .'

'Don't even say it.'

'Sorry. We won't talk about it tonight. But seriously, if you don't like it, I can always take it back and get . . .'

But she cut him off, threw her arms around him and hugged him.

'I love it. It's perfect.'

He hesitated, shifting his weight from foot to foot.

'So are you, Lucy. So are you.'

She froze, sensing the subtle change in their balance. But then second-guessed it. *Is he just being friendly, or dear God . . . please, God . . . is there more to it? Surely not. Don't be a moron, Lucy.*

Before she could question it further he caught her gaze, held it, leaned in and whispered, 'I'm sorry. I'm a bit out of practice but . . .' and then kissed her softly on the lips, lingering for no more than a second. *It isn't real. It couldn't possibly be real. Could it?* And as he pulled away slowly she tried to take it all in. The softness of his lips, the beauty of his sad green eyes, his scent, so familiar, yet so painfully out of reach to her for so long, like a dull, unquenchable thirst.

She trembled, rooted to the spot, unable to find the words to respond. It had finally happened. The thing she'd been dreaming of, like some pathetic, love-struck sixteen-year-old lusting after a pop star, since the second she first shook his hand in the work muster room. Dreaming, never for a moment believing that it could happen. But as the silence grew between them, he blushed and cringed, his gaze dropping to his feet. 'Crap. I'm sorry, Lucy, I didn't mean to overstep the mark. I must have read it wrong.'

Oh God. Do something, you idiot.

He wants you, you moron.

Now.

Mustering every ounce of courage, she stepped in, wound her arms around his neck and kissed him the way she'd spent countless minutes, hours and days dreaming of kissing him. And while the imaginary kisses in the darkness of her bedroom had been delicious, the real kiss made her sigh out loud with contentment. The firm insistence of his lips, the smooth caress of his thick blond hair as it wound around her fingers, the pressure of his palms against her shoulderblades.

The sheer sensuality of it unnerved her momentarily, but once she relaxed, Lucy knew that she wanted nothing more than to stay like that for the rest of her life. No more court. No more suspension. No more sadness. Just him and her, alone, together in the cosy flat, the rain belting down on the tin roof.

She wanted to kiss Cameron Walsh forever.

Two weeks later she sat behind him doubled over with nausea as he was sentenced. Sixteen weeks' jail, out in eight for good behaviour. A result that elicited gasps from the few loyal supporters who had sat with him for the week watching the hearing unfold. The sentence was unprecedented. His lawyer had assured him more than once that if it was custodial, it'd be fully suspended, like it would have been for any other defendant. But as the words fell from the magistrate's lips – *As a police officer you are expected to set a standard far higher than the average citizen . . .* – it was clear, he'd never had a chance. He and defendant Joe Public were worlds apart.

After the magistrate had risen, turned his back and left the courtroom to its stunned silence, she'd gripped his hand, her world tilting and slipping further beneath her feet. She had only seconds before he would be marched to the cells. So much to say, yet time for nothing but the basics. It was eight weeks. For he'd only serve the minimum. They'd cope.

He'd do what needed to be done and when he came out they'd . . .

'Don't visit me,' he whispered, kissing her cheek.

'But . . .'

'I mean it. It's . . . humiliating. I don't want to see anyone while I'm in there. I'll see you in a couple of months. Just go and nail the CIB course, throw yourself into work and before you know it I'll be back. Okay?'

A black hole opened beneath her as his words sank in. She bit back her tears and bowed her head, knowing he'd made up his mind, not knowing if she could stand it. 'Promise?'

'Promise.'

And with a final, lingering kiss, he was gone.

She'd done as he had asked. Aced the course, tried to stay busy, but in the space of a few hours she'd managed to wreck everything with her thoughtlessness, her utter, moronic stupidity. She opened her eyes. The memories fell away, leaving her back at the mercy of the present. And the thought of Nick. She wanted to scream, kick a hole in the plaster, drive her car into a river and feel the icy water fill her lungs. Something. Anything to punish herself for her idiocy. And as she cowered in her bedroom, the hours crawling past, the shadows stretching, shortening, stretching out again, her tears of rage subsided and were replaced with a calm resignation. She was doomed whichever way she turned.

Even if she never admitted to Cam what had happened with Nick, she knew the way the policing community worked. Nick would already have whispered to someone who would whisper to someone else who would whisper to someone else. It would go from shift to shift, section to section, station to station and even now, they were probably all sniggering at her, all the way up to Burnie, Devonport and Launceston. She'd be reduced to nothing more than the latest drunken slut in a long line of police sluts.

She hugged the soft brown bear close to her chest and wept at the thought. It was particularly abhorrent, given that Cam had been her first lover at the ripe old age of twenty-two. And then she wept to think about Cam himself: alone, locked up in some stinking cell, surrounded by hardened crooks and, worst of all, betrayed by the one person in the world he had counted on.

By Sunday night, she was drained, pale and listless. Her stomach rumbled with a hunger she couldn't be bothered feeding and her body screamed for sleep that refused to come. By nine o'clock that night, she'd made up her mind. There was one possible solution. Perhaps, if she was lucky, she could stop it before it started. It wasn't foolproof and it was probably too late, but she had to give it a shot. It was better than just sitting there feeling miserable. What's more, it was all she had.

Reaching for the phone, she dialled the number Nick had given her the week before. She paused, holding her breath in anticipation of the awkward conversation that was sure to follow.

'Yep?'

Oh God. Why am I doing this?

'Nick, it's Lucy,' she said calmly.

'Luce! How you doing?'

'Um . . . good.'

'What can I do for you?' he chirped.

'Um . . . look . . . the thing is, Nick . . .'

'Yeah?'

'The thing is,' *just spit it out,* 'the thing is . . . what happened the other night shouldn't have happened. I had too much to drink and . . . and . . .'

'You're madly in love with your boyfriend and you don't want to jeopardise it, so you'd prefer if I didn't announce it to the rest of the world?'

She felt her shoulders dropping, the tension easing.

'Um, yeah. I feel really bad about what happened. I'm so sorry if I led you on or anything.'

'Luce, it's fine. Don't worry about it at all. I understand. Sometimes these things just happen, okay?'

'Well, it's *not* okay,' she insisted. 'I should've been more careful.'

He chuckled. 'It's fine, Luce. And look, just for your peace of mind, rest assured that I haven't said anything to anyone and I'm not going to be blabbing. That's not the way I operate. What happened stays between us, yeah?'

Haven't.

Said.

Anything.

She closed her eyes, almost collapsed with relief. 'You mean you *really* haven't told anyone? No one at all?'

'Of course not.'

Perhaps Cam never needs to know.

'Thanks, Nick. I really appreciate that,' she breathed.

'No worries, Luce. And hey, if you and your other half don't work out, you know my door's always open.'

She gave another nervous laugh before thanking him again, hanging up and throwing herself face first onto the bed. It was over. All that worry for nothing. She looked at the bear, laughed out loud and chided herself. *You're such an idiot. Here you were thinking it was the end of the world.* Sure, she'd have to live with the fact that she'd deceived Cam, but she would bury it deep down inside her and try to forget it had ever happened.

Sleeping with Nick was nothing more than an accident. A horrid, regrettable mistake.

And on the bright side, if there could possibly be a bright side to the whole damned mess, she'd been so pissed that the few times she *had* found her memory straying inadvertently towards the actual deed itself, she couldn't remember a single detail beyond arriving at his place, having a few drinks and watching some telly and a movie. Nothing of the deed itself.

All in all, a good result.

It was almost, *almost* as though it'd never happened. She could move on, forget Nick's very existence, throw herself into work, welcome Cam home with open arms and start building a life with him.

She hugged the brown bear closely once more and, for the first time since Saturday morning, drifted off into a deep, trouble-free sleep, her second-last thought being that she should make an appointment to see her doctor first thing tomorrow, her last conscious thought, that by some freak of nature she hadn't managed to sabotage her good fortune after all.

For a short while, the denial strategy worked. She lived, worked and slept as though it had never happened. As though the night in the unit at Lenah Valley was merely a figment of her imagination. A D-grade movie starring some poor unfortunate actress that Lucy'd watched and promptly forgotten.

And on the Saturday morning two weeks after her indiscretion, she found herself fully immersed in work, humming, actually grateful for the amount of paperwork overflowing in her tray. As well as taking up a great chunk of her work time, the information reports, search returns, offence reports and court files screaming for her attention ate into her own time which was surprisingly satisfying.

It was a simple equation. More work meant less time to think. Less time to think meant time passed quicker. Time passing quicker meant that very soon, Cam would walk out of the remand centre and back into her life.

But her humming was interrupted when her sergeant, Stu Walters, peered around the corner.

'Lucy, there's a female downstairs, a Suzanne Ward who wants to report a sexual assault. CIB's tied up with a shitload of car burgs in Battery Point and Sergeant Torino wondered if you'd take the initial statement, please?'

It took her a second to process the rather startling request. Sexual assaults weren't normally dished out to junior burgers. She liked Stu with his spiky brown hair, glasses and no-nonsense attitude but couldn't help but wonder if his faith in her wasn't a little misplaced. She might no longer have been the most junior officer on the shift, but in the big scheme of things, she'd still only been out in the real world for about five minutes.

'Ah, of course, as long as you're sure, Sarge.'

'Never been more sure. And quit with the self-doubt,

Lucy. Remember those glowing reports you got from the CIB course? Get out there and show me what you've learned.' He grinned.

'Um, sure. It's just that . . .'

'Just *what*, Lucy? You kicked arse on that course. Richard Moore said so himself and he also happened to mention that you were his first pick for the next secondment. Believe me, he wouldn't have said it if he didn't mean it.'

She grimaced. 'I just don't want to stuff it up, Sarge.'

'You won't stuff it up. Just take your time. Remember what you've learned. Lead her through it chronologically. Cover your points of proof, double-check it and come and ask me if you're not sure of anything. All right?' He turned to leave.

'Sure . . . ah . . . and if we need to do a medical, Sarge?'

'If it's recent, and it's an actual rape, then you might want to do that first. Get her to outline the basics, then make a decision. It might just be an indecent assault, or a historical rape, in which case you won't need to worry about a medical at all. So it'll be your call. If you need to do one, let me know and I'll pop down with a rape kit for you to take over to the Royal.'

She nodded, shuffled her paperwork into a neat pile and made her way down the hallway deep in thought about the level of trust that was being placed with her. A sexual assault was heavy stuff all right.

If only Cam was here, she could run it all by . . .

Stop.

He's not. Deal with it.

But what if I'm not up to it?

29

Stop it.

The self-doubt lingered while she fumbled in her locker and threw the paperwork in her tray. Doing up a mock statement in the warm, cosy CIB classroom environment was one thing, doing up an actual statement in the cold hard light of day, one that would go to court, be tendered as evidence and picked over by lawyers like a vulture with a carcass, was another thing entirely. She kicked herself again. This time, for the last time. *Get it together. It's the next step in your career. You can kick arse on this.* She slammed the locker door shut, headed for the lift.

As the doors closed she pulled herself together and focused, running through the basic steps of the statement in her head, the points of proof that had to be covered to form the basis of the complaint and quell any possible defences if and when they interviewed the offender.

What?
When?
Where?
How?
Why?
ID?
Description?
Alcohol?
Drugs?
Injuries.
Feelings.
No consent. Most importantly, no consent.

As the lift dinged and the doors opened, she pulled her shoulders back, now firmly in work mode, self-doubt banished.

She would take a statement that would make her sarge, not to mention Detective Sergeant Torino, proud.

The open-plan waiting room, crammed with exotic plants and fountains, all the better to soothe the most aggro of crooks upon their reception, was empty with the exception of a fine-featured auburn-haired girl who glanced about nervously, crossed and uncrossed her legs and rubbed furiously at the knuckles on her left hand. Lucy's first impression was that she was young, no more than eighteen or nineteen. Young and shivering, despite her heavy black coat and the central heating.

'Suzanne?' she asked. The girl jumped up, flashed her a nervous smile and extended a hand that shook with gold bangles.

'Hi. Call me Suzy,' she said shyly, one hand clutching her black and white duffle bag tightly.

Lucy returned her smile, determined to make the girl feel at ease. 'Come on through, Suzy. I'm Lucy, by the way, Lucy Howard, and I'll be taking your statement today.'

'Oh, okay.'

'Basically, I'm your first port of call. When we're done, the statement will be forwarded on to CIB who will investigate it,' she explained, leading her through the maze of corridors up to the CIB offices, outlining the process as she went, as much for her own benefit as for Suzy's. Once she found a clear office with a computer, Lucy ushered her in and pulled out a chair.

'Can I get you a tea or coffee?'

'N-no, thanks. I just want to get it over with. If that's okay?'

'Of course,' she said, taking her own seat and firing up the computer. 'Now, first things first, if I can just go through the basics of what happened with you slowly so I can take a few notes . . . then we'll flesh it out, covering everything in a bit more detail. I apologise in advance for making you go through it all again, but it's essential if we're going to get this right.'

Suzy nodded, crossed her hands in her lap and began rubbing again at the knuckles on her left hand.

'I was out at Isobar last night with some friends . . .'

Lucy nodded, scribbling and thinking as the girl spoke. *Recent. Probably have to do a medical then if it's rape.*

'. . . and we were just dancing and having fun. I didn't want to get too smashed 'cause I knew I had a netball game on this morning down at uni . . . which I'm obviously not going to make it to now. Anyway, as I said, I only had a couple . . .'

'Of?'

'Stolis. Orange Stolis.'

'Right.'

'And anyway, there was a group of guys who'd been hitting on us all night, not that we were that interested though.'

'Why's that?'

'Why we weren't interested?' she asked. 'They just looked like total beefcakes. You know the sort. Gym guys. Big biceps, tight clothes, no brain.'

Lucy chuckled but stopped cold as an image of Nick Greaves and his broad, buffed gym body flashed through her mind.

Stop it. Focus.

'A couple of my friends headed home and it was only Mandy and me left. We kept dancing and two of the guys

32

started joining in. They weren't *as* bad, you know. Sort of the quiet ones of their group who'd been sitting over by the bar in the dark.'

Lucy nodded and kept scribbling.

'Anyway, they went to the bar and came back with a couple of Stolis for us and, well, normally I wouldn't accept a drink from a total stranger but . . .'

'Being a broke uni student?' Lucy smiled, remembering the not-so-distant past.

'Exactly,' she said with a roll of her eyes. 'And we were having fun dancing, so I figured what the hell.'

Lucy paused, held the pen aloft for a second. 'Bearing in mind that just because you accepted a drink doesn't mean you were consenting to anything else.'

'Oh, I know that.'

'Good. So what happened next?'

Suzy hesitated. 'Well, that's the problem.'

'Mmm?'

'Well, I remember dancing. I remember feeling a bit out of it on the dance floor and I remember the guy – Tom, he said his name was Tom – taking my arm and asking me if I was okay. I kind of then remember looking around for Mandy but I couldn't see her anywhere. And I was saying, "Where's Mandy? Where's Mandy?" and Tom said, "I think she went home."'

Lucy nodded, the pen scratching quickly on the pad in front of her. *Dancing. Tom. Home.* 'And then?'

'And then . . . nothing,' she said, throwing her hands in the air. 'Absolutely nothing.'

Lucy paused. 'Nothing?'

'Nope. The next thing I know, I woke up in my room at Jane Franklin . . .'

'The student college?'

'Yep. And . . . and . . . I was naked and I realised that I'd . . . you know . . . had sex at some stage.'

Her pen stopped scratching on the page and a strange chill of familiarity trickled down Lucy's spine. She looked up. 'How did you know?'

'Well, it must have been a few hours later. It was just getting light. I woke up, felt a bit . . . I dunno . . . weird . . . and I was freezing cold. I switched my lamp on and realised I was naked. There was what I can only assume was semen on the inside of my thighs and a damp patch on my doona cover. And . . . because I couldn't remember anything, I went downstairs and asked to have a look at the security video taken at the main foyer.'

'And?'

'And I'm on it. At about one o'clock, the guy I met at Isobar, Tom – at least I think it was Tom – had his head down, a cap on and he was walking in with me, kind of holding me up as I staggered. The footage was pretty grainy, but it looked like I was totally out of it and I have absolutely no recollection of it whatsoever. Putting two and two together, I figure he took me up to my room, had sex with me and then left.

'The camera then shows what I think is him, heading back out about half an hour later.'

Lucy frowned, the chill now seeping into her bones. 'So, let me get this right. You have no recollection at all between being on the dance floor and waking up this morning?'

'That's right.'

'And how many drinks in total did you say you had?'

'Three. That's it.'

'Could you be mistaken?'

'No way.'

'So . . . you're not used to alcohol then?'

Suzy gave a snort. 'Are you kidding me? I'm a Jane Franklin girl. I might be small, but I can drink most of our guys under the table. I'm the bloody anchorman for the college sculling team, for God's sake. And we're good too. We won the boat races at the Inter-Varsity Olympics in Melbourne a couple of months back. That's heats, finals and grand finals all in the space of one night, thank you very much!'

'Impressive,' Lucy said with a grimace.

Suzy laughed. 'It's not exactly my parents' idea of making the most of my education, but my point is, I can drink. What's more, I *always* remember things in the morning. Sure, it might be a bit hazy and there might be chunks missing, but even at my worst, which, to be honest, is pretty disgraceful, I *always* remember little snippets, like calling a taxi to get home, chucking up in the bushes outside college, snogging someone cute, trying to find a loo . . . you know, the little things.'

The little things.

'And the problem is, I'm drawing an absolute blank on all of that. Plus, the weirdest thing – I don't have a hangover. If I was *that* blotto, I'd be feeling it today, at least for a few hours after waking up, until I had some Panadol and a McMuffin. I normally get the works: headache, dizziness, nausea, all the good stuff. But apart from feeling a bit stiff and sore, a bit unco and maybe a bit thirsty when I first woke up, I'm fine,' she said with a shrug.

Lucy stopped writing and stared into space, carefully calculating the familiarity of Suzy's words but no longer thinking about Suzy's situation.

'Look, I know this sounds a bit weird, Lucy, but I'm certain I wasn't drunk and I'm certain that I had sex. And I want you to know that I'm not just some drunken slag who goes out and does this sort of thing all the time. And . . . and . . . I know it's not much to go on, but I'm wondering . . . you know how you read stuff in the mainland papers about drink spiking? Well, it might sound a bit silly, but I'm wondering if there's a chance that that's what happened last night?'

Not drunk.

Had sex.

No hangover.

No memory.

Drink spiking.

Lucy trembled, the pen shaking uncontrollably between her fingers.

Could it be?

Had the same thing happened to her?

'Lucy?'

'Yeah, sorry, Suzy,' she spluttered, trying to compose herself. 'I was, um . . . just thinking about what we're going to do next. Drink spiking, you think? It's certainly a possibility.'

And one I should have thought of two weeks ago, the second I woke up in Nick's bed.

Idiot.

You total idiot.

You total and utter moron, Lucy Howard.

You don't deserve to wear a uniform, let alone take a CIB statement and pretend to be an investigator.

You're a fraud.

An impostor.

'Um . . . if you don't mind, I'm just going to leave you here for a sec while I go and arrange for a medical, Suzy. If it *is* drugs, then I'm pretty sure we'll have a limited window of time to test you, so before we go any further with your statement, we really should tee up an appointment over at the Royal.'

'Okay, if you think that's best.'

Lucy nodded blankly, rose from her chair and made for the door. 'I won't be long.'

She snipped the office door shut behind her and walked zombie-like to the end of the hallway before heading for the sanctuary of the ladies toilet. It was quiet. Both cubicles were open and empty. Hands shaking and legs wobbling, she leaned against the basin, turned on the tap and let the cool water run across her hands before cupping them and splashing some onto her face, gasping as it hit her. She shook it off before reaching for great fistfuls of paper towel and patting her skin dry.

She stared into the mirror, peering at the face before her and wondering how on earth she could have been so naive. The longer she stared, the more sense it made, the evidence accumulating with each and every thought, feeling, word and action.

She *hadn't* had that much to drink. Her knuckles whitened as she gripped the basin and thought back to Nick's comments in bed.

We killed that bottle last night between us and . . . don't mean to brag, but I do a mean hangover fry-up, you know.

But they *hadn't*. When she'd walked through the kitchen that morning there'd been half a bottle of Bundy Red sitting on the counter. A fact that only registered at that very moment.

She gulped.

And that wasn't all. What was it that Suzy had said?

I always remember little snippets, like calling a taxi to get home, chucking up in the bushes outside college, snogging someone cute, trying to find a loo . . .

The loo. She cast her mind back to Nick's place. She'd been in the lounge, the kitchen and the bedroom, but not the loo. She thought back to leaving, to the darkened hall with the closed doors. One had to have been a bathroom, one perhaps a separate loo or laundry, and maybe a spare bedroom. But which was which? There was no way she'd used the toilet. Not once that night. And that was unheard of. If she'd been drinking a lot, she would have been in and out of Nick's loo all night. She'd inherited her mother's pea-sized bladder and when she drank, it felt like it shrank to half that size.

If she'd been drinking, *really* drinking, enough to have blacked out, she would have used Nick's toilet countless times before falling unconscious. And even if she was pissed, she would have remembered *something* about it. Searching for an unknown light switch, fumbling with the zip on her pants, sitting forwards and trying not to pee too noisily in case it could be heard in the lounge, checking the seat as she was about to leave, conscious of not leaving any drips or a stray pube, knocking the roll off the holder and giggling. Something. Anything. But there was nothing. Not a single recollection.

No matter how hard she tried to picture it, nothing came to mind. She didn't know which one of the three rooms it was, let alone what it might have looked like.

She had left with a full bladder.

She had not used Nick's toilet.

And then there was Suzy's snogging comment. No matter how hard she strained, there was no memory of a kiss. She thought back to the one time she'd got smashed out of her brain – her Year Twelve formal. She'd passed out and woken up the following day in the glaring morning light on Sandy Bay beach with the taste of vomit in the back of her throat and up into her sinus cavity, remembering full well that she'd been the one uncharacteristically suggesting a midnight swim with a few of her classmates. That night, she'd sunk enough vodka to down an elephant. But despite it being the most drunk she'd ever been, even now she recalled little flashes of earlier points in the evening – like when she'd kissed the slightly nerdy and extremely surprised Michael Harris behind the boys toilets. When she'd burst into tears at the thought that no one would ever love her, and later in the night, the first vomit, the one that had erupted out of nowhere and covered the back seat of poor Michael Harris's brand-new Commodore. She remembered the smack of the icy-cold water as she first waded then dived into the black waters of the Derwent, remembered laughing about how they'd probably freeze to death.

The kiss.

The wailing.

The vomit.

The swim.

All perfectly rational scraps of memory from several years earlier. Yet she'd slept with Nick only weeks ago and there was no memory of even a kiss. No hug, no shoulder to cry on that had accidentally taken a turn for the worse. No stumble to the bedroom, no discarding of clothes, no snagging bra strap, no exploring of each other's bodies, no momentary feeling of self-consciousness at being naked with a stranger. No pangs of regret for what she might have been about to do to Cam.

Nothing.

She splashed another handful of water across her face and tried to focus. How many drinks had she had? He'd handed her one the second she walked in the door. A little strong for her liking, but certainly not too destructive. She'd always planned to drive home and had no intention of staying at the house of someone who was pretty much a total stranger. So she'd sipped it. All the way through *Find My Family*. Then they'd watched a mindless policing reality show, at which point she'd had drink number two.

They'd all laughed.

All four of them. Nick's friends Ange and Dan had been there at the start of the night and she clearly remembered them leaving after the police show. After her second drink. She'd watched the opening credits to *Top Gun*, heard the roar of planes overhead, the jarring bass of the theme music and she recalled Nick heading to the kitchen to get her another drink. Her third. But he'd insisted, despite her protest. *Come on, Luce. The night is young. Just one more drink and half an hour of the DVD . . .*

She closed her eyes, fought to remember what came next. He'd given her the drink in the pink tumbler, she'd sipped, eaten a handful of chips, felt a little sleepy and then . . .

Nothing.

Blackness.

Think, Lucy. There must be something.

Think.

She grabbed the sides of the basin, took a deep breath. She'd had three Bundy and Cokes that night – max. That was it. No more.

Why didn't I realise that before?

Because you wanted to forget that the entire night had happened. No point dredging up details. Remember?

She stared into the mirror one more time before closing her eyes, determined to cut through the cloak of blackness and uncover something. Just one tiny detail, anything that would confirm her worst fear.

And then it hit her. A flash. Like a scene from a movie on a TV without an antenna. Grainy. Dark. Out of focus. She was on a bed, the room swam around her in semi-darkness. Nick leaned over her, his face leering as he pulled her thighs apart and forced himself inside her with a grunt. She tried to cry out but there was no sound. Tried to swing her arms up to his chest to push him off her, but they remained pinned to her side. She couldn't move, just rocked with pain as he thrust deeper and deeper and deeper inside of her, tearing and bruising and smiling as he went.

And before she could recall another detail, the image flickered like someone had turned the TV off, and she hurtled back to the present, to the bright white starkness of the bathroom.

She pushed herself away from the basin, tears streaming down her cheeks. Her back connected with the wall tiles and she found herself sliding, sliding, down to the floor where she crumpled and sobbed.

Nick Greaves, Constable Nick Greaves, her alleged friend, had invited her to his place, slipped something into her third drink and raped her.

No one would ever believe her. Not in a gazillion years.

And there wasn't a damn thing she could do about it.

The Detective Sergeant

8.45 am Sunday 12 June

Will Torino reclined his leather chair, cleared a spot on his desk with one foot, crossed his ankles and shut his eyes. The CIB office was thankfully silent with the exception of a phone ringing somewhere off down the hallway. It would never get answered, at least not by anyone who gave a rat's arse. Not on the weekend. *Especially* not on the weekend. Without the ever-efficient CIB secretary perched behind her desk it would bounce around the station for a while, muster room, sergeant's office, front desk, radio room, where, if the caller was lucky, it'd finally be answered, they'd be told that there was no one available and advised to call back tomorrow. If it didn't make it that far, it would ring out and there'd be an irate member of the public screaming down the phone at the CIB secretary at precisely 8.01 am tomorrow morning, claiming that no one gave a damn about whatever spurious – and it was *always* spurious – matter was worrying them first thing on a Sunday morning. And they'd be right. Personally, he didn't give a flying fuck. If someone was being murdered, they'd call triple-O or wander through the front door of the station. Otherwise, it could wait.

All he needed was five minutes to recharge his batteries. Then and only then would he be ready to deal with the two most important matters at hand – namely, walking across Liverpool Street to his favourite coffee haunt for the first extra grande double-shot latte of the day, followed shortly by the Suzy Ward rape statement he'd just brushed to one side of the desk. But first he needed to sit. Just for five minutes. To conduct the mandatory mental autopsy of the previous night's activities.

His hand strayed to his crotch for a quick scratch at the mere thought of the evening. *Real or imagined itchiness? Not entirely sure. Hopefully imagined.*

But apart from itching like fuck, he wasn't sure how he was supposed to feel about the whole thing. Stoked? Pissed off? Mildly disgusted or just plain old intrigued? Perhaps a combination. One thing was for sure; he needed to digest it and reach a conclusion before he could store it away and get on with the day.

It'd kicked off around nine. They'd rolled on into the pebble driveway of the white rendered two-storey Taroona mansion that overlooked the Derwent River – the good end of town. He parked his well-kept but obviously second-hand beemer among the dozen or so other cars scattered in and around the turning circle and by the time they'd climbed out, his breath forming little wintery clouds before his face, he'd made a few snap judgements.

One. The home owners had money. And not just money, but *money*.

Two. The other guests, Mercedes SLK, Honda Accord VTi, 2007 VW Polo, 2009 RAV4 and a late-nineties Kia Rio, were going to be a mixed bunch.

Three. It was fucking cold.

Four. They shouldn't be here.

Trish, having no such reservations, grabbed his hand and giggled like a thirteen-year-old all the way up the path to the front door. The E she knocked back with a Beam and Coke in the car on the way was doing its job. Her nerves were steady and she was pumped, raring for action. He, on the other hand, had decided to go in cold, not entirely convinced they were going to stay.

It was her idea. She'd heard about it from a friend of a friend of a friend who'd been with her husband the month before and gave gushing, glowing reports. He wasn't so sure, but he loved his wife and was prepared to give it a go.

He trailed behind her and they were greeted at the front door by an older man, distinguished with swept-back grey hair, a neatly trimmed moustache and a casual but undoubtedly expensive shirt, cravat and trousers.

A cross between the major off Fawlty Towers *and the judge off that chef show*, Will thought sourly.

'Come in, come in,' the man insisted, giving Trish the light *mwah, mwah* of an air kiss. 'I'm Roger. It's so nice of you to join us.'

45

Nonce, Will thought, adding to his catalogue of snap judgements.

'Cherie told us about you,' Will said, glancing around the entry way, trying not to look too impressed at the exquisite luxury that surrounded them. The place was enormous, at least six or seven bedrooms, and every centimetre of it was tastefully done. Paintings, sculptures, vases and Persian rugs complemented cream walls, oak staircases and terracotta tiles. And as they followed their host up a set of stairs, Will gawked and snidely congratulated himself on his first call. *Serious money all right.* The space on the upper level was open plan, one wall composed entirely of glass and facing out onto the river itself.

'Ah, the lovely Cherie,' Roger mused. 'She and her husband are already here.' He glanced around the room at the mingling group and waved at the familiar horsy blonde over in the corner.

'Cherie, darling, your friends are here,' he cried, waving her over before heading back downstairs to get the door again.

Cherie dragged herself away from her conversation and approached with open arms. 'Trish, Will, so glad you could make it,' she said with a mischievous grin. 'You two definitely add something to the mix.'

Trish clung to her friend's arm and giggled, a hiccup close on its heels. 'Tell me before he comes back. Does Roger . . . you know . . . get involved?'

She laughed. 'Of course he does. And can I just add, don't be too quick to judge a book by its cover. There's a lot more to Roger than meets the eye. And I mean, a *lot* more.'

A disturbing image of Roger, naked save his cravat and

monstrous erection, flashed through Will's mind and he shuddered. *Ugh*. Trish let out a snort and Cherie gave a conspiratorial giggle, a stupid, vapid noise that grated, made his hair stand on end. Now he remembered why Cherie annoyed the fuck out of him. He sighed. If he stayed another minute, he'd probably end up snapping and insulting her. So without another word he left them to it, his high-as-a-kite wife and her stupid friend.

He grabbed a beer from a young guy who was circling with a drinks tray and backed himself into a dark corner, scanning the room and doing a quick head count. Eighteen in total, nineteen if you included the waiter. A decent number. Best of all, there wasn't a bogan in sight, a thought that had been chewing away at him since Trish first casually mentioned the prospect. In fact, it was quite the contrary.

The women in the pack were generally fit, well dressed and nicely made up, even the ones who had their backs to him. Not a skank among them. The guys also seemed to be reasonably clean and neat, ages ranging from twenties to old Roger himself who had to have been sixty-five. Will sipped his beer and decided to amuse himself by trying to pick Roger's wife out of the crowd. The forty-something brunette in green next to Cherie? The shorter blonde with the slightly thicker than attractive calves? She looked a bit young but then again . . .

'Well, well, well. If it isn't good old Sergeant Will Torino himself.'

He jumped at the voice beside him and turned to see a familiar face peering out of the semi-darkness.

Fuck.

You've gotta be fucking kidding me.

He steadied his voice, stuck out his hand and tried to look casual. As casual as you could look when you'd been totally sprung. 'Ah, Constable Greaves no less. How the hell are you, Nick?'

He'd done a few courses with the big guy over the years, knew him to be a good egg, one of the boys, if not a bit over the top, but hell, that was just about a fucking prerequisite for SOG.

He squirmed at being recognised. *Fuck.* Nick, though, seemed nonplussed. Seemed rather amused actually.

'I wouldn't have picked you for the type, mate . . .' Nick said, giving an upward nod at the others who were drinking, schmoozing and laughing. From the other side of the room a familiar tinkle of laughter distracted him and he looked away. Trish, Cherie and Roger were obviously finding something pretty fucking amusing.

They were the type.

He *wasn't* the fucking type. Should never have been there, a sentiment that was now bitterly confirmed by the fact that he'd been caught out by a fucking colleague.

Should have known this town was too small.

Gotta get the fuck out of here.

Now.

He tried to catch Trish's eye but she was miles away. Beside him, Nick placed a reassuring hand on his arm. 'Don't worry, man, what happens in the mansion stays in the mansion. Know what I mean?'

Oh Jesus.

'Uh . . . look, we were just about to leave anyway, Nick. My wife just wanted to drop in and say hi to a friend before we went out to dinner . . .'

'Mate. As I said, relax. In here, we're just Nick and Will. It's our downtime, yeah? All consenting adults doing whatever the hell consenting adults feel like doing. No one judges anyone. You need to chill.'

He turned and waved over to the other side of the room.

'Hey, Chrissy, Chrissy, come over here and see who I met.'

Will shrank back into the corner, shuffled on the spot. *Why don't you just put an ad in the fucking* Mercury *and be done with it?* His eyes darted about for the closest exit but Nick was blocking his way. A woman approached. And not just any woman. A blonde with fine, porcelain features. Pins like Miranda Kerr. White blouse showing just a hint of cleavage, grey A-line skirt and killer heels. Classy. An absolute fucking knockout. Will gulped. He knew the face. Had seen her about.

Oh fuck. Someone else from work.

Could this get any worse?

'Will, you know Chrissy?' Nick said. 'From Prosecution.'

Oh shit. Of course.

'Hi, Will. Funnily enough, I don't think we've actually met,' she said flirtily, extending a long, slender arm.

'Uh, hi. Good to meet you.' The blood rushed to his face, the stain of his embarrassment flooding his cheeks.

Chrissy looked him up and down and gave Nick a nudge and a wink. 'Nice work. Looks like some fortunate lady will be in for a good night. I'll be crossing my fingers, Will.'

'Slut,' Nick said with a grin.

'You know it, baby,' she replied, giving him a light tap on the bottom. 'Hope to see more of you, Will. Much, *much* more.' Her eyes lingered on his crotch before she spun on her heel and returned to her conversation on the other side of the room.

'Jesus Christ,' Will said, his eyes glued to her arse as she retreated. 'Are you two . . . ?'

'Occasionally.'

'Bloody hell. You're a lucky man.'

'Even luckier than you think, mate. We're just fuck buddies. So I don't have to put up with any of the usual crap.'

Will shook his head and laughed at the younger man's honesty, finally feeling himself relax a smidge.

'Which one's your wife?' Nick asked.

Will pointed towards Cherie and Trish who were downing champers. 'The brunette.'

'Nice.'

His hackles rose at Nick's assessment. But he stopped himself. *Get used to it, buddy. Go with the flow . . .*

'Man, there's some talent here tonight,' Nick continued. 'A couple of times the pickings haven't been as rich.'

'You've been before?'

'Sure. It's mainly Chrissy's thing. But I'm always happy to come along for the ride. I mean, let's face it, who wouldn't be?' He laughed.

Will took another nervous sip of his beer.

Ask him. Just ask him.

'Um . . . does anyone else from work come? I mean, I'm not gonna bump into the fucking commissioner himself coming out of the loo, am I?'

Nick roared. 'Good one. Can you imagine that fucking evil demented little garden gnome here? Nah. Don't quite think it's his scene. Personally, I reckon he's more the closet fish nets, stilettos and pink feather boa type, don't you think?'

He chuckled. The observation was spot on. He could just picture Chalmers strutting around his office, wiggling his arse and brandishing a feather duster.

'But that said, a few of the other SOG guys, not naming any names of course, have been along before. In fact,' Nick said, glancing around, 'I half expected a few more to rock up tonight, but maybe there was something else on in town. Looks like it's just us.'

Thank fuck.

Will's eyes flitted nervously around the room one more time trying to take in all the faces and wondering if he could be so unlucky as to know anyone else. If it was a regular SOG haunt, then there was a chance other coppers might know about it. He could just imagine someone from the fucking promotion board turning up, or God forbid, his immediate boss Richard Moore himself. After all, Richard *was* a bit of a closed book when it came to his personal life. Anything was possible.

But before he could think any further their host for the evening glided smoothly through the crowd, raised a glass high in the air and gave it a series of short, sharp *tings* with a fork.

'If I may have your attention, ladies and gentlemen?'

The chatter died to a soft buzz as Roger took centrestage, obviously in his element.

'Ladies and gentlemen, I'm so pleased to welcome you all here tonight. Before we begin there are some housekeeping matters to attend to. For the uninitiated, we do ask that you adhere to a few basic rules. You are all here of your own free will and if you decide that you have made an error in judgement, now is your time to exit. No one will think anything of it if you choose not to continue on this evening's journey with us and we wish you the very best.'

He paused, his eyes sweeping the room before continuing. Will twitched, desperate to grab Trish and make a break for it, but as he looked across the room and glimpsed the excitement and anticipation in her face, his protest faded. He couldn't bring himself to ruin her night. And he wasn't alone. Judging by the lack of a stampede towards the front door, it looked as though they were all in it for the long haul.

Roger clapped his hands together and grinned. 'Lovely. In that case, let us begin. I hope you all have a delightful evening. And in order to do that, I must ask, on behalf of my wife and me, that you enjoy yourself but respect others, be safe and, most importantly, maintain discretion after you leave the house and go about your day-to-day lives.'

Will snorted. *Yes. Because of course coppers are known for their discretion. Not.*

'Now. As most of you know, there are rooms down the corridor to the right,' Roger continued, pointing like an air hostess to emergency exits. Will fought off a giggle, imagining the debonair host dressed in an airline uniform mincing up and down the aisles. But come to think of it, Roger was younger, not to mention more attractive than most of the old boilers he'd suffered on flights over the years.

'For the more adventurous among you, there are public areas both upstairs and downstairs. However, I would ask you to first discuss this and ensure that both parties are comfortable with the arrangement.'

Will did a visual stocktake of the furniture around him. Grand piano, walnut sideboard, leather couches, drinks cart, bar – all in all, not too promising. He sighed, crossed his fingers and prayed it wouldn't come to that.

Before him, Roger paused again, the ultimate ringmaster revelling in the amateur dramatics. 'If there are no further questions, then I shall call upon the ladies to begin.'

Will held his breath, secretly intrigued. He'd been wondering how these sorts of things actually played out in real life. And here it was, all about to unfold around him.

Roger turned and hit the 'play' button on the stereo behind him, the steady *doof, doof, doof* opening beats of Lady Gaga's 'Just Dance' bursting through the speakers and filling the high-ceilinged room. Will fought back a laugh as the lights dimmed and the room spun around him. It was all unutterably surreal, and Gaga was possibly the last thing he imagined someone like Roger would have on his stereo. Brahms perhaps, a Beethoven concerto, Johnny Mathis at a pinch. But no. It was Gaga, an extended version no less. From behind him, someone cheered and began clapping to the beat. Another couple chimed in, someone whistled, the heat in the room rising. His own toe tapped disobediently along to the beat.

Roger turned back to the centre of the room, now holding an empty fishbowl. It glinted in the spotlight as he raised it high above his head and grinned, the whistles, claps and cheers reaching a crescendo.

Oh my God, this is so clichéd!

Roger lowered the bowl and beckoned to the crowd. 'Ladies, if you please.'

He watched on in astonishment as the women, one by one, came forwards and placed their keys in the bowl. Some, like Nick's fuck buddy Chrissy, luxuriated in the moment, stalking a lap of the centre circle before blowing a few kisses and depositing theirs. Others, like his giggling half-smashed wife, stepped forwards ever more cautiously and flashed shy half-smiles as metal clinked against glass. Will nearly choked on his beer as the last woman to approach turned and smiled at the crowd before placing her keys in the bowl. He'd only seen the back of her, her blonde topknot and short skirt giving off the distinct impression that she'd be in her twenties. But one look at her face said otherwise. She had to be in her sixties and could be none other than Roger's wife, a fact that was confirmed as she leant over and gave him a little peck on the cheek before returning to the crowd.

Oh Jesus. That's so wrong. On so many levels.

'Good luck, mate,' Nick said. 'And don't look so worried – the old battleaxe has got a few decent moves left in her.'

He choked on his beer. 'You've been there?'

'Yeah, mate. Luck of the draw. What can I say?'

Will almost gagged at the thought. He didn't mind older women, had fucked more than the odd MILF in his day, but the woman could have been his mother. *His grandmother, even!* He shuddered and wondered yet again what the fuck he'd let Trish talk him into. Ultimately, he knew that if this was something she wanted to do, then there'd be no way of convincing her otherwise. She could be a stubborn bitch when she wanted to. And hell, if she was giving him permission to screw someone else, then he was hardly going to protest. But deep down, he had to wonder; would the evening *really* spice up their love life as she claimed? Or would it be the start of niggles of jealousy, mistrust and fights? He liked to think he was mature enough to deal with any fallout, but if he was being honest with himself, he wasn't so sure he could stomach the idea of another man fucking his wife.

That said, it was a bit fucking late for regrets.

'What happens now?' he yelled at Nick, struggling to be heard over the music and cheering.

'Watch.' He grinned.

Roger produced a large wooden spoon and stirred the keys in the bowl, smiling all the while at the overexcited crowd. Balancing the bowl in one practised hand, he then reached into his pocket and pulled out, rather too dramatically for Will's sensitivities, something that looked like a handkerchief which he waved at the group.

'Gentlemen. Do I have any takers?'

Will gulped, squirmed with panic as the scene before him became real at last.

What the fuck?

Just like that?

Oh my God.

Someone is about to take my wife off and fuck her senseless. Maybe even in front of everyone.

Gotta get the fuck out . . .

Gotta get the fuck out . . .

But before he could make a beeline for Trish an almighty shove in the back sent him hurtling into the centre of the room. He turned to glare at the ever-amused Nick who had provided the friendly push.

'No way,' he hissed.

'Pussy,' Nick called.

He was only saved when a thinnish, perfectly respectable-looking man in jeans and a polo top piped up. 'I'll get the ball rolling, Roger.'

The throng cheered again and Will escaped back into the darkened corner. Roger beckoned the volunteer forwards, tied the bandana around his eyes and then spun him around. Laughing, he steadied the man and placed the fishbowl directly in front of him.

'Go for it, my man.'

The crowd whooped, someone next to him belted out an impromptu drum roll against a table and polo top guy held aloft a set of house keys on a bright yellow key tag. Will's heart flipped. They weren't Trish's. Polo guy wasn't going to be chockers up his wife in the next few minutes.

Sweet relief.

He peered around expectantly and a laughing thirty-something in a tight black dress pressed forwards to claim him and her keys. Polo guy's face lit up.

She raised an eyebrow, took him by the hand and ushered him off down the hallway to the right, dancing to the beat of the music, the cheers echoing all the way behind them.

Will shook his head in amazement before an idea, a lifesaving idea, hit him. 'Hey,' he said, elbowing Nick. 'What's the go if you pick your own wife out?'

The big guy laughed. 'You get a second dip into the bowl.'

'Oh. Of course.' He nodded, hopes dashed. He'd thought for a moment that he might be able to wrangle picking Trish, take her off to one of the bedrooms for a good fucking and then get the hell out of this weird-arse house. But obviously that was against the rules. And as the guys came forwards one by one, blindfold, dip, cheer and leave, Will fidgeted, the panic rising.

I do not want to do this.

This is wrong.

All kinds of wrong.

He glanced across at Trish who was bopping up and down to the music waiting to be picked and tried again to catch her eye but failed. Perhaps it was deliberate. Perhaps she had no intention of acknowledging him. She wanted to see the game through to the very end without being made to feel guilty or being pressured into leaving. The thought choked him and he watched on glumly.

After three of the guys had neatly paired off, Roger announced that it was his turn. Will looked quickly over to Trish to gauge her reaction, but she continued dancing and giggling with Cherie, giving nothing away. He was sickened by the thought of the old cravat-wearing grandpa climbing on top of *his* wife. But, he rationalised, if Trish didn't mind, then he could hardly object. At the very least, chances of her falling madly in love with him were negligible. And it struck Will that perhaps that's what worried him the most, the thought that she might realise what she was missing out on and dump his arse for someone younger, hotter. Someone like Nick Greaves perhaps.

Roger's wife, the cougar, stepped forwards to take over his role as chief blindfolder and bowl rattler. After giving her a peck on the cheek he withdrew a set and held them high in the air to the cheers of the thinning horde.

This time, the girl with the thick calves stepped forwards, smiled and took his outstretched hand. Roger's eyes sparkled and Will's shoulders sagged with relief. At least Trish had been spared *that*. And judging by her quick whisper to Cherie, he could only guess that she was similarly relieved.

Roger put his partner for the night temporarily to one side while he continued playing at matchmaker, taking possession of the bowl back from the grinning cougar.

'Next!' he called. Nick strode forwards, his huge meataxe figure dwarfing Roger. There was something almost comical about the way he had to bend over to enable the older man to tie up the blindfold. Gaga pumped as his big hand reached into the bowl. The bass pounded. The room swirled. The hand retracted. A bunch of keys on a Brisbane Lions key chain held triumphantly aloft.

Will's mouth fell open.

No.

No.

No.

No.

He knew the keys. Every single one on the chain. Every. Single. Key. He watched on in mute horror as Trish sidled forwards, gyrating with some sort of mock-sexy dance, and took Nick by the hand. The big guy turned, caught Will's eye briefly and gave him a shrug and a grimace before being dragged off to one of the bedrooms.

Yeah, I bet you're really upset, you fucking cunt. A flash of white-hot anger ripped through him. It was one thing to go to a house party and have anonymous sex with a complete stranger, another altogether to have a work colleague, who knew other work colleagues, who he may well have to work with one day, boff your wife.

Fucking arsehole.

Filthy fucking cunt.

He'd been utterly betrayed. Nick should have had the decency to say no, ask for another dip, apologise in advance – something, anything. His entire body reverberated with anger at the thought of Nick Greaves in there peeling her clothes off, laughing, sticking his tongue down her throat and finally, the ultimate insult, fucking his wife senseless. And there was nothing to be done.

Except maybe get smashed.

He turned to the drinks cart, reached for the bottle of twenty-year-old single malt, poured himself a triple nip and downed it in one scorching mouthful. Tears pricked his eyes and the steady *doof, doof, doof* burned through his brain.

A couple of less robust cheers rose and fell as the crowd thinned to nothing. And by the time Will had sculled another three mouthfuls of burning liquor, he turned back to realise that not only were they now down to the business end of things, but that he no longer gave a fuck. On one side, Roger and his patient partner, on the other Nick's fuck buddy, Roger's cougar and a tall guy clad in black leathers who exchanged a quick look with Will.

Who gets stuck with the mutton?

'And then there were four,' Roger cried. 'Who will take the next and final dip?'

Will threw back one more mouthful of Scotch, hoping that he was adequately anaesthetised should he draw the old battleaxe. He took an unsteady step forwards. 'Looks like it's my turn,' he said, winking at the guy in the leathers who was obviously happy to take his fifty-fifty chance. Roger grinned like the Cheshire cat and Will exhaled as the soft cloth of the bandana folded over his eyes. He reached tentatively forwards, feeling the rim of the bowl connect with his wrist.

Please, God, don't let it be the old battleaxe. Please, God. I'll even go back to church again if you just cut me a bit of slack here.

His hands closed around a set of keys and he held them up, whipping the bandana off to judge the women's reactions.

The music continued pumping as his eyes frantically searched both stoic faces.

Bitches. Deliberately making me sweat.

After a few seconds they looked at one another and burst into laughter at the glazed expression on his face.

'Well?' he demanded.

And as Chrissy stepped forwards and flashed him a filthy grin, a flood of relief swept through him.

Thank fuck.

He doubted he'd have been able to get a boner if he'd copped the old duck. But this was good. This was a *bonus*, in fact. Not only did he get probably the hottest chick in the room, but he also got to fuck her knowing that she was with Nick Greaves. Nick 'the traitor' Greaves. That would help dull the pain.

She held out a perfectly manicured hand and whispered, 'I was hoping it'd be you.'

He took an unsteady step towards her, the raw Scotch pounding his brain. In his peripherals he saw leather guy trot off down the hallway with the battleaxe. There was a tug on his arm.

'Come on then,' Chrissy said. 'What are we waiting for?'

Good point.

'Absolutely nothing,' he nodded, the booze sending another pleasantly warm ripple throughout his body.

She made for the hall. Towards where Nick was now presumably fucking his wife. *His wife.* He stood his ground and Chrissy turned back to him, puzzled. 'Well?'

Well, indeed. 'How about . . . we do it right here?' he suggested, nodding towards the plush red and gold rug in the centre of the floor. He had to piss Trish off and it'd piss her off no end if she thought he was having a better time than her. Everyone would wander back in and see what a good time he was having, fucking the hottest chick in the room on the floor, across the couch, on the grand fucking piano for all he cared.

Serve Trish right.

Serve you right too, Greaves.

Chrissy tilted her head to the side and considered for a moment. 'You sure?'

He swung her around, grabbed her arse cheeks firmly with both hands and pulled her towards him, kissing her deeply before releasing her.

'I guess that's a yes then,' she laughed, fingering the top button on her blouse.

But despite giving Chrissy a good hard fucking from one end of the living area to the other, watched over by several curious couples who'd later emerged from their rooms to enjoy the rowdy show, Trish had been, in the end, completely unfazed. In fact, she'd spent the ride home gushing about how cool it all was, how it made her feel horny just thinking about them both with other people and about how she'd love to go next month, if it was okay with him.

He ignored the question. Sulked and cut her off when she started on about the sordid details of her romp with Nick. He didn't want to hear about it. It *didn't* turn him on. And from the endless winding curves of Taroona to the frost-covered slopes of Mount Knocklofty he obsessed over the thought that Nick Greaves might be a better lay than him, that Trish might sneak back for a covert round two.

And he had no idea what he'd do if that was the case.

As they pulled into the driveway, Trish now taking her turn to sulk as a result of his silence, he just wanted to have a hot shower and forget about the whole damn night. His head was thick and aching from the Scotch and he was pretty sure he'd done his lower back in while bending Chrissy over one of the high-backed bar stools.

And when he finally jumped in the shower, to add insult to literal injury, he'd screamed like a bitch when the scalding-hot water slapped the long, deep nail trenches Chrissy had zig-zagged from his shoulders to his arse.

All in all, it was a night he'd rather forget.

By the time he dragged himself into work the following morning, *that* morning, knowing he was going to have to spend the day doing the groundwork on Suzy Ward's rapist, he was pissed off, hazy, disorientated from downing too many Nurofen Plus tablets and totally not in the mood.

For anything.

But apparently the outside world was waiting for no man.

He opened his eyes and shifted in the chair at the sound of a gentle knock on the office door.

'Come in.'

He groaned inwardly at the sight of Lucy Howard's face. Any other time he would have welcomed her in, enjoyed a chat with her. She wasn't a bad chick. Solid, resourceful, a lateral thinker – a rarity itself among coppers of her experience. She was a little serious perhaps, a little *too* squeaky clean for his personal tastes, but undoubtedly one of the rising stars of the junior ranks who'd more than held her own among senior officers on the CIB course a couple of weeks earlier. She'd make a good detective once she learned the ropes and did a few good years of solid front-line groundwork. But no matter how much he liked her, her presence meant only one thing: the fact that Suzy Ward's statement sat before him on the desk, still unactioned. He sighed and pushed all the thoughts of the previous night firmly to the back of his mind.

'Hi, Sarge,' she said a little wearily. 'I just wondered if I could have a chat to you about that statement I took yesterday?'

Ah. Back to reality all right.

The girl looked tired; great bags hung from beneath her unexpectedly dull eyes. No doubt she'd been out on the turps. But hell, as long as she hadn't been anywhere near Taroona, he didn't give a shit. He squirmed in his chair, trying to stave off the itchy tingle that was creeping up his balls.

'Sure. I was going to have a word with you anyway, Lucy.'

She dragged up a chair and perched beside him.

'Oh? Was the statement all right?'

'Yeah, yeah, it's fine. Good, actually. Much better than the crap that some people try to pass off to me. I just wanted to get your impression of the victim. Did she seem legit?'

She didn't hesitate. 'Absolutely.'

'Okay. That's one less thing to worry about then. Oh, and good work getting her over to the hospital so quickly. We should be able to get some sort of confirmation of a drug from the urine test. Sounds like she's on the money with that.'

'Yeah . . . um . . . about that, Sarge . . .'

'Mmm?' he said, fingering the statement and trying to look as though he'd been working on it all morning.

'Um, I just wanted to ask you . . . seeing as you used to work in the Drug Squad . . . what you think he might have given her.'

He paused, tried to ignore the cannon fire blasting from his brain to his temples. 'Well, we haven't had a lot of reported incidents in Tassie involving drink spiking, so it's a bit hard to say. But judging by some of the articles about the drug scene on the mainland, I'd put money on it being either roofies – that's Rohypnol – or GHB.'

'Oh. Can you tell me a bit more about them?'

Coffee.

Must have coffee.

Shut up, brain.

Okay. One minute of explanation to a keen young constable, as a favour to John, then coffee.

He forced a smile. 'No worries. What do you want to know?' he asked, throwing the statement back on the desk.

'Um, I thought you might be able to tell me how they'd be administered, the effects of them, that sort of stuff.'

He swivelled around in his chair to face her and thought back to the bits and pieces he'd learned about them over the years. They weren't especially commonplace in Tassie, but the drug courses he'd done had touched on them. 'Well, put simply, they're both commonly known as date rape drugs. They can both be colourless, odourless and pretty much tasteless, although there have been reports of some GHB tasting a bit salty, but they can basically be slipped into a drink without the person being aware they're there.'

Lucy frowned again. 'Are they liquid or pills?'

'Both,' he said with a shrug. 'You can get a vial of liquid, or if you're popping a pill in a drink it will dissolve anyway, so the drinker isn't any the wiser. That's why you should never let anyone buy you a drink in a club or mix you one, even if you know them. Our alleged rapist bought our victim a drink and therefore had the prime opportunity to slip something in without her noticing.'

'You said we should be able to detect the drug in the urine test, yeah?'

'That's right.' He rummaged around on his desk and pulled out a battered medical magazine that he'd kept from his Drug Squad days. He flipped to the article he'd read to briefly reacquaint himself with drink spiking the day before and scanned it quickly again. 'According to this research, which is a couple of years old now, you should theoretically be able to trace roofies for up to a week, a week and a half max, after ingestion. From memory, GHB leaves the body a lot quicker, within two or three hours, although I remember reading somewhere not long ago that there's an advanced test they can do to trace it up to a day or two after ingestion. So if our girl was given GHB, we might be pushing it but we'll still have a crack.'

'Oh.'

A cloud of disappointment crossed her face and he sought to reassure her. 'Don't be too disappointed, Lucy. You've done a good job. The guys out at Forensic Services should be able to track some residuals in her system either way. Enough to confirm her story at least. We've also got the vaginal swabs, and since she didn't have a shower but came straight to us, then that increases our chances of finding some semen.'

'I guess. But . . .'

'But what?'

'Even if there's semen, it doesn't really prove anything, does it? I mean, even if we manage to track this Tom guy down, couldn't he just argue that they had consensual sex?'

'Yeah, that's right, but it still goes some way to corroborating Suzy's story. She says they had sex; we can prove they had sex. It just supports another part of her allegation. Every little piece counts, you know, Lucy. You don't just go looking for the smoking gun and ignore the bullets, the fingerprints, the DNA, the alibi and the phone records. Every piece is as important as the next. It all adds up to create the bigger picture.'

She sighed and he sensed the but.

Wait for it . . .

'But, Sarge,' *bingo*, 'what if the other pieces of the picture *don't* come together? What if you're only left with his word against hers, and he's saying that she . . . I don't know . . . had been drinking, but that he was still convinced that she was consenting?'

He rubbed one temple, willing the throbbing to stop. 'Look. It's not all as bad as you might think. A few years ago there was an important amendment to the Criminal Code to do with sex offences. It came about because, as you rightly say, when it boiled down to his word against hers – and I say his and hers because that's how it plays out ninety-nine per cent of the time – juries were finding it impossible to prove beyond reasonable doubt that a defendant was guilty. Remember that the burden of proof for the Supreme Court is "beyond reasonable doubt". Fifty-fifty – maybe he did, maybe he didn't – isn't reasonable doubt. Sixty-forty, with her word being the sixty, isn't even reasonable to convict him on. Even seventy-thirty, you're pushing shit uphill to get a conviction.'

'So what happened?'

'Well,' *fuck, I need coffee*, 'let's use Suzy as the example. If we manage to track down Tom and Tom argues that yes they *had* sex but it was *consensual*, then we can fall back onto this amendment which basically says that a person can't actually give consent if they're asleep, unconscious or so affected by booze or drugs as to be unable to form a rational opinion in respect of the intercourse. You saw the video from Jane Franklin Hall. Suzy Ward couldn't even walk properly because of the drugs, or the alcohol, or whatever it was, let alone provide consent, so as much as our man might try to give that a run, we've got pretty good evidence to the contrary. See what I mean?'

'So you're saying that even if you can't find any drugs in her system, then you could still charge him because she was clearly under the influence of something, be it booze or whatever, and therefore couldn't consent to sex?'

I wonder, is it possible, that the veins in my temples could pound so hard that one of them actually explodes? If so, how bad would that be, medically speaking?

'Sarge?'

'Yeah, sorry. That's right. It's certainly not as straightforward as his word against hers in a case like this.' He studied her face, the downturned mouth, the deep furrows that straddled her brow, the remaining, unanswered questions reflected in her eyes and cringed, realising that coffee was still way off in the distance.

Get over yourself. You made a promise to a dead man. You will help them. Train his kids, make them better coppers, look after them. She's one of them.

'What else did you want to know, Lucy?'

'Um . . . I just . . . well, this is Hobart. *Hobart*, for God's sake. How easy would it be for someone to get their hands on these roofies or GHB? I mean, I never heard about them when I was at school or uni.'

'Maybe you moved in the wrong circles,' he said with a smile, thinking of the amazing bag of northern lights he'd had from his own dealer George Casalis only last week and how a smoke might be exactly what he needed to get rid of the headache once and for all. 'If you have the right connections, anything's possible. And it's not like we're talking about coke or heroin. There's bugger-all market in Tassie for those kinds of drugs because basically there's no real money. But stuff like dope, Es, speed – God, I even had a ketamine case last year – it's around. If you want roofies, you can get them. They're big on the party scene and . . . that reminds me . . . GHB is big on the gym scene too.'

'Here?'

'Yeah. We've had a few reports. Body builders like it. They use it as a synthetic steroid.'

Lucy nodded, her eyes distant.

'Anything else?'

Please don't let there be.

'Um, I know the victim told us she has pretty much no recollection, but what about the physical effects of both of these drugs?'

Oh Jesus.

'Well, the main thing to realise is that if it was either drug, according to the nerds in the science magazines, she'd have been incapacitated in anywhere between fifteen minutes and half an hour. Her account is spot on. She might have felt vague, tired, disorientated or even hallucinated before blacking out. She might have been moving and talking but have no memory.'

'Might she have been conscious while he was raping her . . . um . . . and say, unable to defend herself due to incapacitation and then, like, unable to recall the event, or is it more likely she was totally out of it for the whole experience and therefore remembers nothing?'

What the fuck?

It's way too fucking early in the day for this.

He tried to recall what he knew. 'Um, from what I've read, she probably would have been conscious but unable to speak or move. Then the anterograde amnesia would have kicked in, meaning that once she "woke up" she was unable to remember most of what happened. Probably not a bad thing, if you ask me. But look,' *let's wind this up*, 'let's not focus on all of that. It's all hypotheticals. Let's just say Suzy Ward's lucky to be alive. Combined with booze, those drugs can be nasty. Seizures, a coma or even death. Remember the Dianne Brimble case? That was GHB.'

As his last sentence registered, the blood drained from her face and without thinking he reached for her arm. 'You okay?'

She nodded but looked away, her eyes misting up.

I just knew there was more to this. What the fuck is going on here?

'Lucy, what is it? Tell me.'

'N-nothing,' she stammered, reaching in her top pocket, pulling out a tissue and blowing her nose. 'Could have died, you say?'

'Of course. Both drugs are central nervous system depressants. Combined with booze, they've been known to be lethal. But Suzy's okay. And I'm sensing there's more to this than you're telling me. So spill.'

'It's nothing. Don't worry about it.'

She rose to leave but he grabbed her arm to stop her.

It's her. Something's happened to her.

'Lucy, you need to tell me.'

He pulled her gently back down into the chair.

'What happened?' he asked calmly.

She paused and swallowed. 'I think . . . I think . . . that . . . the weekend before last . . .'

He took her hand, gave her an encouraging nod.

'I think that what happened to Suzy . . . the same thing happened to me.'

She put her hands to her face and let out a loud, racking sob.

Oh fuck.

There goes my fucking coffee.

Why did I push it?

I do not want to get involved in this.

This is way too personal.

Fuck, I need coffee before my head explodes.

Too late. You're involved now.

She's one of John's.

Not knowing what else to do, he slipped an arm around her shoulders and sat quietly while she rocked and sobbed. He eventually reached for the hanky in his pocket. It seemed better than just sitting there doing nothing.

'Here, blow your nose and then tell me what happened.'

'There's not much to tell,' she said, giving a huge honk into the hanky and wiping her eyes.

'With Cam in jail, I went over to a friend's place to watch a few DVDs and have a few drinks, you know, to cheer up, and . . . and . . . I woke up in his bed the next morning.'

'And?' he asked.

'And, originally, I thought I'd just had too much to drink and had got drunk and slept with him. I hadn't thought any more about it since. Thought that if I just pushed it to the back of my mind, then it was sort of like the whole thing had never happened. You know?'

Will sighed, thinking of his wife and a virtual stranger practically skipping down a hallway to a bedroom, then of himself, three quarters cut bending a different bare-arsed stranger over a grand piano and fucking her until his dick was raw.

Oh yes. I know exactly what you mean.

'Anyway, when Suzy came in yesterday and told me her story, it rang a bell with me. It was exactly like what happened to me. My so-called friend mixed my drinks. They were made out of my sight. I blacked out on the couch. When I woke up it was obvious that we'd had sex and . . . and . . . since Suzy told me, and I've started trying to remember what happened, I've had this memory, or image, or whatever the hell it is, that comes back to me. It's of him, on top of me, naked and . . . you know . . . and I'm just lying there trying to scream and push him off me but I can't move and I can't talk.'

Will frowned, his mind switching into investigative mode. He felt like a total prick for asking, but he had no choice. *Forgive me.* 'Lucy, I don't want to sound like I doubt you, but is there any chance you could've just had too much to drink and fallen into bed with this guy?'

She shook her head, her nose beginning to run again. 'No way. If I'm drinking, I can usually have four or five Bundy and Cokes before I get wobbly and slurry, and even then, I still remember pretty much everything. I had three. Only *three* that night. There was no chance I was smashed. Plus, Cam and I had just, well, moved beyond friendship into . . . well, you know, and there's no way on earth I would jeopardise that. And, well, they've pretty much gone now, but I was absolutely covered in bruises. Big, black and blue splotchy ones. On the inside and outside of my thighs. It was weird, Sarge. I mean, really weird. I never wanted to have sex with him. Wouldn't in a million years.'

Right. That's that then.

'Okay. Then I guess it would make sense that if there's a batch circulating, we may have a connection. Hobart's a small town after all. Your friend's name isn't Tom by any chance, is it?' he asked flippantly.

She looked away again, fidgeted in her seat. 'No. It's Nick. Nick Greaves.'

The words lingered, before snapping and bursting through his drug-hazed, coffee-deprived, massively fuddled brain.

Nick Greaves.

What the fuck?

Am I still drunk?

What is going on here?

Is someone playing some sort of sick-arse joke?

Does she know what happened last night?

'Um, do you know him, Sarge?'

He gulped, the pounding in his temples doubling in tempo. 'You could say that. Are we talking about the same Nick Greaves from the Special Operations Group? *Constable* Nick Greaves?'

'That's him.' She nodded. 'He just did the CIB course with me.'

He closed his eyes, tried to concentrate through the haze. What the hell would Nick Greaves be doing messing around not only with drugs, but with Lucy Howard? Especially when he could schtoik Chrissy from Prosecution pretty much whenever he wanted? Granted, with her hair out and a bit of make-up, Lucy might have been marginally more attractive, but . . . enough for the likes of Nick Greaves? He glanced at her again. Surely it wasn't even remotely possible.

'You don't believe me,' she said simply.

Oh fuck.

'No, no, it's not that, Lucy . . . it's just . . .'

73

'Look. I'm telling you the truth,' she cried. 'I was down about Cam. I don't really have any other friends. I've always been a bit of a loner, not that that's ever bothered me. Nick started talking to me on the course. He said I looked lonely and asked me if I wanted to come around for a few drinks and DVDs.'

As she talked, Will reflected. He'd dealt with his share of rapists over the years. They usually selected their victims, be it ten minutes in advance, or ten months in advance. It was rarely random. Her story rang true. If Greaves was as conniving a bastard as he was beginning to suspect, he could well have targeted Lucy from day one of the course. Question was, why? When he could sleep with any number of women. He was, after all, a good-looking guy, as far as Will could see. He was huge, muscular, worked out a lot. At the gym.

The gym.

Was there a connection?

Could it have been GHB scored from his gym?

If so, it was a risky stunt to pull with a fellow copper. He glanced at Lucy again and felt a weird pang of protectiveness. She was naive. Dead naive. And so trusting. Had the potential to become a damned good copper, but as far as life experiences went, she may as well have been living in a bubble. She hadn't policed long enough to despise human beings yet, to distrust them every second of the day, realise that they all lied, about *everything*, and that they would all, in their own way, fuck you over for their own selfish motives. Could that have been the main attraction for someone like Nick? Drug her, rape her, convince her that she'd participated in the event willingly, see if he could get away with it and then have a bit of a laugh? Possibly. Maybe it was all about messing with her mind. The idea that he was making her question herself, her morals and her motives.

The smarmy cunt.

A slow-burning rage crawled up the back of his neck. He wanted to storm out of the office, grab Greaves by the balls and twist them until he screamed. Twist them until they came right off, in fact. One for what he did to Lucy, the other his own private payback for being with Trish.

'I believe you, Lucy,' he muttered through clenched teeth.

She heaved a huge sigh. 'Thank you. It's like, by you saying that, it kind of confirms that I'm not crazy after all. I didn't want to believe it when I first put it all together. It was too awful to contemplate. But . . .'

'But now you do?'

'Now I do.'

'I guess my next question is, what do you want to do about it?'

'What do you think I should do, Sarge?' she asked.

He sighed, instantly depressed at the thought of the only two possible paths.

'Well, you can either make it official, in which case we take your statement and crank up an investigation, or . . .'

'Or I just forget about it and get on with business as usual?'

He nodded. Personally, he'd always felt that if it was him, or his wife or a relative, who was the victim of something similar, knowing what he knew of the justice system, then he'd advise them strongly *not* to go ahead with it. An investigation was intrusive and painful, the court procedure, if they actually managed to charge someone, a living nightmare, and the outcome, bound to be disappointing. Convictions were as rare as hen's teeth. The defendant usually walked away. If, by some miracle, they managed to get up on it, the penalty was laughable. A few months in jail for effectively destroying someone's life. Sometimes not even that. A mere suspended sentence, community service, a conviction recorded. The crook waltzed off down the front stairs of the court smirking, more powerful than ever, searching for his next victim to groom.

No. If it was up to him, he'd forget it and live to fight another day. But then again, this was different. The crook was a *copper*. Someone in a position of trust who'd blatantly abused it. Sure, he was no angel himself, but his own slightly dubious extracurricular activities were purely consensual and didn't involve fucking anyone else up along the way.

Nick Greaves had crossed the line and deserved to be tried.

But . . . there was an added complication. He flinched. If there was an investigation into Greaves's personal life, what were the chances that Roger, the house at Taroona and he himself would be exposed? The tiny hairs on the back of his neck rose and prickled.

'Sarge?' she asked softly.

Jesus Christ.

'Sorry, Lucy. I was miles away. You were asking what to do,' he said. 'And I must say, I don't really know what to advise. Um . . . what did they teach you on your CIB course about the process when it comes to sexual assault?'

'Just the basics – how to take the statement, how to do up the file. Not really much about what happens between the file and the DPP and court.'

Will sighed. 'Okay. Well, the thing is, once you disclose that an offence has been committed, then we're duty-bound to invest-igate it. We launch an investigation and when we're done, the file then goes to the DPP for a decision on whether or not the matter will be prosecuted. Rapes are really, *really* difficult to prove and it usually ends up being his word against hers. That said, most times the DPP'll give it a run so the victim can have their day in court. However, if there's something more than just your word against his, more than just a prima facie case, then they'll occasionally get a win. I've got to be honest with you though; the odds on a win aren't great. It's just *so* hard to prove. And it can be a long, lonely road to go down. Especially given the special circumstances of your matter. I guess you have to think of what's best for you.'

'Well, I don't think I can just forget about it,' she murmured. 'As you said, he could have killed me. He could accidentally kill the next person he tries it on if he gets away with it once. And then I'd have to live with the fact that I didn't do anything to stop him.'

'Yeah, but have you thought about how this might all pan out if you go ahead with it? Not that I want to put you off at all . . .'

Actually, that's exactly what I'm trying to do . . .

She shrugged. 'He'll be investigated and charged. I'll give evidence in court. If the evidence for the case is strong enough, we'll win. If not, we'll lose. But, Sarge, I really think that's a chance I have to take.'

God. She's so naive.

He frowned, ran a hand through his hair. 'That's right. To an extent. But . . . you need to think deeper. If this happened to you a couple of weekends back, then we probably won't have any forensics to work with and it might effectively come down to it being his word against yours. Unlike Suzy, we've got no video evidence to show that you were incapable of forming consent. It could be tough . . .'

'But I've got no reason to make this up,' she insisted.

'I know, I know. I'm just trying to explain how it might unfold. He'll say you came around of your own accord, you both had a couple of drinks and ended up in bed together. His lawyer will argue consent and that's usually enough to get him off.'

She bit her lip.

'And then there's the matter of what it might do to your career.'

'How so?'

Careful, Will.

Be very careful.

'Well, if, and I say *if*, you go ahead with it and he's investigated and charged, then people will feel the need to take sides. He's been in the job, what, nine or ten years now? He's SOG. Black pyjamas and storming houses. The cream of the crop. You're . . . well, you're young, inexperienced . . . they'll make you out to be a troublemaker, Lucy, and that's putting it mildly.'

He shuddered, suddenly remembering a sexual harassment incident from years back. A young female constable had made an official allegation about one of the inspectors grabbing her tit in the elevator. She'd been ridiculed. No one had taken her seriously, even though the bloke in question was a known perv, and after an orchestrated hate campaign against her, she'd resigned and topped herself by jumping off the Tasman Bridge a few months later. All covered up nicely by the commissioner at the time, of course.

They'd make a meal out of Lucy. She might have been shaping up to be a good copper, but there was too much against her. When all was said and done, and all the politically correct bullshit was waded through, policing was still a man's world.

'So you're saying I should just . . . let him get away with it?'

I'm not allowed to say that. But yes, of course that's what I'm saying.

'I'm just saying that you need to think this through and be realistic about it. If we had some forensics, even a positive test for GHB or roofies, then maybe . . . but even then, you know what lawyers are like. They'll tear you apart, make you out to be nothing more than a promiscuous liar.'

She chewed at one fingernail, looking pensive, not to mention so damned young. So vulnerable. Deep down, part of him *wanted* Nick formally taken to task for his behaviour. At the very least he'd be suspended pending an investigation. That'd hurt the prick and his ego. But was it worth the price, given what Lucy would be putting herself through?

Given what might be exposed about a certain swingers' party?

Fuck you, Trish, for getting me into this mess.

Whatever.

Fuck.

'Lucy, it's up to you. All you have to do is say the word. If you want it investigated, then we investigate. And we'll do the best possible job. I just don't want to give you false hope that we'll get a conviction and I don't want you to rush into anything without having thought it through. Is there any chance you could run it by Cameron? You'll need his support if the shit hits the fan . . .'

'No!' she snapped. 'I don't want him to know yet. He's got enough to deal with. No. I was thinking about it all last night and . . . and . . . I want to go ahead with an investigation, Sarge. If nothing else, it might help track down this Tom guy. There's gotta be a connection with the drugs. It's just too much of a coincidence. And besides, I can't just sit back and watch Nick go about his bloody job as if nothing happened. He's made an absolute fool out of me, and the system. He has no right to call himself a copper after what he did.'

He smiled, tried to push his own reservations aside. The girl had some balls. Despite all his warnings she still wanted to proceed. Maybe she wasn't such a pushover after all.

He sighed. 'Only if you're sure, Lucy. Because once we start this ball rolling we'll see the investigation right through to the end – until it's handed over to the DPP. No turning back. Got it?'

'I understand all right,' she said, sitting up straight in her chair, a glint of anger flashing across her face. 'Look, I'm not saying it's going to be pleasant. I'm not that silly. I'm possibly the most private person in the world and I know this is going to be embarrassing for me, but if it saves him from doing it to someone else, then there's no choice. I couldn't live with myself if it happened again and I could've done something to prevent it. I want him charged.'

Will nodded slowly, turned to his computer – *goodbye, coffee* – and opened up a fresh pro forma statement. An image of Commissioner Ron Chalmers swept through his mind. The man would have a fucking shit fit when he read it. In fact, they'd probably hear the bellowing all the way down to Huonville. If there was one thing Chalmers hated, it was a scandal in the ranks. He almost giggled at the thought.

Maybe it won't be such a bad thing.

Anything that annoys the fuck out of Chalmers must surely have some merit.

'Right then, Lucy,' he said in his most soothing voice. 'Let's start with the first time you met Nick Greaves.'

The Commissioner

8.57 am Monday 13 June

'Good morning, Commissioner,' Jillian sang, barely looking up from her emails. He strode past, not even bothering with his usual guttural, pre-coffee grunt, and slammed the door to his office with such a tremendous bang that it rattled the walls three floors down. On good mornings those on the floor below knew that he'd arrived for the day. Not-so-good mornings, two. A three-floor rattler was a sure indication that there was no point trying to talk to him for the rest of the day.

Not that he cared.

Once inside, his leather satchel went flying into the far corner of the room, accidentally clipping his beloved peace lily and snapping a flowering stem in the process. He glared at the scene for a moment, too exasperated even to bellow. A lone vein throbbed in the centre of his forehead. Cursing, he turned away, decided to ignore it. It was, after all, only a plant. Admittedly, it was the first time the damned thing had bothered flowering in the three years he'd had it, but still. It was the least of his worries. Hardly worth giving himself a coronary over.

He draped his trench coat across the back of his chair, dug the mobile from its pocket and threw it on the desk, scowling at the fact that the stupid thing had managed to turn itself back on and was in the process of dialling some random number full of ones, fours and sevens. He jabbed at the 'end call' button and glared at it before throwing it back down.

Outside, the grey, low-hanging skies made his office darker and he reached for the light. Winter had hardly begun and already the relentless early-morning sleet was beginning to get on his nerves.

A gentle knock at the door. Jillian appeared with his cappuccino and newspaper in hand. She placed them discreetly on his desk and he watched her leave without uttering a word. She knew better than to attempt conversation when he was in one of his moods. And he liked that about her. It was one of her many redeeming features.

At least *someone* understood him.

But before he could settle and commence the morning ritual of paper and coffee, the mobile rang. He snatched it up, knowing full well who it was going to be.

'Ron?'

'Of course it bloody is. Who else were you expecting, Christopher?' he snapped.

Honestly. The bloody Premier annoyed the crap out of him sometimes. The younger man was as thick as a Salamanca

Market bratwurst. With bun. And extra onions. In fact, Ron had often wondered how the hell he managed to get himself out of bed in the morning and put his underpants on, let alone run a state with his full spectrum of natural handicaps – his utter stupidity, complete incompetence and a level of disorganisation that made Catweazle look like a neat freak with a severe case of OCD. Then there were his piggy, squinty, shifty eyes and, worst of all, his high-pitched, nasal squeak which left one with the impression that he'd be hard-pressed to inspire confidence in his daughter's pet guinea pig, let alone an entire electorate. Still. He was a handy ally to keep tucked away in his pocket for a rainy day.

'Steady on, Ron, I was just checking,' the Premier said.

'Right. Well. Carry on then. Sorry about before. The mobile cut out in the lift.'

A lie, of course.

Christopher's earlier call had got him so worked up that he'd accidentally pressed the 'end call' button while storming from the car park. After several failed attempts to call him back, and much sputtering and cursing, he'd realised with a degree of humiliation, not that he'd ever admit it to anyone, that he'd forgotten how to access his contacts list. He'd subsequently stuffed the phone into his pocket vowing to hurl the goddamn, useless piece of crap off the bridge on his way home that evening.

He detested technology. And this was his first mobile. Ever. Rolled out in bulk to the commissioned officers with no consultation whatsoever. And despite his earlier vehement protests about wanting nothing to do with the damned thing, to his colleagues, wife, children and self, the piece of junk had landed on his desk two weeks earlier with a thousand-page instruction book. He'd immediately vowed never to waste the time reading it. Hence the small issue with the contacts list.

Not only was it an irksome piece of shit, apparently it was a cheap, outdated irksome piece of shit. His son had laughed – something about Nokias belonging in museums alongside the other dinosaurs – but Ron couldn't even begin to imagine using something like Greg's BlueBerry, or BlackBerry, or whatever the hell he called the stupid thing. And Jillian's iPhone, which sat on her desk buzzing and whirring and chirping every time he set foot outside his office, left him with the overwhelming urge to reach for the nearest heavy object and bring it crashing down on top of the irritating piece of plastic, smashing it to smithereens. *That* would be immensely satisfying.

No. Ron couldn't think of the stupid, pointless little hunks of plastic without feeling his blood pressure rise.

And it wasn't just phones. It was the people using them. He hated the way they seemed glued to all sorts of stupid, mind-numbing gadgets this day and age. It was just plain fucking rude, pure and simple. The world had coped without them perfectly well for thousands of years and all of a sudden you had people using them in restaurants, in libraries, on buses and loudly, ever so loudly, for all and sundry to hear in the mall.

Why, people were practically having nervous breakdowns if they couldn't access them for so much as an hour while they were in a meeting or on a flight. Only last week on a return flight from Melbourne three quarters of the passengers seemed to be reaching for the beeping, buzzing detestable objects before the wheels even touched the tarmac, the symphony of bleeps filling the cabin as the flood of messages poured in. And he'd put money on it that ninety-nine per cent of the calls weren't emergencies. Surely everyone on the plane wasn't waiting on life-or-death news.

And that was the other thing that annoyed the shit out of him – the pointless, ridiculous, irritating conversations most people insisted on having so loudly that everyone in the state could hear them. It was never, *Brian has pulled through the major, lifesaving surgery, thank God.* More like, *Did you end up picking up last night?*, *Becky's such a bitch*, and, *Jeremy's soccer match went really well on Saturday.*

There was no escaping the nonsense. Just last week he'd sat down in a nice cafe in the mall for a quiet relaxing lunch, far, far away from the hustle and bustle of the station, only to be subjected to some silly cow prattling on beside him about how little Joey's toilet-training regime was going. Loudly. Of course. After three relentless minutes of her bullshit he'd glared at her until she huffed and hung up.

Once upon a time he'd been convinced there was nothing worse than a noisy, disruptive child in a cafe. Now, you had noisy children, with their even noisier mothers glued to their mobiles talking shit.

It was appalling. Screw getting a fine for using a mobile while you were driving; people should be fined for using the fucking things full stop, anytime, anywhere, unless it was an unequivocal emergency.

And this morning had been just another perfect example of why the world would be better off without them. They professed to be reliable. But when you really, *really* needed them, they fucked you over, stomped on your head and ground cigarette ash into your eyes, laughing all the way.

'I tried to call you back,' the Premier said.

'Mmm. Well. I'm here now. I'm sitting down and better still, I have a coffee in front of me. So tell me again from the top.'

Christopher sighed. 'Right. I had drinkies with Shorty's right-hand man last night.'

Ron frowned. Shorty. The bloated, sanctimonious, self-righteous little prick. They were supposed to be on the same team, but Ron didn't trust the fat moustachioed director of the Department of Public Prosecutions as far as he could throw him. And Shorty never ceased to make it clear that the feeling was mutual.

'And?'

'And, as I said before, he happened to mention that Shorty, his delightful boss, currently has a file sitting on his desk containing a nasty allegation. Specifically about you, my old friend.'

Ron lightly traced the mole on his forehead with one finger. The suspense had been killing him from the second the phone had cut out. Would it be something from years back? Something recent? Something easily deniable or something substantial? The possibilities were endless. All grim, of course, but some far grimmer than others. And the last thing he needed was Shorty on his back carrying on like a pit bull with a toddler.

'Yes, Christopher. We got to that point in the conversation. Now, what you *didn't* tell me was the essence of the allegation.'

The Premier paused. 'Something about blackmail involving the chief editor of the *Hobart Mirror*, Artie Myers.'

Ron sniggered with amused relief. On a grimness scale of one to ten it was a three or four; nothing that couldn't be rectified. There were plenty of other matters that could have been worse. Could have brought him unstuck. Ones that would have left bigger, deeper footprints. His long lunches with the high-flyers at the casino in exchange for a suitable lack of police interference in their operational matters. His silent share in the Men's Gallery, the strip club across from the police station – once again ensuring they were protected from the wrath of the licensing police. Then there were his two eldest children. The prostitute and the drug dealer – the greatest disappointments of his life whose ongoing 'indiscretions' he'd gone to considerable lengths to cover up over the years. Even the relationship between the Premier and himself, which was probably the most complex of them all. Not that there was anything wrong with it though. After all, the commissioner of police should be able to share confidences with the highest ranking public servant in the state. It wasn't his fault if Christopher then went and tipped off the appropriate suspect government officials who were targets of operational investigations so they could change phones, pay off disgruntled whistleblowers, shred documents, stop talking or at the very least take a breath and get their stories relatively straight before matters progressed.

And then there were Christopher's three or four speeding charges he'd magically made disappear, not to mention Christopher's bloody wife who had an even heavier lead foot than he did.

Yes. There were plenty of tricky little situations that Shorty could misconstrue if he chose to do so. But it was all worth it.

In return for his close government connections he received a delightful annual payment from the government coffers. He liked to think of it as his unofficial bonus, one that had bought his wife a new car, put a new wing on the back of the house and was this year just sitting, quietly lining his retirement fund. He earned every bloody cent of it and he'd be buggered if that was going to dry up just because Shorty decided to stick his beak in where it wasn't wanted. The blackmail thing was nothing. Less than nothing in the big scheme of things.

'You had me worried there for a minute, Christopher. But if that's all it is, then there's nothing to it, my friend,' he purred.

'Mmm. Apparently Shorty thinks differently.'

'Well, Shorty's wrong,' he said calmly, throwing his legs up onto the desk. 'That prick has been trying to take me down for years. This'll just be another one of his pathetic, unjustified attempts. He can dig all he likes. He's not going to find anything.'

'He says the newspaper editor made a written statement about it, claiming that you'd threatened him and that he was forced to destroy some article he was going to run in return for you sitting on charges you knew he had pending.'

Ron frowned. *So, Myers has gone and opened his big gob. Obviously he wants his wife to know that he's a filthy little pervert. Interesting.* He dug deep in his top pocket for a small silver key, stuck it in the bottom drawer of his desk and withdrew a manila folder with the standard yellow Prosecution brief plastered across it. The cover name was clear: *Arthur Joseph MYERS, Offensive Behaviour.* He ran a hand over the folder, smoothing off the dog-ear on the top right.

'It's a crock, Chris,' he lied smoothly. 'Do you know how many people are charged by TasPol every day? I can't be expected to keep track of all and sundry. And I certainly don't know anything about any charges for anyone down at the *Mirror*.'

'Well, Artie Myers says differently and as I said, he's allegedly made a statement to that effect. Is there anything I need to know here, Ron?'

'Oh, for God's sake. When did Myers supposedly make this *dastardly* allegation?'

'I don't know. A few months ago, maybe?'

'Think about it, Christopher. If that was the case, why on earth would he be jumping up and down about it now?'

The Premier sighed again and Ron sneered.

Even his sigh sounds squeaky.

'I don't *know*, Ron. Maybe the journo who wrote the supposed article in the first place started putting pressure on him to run the story and it's all erupted from that. I'm pretty sure the *Mirror* crew has some contacts up at the DPP.'

Ron's eyes narrowed. Christopher was probably right. The journo probably *was* behind it, arsehole that he was.

Tim fucking Roberts.

Tim 'I'm such a hot shot journo' Roberts.

Tim 'watch me bring down a government' Roberts.

The little prick has been quiet lately, come to think of it.

He cleared his throat. 'Well, look, as I said, Christopher, I don't know anything about it, so it's case closed as far as I'm concerned and unless Shorty has any evidence he'd like to present to me, then I'm quite sure that'll be the end of it.'

The Premier sniffed. 'He reckons he does and he's planning

on starting up an inquiry into it. That's what I'm trying to tell you, Ron. Apparently there *is* a file relating to Myers. And apparently that file is missing. It never made it to court, which firms up his story a bit.'

A quiver of uncertainty danced in his stomach. 'Bullshit,' he snapped, running a finger down the length of the file before him. 'It confirms nothing. Just that Prosecution are a bunch of incompetent morons who couldn't put together a case and present it to a court if their arses were on fire. Files go missing all the time. Why, only last week the Prosecution inspector gave a counselling report to one of the constables about losing a file. When you're dealing with thousands at a time, one or two are bound to go AWOL. Not to mention the fact that sometimes files just simply don't get done. If it's just a summons matter, it can be overlooked if an officer has a huge workload. Lost in their workload. It's perfectly legitimate. Not good, but legitimate as in, it's been known to happen. Now, if there's nothing else, Christopher, then I'm busy. I've got a CMG meeting this afternoon and I need to prepare.'

'No worries, mate, but don't bite my bloody head off. I'm just the messenger.'

'Well, that's all very well and good,' Ron hissed, suddenly furious at the Premier's casual tone. 'But do you know something, Christopher? This . . . *mess* we're talking about is as much *your* fault as anyone's and it was going be *your* nuts on the chopping block if Myers ran the story he had planned. I know exactly what was in that article. And let's just say that that particular little nugget of journalistic brilliance was more about *you* and your dirty colleagues than *me*. So let's also just say that once again, I've been forced into cleaning up your . . .

fucking . . . mess. And to tell you the truth, I'm getting a little tired of it.'

He slammed a fist onto the desk, and listened to the silence on the other end of the phone before immediately regretting giving anything away to Christopher. He should have known better. He liked the guy, but at this point in time he shouldn't be trusting anyone. Not if fucking Shorty had him in his crosshairs.

'Oh Jesus, mate, what have you done?' Christopher eventually groaned.

'Nothing that can't be undone. Now forget this conversation and leave it with me. I'll sort it,' he said calmly, terminating the call and eyeballing the folder before him.

What to do with it?

What to do with it?

Shred it?

No. If Shorty was about to initiate an investigation, then they'd turn his office over sooner rather than later. Nothing was more sure.

Dump it on the way home?

Too risky. He might be seen. Someone might find it and put two and two together and if Shorty was serious about an investigation, there was a chance they might put the dogs on him. He groaned, imagining the surveillance footage appearing on the telly, of him stealing down a back alley and dumping the evidence in a bin. And then, a moment of clarity.

If he took the folder back over the road to the Prosecution section and stuffed it somewhere unlikely in the cramped, overflowing office that boasted floor-to-ceiling cabinets full of files, then his theory about it simply being lost would have some credence if and when they did a search and uncovered it there. Losing it in there would be a bloody sight easier than finding it had been all those months back. He'd have to make sure it was clean of his prints. There were no problems with DNA. He might have managed to convince every other member of TasPol to give a swab sample to go on record for 'forensic elimination' purposes but he hadn't been silly enough to do it himself. Then it'd just be a matter of denying his conversation with that prick Myers and *voilà*, that would be the end of it.

If Tim Roberts's article about corrupt politicians and public servants ever looked like making the light of day, he would rethink his campaign of suppression. Come up with a plan B. But first things first.

He slid the file back in the drawer and made a mental note to have a trip down to Prosecution later that afternoon – *those lazy pricks are always gone by four* – to get rid of it for good. Feeling somewhat placated, he sipped on the now lukewarm cappuccino and slumped back in his chair.

Monday morning and already he'd had a gutful.

Fortunately there was a hint of sunshine on the gloomy horizon. The Corporate Management Group meeting later in the day. Always something to look forward to. The prospect of a CMG never failed to put him in a slightly brighter frame of mind. It was like looking forward to a tropical holiday, or planning a lazy weekend on his boat with just the fish for company, or salivating over homemade cheesecake before sinking his teeth into that first exquisite mouthful. Infinitely pleasurable, with the anticipation of the event being as exquisite as the event itself.

The primary role of commissioner at CMG was a cross between chairing and admonishing, with the emphasis on admonishing, and Ron always savoured the prospect of sending a few good hard kickings right down the line to those lazy good-for-nothing inspectors whose sections had failed to meet their quarterly benchmarks. Kickings, topped off with a generous lashing of public humiliation. The combination was heady, almost sensual.

He was the star of the show, of course, lording it over them all, making the subordinates squirm and stutter their pathetic excuses as to why their bone-lazy shifts and sections had failed to meet the quotas the government so desperately needed to make the state's books balance. A lack of traffic infringement notices for the quarter meant a lack of dosh in the coffers and the effect was passed right down the line. Light coffers meant a light police budget which meant that everyone had to tighten their belts. Not to mention the fact that Ron would miss out on his actual legitimate bonus, the one dished out for meeting the set targets.

Indeed, some days he felt like he was the only one who truly understood that the state police force – *service*, he reminded himself with a snort – needed to be run like a business and that idle, deadwood coppers who weren't pulling their weight were the quickest means of bringing down the empire. He often chuckled to himself about the quaint public perception that police existed solely to protect and serve. The cold hard truth was that their principal function was to raise the funds to keep the state ticking over. Anything else, such as keeping the streets safe, was simply a bonus. And those who protected the underperforming part-time mummies and full-time malingerers could be expected to cop a reaming at CMG. It was only fair.

And the last CMG had been a doozy all right. He'd handed out the usual spankings.

You're telling me that your section has issued one hundred and fifty-eight inattention infringement notices this quarter, when you know full well that your benchmark is set at two hundred and ten. Where are the other fifty-two, Inspector? What's that? Five on long-term sick leave, three on second-ments and three on month-long courses? That's not really my problem, now is it? You know your benchmark well in advance. There's no reason why you couldn't have taken that into account at the beginning of the period and worked harder on inattentions. You're not doing much to convince me that you are an effective leader. If you can't manage your troops and your benchmarks properly, then maybe we need to look at putting someone in your place who can, eh? Someone with some brains. Some nous. A sense of drive, perhaps?

He'd watched with smug satisfaction as the inspectors grovelled, bleated and snivelled their pathetic excuses for their dismal numerical performances before accepting their inevitable bollockings and returning to their seats, heads hung low. Ron'd been on such a roll and was having such a good time tearing one of the few female inspectors a new arsehole that she'd actually burst into tears in the middle of the session.

It was a new high.

Never before had he witnessed tears.

He'd barely believed his own eyes when he looked up in stunned silence, her humiliation on display for all her high-ranking colleagues to witness. He'd given one final growl and told her to go and sit down before she embarrassed herself further, but not before glancing around the silent room, hoping to catch an amused wink or twitch of a smile from any of the men gathered there. He'd been bitterly disappointed to note the sea of bowed heads and clasped hands. Not so much as a smirk of male solidarity.

Not that it put him off. It showed that they were all in their places.

Oh yes. He enjoyed the theatrics of a good old CMG all right.

The phone on his desk rang and he grabbed it, wondering if Christopher had been dwelling on their conversation and had decided to continue on with his blubbery, doom-and-gloom hissy fit.

'Sir, I have Detective Sergeant Torino and Constable Lucy Howard here to see you.'

'I'm busy, Jillian,' he said quickly. The last thing he needed was some unplanned interruption. He needed to relax so he could go over his CMG figures one more time.

A pause. 'Uh . . . I left a note on your desk first thing this morning, sir. They phoned earlier and said it was urgent. They need to see you right away.'

He glanced across the sprawling mahogany desk and spied the yellow sticky note covered in Jillian's loopy, childlike handwriting. He snatched at it and snarled, irritated beyond belief.

'I *really* am busy, Jillian . . .'

'I know, sir, but Detective Sergeant Torino insists.'

He glanced at his watch, looked back to the lukewarm coffee which was irredeemable now and growled. 'I can give them five minutes. Send them in. And get me another coffee.'

He pushed the newspaper and coffee to the side of the desk and rose to greet them. Torino was one of the two token wogs in the force, a solid bloke who seemed to keep his nose relatively clean. He was slightly less annoying than the other wog, the Greek who was currently out on some weak-as-piss stress claim. *Sleeping in and watching TV on full pay more like it.* Aided and abetted by his wife the psychologist no doubt, a thought that annoyed Ron to the point of exhaustion.

What the hell had the police department been thinking when they'd hired a bloody female psych? What the hell did women know about men's minds? He hated psychs at the best of times, what, with all their mumbo jumbo, all their namby-pamby, warm-and-fuzzy bullshit, and a woman in the post was a complete insult to his hardworking men.

Not that they should have been seeing a psych, anyway.

Why, in his day, you just got on with the job. And if you weren't cut out for it, you took it like a man, handed in your warrant card and found yourself a new job. But no, not anymore. Nowadays they sat around on their arses on full pay crying like pathetic little bitches. And the Greek was no exception.

But at least Torino was a worker and Ron had nothing against the man himself, apart from the fact that he was interrupting the morning routine. Howard, on the other hand, was and would always be the troublemaker who'd stood by and watched her sergeant get killed. He'd had nothing to do with her since that fateful, black day in TasPol's history some five months earlier and had aimed to keep it that way. He hadn't been sure he could keep his disdain to himself if he had to be in the same room with her. But apparently the time had come.

He flashed them an insincere smile.

'Sergeant, Constable, come through, please. Nice to see you both.'

He noted the file in Torino's hand, the way the girl's shoulders slumped and he twitched in agitation, fighting the urge to spin her around and shake her.

You should look proud to wear that uniform, you blundering girl. It's a privilege. Not something to be embarrassed about.

And Torino didn't look much better. Ruffled, edgy, fidgeting, and badly in need of a haircut.

Ron proffered them a seat and took his own, leaning forwards, like his wife told him he should in situations like this, to show them he was open to whatever they had to say.

'How can I help you both?'

Torino cleared his throat, had the decency to look vaguely apologetic. 'I'm sorry to disturb you, sir, but it's a rather delicate matter.'

Ron waved a hand dismissively. 'Not at all. You know my door is always open. Now what can I do for you?'

'I'll get straight to the point, sir. Lucy came to me yesterday morning to discuss a statement she'd taken for a rape that I'm working on. A uni student. One that happened over the weekend. The statement was good. Lucy came top of the CIB course, you know.'

Ron glanced surreptitiously at his watch and tried to feign interest.

Torino cleared his throat again and continued. 'Anyway, during the course of the discussion, she made an allegation of a personal nature.'

Ron's ears pricked up and he leaned even further forwards. Personally he didn't give a fig that the girl was the top of anything. He'd seen it all before. Female officers, uni grads who came and went, thought they knew it all, only didn't have so much as a scrap of common sense to enable them to do the real job properly. You couldn't recite university theories to a drugged-up, rampaging nutcase and expect to solve the situation anytime soon. But an allegation of a personal nature was something else.

What the hell is she up to?

'The rape of the uni student was facilitated by drugs. GHB or Rohypnol, we believe,' Torino continued. 'Lucy has alleged that two weekends ago she was subject to the same . . .'

Don't say it, Torino.

DO NOT GO THERE.

Ron closed his eyes and held up a hand, now fully aware of what was coming. 'Please, Sergeant. I'm going to have to ask you to stop there. If an offence is disclosed, then I'm obliged, as per the code, to have it investigated. And if it turns out to be what I think it's going to be and she then changes her mind about reporting it . . .'

'I'm aware of that, sir, and I informed Lucy of that before we took this any further. The fact is, she alleges that she too was drugged and raped, she wishes the matter to be pursued and has made a statement detailing the allegation.'

He closed his eyes briefly, each word slapping him about the face.

You stupid girl.

You stupid, stupid girl.

Do you have any idea what sort of can of worms you're opening up?

He glanced over at Lucy, tried to remain perfectly composed so as not to betray his thoughts. She sat straight-backed in her chair, her hands gripping the arms and her eyes staring defiantly straight into his.

You fucking troublemaker. Trouble with a capital fucking T. You stupid little girl.

The last thing he needed, on top of the shit with Christopher, was a female constable screaming rape. What the hell sort of message would that send about the training and professionalism of Tasmania Police?

He cringed just imagining the headlines: *Police Not Even Capable of Looking After Themselves; How Can the Public Trust Them?* For her to allow herself to have got into that position in the first place was . . . was . . . well . . . folly at best, thoughtless, negligent stupidity at worst. That she should display such little regard for her own personal safety and wellbeing. It made him want to grab her by the hair, smack her around her stupid, insipid cow face and scream.

He closed his eyes again, silently cursing the day women had been allowed to join the rank and file.

'Sir?' Torino asked.

'Yes, yes. Sorry. I was just thinking. I must say, this has never happened to me in all my years of service and I'm wondering about the best way of dealing with it.'

Not to mention wondering why the hell you didn't manage to talk the silly bitch out of taking it further, you stupid wog. I thought you had some brains.

'With all due respect, sir, we just wanted to let you know before we commence an investigation. I've already spoken with Detective Inspector Moore about it . . .'

100

'And?'

'And . . . he agrees that if Lucy wishes to go ahead, then we treat it exactly the same as we would any other allegation of rape.'

Great. Just fantastic. Wonderful.

Don't roll your eyes.

It's happening. There's nothing you can do about it. Apart from some damage control down the track . . . maybe.

Breathe.

'Precisely, Detective Sergeant Torino. So, thank you for bringing that to my attention and make sure DI Moore gives me regular updates on the matter. If you need to speak to the police psychologist, Constable Howard, then you only need to ring Temple House and they'll arrange an appointment for you. Anna Tsiolkas is very good and it's all confidential, of course,' he said crisply, rising from his seat, determined to get them the hell out of his office so he could think.

But they remained.

'Uh . . . there's more, sir,' Torino said flatly, pushing the file across his desk.

More? Isn't it enough that some idiot girl who should never have been a police officer in the first place gets herself sexually assaulted and is determined to make a public laughing-stock of my police force? I don't want to know the details of it all. Just go and fucking investigate it, like I pay you to.

Frowning, he pushed up his glasses and sat back down, file in hand.

'Well?' he asked, pretending to flip through the statement.

'The suspect, sir.'

'Yes, what about him?'

'It's Nick Greaves, sir.'

Ron looked up, caught the twitch on Lucy's face and felt his nostrils flare. He placed the file squarely on the desk, took his glasses off and folded them before staring into the distance.

Nick Greaves.

Constable.

Special Operations Group.

Highly trained professional.

One of their most elite.

Ten years' experience.

Well respected.

Liked.

Admired.

He looked back at Lucy who stared, her eyes daring him to challenge her, and he glowered with rage. If he was a younger man, in an office alone with her, he would have picked her up by the shirt front and shaken her until her teeth rattled in her empty head. Had she *any* idea what an allegation like this meant? Was she so utterly naive to think that she could just swan around, spout off about some alleged fantasy of screwing someone of the . . . the . . . calibre of Nick Greaves, have him charged, and they would all live happily ever after? Was she that big a village fucking idiot? What the hell was she playing at?

'It's true, sir,' Lucy said, shifting uncomfortably in her seat. The silence was obviously testing her, but he wasn't the least bit impressed with her little show of bravado.

Don't you fucking talk to me unless I tell you you can, you fucking halfwit!

He took a deep breath and fiddled with his glasses.

'I don't doubt you for a moment, Constable. It's just that . . . well . . . this changes things, doesn't it?'

'With all due respect, sir, it shouldn't,' she said. 'Nick Greaves drugged me and raped me. He is a rapist. The fact that he's a police officer shouldn't change anything. I know it sounds awful. It took me a while to get my head around it as well, but that's all there is to it. And if anything, it makes me even more determined to follow it through. Someone in his position shouldn't be allowed to get away with it.'

A little hiss of anger escaped from between his teeth and he calmly placed his hands underneath his thighs, fearing he might just jump up and smack her.

Shouldn't change anything, my fucking arse.

Do you have any idea what this is going to look like splashed across the front page of the paper?

Do you?

'That's correct in one respect, Constable,' he said through gritted teeth. 'But on the other hand, it does pose something of a difficulty.'

'Why, sir?'

Dear God. Are you really that stupid?

'Well . . .'

Torino cut in, his face grim. 'With all due respect, sir, I understand how sensitive this will be. It will need to be handled with the utmost discretion both from an investigative point of view and a media point of view. I've explained all that to Lucy, and we've talked over some of the potential problems she may face in house because of it, but she's determined to go ahead. And surely, at the end of the day, the overriding fact is that she wishes to make an allegation of sexual assault and she has just as much right to do that as any other member of the public. Any concerns over the potential backlash both in house and out of house that something like this might generate need to be pushed to the background.'

Got your union hat on now, haven't you, buddy? he thought with a sneer.

'I assure you ... Sergeant ... Constable ... that the last thing on my mind is, as you infer, the media. I am more concerned about your welfare, Constable.' *Yes. Go the welfare angle. Makes it sound like you give a shit.* 'Nick Greaves is a popular figure. You know he'll have supporters. You know they will not take something like this lying down.' He paused, battling to keep a straight face at his unintended pun. 'They have the potential to make your life very difficult.'

Torino chimed back in, sitting forwards in his chair. 'Well, surely it's up to you and your fellow commissioned officers to step in and make sure due process is followed . . . which includes the fact that witnesses, including Lucy, aren't tampered with or harassed in any way.'

Yes, because it'll be so fucking easy to step in and tell a pack of SOG thugs to behave themselves. Fuck off, Torino. You're as stupid as your little friend.

The anger boiled over and he fought to contain it. On his forehead, the mole gave its telltale itch.

'Yes, yes, I understand that, Sergeant. I was just wondering if there was possibly a more . . . *practical* way of handling the matter in house. So it doesn't get out of hand.' *And out into the media.*

'Such as, sir?'

He shrugged. 'A mediation session between you and Greaves, perhaps?'

He caught the look of utter surprise on both their faces.

'Sir, again, with all due respect, we're talking about the drugging and sexual assault of one of your officers,' Torino said, his face flushed. 'A *crime*. It should be dealt with via the appropriate, established legal process.'

Ron backpedalled rapidly. 'Of course, of course. I was just musing out loud, seeing if we couldn't come to some internal arrangement before it all gets out of hand and people, mainly you, Lucy, get hurt.'

'I've already been hurt, sir.'

He checked himself, adopted his most soothing, sympathetic voice. There was nothing else to be done. They weren't going to back down. Not yet. He would think it over and come up with something. 'Right. Well. I suppose that if you're certain you want to go ahead with this, knowing all of the possible ramifications, then . . . then . . . it goes ahead,' he said with a grand flourish of his hands.

'Thank you, sir. There's a good chance it's linked with our uni rape, because of the drugs, so we'll run the cases pretty much side by side, with some help from Internals,' Will said, getting up to leave. Lucy followed, head bowed, face pale.

'Very good. Yes. Keep Professional Standards in the loop. Maybe make it a joint operation. I'll have a word with Detective Inspector Moore later. Thank you for letting me know so promptly,' he said, ushering them out of his office.

He watched as they entered the lift and the doors closed behind them. The smile dropped instantly from his face and he turned to Jillian who was also watching them leave.

'Get me Richard Moore on the phone immediately,' he demanded, before turning on his heel and storming back through his door, slamming it behind him for the second time that morning. He wanted to scream, yell, abuse someone, tear some hair out. Instead, he paced the length of the office fuming. Mulling it over. Trying to comprehend what had just happened.

What the hell would a big, fit, popular, good-looking guy like Nick Greaves be wanting with a plain, irritating, incompetent like Lucy Howard? The man could have had anyone he wanted, and from all accounts on the rumour mill, he had no shortage of admirers. Soggies were pussy magnets. Had Howard come onto him and been rebuffed? Was this some sort of revenge? What other possible motive could she have had for coming up with such a crock of shit?

He threw himself in his leather chair and snatched at the file before him, flipping randomly through the pages of her statement.

At his house.

Having drinks.

Blacked out.

Woke up.

Semen.

Bruises.

He'd been polite, respectful the following morning.

Ron slammed the folder shut, closed his eyes and conjured up what he knew about Lucy Howard. She was unreliable. She'd done nothing to help John White. She'd been friendly with that other idiot copper who'd managed to get himself charged with assault months ago. The one who was currently in jail. *What is his name? Wells? No. Walsh. Charlie? Callum? Cameron. That's it. Cameron Walsh.*

Come to think of it . . . Yes. He'd heard the rumour that they'd become a little more than friends during Walsh's bloody court case.

That's right.

He almost snorted with glee. Lucy Howard was banging that no-good son of a bitch who'd also managed to drag TasPol's reputation into the gutter by pummelling the shit out of some innocent man at the pub one night.

Lucy Howard and Cameron 'at Her Majesty's pleasure' Walsh.

He let out a little 'Ha' and slammed a fist on the desk, proud of his deduction skills, thrilled to think that he still had it. Wasn't it obvious to Torino and his crew? Lucy Howard had been screwing Nick Greaves – although he still couldn't work out why Greaves would want to go there – and she was covering her arse in case her jailbird boyfriend found out. That, and the fact that she stood to make a few dollars if she put forward a claim for Victims of Crime compo.

He pushed the folder away in disgust. It was hardly rocket science. Lucy was looking after number one and trying to make a few bucks and Nick Greaves was nothing but collateral damage. It made him want to spit.

The shrill ring of the phone interrupted his train of thought.

'I have Richard Moore on line two, sir,' said Jillian.

'Well, put him through then.'

A click. A tinkle of piano. Then Moore.

'Commissioner. How are you?'

How am I? How do you think I am, you twit? Call yourself a DI?

'Fine, Richard. I've just had Detective Sergeant Torino and Constable Howard up to see me,' he said, picking a pen from his holder and rubbing it absentmindedly between his fingers. It was his favourite pen, a souvenir from Paris with a scantily clad brunette on one end. When tipped upside down, her black bathing suit fell away leaving a huge pair of tits and a well-thatched pubic region – *très* European, just the way he liked it.

'Ah yes. I'm aware of the situation.'

'Good, good.' He paused. 'It's a terrible business.'

'It certainly is. Made even worse considering the suspect.'

'Mmm. About that, Richard . . .'

'Yes?'

'Um . . . I don't mean to sound insensitive, but . . . what's your overall impression of her allegation?'

'I'm not sure I know what you mean, sir.'

Ron rolled his eyes. *So you're going to make me spell it out. Make me out to be the insensitive, politically incorrect prick for not swallowing her story hook, line, and sinker.*

'I just meant . . . is there any chance that Constable Howard's allegation might be . . . how do you say . . . a little off the mark?'

He listened to the pause on the other end of the phone. 'Off the mark? Well, what can I say, sir? Lucy strikes me as quite a forthright, earnest sort of girl. She's young, sure, but she seems to be developing into a good copper. We headhunted her for the CIB course and by all accounts she did an amazing job on it. She's got a keen lateral thought process that blokes twice her age lack.'

Blah, blah, top of the course, blah.

Ron threw the pen on the table and drummed his fingers impatiently. 'Yes, so I heard. But what I was more interested in is . . . and once again, I don't mean to sound insensitive, but I have to cover all angles here . . . is there a chance that there could be a little more to her allegation than she's saying, that it's not quite . . . accurate?'

'What do you mean, sir?' Moore asked slowly.

He took a deep breath. *Try not to sound like a total bastard.* 'Well, it's just that Greaves is a damn good copper with an immaculate record. Ten years' service. Promotional qualifications, Part-time Dignity Protection, full-time Special Operations Group. Commendations. I mean, he's very good at what he does and he's kept his nose clean and I just can't see it unfolding the way she's told it. Is there a chance that, say, she's ended up in bed with him and now doesn't want her boyfriend to find out about her little *indiscretion*, shall we say?'

His speech was met with a silence on the other end of the line and he jumped to fill it.

'Look. All I'm saying, Richard, is that I know you thoroughly investigate the complainant's side of things in these situations and I'm just trying to maintain a semblance of impartiality – double-checking, shall we say,' *before the media gets hold of this shit*, 'that her story adds up.'

Moore spoke calmly. 'I spent an hour this morning going over it all with her, sir, and her story checks out. She's a smart kid and a credible witness. That's not to say it's going to be easy to prove . . .'

'Why?'

'Well, it's a rape,' he said flippantly. 'They never are. But I've made sure she's very clear on our chances of a conviction. We've talked it through and she's under no illusions that it'll be easy. There's no forensics due to the time lapse. She had some bruising, but that's gone now and wouldn't have meant much in the big scheme of things, anyway, as you'd be well aware. I've had victims who were beaten half to death and the defence just argued that they liked it rough.'

'Anything else?' Ron sighed, marvelling at just how disastrous the whole thing was panning out to be.

'Well, as you'll see on the file, we've got her clothes from the night. They were at the bottom of the laundry basket which was a bonus, and with any luck we'll get a semen sample from them.'

'Which will be useless if he argues consent,' Ron said, turning the pen upside down and watching, mesmerised as the bathing suit slid off his brunette again.

There was another long pause. 'Yes. I'm aware of that, sir. But it goes some way to at least corroborating her account.'

Corroboration. Fantastic.

'Any sign of the drugs?'

'No. She left it too long. Anything will have dissipated by now.'

'But even if you did find something, the defence could simply argue again that she's, say, taken drugs of her own volition, right? I mean, the young ones pop all manner of party drugs these days, don't they?'

'Yes, sir. Although if we had been able to confirm that there was something in her system, it would have further corroborated her story. Every little piece of the jigsaw puzzle counts.'

Oh, spare me. You've got jack shit. End of story.

'And there's one other thing, sir. Something I was just going over now.'

'Mmm?' he said disinterestedly, tipping the pen back up and re-dressing the brunette.

'I've been checking the system for information reports, seeing what we have on date rape drugs over the last few years and we've got a few hits.'

'And?' Ron snapped.

'Well, there are three IRs relating to the sale of GHB at a gym called Apollos in Glenorchy. One three months ago, one about nine months ago and the other, a couple of years back. An A1 and a couple of B2s.'

Ron snorted. 'Sounds like you're drawing the longest bow in the history of the world there, Detective Inspector. So what? There've been allegations of the existence of date rape drugs in the south of the state. It's hardly conclusive, is it?'

'Perhaps not on its own, sir, but when you add to it the fact that I'm reliably informed that Apollos is the gym that Nick Greaves frequents at least three times a week, then it's defi- nitely a link. And a link worth investigating.'

Ron paused, closed his eyes. *So there have been, in the past, drugs at a gym where Nick now works out. There are always drugs floating around gyms. Doesn't mean he's ever seen them, let alone used them. It doesn't mean shit.*

But Moore was clearly determined to kowtow to the girl and go in hard with this.

Poor Nick.

'Right,' Ron said brusquely, not prepared to leave Moore with the final word. 'One final thing, Richard. Um . . . I haven't read the statement yet, but I'm guessing that she didn't put up much of a struggle?'

He was met by another uneasy silence before Moore's voice cracked, his irritation obvious.

'That's right, sir.'

'Oh. I only ask because a few weeks ago that lawyer, what's-his-name . . . O'Donnell?'

'Yes, sir. Sean O'Donnell?'

'That's the one. He managed to have a win with that last rape case you had with the young girl . . . what was her name again? Chloe Morris? He argued that she didn't really put up much of a struggle and that therefore she couldn't have been too concerned about what was unfolding.'

His words hung in the air. When Moore finally replied there was no disguising the raw fury in his voice. 'Lucy alleges she was *unconscious* at the time, sir. It would have been a bit difficult for her to struggle. And more to the point, with all due respect, sir, it's really not very helpful when dealing with these cases to infer that there should be some sort of struggle-o-meter employed. You can't say, "Oh, I'm sorry, but you only registered a six on the struggle-o-meter, so unfortunately, you must have wanted to have sex." There can be a whole host of reasons why a victim, particularly a tiny inebriated eighteen-year-old like Chloe Morris doesn't struggle when she's got a hundred kilos of violent, threatening bartender wedged inside of her against her wishes. And I think that being unconscious at the time, as Lucy was, is a reasonable excuse.'

Ron's eyes bulged. Moore's thinly disguised attack was astonishing. Clearly he was siding with the girl, and clearly poor Nick Greaves was going to be considered guilty until proven innocent. 'I was just trying to cover this thing from all angles, Inspector. Playing devil's advocate. It's nothing personal. And yes, I see your point. Enough said. So, I trust you'll be onto it right away then?'

'Yes, sir. The plan at this stage is to tread gently. If we pull Greaves in now, he's only going to deny it and argue consent. We'll make some inquiries around the gym, see if anyone wants to talk. We're also going to do up a telephone intercept warrant, see who Greaves himself is talking to. That might also lead us towards our uni rapist. And I've also discussed the possibility of having Lucy wired up to go and see him, put it on him, see what he says. She's quite amenable.'

He's been a copper for a decade.

He'll see it coming a mile away, you fool.

'Sounds like you've got all bases covered,' he said. Then a thought occurred to him. 'You're not trying to pin this uni rape on Greaves as well, are you?'

'No,' Moore said calmly. 'He doesn't fit that victim's description and it definitely doesn't look like him on the CCTV footage we have of him from the college.'

Ha.

See. Bet you're barking up the wrong tree with it all.

'One other thing before you go, Richard,' he said, tipping the pen back to disrobe the brunette once more. 'Keep it covert, please. The fewer people who know about it the better. Because if there's the slightest chance Howard's not being up-front with us, then I don't want it ruining a good man's reputation. I *especially* don't want to see it plastered all over tomorrow's newspaper.'

'No, sir. We'll leave that for when we've arrested and charged him at least,' Richard said.

Ron closed his eyes and groaned inwardly at the thought of the circus that would stir up. 'Right. Well, thank you, Richard. I'll leave it in your capable hands and please keep me updated on the investigation.'

'Certainly, sir. Goodbye.'

He plonked the phone down, swivelled around in his chair and stared at the wall for a moment. Moore was determined to go ahead with it, not that he had any choice if the silly cow wanted to push it. The media would get hold of it. A good copper would be ruined and there was fuck-all he could do about it.

Fuck.

All.

What an absolute prick of a day.

And it's not even lunchtime.

He shook his head trying to rattle the DPP, the Premier, Artie fucking Myers and Lucy Howard out of his mind. He reached for the phone again. 'Jillian? Where's my fresh cappuccino? And make sure you put extra chocolate on top.'

He pulled out his CMG notes, put his feet up on the desk and perused the appalling quarterly figures while he waited. At least the afternoon would be something of an improvement on the morning. The lazy sons of bitches had given him plenty to work with. Thank God for small mercies. And perhaps with any luck, he might be able to make the female inspector cry two CMGs in a row.

The Detective Inspector
10.15 am Monday 13 June

'Arsehole,' Richard muttered, placing the phone down and gazing up at one of the two personal items in his small, cold, south-facing office. The framed print of the Magna Carta hung directly above his desk. He'd bought it years back in Salisbury and hauled it lovingly all the way home. Not an easy task, but one well worth the effort. It was more than just a decoration. The document symbolised the beginning of constitutional law in England, in the English-speaking world for that matter. And for Richard, it was an all-important symbol, one that reminded him day after day that the powerful, like King John himself, were bound by the law, by the common people.

'Everything all right, Rich?'

Will Torino poked his head around the doorframe.

'Yeah. Just had the Prince on the phone.'

'Oh, that explains it then,' Will nodded.

'Explains what?'

'The whole "arsehole" thing,' he said, wandering in and pulling up a chair. 'He made a right prick of himself in front of Lucy. We only just got back, so I'm guessing he was straight on the phone to you?'

'Yep. He decided to play devil's advocate with me and ended up bringing up Sean bloody O'Donnell. Among other things he implied that we'd be battling to prove it because Lucy didn't struggle enough, because of course, being unconscious has no bearing on it. God, that man is infuriating! Obviously he's concerned about the ramifications of all this but, jeez, he could at least try to appear a little bit sympathetic to Lucy.'

'Yeah. She might be putting on a brave face, but she's pretty gutted.'

Richard nodded. On top of the usual feelings associated with this type of victimology, Lucy was berating herself furiously, feeling so damned stupid for having it happen to her. He'd raked over her statement with a fine tooth-comb and her brutal, self-deprecating honesty, her utter humiliation about the whole situation was almost too painful to read.

Can't believe I put myself into this position.

Feel like such an idiot for not realising what he was doing.

Feel like an even bigger idiot for not realising what had actually happened until so much later.

Wouldn't be surprised if my boyfriend dumped me, anyway. Just for being so stupid.

I'm supposed to prevent and detect crimes. What a joke.

The low-down stunt Greaves had pulled was matched by the flogging she was giving herself.

'I know,' Richard said, running a weary hand through his hair. 'All the more reason to make sure we do a damned good job on it. You happy to run with it, Will?'

'Absolutely. It's gonna be a bitch though. You know how hard these are to prove at the best of times. Let alone when the suspect is a copper who knows exactly how it all works. And not just any old run-of-the-mill copper.'

Will was spot on. Richard remembered Greaves from the CIB course only a couple of weeks back. He'd been a cool customer all right. Seemed to have his head screwed on and certainly knew his stuff. He was also as keen as a pack of starving greyhounds after a rabbit, approaching Richard after their final mock interview exam and asking straight up if there was any chance of a secondment to CIB. He hadn't thought much about it at the time. Greaves was a bit cheeky maybe, ingratiating himself and angling for the inside scoop. But, now that the allegation against him was staring up from his desk, Richard felt a twinge in his gut. Just for a split second. Greaves was *too* cool. Too cocky. A bit of a lad and overall, just a tad too eager to please. But the one thing he wasn't was stupid. And that was going to be an issue. It gave him a head start on every other crook whose file crossed Richard's desk.

'Mmm. I know. And when I spoke to Lucy before you went to visit the Prince, I made sure I let her know just how difficult sexual assaults are to prove. But she's determined.'

Will grimaced. 'I know. I had the exact same conversation with her when she first told me. I tried to totally talk her out of it, but she wasn't interested.'

'Oh well,' Richard said, 'she might come across as a bit of a softie, but she's a smart girl. She's thought about it, she understands the potential difficulties and the ramifications, so really, we have no choice but to do the best we can with it. Plus, anything we uncover might help us out with the Ward rape as well. Not to mention the fact that there could be more victims out there. So, we'll need to tread carefully but I want to throw everything we can at this. Let's start building up a picture of our man – work and downtime. We've got multiple IRs suggesting GHB has been available at his gym in the past. Supposing Greaves has had access? Could his nasty little trick on Lucy have been a once-off or is he regularly in contact with the stuff? Has he used it on anyone in the past? Is he dealing perhaps? If he's buying, selling, using drugs or even bragging to his mates about what he *thinks* he's got away with, then there's a chance someone up at that gym will know about it. That will be the starting point. Some discreet inquiries, of course. No point tipping him off too early.'

Will nodded.

'Also, I want listening devices. One in his house, one in his car. We're still not exactly sure at this stage what we're looking for in terms of drugs and won't be until Forensic Services gets Suzy's test results. Even then we're still only assuming it was the same thing. But, for argument's sake, let's say it was. If he's talking about it, I want it on tape.'

'Bit of a long shot, don't you think?' Will asked, chewing the end of his pen.

'Maybe, maybe not. We might pick up something. He might, at the very least, be talking about Lucy or what he's going to do next. Which reminds me, we'll also need phone intercepts. House and mobile.'

Will sat back, a cloud of doubt crossing his face. 'TIs? You reckon we'll get the warrants signed off? An op like that'll cost a bomb and you know Chalmers'll resist paying anything more than he has to.'

'Of course we'll get sign-off,' Richard said dismissively. 'It's all in the wording. Just remember when you're doing up the warrant applications, that it's not just Lucy we're dealing with here. There's a good chance it could be linked to your uni rape, and if there's a batch of whatever the hell drug it is floating around out there, then there might be more to come. There might already be other victims who don't want to come forward, due to, say . . . *embarrassment*, or, like Lucy, for the plain simple fact that they're not even aware of what happened to them.'

'True.'

'Which leads to my next strategy. Once the warrants have been signed off and the devices are in place, we'll do a press release about a possible epidemic of drink spiking in town. Not only do we run a chance of dredging up another victim or two who might be able to give us some leads, but it might generate some chatter on Greaves's phone.'

'Mmm, but we can't guarantee that he'll read a paper or watch the news though.'

'Of course not. But on top of that, I'll send out a generic email to all staff regarding the situation, a reminder on how to handle it if they're the first point of contact for a victim in the station.'

'Okay. And if that gets nothing?'

Bloody hell, Will, and what if you get hit by a bus on the way to work tomorrow? It was odd. Normally Will would be

119

all over something like this, but suddenly everything was a potential obstacle.

What gives?

But he said nothing, merely shrugged. 'We stick with the original plan. Give it a week or so. If there's nothing forthcoming, then we'll send Lucy in to talk to him. See how she plays it. If he doesn't put himself in it directly to her, then we might get some chatter on the phone afterwards. If we still get nothing, then we interview him, release him then see if he talks. Either way, I'm gonna want those devices in for at least . . . a month, yeah?'

'Sure, Rich. I'll go start the paperwork,' Will said, standing up, an odd expression on his face. Richard couldn't pick it despite their years of history.

Doubt?

'Happy with that?' he asked innocently.

'Yeah. Well, actually, no. There's one thing bugging me in all of this.'

'Shoot.'

Will paused and frowned. 'It's just that, well . . . why Lucy? I mean, he probably picked her out right from the beginning of the course and groomed her, but . . . why *her*? I dunno. It's just not sitting well with me and I can't put my finger on it. Something to do with his motive, or lack thereof perhaps.'

Richard chuckled. 'Oh, boy. You really were in the Drug Squad too long, weren't you? Okay. Do you remember old Kenny Appleton?'

'Sergeant Appleton?'

'Yeah. He was my boss in CIB when I first started out.'

'Uh-huh,' Will said. 'Old guy. Grey hair, pot belly, gruff old bastard.'

'Yep. Well, I worked a few rape cases with him back in the day. And I remember asking him a similar question once.'

'And?'

'And . . . maybe it's easier to show you.' He stood up and beckoned Will out into the hallway.

'Helen,' he hollered towards his secretary's tiny office some twenty metres up the corridor. 'Can you bring me that file for the CMG, please?'

He leaned against the wall and winked. 'Watch.'

Sure enough, within seconds the uber-efficient Helen, who he couldn't have made it through the day without, strode briskly down the corridor, heels clacking with a fierce metronomic rhythm, a file in one outstretched hand.

'Anything else, Richard?' she asked crisply.

'No, thanks, that's all.'

She nodded and trekked back along the hallway, her mind clearly already on the next three jobs she had to complete.

He turned to Will. 'Now tell me what you just saw.'

'Uh . . . Helen in work mode?'

'Yes, and?'

'Uh . . . a very confident woman who has a very busy day, obviously on a mission to get your file to you as quickly as possible and then get on with it.'

'Aha,' he said. 'Got it in one. You noticed the way she walked. The aura of confidence. The way her hips moved, the pace of the stride, the way everything about her says, "I'm busy, so make it quick and don't mess with me." Yeah?'

Will nodded.

'Now compare that to the way Lucy walks. When she's in public, in work mode as Constable Howard, it's different, of course; she pulls her shoulders back, plasters on her most confident face and comes across as relatively authoritative, ready to help anyone with anything. No problem is insurmountable. However, the second she thinks no one is looking she reverts back to plain old Lucy, the person beneath the blue skin, a different physical entity altogether. Her entire demeanour yells, "I'm totally lacking in confidence, I don't really like myself and if I bow my head, slouch and shuffle on past you really, really quietly, you might not notice me."'

Will nodded. 'Spot on.'

'Ah. Not me. That was Kenny's theory. His idea was that perverts and rapists, to a certain extent, pick their victim based on something as seemingly innocuous as their walk. And if you think about it, Lucy is the ideal victim from Nick Greaves's point of view. She certainly isn't the type of woman to hit on him, so immediately she's perceived as being a challenge. She's depressed about her boyfriend being in jail, obviously has bugger-all self-confidence and isn't exactly a social butterfly – something he would have picked up right away.

'She's the perfect choice. Not only does he get the thrill of playing his sordid little games on a colleague, but he plays it safe by choosing someone who he guesses won't kick up a stink about it, someone who carries around so much self-doubt that she'll naturally think it was her fault and will just want to forget about it. So for him, it'd be a high thrill factor combined with a low risk factor. Make sense?'

'That's quite a theory all right,' Will said with a whistle.

'And there *is* one other thing,' Richard said slowly. 'In case you hadn't noticed, I reckon that out of her dowdy blues, with her hair down and a bit of make-up, our Lucy wouldn't be quite as ordinary as she or the rest of the world thinks.'

Will grinned. 'Maybe you're onto something there, Rich. Can't say I noticed.'

'Yeah, right. You're forgetting that I know you too well.'

'Hmm. I'm sure I don't know what you're talking about, boss. But . . . I think that's my cue to go get cracking on those warrants.'

'Good work,' Richard chuckled. 'And Will?'

'Yeah?'

'I took the liberty of ringing Internals while you were over with the Prince. You'll be teaming up with Sonya Wheeler.' He paused, anticipating the inevitable grumble.

'Jesus, Rich, give me anyone but the fucking Rottweiler,' he pleaded.

''Fraid not,' he said. The tough-talking, prickly DS Wheeler was as infamous for her hard-arsed attitude as she was for her colourful, much-gossiped-about personal life. But even though she was a little over-officious – *in fact, make that downright rude* – she was the person for the job and Richard was quietly pleased to have her on board. Will, judging by his scrunched-up face, was less thrilled.

'And make sure you play nicely, Detective Sergeant,' he called after him, before wandering back into the office and throwing the CMG file onto his desk with a sigh. He had to go over it before the meeting. Had to try and come up with some intelligent ripostes for the commissioner's inevitable attack. But no matter what excuses he came up with, he was still going to be in the firing line.

It'd been a bad three months for CIB. A murder, a man-slaughter, two robberies and a series of substantial arsons had taken their toll on the team. Each detective was expected, as per the commissioner's directives, to produce a minimum of four arrests a month, a total of twelve per officer for the reporting period. Eight on the team meant they should have ninety-six arrests. But as usual, the actual crimes for the quarter didn't naturally lend themselves to quick runs on the board. The painstaking hours and hours of manpower had resulted in one arrest for the murder, one for the manslaugh-ter, three for the robberies and none thus far for the arsons, a bitch of a crime which, like most arsons, was proving impos-sible to solve.

He sighed again, did the maths quickly in his head. It wasn't nearly good enough and even with the swift arrests they'd managed to snavel from the uniform section by racing down-stairs and poaching a few of their shoplifters, they were clearly well short for the quarter. He was going to be crucified. It'd be pointless trying to argue that his team had been tied up on a murder and therefore didn't have the time to chase the smaller stuff. Ron was never interested in that argument. There'd be no 'well done on putting a murder to bed', no 'thank your team for all their hard work on getting those robbery results'.

He ran another agitated hand through his hair and mulled over the injustice of it all. His team worked like Trojans and it certainly wasn't their fault they couldn't reach the outrageous targets. Ron was only interested in numbers, in reporting back to the government that Tasmania was living up to its hallowed reputation as the safest state in the nation. And collecting his bonus accordingly.

He looked up at the Magna Carta. *Bet they didn't have to put up with all this stats crap in 1215.*

He'd occasionally dreamed of going to the media, of exposing the stats for what they really were and informing the public that the benchmarks actually *prevented* them from getting out there and doing real, quality police work like they used to in the good old days, back when he'd first joined. These days it was all about quantity. Everything was geared towards making the public feel good about the 'safety' of their state. And the dishonesty of the entire benchmark system, not just the arrest figures, stuck in Richard's throat like a gigantic fur ball. If the public knew, for example, that house burglaries were down across the board, not because house burglaries were actually down, but because they were, under instructions from the commissioner, now officially being classified in the 'injury to property' set of figures, there'd be a riot.

Likewise, the unsuspecting public would be less than thrilled to know that many burgs on motor vehicles were being dodgied up under the much more appealing and certainly less threatening criterion of 'tamper with a motor vehicle'. And by the same token, robberies were, depending on the nature of the specific incident, being downgraded to the much less abhorrent 'assault against the person', another seemingly petty criterion to which the media paid less attention.

They wanted to know about the burgs, the robberies, the murders and the arsons afflicting the community, not the petty stuff. And as long as the big crimes were seen to be falling, no one seemed to pay much attention to the pettier ones; certainly no one scrutinised them closely enough to see that they were rising, let alone put two and two together to realise that the big stuff was being masked by the small.

Richard snorted. Hell, if Chalmers could get away with reclassifying murders into a lower, more publicly palatable category, he would. But regardless, the system existed, and there was no choice but to work within its dishonest confines and suffer its indignities. And if the public *felt* safe, then maybe that was almost as important as actually being safe. Who was he to quibble?

Feeling empty, jaded and not to mention immensely dissatisfied at the prospect of the day unfolding before him, he opened the CMG file. And was promptly interrupted by the phone.

'DI Moore?'

'Boss, it's Mick.'

'Ah. Morning, old boy. How's it going?' he inquired, pleased to put the figures off for a tiny bit longer, even more pleased to hear from one of his hardest workers, Sergeant Mick Lyons.

'Good. Excellent, in fact. I've been trying to get hold of you for a little while . . .'

'Yeah, sorry, I was on the phone to the commissioner.'

Mick laughed, a deep, throaty, smoker's laugh. 'Ah, the irony of it all. I was ringing to let you know we've got something. You'd better pop up and see us if you've got a minute.'

Richard raised his eyebrows. Good news indeed. 'See you in a sec then,' he said, grabbing a set of keys from his personal safe and waltzing out of the room. He stopped long enough to peep around Helen's door. 'I'll be on the mobile for a bit if there's anything urgent.'

Without waiting for her response, he made for the lift and pressed the button for the top floor, humming as he stepped in for the short ride. Nobody of any importance *usually* graced the floor. It was the sole domain of the radio room operators who were barely given a second thought by the rest of the operational police force. But over the past few weeks, things had changed. The large, open-plan and perpetually empty office beside the radio room had undergone a transformation, literally overnight, as a handful of trusted workmen moved in desks, filing cabinets, lockable storage units, computers and boxes of office paraphernalia, all under the cloak of darkness. The locks had been changed, six expensive, uncuttable keys specifically moulded and a high-tech alarm system installed. The covert camera in the hallway facing the door alerted the staff on the other side to potential intruders and no one, not even the commissioner himself, *especially* not the commissioner himself, was to enter the space.

Not that it had become an issue yet. The five people inhabiting the office had been quietly seconded away from their regular duties to work on a task force, one that they were instructed to inform curious colleagues was focusing on a vague, ill-defined fraud matter. It always amused Richard how quickly coppers' eyes glazed over at the mention of cheques, forging, uttering, business loans, dodgy overseas transactions and a paper trail as long as the Amazon. If it wasn't brothels, bikies or firearms, most coppers didn't give it a second thought.

Richard rang the doorbell and stuck his key into the lock, calling out as he came. 'Only me.'

He waited for a second and watched the door close quietly behind him before striding up the narrow corridor towards the main office space. Its pale yellow walls, previously unadorned, were now littered with all manner of charts and graphs depicting dates, events and subjects. In the centre of the room sat an island of desks, pushed together and littered with boxes and an air of optimistic industry.

'Morning, Mick,' he said, throwing his suit jacket on the main desk and greeting the tubby detective and his minions, all personally selected by Richard and Mick themselves and overseen by a single commander and the amenable, perpetually cheery assistant commissioner, both of whom trusted the team to get on with the job at hand and thankfully, didn't feel the need to micromanage.

'Coffee?' Mick asked.

'Sure. You're right – I'll get it,' Richard said, heading for the kitchen.

The long black was his fifth for the morning. He stirred his second sugar in, knowing it was going to be the death of him, but thought it was probably quite a respectable way to go, considering some of the methods he'd witnessed firsthand over the past decade.

'So, what have we got?' he said, perching on one of the analyst's desks.

Mick handed him a scrap of paper, a standard pro forma report from the Telephone Intercept team.

'Don't tell me our little ruse got him talking?' he said, scanning the document, his eyes nearly falling out of his head as he read the transcript of the phone call.

'Worked like a charm, boss. Shorty called me last night and told me his bloke was meeting with the Premier for drinks as per instructions. He passed on the scenario about the file and . . . bingo . . . Mr Premier himself phones our good friend first thing this morning and gives him the heads-up.'

'Dear Lord . . .' Richard said, pausing over the last para-graph. 'And look at this. It's not quite an admission, but . . .'

'Well, that's all very well and good. But do you know something, Christopher? This . . . mess we're talking about is as much your fault as anyone's and it was going be your nuts on the chopping block if Myers ran the story he had planned. I know exactly what was in that article. And let's just say that that particular little nugget of journalistic brilliance was more about you and your dirty colleagues than me. So let's also just say that once again, I've been forced into cleaning up your . . . fucking . . . mess. And to tell you the truth, I'm getting a little tired of it.'

'Oh Jesus, mate, what have you done?'

'Nothing that can't be undone. Now forget this conversation and leave it with me. I'll sort it.'

He read the conversation out loud, hardly able to believe the words jumping off the page. So there *was* something to the allegation after all. A twinge of excitement, tempered with a hint of regret, coursed through his body.

'This is *good*, Mick. *Very* good.'

'Is it good enough though?'

'No. But it gives us something to work with,' he said, mulling over the information. 'Think about what he's said. *Nothing that can't be undone. I'll sort it.* He's going to make a move. I'll put money on the fact that the silly bugger still has that file on Myers.'

Mick's eyes lit up. 'Surely he wouldn't be that stupid?'

'Why not? He'll want to make sure that piece on corruption never comes out, which means hanging onto his bargaining chip just in case. He's still got it. I just know it.'

'So, what do you think he'll do? Try to destroy it?'

Richard paced, his mind ticking over. 'Nope. He's a cunning bugger. He'll know that if he destroys it, it'll add weight to Myers's allegation and therefore there'll always be doubt cast over his innocence. No. I'll put any money on it that he'll try to slip it back unnoticed into the Prosecution office, so he can put the blame on them when it's miraculously discovered. It'd be the only way of fully covering his tracks. Hell, it's what I'd do if I was in his shoes.'

'You want me to get the techies back on board asap?' Mick asked.

Richard nodded. 'Amend the warrant right away to cover the Prosecution office. There's never anyone around there at lunchtime. Plus, I know for a fact that the inspector will be heading out for CMG shortly. I want them in and out of there quick smart with video and audio covering every angle.'

'Done.'

'Anything else before I go?' he asked, grabbing his suit jacket and setting the mug in the sink.

'Not yet. The financials are slow. I had a meeting with our liaison from the tax office yesterday, but they're still trawling through years of his paperwork and have only just got their hands on the ownership documents for the strip club. They want to meet again next week and might have something for us then.'

'Excellent. And the infringement notices?'

'Cat and Benny are still working on it,' Mick said, giving a nod to the two constables who were surrounded by a sea of infringement notice books. They were spread across at least four desks in neat piles, the connies scanning each and every

130

original ticket in each and every ticket book that had been completed and returned to Traffic Liaison.

'They're doing 2011 at the moment but we plan on going back at least four years – back to when the Premier actually took office. So far they've come up with one original ticket issued to the Premier in January and two issued in his wife's name in February. Both issued in the Hobart area.'

Well, well. There might really be something in this after all.

'And have you had a chance to cross-reference them with the Prosecution system and Traffic records?'

'Yep. And guess what? Zilch. Not a single thing pending. It would seem that the tickets never made it to the Prosecution system.'

Bingo.

'So it's looking good that they've been pulled prior to the Traffic Liaison Office getting hold of the admin copy?'

'Correct,' Mick said. 'And I'm sure they'll come up with a few more before they're done with that pile. I'm curious to know at what point Chalmers has been pilfering them though.'

Richard smiled. 'And I have no doubt that you'll work it all out. When you think you have a full list, then we'll look at grabbing each watch sergeant's personal records to see if they've been recorded in their books. That'll narrow down the time frame a bit. Bearing in mind . . . it could be happening at any point, really; he could be pinching them from the sergeant's trays, the outgoing correspondence tray, the Traffic Liaison Office itself . . . the possibilities are endless.'

'True. We've got a lot of work to do yet.'

'Yes, but you're doing a great job already,' Richard said. A pat on the back always made them work ten times harder for him and Mick's grin confirmed it. 'So keep it up, get onto those other matters and let me know if we have a result on the Prosecution office. If he's gonna dump the Myers file, it'll be sooner rather than later.'

He waved them a quick goodbye, strolled back out the door and hummed while he waited for the elevator. At the last second, he changed his mind and opened the door at the stairwell. A walk back to the office before CMG kicked off at twelve might be just what he needed. And as he clacked down the concrete stairs, his footfalls echoing above and below him, he mulled over the job at hand.

The DPP trusted him to come up with the goods on the boss. Shorty was convinced that Ron Chalmers was rotten to the core and Richard hardly required much convincing himself. There was something decidedly off about the man. He'd never been a great fan but had always figured that as long as he was in charge, it was easier simply to get on with the job and give him what he wanted. Ergo, the bloody benchmarks.

When he'd been called into the first hush-hush meeting with the assistant commissioner and Shorty a few weeks earlier and heard the allegations outlined in detail, he'd come away feeling distinctly ill at ease. Part of him hoped the boss *wasn't* filthy. It'd be a complete kick in the guts if that was the case. Granted, the majority of the rank and file detested the man. But there was something bigger at stake. Having a threatening, belittling bully as top dog was one thing, but to have him publicly outed as a crook was something else altogether. It would tarnish *all* of their reputations, regardless of how hard-working they were. He could just hear it now.

They're all dirty.

You can't trust any of them.

Lying pigs.

He sighed, thinking over his conversation with Mick. There was also the problem of how the investigation itself would unfold in the long term. It would get ugly. No doubt about it. When they pooled everything they had and approached Chalmers for a video interview, there was no way in hell he'd play nicely. That had never been his modus operandi. The only possible scenario was that he'd make a prick of himself. Which was why they had to be *damned* sure. They had to go in armed with three, four times as much evidence as they normally would, having dotted every i, crossed every t and covered off every possible angle of defence. Because if they charged him but he walked, he'd make their life a living hell. As sure as the sun rose in the east, the pope was a Catholic and bears shat in the woods.

By close of business, Richard was knackered but on a high. He'd spent the afternoon copping the predictable arse reaming at CMG. It wasn't all bad though. He'd come out to find a missed call from Will and had rung him back immediately.

'You know those IRs about GHB at Apollos?' Will asked excitedly.

'Yep,' Richard said.

'There's more. I did a bit of digging and found an old file in the archives. Seems that a couple of years ago, a woman named

Heather Anderson made a complaint of rape to Glenorchy Police. It was alleged that she'd been out at the Mustard Pot, met a guy who she thought was quite nice and had a few drinks with him. The next thing she knew, she was at home, waking up, knowing that she'd had sex but had absolutely no memory of it. The long and the short of it was that he'd disappeared and she had no idea who he was. Glenorchy CIB got onto it right away and she tested positive for GHB. They did what they could to try and track him down but all she had was a name which was most likely false, and she remembered him saying, before she passed out, that he'd worked out up at Apollos before.'

Apollos.

The tiny hairs on the back of Richard's neck tingled. *Another coincidence.*

'Anyway,' Will continued, 'they never managed to track the guy down – seems they weren't too cooperative up at the gym – and the complaint was eventually filed due to the fact that there was no suspect. But there you go – yet another little piece of the puzzle to suggest a link between Apollos and GHB. And not only a link, but a link between the fact that the drug has been used as a date rape drug, rather than just a steroid.'

'But why wasn't there an IR on it? I should have found it earlier.'

'Someone being slack, no doubt. It's just fallen through the cracks.'

'Who was the investigating officer?' Richard asked.

He heard Will flicking through the file that was obviously lying in front of him. 'Um . . . Rory Fitzgerald.'

Richard frowned. 'Is he still around? It'd be worthwhile picking his brains.'

'I'm pretty sure he resigned last year. Went off to the mainland to do something with the Building Inspectorate.'

'Damn,' Richard said. 'Oh well, on the bright side, it's quite something, isn't it? Things are beginning to add up.'

'That they are, Rich. Anyway, I'll head off. Oh, but before I go, I've got something else in the pipeline. I've teed up a meeting with a bloke tomorrow morning. Duane Macallister. A guy I locked up six months back. Not only does he have a finger on the pulse up at Apollos, but due to his own pathetic little indiscretion, he has a very good reason to want to help us out. And he's agreed to meet. Could be our big break.'

Richard took a deep breath, tried not to get too excited. The case might have started out as nothing more than a good old 'he says, she says' which was certain to result in Greaves walking, but thanks to Will it was shaping up beautifully. And for the fiftieth time since he'd poached him back from Drugs to CIB, Richard offered up a quick prayer, thankful for his nous, not to mention his connections.

It'd turned out to be a good day after all.

And as he left the office and started the walk home through town, he experienced an overwhelming feeling of calm. He might have doubted it from the outset, used as he was to even the best of rape cases being virtually unwinnable, but there was an air of optimism forming around this one and he had a good feeling that maybe, just maybe, they'd get Lucy her pound of flesh.

Leaving the office, he zigzagged down to Macquarie, headed over Davey and across into the still darkness of St David's Park, its winding paths already damp with early-evening dew. He enjoyed the walk to and from work. It was only fifteen minutes and it always cleared his mind, prepared him for the day and wound him down in the evening. His crew thought him a little odd, particularly during the winter when the morning ice snapped at his fingers and nose and the ever-present showers descended, drenching him from head to toe. But it never bothered him and nights like tonight made it all worthwhile. Today might have begun with drizzle, but it was now the perfect clear, crisp, freezing winter night, the type that reminded him that despite the rigours of the day, he was alive.

Midway through the park, he stopped and took a deep breath through his nose. The scent of freshly mowed grass wafted before him and the rotunda loomed large in the darkness, empty, cold, yet still grand. An incongruous reminder of summertime and garden weddings.

He wrapped his scarf snugly around his neck and stepped out the other side onto Sandy Bay Road. It was alive with flashes of white and red. The bumper-to-bumper headlights and brake lights of knock-off traffic. He inhaled deeply as he walked, soaking up the glorious evening smells: wood-fired pizza from somewhere down in Salamanca Place, pub meals from St Ives on the corner and the heady aroma of fresh, home-cooked Chinese food from the student accommodation blocks further down near the university. Smiling, he stuck his hands in his pockets and continued, turning left onto his beloved Quayle Street.

He adored the majestic, tree-lined street and rejoiced in the fact that he'd bought his neat, split-level brick unit in the prime location when prices had been lower. It was two minutes' walk from the beach at Marieville Esplanade, three minutes' walk from Brew, the best coffee shop in town, in the whole south of the state for that matter, ten minutes' walk to the uni and not much further into the heart of town.

As he turned up the driveway he caught sight of his slightly oddball, extremely introverted neighbour with his lank dark hair, thick black glasses and darting, nervous eyes. Gil bore more than a passing resemblance to the weird bearded guy from the movie *The Hangover*.

'Evening,' Richard called with a friendly wave.

Gil nodded his usual silent response and shuffled in through his front door, closing it quickly behind him so no one would catch a glimpse of the interior he kept so perfectly guarded. Despite saying hello to him for five years, Richard had no idea what the man did for a living and had never seen the inside of his unit. The blinds remained permanently shut, even during the bluest of summer days. He often laughed to himself, thinking Gil could have been a reclusive genius, or a terrorist, or something in between. Maybe both for all he knew.

And for the first time ever he hesitated, stared back towards Gil's unit. *I wonder what he makes of me. Loner? Workaholic? Odd perhaps?* And he grinned. Maybe he was as much of an oddity to Gil as Gil was to him. Mulling over the thought, he climbed the stairs to the living area and threw his bag on the kitchen counter, pleased to be home in the warm cosy unit.

He was halfway through pouring a glass of cab sav when his mobile rang. Mick's number. Apparently work wasn't content to stay at work tonight.

'Hi, Mick,' he said, taking the glass over to the couch, kicking off his shoes and settling back. 'What's up?'

The sergeant could barely contain his excitement. 'You wouldn't read about it.'

'Don't tell me we got him.'

'Yep. It was exactly as you said. No sooner had everyone left for the day and suddenly, bam, there he is in the Prosecution office, folder in hand.'

'Good God,' he chuckled, amazed and not to mention a little disappointed. 'What did he do with it?'

'Wedged it down between a couple of filing cabinets in the secretary's office and walked out cool as a cucumber.'

'Right. When Surveillance are sure he's gone from the building for the day, I want you to retrieve, bag and tag it, and of course verify the fact that it's the actual Myers file. Was he gloved up when he dumped it?'

'Yeah, but if he's had it in his possession for a little while now, we'll probably get something off it, even though it's pretty clear from the tape where it's been all this time.'

'I know. But we need to make sure we're covering off on everything. It's going to be an absolute bitch when we put it all to him, so I want every shred of evidence possible and I *don't* want to leave any room for error. So at this point in time, tell me what we've got exactly.'

'Re the Myers file, we've got a copy of the journo's article, Myers's statement about the threat, the TI product re the call between the Premier and Chalmers, the corroborating surveillance product and the recovered file itself.'

'Brilliant,' Richard said, breathing a little sigh.

'It's pretty cut and dried, yeah?'

'Well, you never know, but as far as I can see it's looking good. So we've got the infringement notice side of things still on the boil and financials still fishing.'

'Yep. And as per the journo's original accusations, I'm going to get Cat and Benny to go back through some old operations, anything where there was so much as a hint of a member of the Department of the Premier and Cabinet involved, and then suddenly, magically, uninvolved. You never know what we might dig up.'

He took another sip of the cab sav. 'Good. And I know I'm telling you how to suck eggs, but make sure you leave it till the very last before you pull any of them in for interview. I don't want Chalmers tipped off beforehand.'

'Done, boss.'

'Okay. What I propose at this point in time, then, is that we keep chugging along with surveillance and TIs for a few more weeks at the very least. If that man so much as farts, I want to know about it. I want to know just how buddy-buddy Chalmers and his mate the Premier are, and I get the distinct feeling that if we sit back and watch, we'll give him an ample supply of rope. Happy with that, Mick?'

'As a pig in shit, boss. Leave it with me.'

'And by the way, if I haven't said it yet, awesome work, Mick,' he said. 'Oh, and Mick?'

'Yeah, boss?'

'Bring the tape down for me tomorrow morning so I can have a quick squiz. Around seven-ish?'

'Done.'

Immensely satisfied, Richard hung up, glanced at the time, and sank back into the comfy soft blue couch. It was his favourite time of day. Seven o'clock. *Home and Away* time. He took another gulp of his wine, switched on the telly, banished Ron Chalmers from his mind and drifted off into Summer Bay, a world full of complexities, but far, far removed from the complexities of his own life.

Home and Away was followed by *Packed to the Rafters* and finally, an SBS documentary about epigenetics. But regardless of how mind-numbing or fascinating the shows were, he found it impossible to focus. No matter how hard he tried to switch off, his mind drifted back to young Lucy Howard. He pitied her, even though pity was the last thing she'd want. In the dealings he'd had with her he truly believed that she'd be the type of person who literally wouldn't hurt a fly. He wondered, therefore, how she'd fare if she stayed with TasPol after the whole Greaves matter was over. Win or lose, was she strong enough to cope?

His thoughts then switched to Greaves, his mind wandering, the wine making him philosophical. Why would someone do something so awful to another person? Why did human beings engage in such behaviour? Why were they so dreadful to one another? Why couldn't people just respect one another and get on with it? Live and let live. In the end, after much thought, he'd switched the telly off, read a few more chapters of his Patricia Cornwell novel, turned off the light and tried to forget all about it till the morning.

Sleep hadn't come easily. Lucy was replaced by Chalmers again. He'd tossed and turned most of the night trying to come to grips with the fact that the boss was obviously deeply under the bedcovers with the Premier, more so than anyone could have imagined perhaps. The Myers file was probably only the tip of the iceberg. If he was bold enough to pull a stunt like that, then chances were it wasn't the first time he'd abused his powers. It was kind of like a paedophile. They didn't start by waltzing out into broad daylight and raping a child. There were steps to be taken first. Courage to be worked up. Grooming to be done. A touch here. A period of waiting there to check reactions. A gift. A kiss. And it bothered, even amazed, Richard that they were probably going to find a whole lot more than they bargained for once they *really* started digging into Ron Chalmers's life.

The thought rattled him on every level. Did Chalmers really think he could get away with using and abusing his powers? Did he think the voters were that apathetic about the impartiality of police and government? And did he really not notice what had been going on in the mainland states over the past decade with their anti-corruption commissions? Could he be that . . . arrogant? Stupid? Deluded perhaps?

The following morning, as he sat through the footage taken from the camera in the Prosecution clerk's office, Mick hovering excitedly behind him, he was dismayed to realise that the answer to all of his questions was a resounding yes. His heart dipped as he watched the slim, grey-haired dictator who'd been such a presence in his daily working life for so long, sneak into the clerk's office, folder in one gloved hand. A pause. A glance. The selection of a location. The folder was then dispatched in between a couple of filing cabinets where it would appear to have accidentally slipped, months earlier.

He grimaced and pressed the 'pause' button. 'Bloody hell. I was hoping I was wrong, but it looks like we've got our first serious run on the board. Can I just watch it one more time?'

'Sure, boss.' Mick reached over and pressed the 'rewind' button, but instead of watching the footage jump back frame by frame, it whirled back at ten times the speed. 'Oh, shit,' he said, fumbling with the controls and attempting to right it. 'Sorry. I'm all thumbs this morning.'

Richard watched as the footage showed the leggy blonde Prosecution clerk moving in and out of her office in reverse and the office behind her slowly filling again. He sat forwards suddenly in his seat. Something caught his eye. 'Stop it there. Let me watch the whole thing.'

Mick, still swearing and cursing, finally managed to stop the footage and pressed 'play'.

Richard turned the volume up and watched intently as the office in the background emptied again. The clerk waved a couple of times over the top of her computer, typing quickly with a frazzled look on her face, as though she was in a hurry to go. When the office had grown silent and empty a male came into shot and perched casually on her desk.

'Ready to go, Chrissy?'

Richard hit the 'pause' button and turned to Mick. 'Is that Nick Greaves?'

Mick squinted. 'Yeah, looks like him.'

'Thought so,' Richard muttered, taking in every detail of the cocky, arrogant man leering across the desk. He pressed 'play' again.

'You coming or what?' Nick said.

'I'm doing the best I can. Inspector Sherwood wants this first thing in the morning.'

'Fuck Sherwood. Come in early tomorrow. I wanna go now.'

'All right, all right,' the flustered Chrissy said, saving whatever she was doing on the computer before closing it down and grabbing her bag. 'I have to get changed first though.'

Nick folded his arms. 'Can't you just change at the fucking gym?'

She glared at him, grabbed a backpack and headed out the door. 'Jesus Christ, Nick. I'll be two seconds.'

'Hurry up then.'

Richard held his breath as she exited and left Nick to his own devices. The second she was gone he pulled out a mobile phone and pressed a pre-programmed number. Richard strained to hear the hushed, one-sided conversation.

'Yeah, it's me.

'Good, mate. We're on the way up shortly.

'I know. I've been fucking flat out.

'Yeah, good.

'Nah, not just yet. Where were you the other night, anyway? I was gonna tell you all about it then.

'Your loss. Anyway, it was fucking awesome actually.

'Yeah, yeah. Really. '*Course* I fucking did.

'Yeah.

'Yeah.

'Nuh, only about fifteen minutes and she was out for the count.

'You're not wrong.'

At that moment Chrissy glided back into frame kitted up in her sneakers, tiny shorts and tight T-shirt.

'No worries. See you shortly,' he said, snapping the phone shut and sticking it in his top pocket.

'Who was that?' she asked.

'George Clooney.'

'Ha-ha. Very funny. And what did he want?'

'He was just letting me know that he's relinquishing the title of World's Sexiest Man to me.'

'Oh, Nicholas. You can be such a wanker sometimes.'

'Only when there's no one else around to do it.'

'Ha-ha.' She smirked. 'But you're still avoiding the question.'

'Who's my little green-eyed beast then?'

'Oh, piss off,' she said, giving him a swat.

'It's okay. I like it when you get jealous. Besides, it wasn't even that exciting. Just Danny boy. I was letting him know we're on the way.'

'Oh. Okay. Well, come on then, what are we waiting for?'

She switched the light off and they wandered out of the office, leaving the place in gloomy grey semi-darkness.

Richard hit the 'pause' button and sat back in his chair contemplating the footage.

Only about fifteen minutes and she was out for the count.

It had to be about Lucy. Goddamn it. How bloody infuriating. To catch him talking on a listening device was something, but it didn't compare to a telephone intercept. If only they'd had the TIs up and running on Greaves, they'd have both sides of the extremely dubious phone conversation. It had to be about Lucy. There was no other logical explanation. He drummed his fingers on the desk in frustration. *Damn it.*

'Everything all right, boss?' Mick asked.

'I think so. Maybe better than all right actually. It might relate to something else I've got on the boil at the moment. Could I be a pain in the butt and get you to run a copy of that off for me?'

'Sure. I'll go do it now if you like,' he said.

'That'd be great. Much appreciated.'

Mick flipped the disc back into its case and headed off upstairs to the technical support unit. Richard reclined even further in his chair. Could he be that lucky? Or was there something completely different at play here? Surely it had to be a reference to Lucy. If so, then it could be their first tangible break and he needed to jump on it. The gym *had* to be the connection. He reached for the phone.

'Will?'

'Hey, Rich, what's up?'

'I think we've got another starting point for the Greaves matter.'

'Superb.'

'Can you get onto Telstra and get CCRs for Greaves's mobile for the past month? And then get a complete list of members up at Apollos.'

'Riiight . . . what's brought all this on?'

'I've just seen footage of our delightful Mr Greaves having a phone call yesterday with someone called Danny, who is most likely one of his buddies from the gym regarding what I suspect will turn out to be drugs.'

'Ah. That'd be Dan Williams then. He and Nick are best mates, have been for years. They're both SOG.'

Richard groaned. Of course. He knew Williams all right. Built like the proverbial shithouse, the hulking blond giant would have looked perfectly at home dropping out of a helicopter in Iraq or Afghanistan. He'd exchanged pleasantries with him a few times over the years at various junctures – mainly formal functions and courses. Williams came across as cocky. Walked with a swagger, talked tough with the guys, was a man's man through and through. Generally looked down his nose at any policing role that didn't involve smashing in doors and using brute force.

It made sense that they'd be gym buddies, not to mention partners in other more nefarious activities.

'Right. Williams is in the picture too then. I want you to dig up everything you can find on him. Also, what do we know about Greaves's involvement with Chrissy, the Prosecution clerk? Looks like they go to the gym together. She could be the girlfriend. Let's have a good look at her as well – personal details, counselling reports, anecdotal notes, anything.'

Will cleared his throat. 'Ah . . . Chrissy Matterson? Um . . . sure.'

'Good. And Will?'

'Yeah?'

'Let's start planning this out a bit. Start drawing up the warrant applications to search his house, his work locker, a gym locker if applicable, and a warrant for Lucy Howard to wear an LD. Hold off on getting them signed.'

'Sure. We're gonna put her in the hot seat then?'

'As a last resort, maybe. But I just want to have all the paperwork ready to go in case we need to move on this in a hurry. If we can at least get him on tape agreeing that she was out of it, then we might be able to get him under section 2A of the Code, regardless of whether we uncover any drugs or not.'

'Yeah, I kind of already outlined the whole "unable to consent" bit to her,' Will said.

'Cool. I'll leave you to it. Oh, before you go, what time are you meeting up with your contact from the gym?'

'Four.'

'Bewdy. Let me know how it goes. See ya.'

He hung up the phone, Nick's voice echoing in his mind. *George Clooney. He was just letting me know that he's relinquishing the title of World's Sexiest Man to me.*

Smarmy bastard.

He glanced at the second personal item in his office, a silver-framed photograph of three men. Smiles, suntans, tinnies and broad grins. Him, Will and John White. The Three Musketeers. Undefeatable. Superhuman.

And then there were two.

A hint of sadness, tinged with a fleeting sense of something darker, crawled across his skin.

John.

To the outside world, even to his inner circle of friends, Sergeant John White had presented as the ultimate copper. Knowledgeable, calm, humorous, a teacher, a problem solver. To the outside world it seemed as though he'd had it all. Loving wife, gorgeous kids, a house many would kill for. But on the inside, as Richard had discovered after his death, there'd been a whole lot more to him. Something dark, ugly, festering.

Richard couldn't help but draw a comparison with Greaves. Good-looking, hot girlfriend, SOG career many less fit and able coppers would kill for.

John and Nick.

Two peas in a pod.

The thought rattled him. If there was one thing in life Richard detested, it was being made a fool of. It didn't happen often, but when it did, it lingered and ate away at him. And despite the fact that he'd covered for John when he could no longer do it himself, he'd still never really forgiven his mate for being dirty. For being up to his nuts in it with that filthy rotten drug dealer George Casalis.

But this time it will be different, Richard thought. *There's no room in this job for bent coppers.*

And as he stared at the photograph, he made a vow, not only to himself, but to Lucy, Suzy Ward and any other poor victims of the current spate of drink spiking.

I will bring you down, Greaves, and I'll sure as hell make sure you pay for what you did.

The Psych

7.10 am Wednesday 22 June

'Costa, can you *please* hurry up and get out of bed? Remember? I've got an early appointment. I need you to take the kids to school.'

She snapped the master bedroom blackout curtains apart, dragging them to their respective sides and flooding the room with early-morning sun. A muffled groan of protest emanated from under the doona and she tried again, her tone now sweet and pleading.

'Costa? Did you hear me, hun? I need you to get up *now*. I'm already late. The kids are just finishing breakfast and . . .'

'All right, all right . . . quit harping, for fuck's sake. I'm getting up,' he grumbled, shoving a pillow over his head.

A reply lingered unspoken on her lips. *If you'd got up the first time I asked you an hour ago, I wouldn't have had to ask*

149

you for the fifth time. But she let it go through to the keeper. She reached for her earrings and watch on the bedside table before striding to the walk-in and hunting for her favourite crimson handbag.

'Don't forget your pill,' she sang out over her shoulder before realising what she'd done and cringing. *Shit.* But it was too late. In the morning chaos she'd gone and unthinkingly committed the cardinal sin. Again. *Idiot.* The angry rustling of bedclothes and stomping of bare feet on wooden floors confirmed it.

'*Don't forget your pill,*' he mimicked in his stupid, piss-taking falsetto, the one that made her clench her fists and bite the insides of her cheeks.

'How *could* I forget, Anna? In case you hadn't noticed, I've been taking the fucking pill for the past five months now without actually needing to be told by you or anyone else. But no, obviously you've had your head jammed so far up your arse that you failed to notice. Well, here I go now! Want to come out and witness me taking it? Just to make sure? Huh?'

She heard the rattling of the foil packet in his bedside drawer but stood her ground in the walk-in, one hand resting on the shelf, the other on the bag. She closed her eyes, willing the tears away.

I will not cry.

I will not let you make me cry.

You are not well.

And I will not take it personally.

Three seconds later she heard him storm off towards the shower, muttering as he cranked the water on full blast. Knowing the coast would be clear, she grabbed the bag, switched off the wardrobe light, pulled the doona back up, stuck her head around the bathroom door and forced a smile.

'Thanks, hun. I'll let the kids know you're on your way down.'

But it was met with cold silence. He was ignoring her and that was fine.

Whatever.

By the time she headed out the front door and cracked the car door she felt calmer. Lately, just getting away from the house was the daily activity she looked forward to the most. Her mother joked that work must be a drag for her, but she never let on that it was actually her greatest escape. It was home that was the drag. Home that made her tired and irritable. Home that did her head in. And the irony wasn't lost on her.

Anna Tsiolkas, wife, mother, primary carer of a severely depressed PTSD-suffering cop, was infinitely less glamorous than Anna Tsiolkas, psychologist to the Tasmania Police Service. Sure, she might spend her day dealing with other people's crap, but that was just it. It was *other* people's crap. And being dumped on professionally was a hell of a lot easier than being dumped on personally.

She sighed.

No point dwelling on it. This is your lot.

For the time being, anyway.

As she backed out of the driveway onto the dark, ice-covered and still empty Channel Highway that wound waterside from Taroona along into Sandy Bay, she cranked up the heat and flicked the radio on, rolling her eyes as the regular breakfast show hosts engaged in the usual hard-hitting morning debate-cum-banter. The topic of the morning: Do you let your pets eat off human plates? Kim, the argumentative, loud-mouthed whinger, stated a firm and unsurprising, 'Under no circumstances; it's totally disgusting'; Eddie, her long-suffering and decidedly more laid-back offsider, an equally as firm, 'Who cares as long as you wash them up?'

She tutted and switched it off. The last thing she wanted to hear was sodding breakfast show hosts yabbering on about the most inconsequential crap in the world.

If that's all that bothers you, if that's your single greatest dilemma for the day, then you should be bloody thankful.

She'd met DJ Eddie once, at a fundraising dinner at the Wrest Point Casino. She couldn't remember what they were raising funds for exactly, having been to so many of the damned things over the years, but she remembered Eddie clearly. Remembered shaking his hand and thinking how he looked nothing like he sounded on the radio. She'd always pictured him as tall, rugged, broad-chested and big-grinned, possibly with a surfboard tucked under one arm. In reality, DJ Eddie was disappointingly small and spindly, sprouting a rather alarming crop of Krusty the Clown hair. Worst of all, he was kind of sad-looking, probably as a result of having to sit next to loud-mouthed Kim for all those years. All in all it was something of a surprise. She knew perhaps better than anyone that people didn't usually live up to their public representations, but Eddie was more disappointing than most.

In some ways he was like Costa.

To everyone around them, her husband had always radiated strength, wisdom and reliance. He was Costa the career copper, the problem solver. Nothing was too hard, ranging from a sobbing child's broken rocking horse to a sobbing colleague's broken and battered personal relationship. And everything in between. He'd always been solid. Dependable. A survivor. She'd joked more than once to family and friends that if a plane went down and ninety-nine out of a hundred people were killed, then Costa would be the sole survivor.

These days she wasn't so sure.

These days, when the front door was firmly closed, he was anything but. For twelve months he'd been a stranger to her and a ghost to their children. Not that she'd seen it right away, for you don't always notice what's going on right under your nose. Even with all your fancy training and professional insight. She'd only realised just how sick he was some five months earlier and she shuddered with terror at the memory of that late January Sunday afternoon.

They'd returned home from the funeral of John White, one of Costa's colleagues who'd been killed on duty, and he'd immediately picked a fight about something completely inconsequential – the way she'd shut the car door in the driveway.

There's no need to slam the fucking thing.

As soon as the words left his mouth a prickly heat coursed through her. She looked at the doorhandle, reviewed her action and stopped dead. She certainly had *not* slammed it. But she knew with a sinking feeling of dread what was coming. He was tetchy about the day and itching for a fight. This was how it began. How it'd begun for a while now. But there was no way she was going to ruin the rest of the day. She'd be damned if she was going to give him what he wanted.

'Sorry, love, I didn't mean to.' She started to walk towards the front door and he followed, a scowl etched across his dark, brooding features.

'Well, you *did*. What the *fuck* is with you anyway, Anna? You've been a bitch all afternoon,' he snarled.

As she entered the hallway she bristled, startled by his attack.

'Sorry?'

'You heard. You've been giving me the cold shoulder all afternoon. What is it that I'm supposed to have done now?'

She paused before skipping to pacification strategy number two. Calm denial. 'Nothing, Costa, everything's fine.'

'Why haven't you said so much as two words then? And don't just say *nothing*. I hate it when you fucking well fob me off with nothings,' he said, throwing the keys into the bowl on the counter, unbuttoning his tunic and casting it over the back of the couch. She froze, her eyes silently following the item of clothing.

'What? Now I'm making a mess? *So-ree*. I'm such a fucking pig. Such a pain in the arse, messing up your nice clean home . . .'

Ignore it.

Ignore it.

Ignore it.

She bit down on her bottom lip, powerless as he paced before her.

'Oh, so now I get the silent treatment, do I? Charming.'

'Costa, please . . .'

'Oh, just shut it, Anna. I know you resent the fact that I live here too. It's bad enough having two kids to clean up after, let alone me as well. Don't worry . . . you've made *that* perfectly clear over the years, Anna.'

'That's not true.'

'Oh my God. You're such a lying cunt. What else do you lie to me about, huh? Huh?'

She stared at him, the familiar chill creeping through her veins. Once he reached this point, there was nowhere for him to go except to explode. That was how this same scenario had played out over the past six months. *Pick, pick, pick, boom.*

Trembling, fearful that one day he might just take it one step further than the usual verbal tirade, she kissed him softly on the cheek and tried one last time to soothe him.

'Costa, I love you. But it's been a shit of a day with the funeral. That's why I've been quiet. That's all, I promise. And to be honest, I really don't care about the tunic. Okay? I'm going to make a pot of tea and try to relax a bit before the kids get home from Mum's. Would you like one?'

He paused, glowering at her, his black eyes flashing with anger. 'So you're just going to sweep it all under the carpet, are you, Anna? That'd be right. Do what you do best. Honestly. You call yourself a fucking mental health professional, a fucking psychologist, and you can't even take two seconds out of your life to talk to me. You just mope around . . .'

'I *haven't* been moping. I told you . . .'

'God, you're full of shit! You walk around with a face like a cat's arse, hardly say two words to me all day, slam the car door . . .'

'I *didn't* slam the car door . . .'

'You fucking *did* slam the car door. Why do you always have to argue and make me out to be the bad guy? Why can't you just accept that for once I might be right? For once, I might *actually* have a valid point to make in this relationship?'

She cursed herself. She'd gone and done exactly what he wanted. She'd bitten and he'd swooped on her. His usual style. Poke, poke, poke until she reacted.

How to make him stop?

Without thinking, she moved into the latter stages of their chess game, the final strategic call, the comment she used when her temples were pulsing, her stomach was flip-flopping and she was convinced he might just take a swing.

'What do you want me to say to you, Costa?' she pleaded, hearing the tremor in her own voice and hating herself for caving, for sounding so needy and pathetic. Not that she had a choice. When it got to this point, all she wanted to do was stop it dead in its tracks. She didn't care what she had to do or say. She'd admit to anything, apologise for anything, say *anything* just to have him calm down and return to being Costa, the man she'd married, the father of her children, the strong Greek man she adored, instead of this Mr Hyde who seemed to slip in when she was distracted, take over her husband's body and provoke the mother of all arguments over nothing.

'And here we go again,' he spat, throwing his hands in the air. 'You're so fucking predictable, Anna. The second I try to talk to you about how I'm feeling you clamp up and that's it. Discussion over.'

Discussion? Discussion?

Oh God.

I'm so tired.

Nowhere left to go and he's still hammering away.

It's never going to end.

She shook her head, moved into the kitchen and went through the motions of making a pot of tea while trying to sniff back the tears that threatened to betray her.

'Got nothing to say now? Fucking typical,' he yelled. 'It's hilarious that you claim to spend all day working out other people's issues when you haven't got a fucking clue how to deal with your own, Anna. And I for one am sick to fucking death of it.'

She stood motionless, one hand on the kettle as he grabbed his tunic and stormed up the stairs ranting all the way about her alleged moodiness. She waited, eyes closed, as the bedroom door slammed shut. *One.* The ensuite door slammed shut. *Two.* Another unidentified bang – *three* – and the tap was turned on full bore. He was the only person she'd ever known who could turn on shower taps aggressively; she could actually hear the anger in the turning. After a few seconds of relative quiet, her shoulders sagged and the tears raced down her cheeks.

It was the speed and the ferocity of his explosions that took her by surprise. Deep down she knew it wasn't her fault. The professional Anna Tsiolkas soothed her in that respect. He was depressed. It was becoming clear that he was suffering from an accumulation of God-awful jobs he'd attended over the years. One of his colleagues had just been murdered. And the only way he knew of coping was to lash out. It was understandable. Unpleasant, soul-destroying sometimes, but understandable nevertheless. But it felt like there was no end in sight.

Here she was, the crack mental health professional, able to leap tall buildings in a single bound and all that, but when it came to her own home, she was utterly powerless. Costa didn't think he had a problem; everyone else had the problem and until he wanted help, there was nothing she could do apart from sit back and be the punching bag.

She'd thought about leaving. Running away and starting fresh. There was only so much a wife could take and sometimes late at night when he was out in his shed hammering away on one of his never-ending carpentry projects, having spent the evening screaming at her about an apparently misplaced word or deed, she fantasised about life without him.

She'd no longer have to walk on eggshells in her own home. She could have a normal conversation knowing that nothing would be misconstrued in the worst possible light. She wouldn't have to worry about accidentally slamming a car door, forgetting to water the vegie pots, failing to check the mailbox on the way in or any other everyday action which stoked his rage and brought her to tears.

She might even stumble across a man who made her feel loved, warm, safe and unthreatened. A man who would make her tea, massage her shoulders when she was knackered and get the kids organised without having to be asked a thousand times. They could sell the house, split the proceeds; after all, she'd more than contributed financially over the years. There probably wouldn't be enough to get her into a new house, so she might have to rent. Then again, her parents would probably insist that she and the kids move in with them *just until things got sorted*. And with that, the fantasy vanished. Moving back in with her parents would be a monumental step backwards.

She was kidding herself. She'd come too far and invested too much time and energy to bail now. Besides, she knew that *her* Costa was in there somewhere and might come back one day.

If she was lucky.

She snapped back into focus as the shower stopped running upstairs. Her stomach twisted again, knowing he'd be on his way back down shortly and would want to pick up where he'd left off. But she paused. From upstairs, an unfamiliar sound. She could have sworn it sounded like sobbing . . . but . . . but . . . surely it wasn't. In all the years they'd been together she'd never witnessed a tear. Not even when he took the stilted late-night call from his father to say that his mother had died of a massive, unexpected heart attack.

She switched the kettle off and crept out of the kitchen, the house silent apart from the sobbing. She climbed the stairs, tentatively opened the bedroom door and walked towards him with open arms. The sight of her husband, the grown man, the copper, the hard guy, the reliable one, alone, head in hands, crying his eyes out in defeat was heartbreaking. Of course she could never leave him. She sat on the bed and placed her arms around him but he shrugged her off.

'Costa . . .'

'Just *don't*, Anna,' he cried. 'I'm not good enough for you. I'm a total failure, a useless piece of shit. You and the kids would be better off without me.'

He shook her off, pulled on his beloved tatty old Ramones T-shirt and wiped the tears from his face. Behind him, beside the window, she noted the new fist-sized hole in the plaster – *the third bang* – and cringed.

This needs to stop now.

'Costa. We need to talk about . . . well . . . this.'

'There's no need. I know how fucked up I am. I'm a liability. I'm done talking. I'm no good at work anymore. I'm no good at home. I'm beyond repair, Anna. This job has completely fucked me up. You need a man you can depend on. You deserve a real man, Anna. The kids deserve a real father.'

His tone sent a wave of pinpricks up her spine. Was he leaving her? She tried to remain calm, took a deep breath and a step towards him.

'Costa, the kids and I love you. We're a family. Yes, things have been a bit rough over the past few months,' *that's the understatement of the century*, 'but we'll get through it. I love you, honey; we all do. Please don't talk like you want to leave us.'

He snatched his favourite blue jeans off the bureau and pulled them on, eyes full of tears. 'Trust me, Anna. You'll be much better off without me. Now listen to me, because I'm only gonna say this once. My will is in the top drawer of the desk in my office. It's the only one in existence . . .'

The ripple of pinpricks at the thought of him walking out on them converged into a tidal wave of chaotic heat crashing through her entire body.

Dear God.

He's not talking about leaving.

He's talking about . . . leaving. For good.

She froze, tried to speak, but could manage nothing more than a vague stutter.

'D-don't say that.'

'Just shut up and listen to me.'

160

'No! You're talking crap!'

He laughed coldly, wiped an already tear-streaked forearm across his face. 'Believe me, Anna. This is the most sensible thing I've said in ages. I've been thinking about it for a long while now. I just haven't been man enough to do it.'

She could only stare blankly as his words confirmed it. How had she not seen how bad things were for him on the inside? She'd been so selfishly focused on her own misery that she hadn't noticed that he hated his life to such an extent that he'd been contemplating leaving it. Permanently. He whipped his wallet off the bureau, pulled out a handful of fifties and threw them on the bed.

'Here. Go out and do some shopping or have a coffee or something.'

'What are you talking about?' she shrieked.

'Just go out. The kids won't be home for a few hours at least, so . . . just . . . please . . . go out. And tell the kids I love them, okay? And that I really tried, and I'm so sorry, but I just wasn't good enough. You can't argue with that.'

She took a step backwards in horror. How had they arrived at such an absurd point, him offering her a fistful of cash to get her out of the house so he could calmly go about killing himself?

Costa the pragmatist.

She threw a hand over her mouth and suppressed a hysterical giggle, but it died as the horror of the situation unfolding before her sank in. He was going to kill himself.

Get a grip, Anna.

Get a fucking grip for once in your life.

'Right. No one's going anywhere, Costa. I can see that you're hurting, but we can deal with this. I know a really

161

good psychiatrist . . . Peter Fox . . . you remember? We had him and his wife Lil over to dinner a while ago. We'll go see him together.'

He laughed, a joyless laugh. 'I'm not seeing a shrink, Anna. It's beyond that.'

'It's *never* beyond that. In fact, it's exactly what you need to do. What *we* need to do. I'm pretty sure you've got PTSD. If not, then you're *depressed*, Costa. It's bloody understandable, given the job you've been doing for so long. It's normal; for God's sake, one in six men in Australia experiences it at some point in their lives. Eight hundred thousand new cases are diagnosed each year. You're not alone, Costa!'

'Quit with the stats, Anna. It's not an illness. I'm just a pathetic loser who can't do his job anymore, can't be a proper father or husband and can't stop being a total misery guts. It's affecting everyone around me and no amount of psychobabble is going to make that right.'

She tried to grab him as he pushed past, but he was too strong for her and with one simple move, practised over years of fighting off drunken patrons outside nightclubs at two in the morning, he'd untangled her grip and pushed her onto the bed. He strode out the door and she scrambled up, taking the stairs two at a time in an attempt to catch him up, not knowing what she could do even if she managed to. Her sweaty palm slipped on the balustrade and she careened awkwardly down the last few steps, landing at the bottom with a heavy thump, a stinging pain ripping through her right ankle. She shook it off and hurried towards the back of the house after him, a feeling of total helplessness overcoming her. She had no idea what to do, only knew what to do well *before* it ever reached this stage. All of her training and years of prac were pointless.

'Costa, where are you going?' she cried.

He slid the glass door to the deck open, ignoring her cries. Suddenly she knew. *The shed.*

Of course. All his tools were down there. Ropes for hanging, power tools, not to mention probably a firearm stashed among the junk somewhere. Frantically, she grabbed the cordless phone from the kitchen bench and chased after him, not stopping to put on shoes. The grass was soft, springy, summery under her feet.

'Costa!'

But he didn't turn. There was only one threat left to make and she didn't even know if that would work.

'Costa . . . don't make me call the police, please . . .'

He turned and paused, surprise clouding his previously determined face.

'Don't.'

'I *will*, Costa, unless you come inside now and sit with me while we ring Peter to come around.'

'You wouldn't. You wouldn't humiliate me in front of my colleagues,' he challenged.

'Try me,' she dared, holding the phone aloft and attempting to mask her relief at having found his Achilles heel.

'Don't drag them into this, Anna.'

'You're not giving me a choice, Costa. *You're* the one controlling this situation. *You* dictate whether I bring them into it or not. And if you keep going, I *will* call triple-O. I'll get them to section you right here and now if that's what I have to do to keep you alive.'

She raised a single finger to the '0' button.

And with that simple gesture, his shoulders slumped and he fell to his knees on the grass sobbing.

Thank God.

She pocketed the phone, raced to kneel beside him and rocked him as he cried. This time he didn't fight her off. He had nothing left. She'd won.

She'd called Peter straightaway and he'd dropped everything to come around and help. Once they'd begun treatment, Costa had been compliant. Fifty milligrams of Zoloft had made him nauseous but day after day she'd cradled him in bed, kissing his forehead until it passed. The step up to one hundred milligrams had made him tired, but it wasn't a problem considering Peter had signed off on a few months of sick leave. One hundred and fifty milligrams made him quieter, thoughtful and almost obliging around the house, and when he hit two hundred, the dose Peter recommended for at least twelve months, it was like he was a different person. Sometimes he was a zombie, sleeping all day, walking around in a daze, oblivious to anything that went on outside his immediate personal space – a stark change from the vigilant, almost frighteningly perceptive man she'd married.

On two hundred, and with his fortnightly visit to Peter for therapy, he was calm, reasonable and, above all, manageable. He appreciated the intervention, thanked Anna on a daily basis, and even learned to cook, one less thing for her to worry about. He even managed to fix the hole in the plaster.

She pulled the car into the Bathurst Street car park underneath the police station and switched off the ignition, sighing as she reached back for her briefcase. But just as she was learning to like Costa again, he was dropping hints about how well he felt, how balanced he was.

Perhaps I don't need so much medication, after all.

Perhaps I can cut back on my visits to Peter and try to keep on an even keel using more of my own inner resources.

The pills are destroying my libido; it makes me feel like less of a man. I can't even pleasure my wife.

She stopped short of pointing out that prior to him taking the pills they'd hardly been sleeping together, anyway, due to the fact that she'd come to detest the man he'd become and didn't want to be intimate with him. It would have destroyed him.

And over the last few weeks, his grumblings had grown.

I'm sick of the pills.

I'm sure I can come off them, do it on my own.

You don't understand how it makes me feel like a failure every morning having to wake up and reach for that packet.

The pills make me dull, flat, numb. I don't see anything, smell anything, feel anything anymore. It's like watching a black-and-white movie in slow motion.

She'd tried to explain the importance of staying on the meds, but he stonewalled her with *you don't understands.*

So in the end she'd simply stopped trying to convince him. Changed the subject. Refused to agree, for she couldn't. Going off the pills and turning back into Mr Hyde would destroy them both. And it seemed as though it would only be a matter of time, given his insistence. A sick, jumbled feeling of dread wound its way through her body at the mere thought of him ditching his treatment.

And when she stepped out of the cold grey car park onto Bathurst Street, Costa was filling her thoughts, eating away at her peace of mind bit by bit. She would ring Peter before her first appointment walked in the door, to let him know it was getting worse, that he needed to reason with him. Costa had a begrudging respect for Peter. He'd listen to *him*.

As she walked down Argyle Street past the Jewish temple, the oldest synagogue in Australia that had miraculously been saved and incorporated in among the cluster of police buildings, she felt a familiar sense of calm amid her rising anxiety. She loved the beautiful white building finished in the Egyptian Revival style, complete with original cast-iron railings, and it intrigued her to think that such a tiny, inconspicuous place of peace could be wedged in the midst of the great sprawling police estate which hummed with life and energy twenty-four hours a day.

She shivered, pulled up the collar of her smart cream woollen overcoat and continued on towards her office in the nearby Temple House. But as she swung open the gate she knew that Peter and Costa were going to have to wait; for there, huddled on the front step, was Lucy Howard – early.

Damn.

She hid the flicker of irritation behind a broad smile. 'Hi, Lucy, nice to see you bright and early.'

The girl smiled back, jumped up and stretched the kinks out of her legs before yawning. 'Sorry about that. I was on night shift and just knocked off. I can go and grab a coffee and give you a chance to get organised if you like?'

Anna hesitated. *Tempting.* But then again, when she rang

Peter she needed to be focused, not in a rush and expecting a knock on the door any second. 'No, no, it's okay, Lucy, come through now. The sooner we get started, the sooner I can send you home to bed.'

She unlocked the door, disabled the alarm and ushered the bleary-eyed girl in. 'How was your night, anyway?' she asked, flicking on the reception area light and making her way up the grand old-fashioned carpeted staircase.

'Not too bad. Pretty quiet actually.' Lucy yawned. 'A couple of car burgs in West Hobart around three which kept us busy, but that was about the extent of it. A typical Tuesday, winter night shift. Or so I'm told.'

'Must make it even harder than usual to stay awake,' Anna commented, opening her own office door and wondering how the hell anyone managed to stay awake much past midnight. But Lucy was still young enough and junior enough to be upbeat about it.

'It's not so bad. It's kind of nice in a way to creep around the backstreets with your headlights off knowing that there's nothing much moving out there. It's like you have the whole world to yourself. Apart from the bakers, the butchers, the newspaper delivery guys, the dog walkers and the insomniacs, of course. Hmm. On second thoughts, I guess it's pretty crowded out there.'

'True. Have a seat,' Anna said, placing her briefcase behind her desk, draping her coat over her chair and pulling out a notepad and pen before joining her. She took a quick glance at the coffee table between them, pleased she'd already put out the box of tissues, the frequently ransacked box of tissues. She crossed her legs, pushed Costa to the far reaches of her mind and switched into professional mode.

167

Focus.

'So, I must say, despite the whole lack of sleep thing, you're looking really well, Lucy.' She skimmed her first lot of notes taken the week before. *Neat. Well-groomed. Composed, overly grateful, obvious punitive conscience, distressed but remarkably contained.* She remembered the first visit they'd had, the defeated, almost haunted look that shadowed the girl's face, the way she'd been embarrassed about reaching for a tissue as she outlined the whole sorry mess. But today was different. Today she radiated strength. It was almost like there was a different person sitting opposite her.

'I guess I do feel a lot better,' Lucy conceded. 'I've had the week to think everything through and all in all, I'm really happy with my decision to go ahead with the case. Nick needs to be brought to account. If he's not, then, it's like you said before, he could do it again.'

Anna nodded, pleased that Lucy had taken that particular gem of wisdom away with her. She'd dealt with more than her fair share of SOG operatives during her career and personally found the majority of them to be boorish, testosterone-fuelled gun nuts with egos the size of China. If Nick wasn't made accountable for his actions, there was every chance he'd feed off the power trip, repeat his actions or, worse, up the stakes next time around.

'So how's the investigation going then?'

Lucy's face brightened. 'Good, I think. Richard . . . I mean . . . Detective Inspector Moore is so lovely and he's been keeping me in the loop every step of the way.'

Anna flushed at the mention of the DI. She remembered him well. Richard Moore wasn't handsome in the conventional

168

sense, but he was intriguing with an intellect vastly superior to most of the senior officers she dealt with. His offbeat sense of humour fitted so snugly with her own world view, and then there were his glasses. She'd always been a sucker for a man in a good pair of frames.

He was the complete package, all right, so much so that the last time she'd spoken to him, prior to Costa being medicated, she'd spent the night clinging to his side at some corporate do at the academy, flirting up a none-too-subtle storm. He'd stirred such a long-forgotten desire in her, a feeling that had been lost over the years, misplaced among the humdrum of school lunches, the gymnastics, the soccer training, the piano lessons and the fights. Those endless fights.

In fact, she'd been so drawn to the witty detective that by the end of the night she'd glanced over the rim of her glass, laughed heartily at another of his jokes and had contemplated, just for the briefest of seconds, asking him to take her back to his place and make love to her. It was the booze talking, of course, but even more than that, it was his charm, his warmth, his lack of criticism, his compliments and the way he made her feel as though she was sexy and young again – the complete opposite of how Costa made her feel: ugly, tired, unsexy, pathetic and beaten into submission.

But as she flicked her long dark hair across to one side and sidled closer to Moore he'd taken a casual, discreet step backwards, looked her in the eye and whispered, 'Ah. Costa is one hell of a good bloke. You're a lucky woman, Anna.'

She'd laughed, a little too loudly, and agreed with his assessment. The unspoken message in his comment smacked her across both cheeks, leaving a sting of humiliation. Making a break for it, she'd scurried off, locked herself in the loo and sat quietly for a moment berating herself for her gross display of desperate, childish neediness.

She swallowed as Lucy continued talking. Oh yes. She knew Richard Moore was lovely. Then, a thought. What would Costa make of this business between Lucy and Greaves? She frowned and turned it over in her mind. Who would he support? Would he understand that there'd be no other possible reason a copper would put herself in this position, other than the fact that it had actually happened? Or would he, in his paranoid hatred of the department, see Nick as just another victim of a vindictive hierarchy – another sacrificial lamb to be roasted on the pyre of political correctness? But try as she might, she couldn't form any sort of thought process. What *would* Costa think? She honestly had no idea.

Dear God. You really have drifted apart, haven't you?

'. . . and what's more, Richard's honest,' Lucy continued. 'You know? He's been really careful not to give me false hope and has sort of been making sure he errs on the side of caution when he's talking about how the case might unfold once Nick's been arrested and charged.'

Anna cleared her throat. 'So, there's a good chance he'll be charged then? Don't they need to weigh up all the evidence first to see if they have enough to charge him?'

'Funnily enough, no. It's not like a burg or a robbery or whatever. It doesn't take much to make a prima facie case when it comes to rape. As long as I make a statement and I'm prepared to give evidence, then CIB puts together a file. Then it's forwarded on to the DPP to make the final decision. So, provided I want to go ahead with it, Richard will make sure a file gets done. Of course, the more evidence we have, the better. And in that respect, it's shaping up *really* well.'

'Oh?'

'Yeah. Between you and me, I was talking to Will – oh, I mean Sergeant Torino – yesterday and they've had a really promising breakthrough. An *amazing* breakthrough actually. He's got this informant who, as it turns out, goes to the same gym as Nick. Anyway, the informant overheard Nick and a group of his friends talking in the gym about using some drugs they'd got hold of. They were, like, laughing and stuff about how easy it'd be to render a chick unconscious.'

'Good God,' Anna exclaimed.

'I *know*,' Lucy said. 'It's just horrid, isn't it? Anyway, this guy has made a statement and is prepared to give evidence about the conversation he overheard, so that goes a really long way towards corroborating what they already had. Suffice to say, I was practically doing cartwheels when I found out. Richard's pretty excited too. He reckons it's a very strong circumstantial case at this stage. I mean, it's an independent person, Anna. *Independent*. That's so valuable, it's like, *gold* in terms of evidence. Plus, they have a recording of Nick talking to his friend about drugging me. Not specifically, but the inference is definitely there. So, you see, it's all going our way.'

'Well, it certainly sounds promising,' Anna said with a nod.

And thank God it's going to be more than just he said, she said.

'It *is* promising,' Lucy said, her eyes lighting up with excitement, despite her lack of sleep. 'He's really happy with the way it's falling into place. Reckons, just between us, that we've got more of a chance than most cases he's done. Although, that said, he'll keep working on it. It'd be great if they could get something even more concrete before the file goes together. Richard said they'll keep Nick under tabs for a few more days to see if they can gather any other evidence. And there's a chance they might wire me up and send me in to have a conversation with him about what happened. To try and draw him out a bit, you know? Get him to make some admissions. After that, they'll bring him in for an interview.'

Anna paused. She was familiar with pretext calls. Not entirely supportive of them as an investigative technique though. They could be hard on a victim, confronting the offender, trying to get him to admit his guilt, being doubly distraught if nothing was forthcoming from the situation. Being wired up and coming face to face could be potentially catastrophic for a victim who wasn't in the right headspace.

'And are you all right with that, Lucy? It can be a traumatic, pressurised situation to find yourself in, on top of everything else that's already going on in your life.'

Lucy shrugged. 'I'm happy to do whatever needs doing and . . . hey . . . it's what I do – talk to people for a living, I mean. The CIB course taught me a lot more about eliciting information from suspects, so I figure I'll be right if I just stay professional about it all.'

The girl was tougher than Anna had originally thought. She seemed to be taking it a little *too* well in her stride and it crossed her mind that she might be bottling.

'You know, Lucy,' she said pensively, 'it's okay for you *not* to always think about being the consummate professional. You're allowed to just be you too. From what you told me in our first session, you have every right to feel the same way as any other person who has been the victim of this sort of behaviour. You don't necessarily have to be the tough cop all the time.'

Lucy chuckled. 'Thanks. I know. And believe me, I have been taking time for myself as well. In fact, I reckon I should just about get shares in Kleenex. But when I lay it all out and analyse what happened I actually consider myself kind of lucky in many ways.'

'Lucky?'

'Yeah. It sounds stupid, I know. But it could have been a lot worse. What happened was shitty. No doubt about it. But I'm also thinking that compared with a lot of people who go through this sort of thing, I'm pretty fortunate. On the upside, it didn't happen at my house, so I'm not going to be constantly reminded of it every time I close my eyes and try to curl up in my own bed. And maybe, just maybe, being unconscious for the worst of it means I can sort of *almost* forget that it ever happened. I mean, aside from one flash I have, the one I told you about where he's on top of me, my recall of the whole thing is pretty much watching the start of the movie, *Top Gun*, and then waking up the next morning feeling embarrassed.'

Anna frowned, her pen skipping lightly across her notebook. Lucy was still clearly in suppression mode. Glossing over it wasn't going to help anyone in the long run. It was one of the most destructive ways of dealing with it. She'd seen it before. One of her first patients, in fact, a girl who'd been date raped in a similar situation in 2001 had recently been in touch with her about her case. She too had tried to brush her particular incident aside, get on with life, not deal with it properly and had found herself ten years down the track, living in Canberra, out at Wagamama one night enjoying a meal with her husband when she caught a glimpse of a man who was a dead ringer for her rapist at the table beside them. She'd completely fallen to pieces on the spot. Had to leave. And this, a good ten years after the event. Ten years of telling herself she'd been one of the lucky ones to come away comparatively unscathed.

She cleared her throat. 'Can I point out, Lucy, that in many ways, it's good that you're feeling so positive about what's happened? However, I don't want you to underestimate what's happened to you. I especially don't want you to bury your feelings about it. It *is* a big deal. It *was* a shitty thing, particularly when you think about the trust you placed in Nick as a friend. It *was* a betrayal, the ultimate form of betrayal actually. And while I don't want to suggest to you that you *have* to be feeling anything other than what you feel, you need to know that it's okay to feel pissed off or ripped off, or furious or even vulnerable. You're thoroughly entitled to feel all that and more.'

'I know. I *am* pissed off with him for what he did. I feel like the stupidest person on earth for having trusted him . . .'

'No,' Anna said firmly. 'He was a colleague, a friend. You should have been able to trust him. You have no reason to feel stupid. He's the one in the wrong, remember?'

Lucy sighed. 'I know. But still, I do feel silly for having got myself into the situation and I'll certainly be a lot more wary about who I make friends with in future. But hey, maybe I won't need to worry for long. Cam will be out in a few weeks.'

Anna frowned again. There were a few points she still needed to bring home, but Lucy had inadvertently given her another opening she needed. 'So . . . have you told him yet?'

'No,' she said quickly. 'He didn't want anyone to contact him while he was . . . you know. He was so embarrassed about everything. And honestly, I think he's got enough of his own troubles to deal with at the moment without me dumping my problems on him as well. I'll explain everything properly when he gets out.'

'Okay,' she said, agreeing with the logic. The boyfriend probably couldn't be much of a support, anyway. 'So, have you told anyone else? Your mum, a friend? Remember we talked about the importance of having a support person throughout the investigation and the court proceedings?'

Lucy's eyes dropped to her feet and a hint of pink crept up along her cheeks. 'No. To be honest, I really don't have any close friends. And I've tried now a couple of times to broach the subject with my mother, but the thing is, she doesn't really do emotion.'

'What do you mean?'

'Oh, sorry, that probably sounded bad. I'm not criticising her. She was brought up in quite a strict household and unfortunately she's more comfortable with conversations about the weather, politics, her charity work, that sort of thing. She's right into all that community work and is very much about . . . um . . . how do I describe it . . . um . . . saving face. She's, like, the ultimate people pleaser. And I think she'd probably be pretty embarrassed about what's happened. It'd be like losing face, having a daughter who found herself on the receiving end of something like this. I think it might all be a bit too much for her. You know? So, I'm just going to sit on it for the time being. I know I'll have to tell her before it becomes public and we go to court, but I just don't think she'd cope very well with it at the moment.'

'And your father? Could you talk to him?' Anna asked with a frown.

Lucy squirmed. 'Uh, it's quite possible that he does even less emotion than my mother. But look, it's cool. I've got Richard and Will for the time being and they've been great.'

Anna nodded, imagining how thoughtful Richard would be, but the situation was far from ideal. 'You know that when this all becomes public knowledge, as I assume it will before much longer, you're really going to need someone you can rely on twenty-four seven, someone you're comfortable ringing any time of the day or night to have a cry or a vent if needs be. And while Richard's great, I can't help but feel that he might not be able to give you everything you need.' But as she spoke an image of Lucy wrapped in Richard Moore's arms danced before her.

At least I hope he won't.

Wait a minute.

Am I . . . jealous?

Ridiculous.

Stop it.

'Well, hopefully by then Cam will be out and I have no doubt that he'll support me the way I supported him through his court case.'

Anna stared at her book, tried not to raise an eyebrow. There was every chance in the world that the boyfriend was going to come out of prison even more damaged than when he went in.

'Okay. Well, hopefully between him, Richard, Will and myself, you'll have plenty of scope for talking things out if needs be. And I say that because of what I want to raise with you next.'

The hardest bit of all.

'Mmm?'

'Well, once this comes out, Lucy, you know there'll be a certain amount of interest, not only from the media, but your colleagues as well.'

'Sure. That's only natural, I guess, given what we do for a living.'

Anna nodded again. 'Of course. But in your case, the scrutiny might be pretty intense. Have you heard of the saying "the second rape"?'

The girl shook her head.

'Well, in a nutshell, it's an expression that's utilised in cases such as yours when the actual responses from family, friends, colleagues and the like are, shall we say, less than supportive. And I'm not necessarily saying that's the way it's going to play out, but you should be prepared for any eventuality.'

'I know that not everyone's going to believe me,' she said, eyes downcast. 'Despite the fact that there's an independent witness to back it up.'

'True. And sometimes their reactions can be a lot more disappointing than you might expect. Not only might they *not* believe you, but they might feel the need to ridicule you, blame you, ostracise you, threaten you, sabotage your career or even abandon you altogether.' *Jesus, Anna. That sounds crappy. Crappy but true.* 'Now I'm not saying this is always the case, but . . .'

'I know, I get it. Coppers have loyalties. Long-established loyalties. And it might come down to them choosing between him and me.'

Anna bit her bottom lip and paused. 'Yes. No matter how much they claim the service is modern, equal, inclusive and all the other politically correct palaver, it's still a very male-dominated and in many respects old-fashioned beast, as you know. They're not all good guys like Richard and Will.'

'I know, I know. But like I said before, it boils down to one simple fact: Nick should be held to account for what he did. If people feel protective of him, and feel the need to choose sides, then there's not much I can do to dissuade them, apart from just getting on with the job and telling the truth. And if people don't want to work with me, or choose to give me the cold shoulder in the corridor, then that's their prerogative.'

Oh, you make it sound so easy, my darling.

You have no idea what sort of a hell storm you're conjuring up.

Anna closed her eyes briefly and thought back to a woman she'd taken on as a patient a few years earlier, a junior ranger with Parks and Wildlife who'd been sexually assaulted one night after work by her boss. It wasn't just a matter of people no longer wanting to work with her, or giving her the cold shoulder in the corridor. The vicious hate campaign they'd subjected the poor woman to led her to resign only days after she made her initial complaint to the police. She'd received phone calls with death threats in the middle of the night, had a dead possum nailed to her front door, had posters picturing her face put up all over town one night with the words *This woman is a slut and a liar* on them. Eventually she'd been forced to pack up her belongings and catch the first plane to the mainland to begin a new life, dropping the charges on the way as she'd been terrified of going through with them.

Lucy, in her youth and naivety, might have imagined the second rape would be unpleasant but trivial, but Anna was afraid she wouldn't know what had hit her. Anna knew coppers. She understood the psyche of the tight, impenetrable band who called themselves the SOG. She'd also been watching and listening to Costa for almost twenty years, knew how men *really* thought, even the most decent of them. And she'd seen with her own eyes how, over the past couple of years, their general attitude towards women in policing was becoming worse.

Even the 'good' blokes were becoming disgruntled with women taking the quality non-operational positions on the pretext of being pregnant or breastfeeding or having to pick kids up from school. They were tired of being overlooked for specialist and promotional roles, aware that the hierarchy had a political agenda of automatically promoting more females into higher and better positions. They were grumbling about instances of reverse discrimination.

She recalled one of Costa's stories about a particular female constable going into an interview for a sergeant's position and exclaiming on her way in that if any of the panel so much as looked at her pregnant belly and didn't give her the job, she'd be screaming discrimination from the high heavens. And they'd better change the job to a part-time sergeant's position while they were at it; the full-time job didn't fit in with her maternity plans.

Anna would bet a thousand bucks that when it all came out, Lucy would become the ultimate scapegoat for all of the ills of women in contemporary policing. The thought was bloody depressing.

She opened her eyes and studied the girl before her. Was she was incredibly naive or, alternatively, incredibly courageous?

'I'm glad you believe in yourself enough to see this through, Lucy. Not everyone does, and once people find out, they could be really hurtful. But remember that even if worst comes to worst and people seem to be giving you a wide berth, there are a few basic reasons for that which you can't control.

'Firstly, in a situation like yours, it's always a lot easier for people to side with the offender. If they take your side, then they're deliberately having to take a stand. Taking Nick's side is easier; it means that they only have to let their friendship with you slide. Secondly, offenders in scenarios like this are inevitably bullies, liars and manipulators. He's used to employing these sorts of strategies and may do so again to convince people to side with him rather than you.'

'Great,' Lucy said, rolling her eyes.

Careful. Don't scare her off completely.

'I don't mean to be the voice of doom and gloom, but do you see what I'm saying? How I'm trying to be realistic?'

'Of course. And I guess on top of that there're the usual old sexist stereotypes that come into play. It'll be easier for people to believe that I was asking for it, that I'm a bit of a slut, that since I went around to his place on a Friday night I must have known what was going to happen . . . blah, blah, blah.'

Anna nodded. 'Sad, but true. Stereotypes provide people with an easy out. It means they don't have to think too much about who's in the right and who's in the wrong. And at the end of the day, it's easier to believe that a big burly male police officer would never do the wrong thing. It fits with their world view. It's comfortable for them to believe that. To believe

180

the opposite, i.e., that a police officer, like a rugby player, rock star or other sort of public figure, is capable of such a thing, doesn't sit well. It's mentally unsettling for many people.'

Lucy sighed and then threw a hand in front of her mouth, stifling a yawn. 'Well, I guess all we can do is go ahead and see what happens. And hey, who knows? Maybe it won't be as bad as we think, eh?'

Anna caught her drowsy grin and returned it. It was all she could give her. And hey, perhaps she was right. Perhaps it wouldn't be so bad. Lucy seemed mentally tougher than other victims she'd encountered. Hell, if anyone could withstand the flak the department would start churning out the second it became common knowledge, then it would be her.

Still.

'Okay. Is there anything else we need to go over before you fall asleep face first on my couch?'

'No . . . I'm good. It's the right thing to do. And that is, after all, exactly what I signed up for; doing the right thing, I mean,' she said self-consciously.

'True. Now head home and get some sleep. Oh, but on your way out, make another appointment to see me. Maybe next week, yeah? Jenny should be down at the front desk by now,' she said, glancing at her watch. 'And if anything unfolds before then and you need to talk, just call and I'll make a spot available. Okay?'

She rose and followed the yawning girl to the door.

'Thanks, Anna. I really appreciate it. More than you could know,' she added.

'No worries. See you next week.'

She closed the door softly behind her, placed the file on her desk and paused, trying to brush away the heavy, impending sense of doom that was invading her headspace. Anna wondered again what Costa would have made of Lucy Howard and her allegation. Would he have been pissed off, sided with Nick Greaves and thought her a troublemaker? Or would he have been sympathetic, understanding that there was no way on earth a woman would make this sort of thing up, knowing that she was placing herself in the most horrific of positions by doing so? She toyed with the idea for a moment before reaching the same troubling, uncomfortable conclusion.

I still have absolutely no idea what he would make of it.

In fact, I have absolutely no idea who my husband is any-more.

Somewhat despairing, she shrugged the thought off and reached for the phone, relieved to finally begin taking care of the most important business of the day. Hopefully Peter would be in by now.

The Toecutter

3.15 pm Thursday 30 June

Augusta Road pulsed with the steady flow of midafternoon traffic. The main stretch of road was the inner artery that ran through the heart of Lenah Valley, the northernmost suburb of Hobart city. Residents classified themselves as Hobartians, fiercely ignoring the fact that their burb lay nestled within spitting distance of the southern boundary of the city of Glenorchy, a boundary rather scathingly referred to as the Flannelette Curtain.

The black, unmarked sedan was inconspicuous on the corner of Montagu Street and Augusta Road and from the three metres of bitumen she'd claimed as their own, Sonya Wheeler propped behind the wheel, watching and waiting. She sat rod-straight and unmoving in the driver's seat, ignoring the low-slung sun in the western sky which glanced off the bonnet and pierced the backs of her eyeballs. Discomfort could wait. It was more important to be ready to spring into action should the need arise.

Her gaze, quick, measured and unrelentingly judgemental, jumped towards the rear-vision mirror at the wail of an approaching ambulance siren. It slowed, flashing roof lights barely visible through the blackened sun spots dotting her vision, and entered the shrub-lined driveway of the Calvary Hospital behind them, the third such arrival since they'd propped an hour earlier. A sound, closer this time, brought her back. On the footpath beside them, the brown, maroon and white uniforms of a pair of local schoolgirls bobbed. They giggled as they passed. One let out an almighty shriek of laughter while the other let a spent blue chip packet slip through her fingertips without a care. It danced lightly on the footpath before bobbing along behind in their wake, caught in a flutter of afternoon breeze.

Sonya watched it. Her eyes narrowed, her lips tightened. It didn't even register on the girl's 'give a shit' radar. Apparently littering was as natural as breathing, even to supposedly well-educated private school girls. She resisted the urge to wind down the window and call, 'I think you dropped something!'

Not that they'd care, anyway. They'd probably just flip her the bird.

'Sooo, what's your take on all this, then?' Will Torino asked from the passenger side, breaking her train of thought and cracking the frosty silence that had crystallised between them. He lounged in the seat, his slumped, carefree form grating on her nerves almost as much as his size elevens on the dash did.

Her face remained stony, impassive. The guy was seriously mistaken if he thought she was going to get embroiled in any sort of personal, social discussion over it. Let him dissect it with his gossiping buddies over a beer if he wanted, but she wasn't having a bar of it. She turned away from him, lips tightening again, and pretended to study the traffic flow.

'My official verdict thus far, Detective Torino, is that an officer has made a formal complaint against another officer and we're here to investigate it. As the complainant, she has every right to pursue it and clearly she's determined to do so. It's our job to support her by finding as much evidence as we possibly can to substantiate the allegation. The offender will be charged, the file will go to the DPP for decision and we'll move onto the next one. Nothing more, nothing less.'

Without looking back, she could feel his 'fuck you, then' smirk. But at least her curt response shut him up. She detested being cooped up in the car with the Italian Stallion. He was a good-looking son of a bitch and he knew it. Good-looking and arrogant. But as far as she was concerned, both qualities paled into insignificance when compared with his greatest crime of all: his cavalier attitude. Torino was not a professional. He was one of the boys, the *maaaate*, the back-slapper extraordinaire, the *trust me* guy in the room, the feel-good, *tell me everything* man. Smooth as a bucket of snot. And despite having known him for years, she'd never warmed to him. In fact, Will Torino embodied everything she despised in a colleague and the mere idea of spending another hour trapped beside him in silence gave her a throbbing bitch of a headache.

Fingers crossed they'd be out of there before (a) her temples exploded or (b) she punched him.

Howard, approximately two blocks west of their stationary car, was wired up and ready to go. All they needed was the shout from the dogs to say that Greaves was home and they'd send her in. A quick chat, an admission of guilt – *pffffttt* – and they'd move in for the search. The interview would be brief, painfully brief no doubt, and with any luck she'd be home in time for dinner, a first for the month.

'Do you always get this emotionally involved in your cases?' Will remarked, sliding his seat back further and crossing his ankles on the dashboard. She noted the bright yellow, smiley face socks peeking out beneath his jeans and dropped her opinion of him yet another notch, something she hadn't thought possible.

'Do you always rely on the lowest form of wit to get you through everyday social intercourse with other human beings?' she asked drily.

'Only the prickly ones,' he said with a casual smile.

Arsehole. Her fingers twitched in her lap. It'd be a pleasure to smack the smarmy grin off his face, or at the very least, smack his sneaker-clad feet off the dash and remind him, as she frequently had to with her colleagues, that they were supposed to be professionals. They had a job to do and as far as she was concerned, if everyone just took things a little more seriously in this tin-pot police service, then they might actually cultivate some respect from the public. A novel concept, but one she hadn't given up hoping for.

'It's not about being *prickly*, Detective Torino. I believe the word you're looking for is "*professional*".'

He threw his arms up behind his head and grinned. 'Mmm. Pricks and pros. Some might suggest there was a link there somewhere.'

She was saved from engaging in his banter by the crackling surveillance radio.

'Target has arrived.'

Will sat up, finally ready to be serious. 'Roger that. Stand by.'

Sonya punched Lucy's pre-programmed number into her phone and held her breath. The dial tone was shrill in her ear.

Once.

Twice.

Three times.

Four times.

Where the bloody hell is the silly girl?

Five times.

'Hello?'

'Hello, Lucy. It's Sergeant Wheeler. He's in. You ready to go?'

'Ready as I'll ever be, Sarge.'

She bristled at the young woman's familiarity. *It's sergeant. Would it kill people to be a little more respectful?*

But she bit her tongue and kept her voice even. 'Good. Is the DAT on?'

'Just doing it now.'

In her left ear Sonya heard a rustle as the recorder was switched on. 'Right. I've got you, Lucy, loud and clear. We're ready when you are. Remember what we discussed. No leading questions, no emotions. Just keep it together, get as much as you can from him. An admission of sex is good, a volunteered admission of alcohol or drugs will be outstanding. But if you're clearly not getting anywhere with him, don't bring up the drugs. We want to keep that up our sleeves for the interview so we can catch the look on his face. Got it?'

'Got it, Sarge. Wish me luck.'

Her hackles rose again. 'Good luck,' she said through gritted teeth.

Will threw her a condescending look which needed no interpretation. *Lucy's not an idiot, you know.*

She ignored him, put the phone onto loudspeaker and focused on the scene playing out on their dashboard. A car engine. Silence as it was cut. A car door opening, slamming shut.

Footsteps.

Knuckles on wood.

A pause, followed by a deep, nervous exhalation and a door thirsty for a splash of WD-40.

'Oh? Hi, Luce. How you doing?'

She noted the tone. So, Greaves was surprised. She sensed his mind ticking over in the pause. If he was guilty, he would have twigged that something was up the second he saw the girl standing on his doorstep. Sonya held her breath, mildly surprised at her own anxious anticipation.

'Hi, Nick. I'm fine. Well, actually, no, I'm not fine. I need to talk to you. Can I come in for a second?'

Everything hung on his next sentence, on the inflection.

The hesitation lengthened, stretching out before them like a piece of gum, then snapped.

'Sure. Come on in.'

Shit. There was no concern in his words. No surprise. He was too chirpy. *Too* in control. He was onto them. There was no way he was going to put his foot in it or give anything away and if he had something to hide, then he'd hide it well.

Shit.

This whole bloody operation is a waste of time and money.

And from the look on Will's face, a disappointment that mirrored her own, she knew she was right. Nevertheless the futile encounter continued before them, Sonya leaning in to hear every word, analyse every syllable.

'So what can I do for you, Luce? Changed your mind already, eh?' Nick asked.

'Not exactly. Um . . .'

Get it together, Howard. Think about it.

'Um . . . I was thinking about what happened between us . . . when we slept together . . .'

'I haven't stopped thinking about it,' Nick said.

Sonya heard the sly grin on his face and her eyes narrowed. *Smarmy prick. But at the very least that's admitting that you've done the deed. Strike one, Nicholas.*

'Well, me neither,' Lucy continued. 'In fact, that's what I wanted to talk to you about.'

'Yeah?'

'Well, the thing is, Nick, like, I'm sure we had a really nice night . . . but . . . I'm having trouble actually remembering it.'

Silence.

Sonya leaned further forwards, desperate to block out the residual traffic noise.

But there was more silence. *Shit. He's onto her for sure now.*

Beside her Will grimaced.

There was a rustle of clothing before Lucy chimed in again, the discomfort echoing in her every word. 'Look, I don't mean to be rude or anything, and I'm sure we had a great time, but I was just wondering . . . um . . . how much did I have to drink, Nick?'

More silence.

'He's totally onto her,' Will whispered with a shake of his head.

Sonya threw him a look. *Of course he is. But will you shut up?*

'What do you mean you're having trouble remembering it?'

'Well, exactly that. How many drinks did you give me?'

'Three. Only three.'

A pause.

'Um . . . are you sure? It's just that I remember the next morning you said something about us having killed the bottle.'

'No, I don't think so.' Calmly. 'You had a few quite strong ones, I had three, maybe four, but I'm sure we didn't kill a whole bottle.'

Lucy struggled, searching for words.

'Um . . . three, you say?'

'Yeah, three. Look. What are you trying to say, Luce?'

'I'm just trying to work out why I can't . . . um . . . remember things properly.'

He laughed. 'Well, I don't know. What I do know is that we had a few drinks, you kissed me . . .'

'What?' she shrieked.

'You kissed me. When we were on the couch. Watching *Top Gun*. Remember?'

'No! I don't remember, Nick, and that's the problem.'

Sonya shifted nervously. *Steady, Howard. Don't let him get the better of you.*

'Look,' she said, taking a deep breath and regaining control. 'I'm not mad, Nick. As I said, I'm sure we had a really nice night together, but what I need to do is get to the bottom of why I can't remember anything. Is there a chance I was really pissed? I mean, really, really pissed – that I had more than three drinks?'

Another pause.

'No, Luce,' he said calmly. *Too calmly.* 'You only had three. As far as I could tell, you were totally compos. You kissed me. I kissed you back. I asked if you wanted to stay the night. You agreed. We went to the bedroom and we had sex. End of story. I don't understand where you're coming from with all this.'

'This is pointless,' Will hissed. 'It's like he's reading from a fucking script.'

Sonya resisted the urge to clock him. 'Shush.' But Will was right. Greaves had covered the works. Every single point of proof he would need to cover in court. He'd left them no defence. *Totally compos. Lucy initiated sex. Consensual sex.*

It was game, set and match Greaves. *Shit.* But Lucy missed it, pushed on.

'Nick, it's fine if I was smashed. I don't care. I just need to know so I can put it straight in my own mind, yeah? It's really freaking me out, the not knowing.'

'Sorry, Luce, but I don't know what you're on about.'

Another rustle of material. The girl was up and pacing.

'Nick. Just tell me. Between you and me. It goes no further. I just want to know for my own peace of mind. Was I totally out of it? I'm just . . . embarrassed, I guess. I hate to think that I made a fool out of myself in front of you.'

His tone altered like a train switching tracks, annoyance penetrating casual calm.

'Lucy. I told you what happened. Now I don't know what game you're playing at, but I think it's time you left.'

'No!' she snapped. 'You're lying, one way or the other. Just tell me, Nick, was I pissed or was it something worse?'

'Worse?'

'Did you slip me something? A pill?'

'Oh shit, she's done it now,' Will groaned.

And she had. She'd overstepped the mark. If they'd ever had a chance of ambushing him with the drug issue and capturing his look of surprise in a video interview, it had just vanished into thin air. Howard'd gone and played their final hand. *Theirs*, not hers.

Sonya picked up the radio, hand shaking with fury. 'All units, we're moving in.'

'Pills? What the *fuck* are you on about, Lucy?' Nick cried. 'How dare you come barging in here . . .'

'Oh, just stop it, Nick! I know what you did. I know,' she finally yelled. 'What was it, huh? GHB? Roofies? Something else?'

Sonya slammed the 'transmit' button again. 'All units, I repeat, all units, go, go, go.'

The live staccato exchange continued firing from the phone as she reefed the car out of its parking spot and accelerated towards the ugly brick unit two blocks up.

They were out of the car and hurtling through the open front door within seconds, Lucy's hysterical accusations and

Nick's angry protests bouncing off the inside walls and out into the street.

Will, one step ahead of Sonya, made straight for Greaves and flipped the search warrant up into his flushed, incredulous face.

'What the hell is going on?' he yelled.

'Nick Greaves, we have a warrant to search this premises in relation to an allegation of sexual assault.'

'You've got to be kidding me, Will,' he cried as the six-person team filed into the tiny flat and spread out, commencing the search. He stood in the middle of the lounge, hands on hips, his anger slowly being tempered with wounded confusion.

Sonya zeroed in on Lucy and made a grab for her, a little rougher than she'd intended. But she didn't care. Hoped she left bruises actually. The girl was too stupid to follow even the most basic of instructions. *No emotions and if you're clearly not getting anywhere, don't bring up the drugs.* It wasn't fucking difficult. But no. She'd gone and blown it. She pushed her out the door towards a waiting officer. 'Put her in the car,' she barked. She turned back and faced Nick, eyed him up and down.

'If you don't already know, Constable Greaves, I'm Detective Sergeant Wheeler, from Professional Standards. Detective Sergeant Torino is from the Hobart CIB. We've received a complaint of assault and intend to search your residence. You can cooperate and save everyone a whole lot of time by handing over a number of select items we require. Or you can do it the hard way. Your choice.'

He glared at her, but she stared back defiantly, holding his gaze. *Oh yes, tough guy. That's right. I'm a woman who*

193

isn't intimidated by you. One who isn't going to fall for your charms. One who isn't going to trip over herself and throw her knickers at you just 'cause you're SOG. One who you're not going to fuck over. You can eyeball me all you want and I'm not going to budge, you son of a bitch. Like that, tough guy? Something a bit different, eh?

He might have been a head taller, but when she didn't budge he eventually cleared his throat, took a step backwards and crossed his arms, obviously deciding it was better to cooperate. 'Whatever you want. *Sergeant.* As you no doubt heard, I've already discussed the situation with Constable Howard and I have nothing further to say on the matter. I take it she's the one making the accusation?'

'Correct.'

He scoffed. 'What a joke. What an absolute joke. Will, you know me, man . . . Come on . . .'

But Will ignored the appeal and headed for the kitchen.

Greaves shook his head, turned back towards her. 'Fine. Let's get it over with then. What are you looking for?'

She pulled out her clipboard, scanned the list of items. 'Right. First of all, sheets and doona cover from the evening in question.'

'Washed,' he said with a casual shrug. 'It was a fair while ago, you know.'

Don't react. Don't bite. Remain professional.

'Right. A plastic tumbler. Pink. From your kitchen, I believe.'

'Gone.'

'What do you mean gone?'

'Binned. Went out with the rubbish the next day. I had half-a-dozen temporary ones I was using while I was unpacking. Feel free to check the kitchen.'

She frowned. 'Oh, we will.'

'Next?'

She hesitated, prickling with a fresh burst of anger.

This is ridiculous.

What's the point in even asking?

Damn you, Lucy Howard, for putting me in this position and making me look like a bumbling fool in front of this prick.

She slowed her breathing. 'A bottle of Bundy Red.'

'Gone too. I drank the rest of it over the following week and threw it out as well.' He shrugged, his eyes never leaving hers.

Oh, you reckon you're pretty good, don't you, tough guy?

Her grip tightened around the clipboard. 'Fine. No offence, but we'll have a look anyway. Oh, and I'll be needing your mobile and the hard drive from your computer as well. Hope that doesn't inconvenience you too much.'

'Not at all. Take what you like. I've got nothing to hide.'

'Good,' she said, her heart sinking. It was definitely over. If he wasn't putting up any resistance, then they'd be clean. They were going to come away from the whole mess with sweet FA. 'Give them to Constable Miller and he'll bag and tag them for you.'

She turned him over to a couple of the CIB guys before heading off into the bedroom still seething. By the time she arrived the officers were busy going through the bedside drawers. 'Anything?'

'Nope. The bedding is different to what's described in Howard's statement. And the laundry basket is empty. The sheets and doona cover she described are nice and clean and folded up in the linen closet.'

Of course. Perhaps if Howard had thought to report it earlier . . . But she cut the thought off dead. It wasn't worth speculating. They could only do the best with what they had, not what they didn't have, and at the very least, the mere existence of the bedding described further corroborated the allegation.

'Oh well, we expected as much. Bag them anyway and keep looking.'

She took a step back towards the doorway and scanned the room. Like the lounge, it was extraordinarily neat and tidy for a single man living by himself. She thought of her younger brothers, of her ex-husband when she'd been away for a week. Piles of clothes, dirty or merely clean and discarded, piles of books, a coathanger, a comic, the odd shoe, dust. But there was nothing. Every centimetre of Greaves's floor was visible around the bed. The bed itself was neatly made, the corners almost hospital in style, the side tables spotless. Not even so much as a half-drunk glass of water. Curious, she meandered into the bathroom, opened the medicine cabinet and perused the contents. There was no mess, no clutter, each and every item neatly displayed.

A razor.

A can of shaving cream.

Roll-on deodorant.

Bottle of aftershave.

Tub of hair product.

Mouthwash.

Sunscreen.

Talcum powder.

Tube of Deep Heat.

All equally spaced, labels facing out. Not a fingerprint smear, a stray drop of product or a misplaced splash in sight. She sighed. Anyone *this* organised wasn't going to leave incriminating evidence relating to nefarious activity just carelessly lying around. The search was pointless. Absolutely pointless. They were being made fools of.

She made her way back along the hallway and frowned at the hushed voices in the lounge. Her pace quickened. She rounded the corner of the kitchenette, stopping dead at the sight, Torino shirt fronting the taller Greaves, his eyes ablaze with rage. Their conversation tailed off. 'You wouldn't dare . . .'

'Wouldn't dare *what*, Sergeant Torino?' she asked abruptly. Both heads turned to face her. Will, still glowering defiantly, released his grip and gave Greaves a small but discernible push backwards. He adjusted his clothes and they exchanged a mutual scowl.

'Nothing. Constable Greaves and I are having a friendly chat – that's all.'

Nothing, my arse. 'Can I see you outside for a moment, please?'

'Sure,' he said casually, walking towards the door without so much as a glance back at Nick.

'What the hell are you playing at?' she hissed.

'Nothing. I told you. He was just winding me up.'

She met his stare. *I seriously doubt that. God knows what you're up to.* 'For the record, Sergeant, I'm officially watching you. This is going to be done by the book, okay? If I get so much as an inkling that you're deviating, I won't hesitate to put you on paper. I don't give a damn that we're the same rank. Do I make myself clear?'

'Oh, chill out, Wheeler. I want this prick as much as you do.'

'Don't call me Wheeler. You can want him all you want. But until we've got as much evidence as we're going to get, he's to be treated exactly the same as any other suspect. Now let's finish this up and get him back to the station.'

She turned and headed back inside, but not before hearing the mutter of a '*Sieg Heil*' behind her. She ignored it, strode on. To do otherwise would have been futile. And besides, it was hardly the first time. She'd heard worse. She wasn't stupid. Knew their nickname for her. *The Rottweiler*. But whatever. Let them think she was a ball breaker. It was, after all, the only way to be taken seriously in their world.

By knock-off time, her entire body was screaming with exhaustion and spent emotions. All the Red Bull, Clear Eyes and Panadol in the world wouldn't have a hope of touching the aches or numbing the tension she'd accumulated during the afternoon. Howard's conversation with Greaves had been a waste of time and manpower. If anything, it'd gone in his favour, giving him the chance to neatly lay his tale out for the world to hear, outside the confines of an interview room. A jury would find it calm, methodical and plausible. The search had also turned up bugger-all. Hardly surprising.

Once back at the station Greaves was unshakable, having stuck rigorously to his story throughout the video interview.

He'd provided what a jury would consider to be an adequate account of his phone call with his mate Dan Williams that day in the Prosecution office, a fact that had Sonya almost tearing the hair out of her scalp in frustration. It was bullshit, for sure, but was unfortunately perfectly adequate.

There was no way he and Dan would have been talking about Lucy.

Sure, he and Dan were mates. Sure, they went to the same gym. Sure, they talked about shags. Sure, Dan knew Nick and Lucy had done the deed, but that was the extent of it. The phone reference about someone being out of it didn't ring any bells. It was probably just meaningless banter. On second thoughts, it could have been about Greaves's pseudo girl-friend Chrissy. Probably *was* Chrissy actually. She was always around at his place, always knackered, especially after a hard work-out at Apollos.

Ask Chrissy. She'd back him up.

Dan Williams would back him up.

There was no way he'd ever do something as revolting as what they were suggesting. He genuinely liked women. Loved them. In fact, he was suitably outraged at the suggestion, suitably cool and suitably deferential.

Rumours of drugs at the gym? Not to his knowledge.

Semen from Lucy's clothes? Well, of course. They had, after all, had consensual sex.

Duane Macallister? A guy from Apollos? Never heard of him. Then again, he *had*. He knew *exactly* who they were referring to. The loser who was always hanging about them at the gym, trying to sleaze his way into their circle of friends. A statement? He was probably jealous because they excluded him. Because he was a weirdo. If he'd made a statement against him, it'd be utter bullshit, motivated by pure jealousy. Nothing more.

In the end Sonya had concluded the interview, signed the tapes and fled the room to the sanctuary of the CIB kitchenette. The seized mobile and hard drive would be examined in time, but there'd be nothing of interest on them. The whole thing was infuriating. Moore thought it was a good circumstantial case and she couldn't argue. But that's all it was. Circumstantial. If only there'd been more. If Howard had reported it earlier, they might have had drugs. If CIB had got their act together earlier and had the fucking TIs up and running, they would have had both sides of the call between Williams and Greaves and it would have been all over, red rover. Greaves bragging about Howard being out of it. One count of rape. Thanks for coming.

If Nick Greaves had done what he was accused of doing – and Sonya had never been more certain of anything in her life – he'd covered his tracks like an avalanche.

The best they could do was a circumstantial case. A strong one, but circumstantial all the same. If it was any other rape case, she'd be stoked. But it wasn't just any old rape case involving any old victim or any old suspect, and as such, she just wished they had something more tangible. Something that would put an end to the doubt and speculation that would naturally do the rounds once it went public.

She put her elbows on the desk, rested her thumping forehead on her hands and closed her eyes. Greaves must have talked to someone, laughed with someone, written, recorded, photographed something as a future memento. What the hell had they overlooked?

And what about the other rape? The uni student. She recalled the file, having scanned through it only a few days earlier when she was getting up to speed on Greaves. But it, too, had too many holes. A positive result for GHB, a grainy, unidentifiable CCTV image from the college and a hazy, ill-defined identikit that could well have been half the men in Hobart. That was the sum total of the evidence. The victim hadn't picked Greaves or Williams in the photo board. The database failed to provide a match for the DNA sample. That immediately counted Greaves out. Like every other police officer in the state, he'd given a voluntary sample years earlier for 'forensic elimination' purposes.

The handful of Isobar patrons they'd tracked down recalled nothing, the club staff, never particularly eager to assist, ranged in opinion from a brown-haired man to a black-haired man to a crew cut, colour-indistinguishable man anywhere from one-seventy to one-ninety centimetres and wearing either a blue shirt, a green shirt or possibly a khaki T-shirt. And of course their own CCTV footage was conveniently 'unavailable', the system unfortunately malfunctioning that night. *More likely to be related to the fact that they'd had three separate complaints of bouncers beating the shit out of people that very night and some bastard had wiped it . . .*

Even though he clearly hadn't been the rapist in this case, she'd put it all to Greaves, wondering if it might be one of his mates. If he might not have been standing next to a friend, egging him on to spike the uni student's drink. But he'd denied it. He'd sat back, folded his arms and declared that he'd never been to Isobar in his life, had never met anyone by the name of Suzanne, or Suzy, Ward and if they could prove that he had, then good luck to them. Sonya had no comeback. Had nothing else to throw at him. And it made her head ache just to think about it.

Her train of thought was interrupted by a knock and a polite cough. She looked up. Richard Moore hovered in the doorway.

'Oh, hi, Inspector. Sorry, I was just having a moment to catch my thoughts.'

'No worries, Sonya. I just wanted to say well done.'

'Well done? Ah . . . correct me if I'm wrong, but Greaves did a good interview. He's got answers for everything.'

Moore chuckled. 'I know that, but it's not over yet. We might not have as much as you'd like, but the TIs are still running. Forensics have almost finished with his phone so we'll give it back before we throw him out the door. Then we sit back and see what he does next.'

Keeping in mind that if he hasn't talked about it yet, he's hardly going to now.

'So he just walks out the door?' she asked despondently.

'No, no. We'll charge him . . . and then let him walk out the door.'

'*Charge* him?' she cried, nearly falling off her seat. It hadn't even crossed her mind that they'd be contemplating that. But then, of *course* they would. It was the next, inevitable step. After all, it was up to the DPP to make the final decision – not them.

'Sure.'

'But . . . but . . . it's a pretty circumstantial case, and even though I know we can, um . . . do you really think we should? At this stage?'

Moore shrugged. 'As far as I can see, we've got just as much as we have with most other rape cases we've gone ahead with before. More, actually. They agree on everything that happened up until a point. Then they diverge. He says it was consensual, she says it wasn't. We can show the gym has a history of drugs. We've got records to show that Nick has been a member of that gym for seven years and that he goes at least three times a week. We have the extremely dodgy phone call between him and Dan Williams. We have an independent witness who's prepared to give evidence that he overheard Greaves and Co. talking about using GHB as a rape drug. Best of all, we have Lucy, who'll be far better in the box than ninety-nine per cent of civilian rape victims.'

Sonya stared at him open-mouthed. Of course it was shaping up well, but . . . but . . . this was no ordinary case. There was a hell of a lot at stake.

'Sir, I agree that if it was anyone else, we'd give it a run, but . . . well . . . it's *not* just any old rape victim, is it? And it's not just any offender. There's a lot at stake . . . for him.'

He looked taken aback. 'I know what you're saying, Sonya, but she has every right. If she wants her day in court, then so be it. She's credible, she's given a good statement, he's corroborated that intercourse took place . . .'

'Yes, I'm not talking about that. I know it's a strong circumstantial case. But . . . but . . . Greaves'll probably be suspended if he's charged. That's pretty high stakes.'

'Of course. But what about every other offender who's charged? They all have things to lose. Jobs, family, friends . . . We can't just ignore these things or go around perverting the course of justice, or bending it to our needs, just because we're worried about what might or might not happen. Our job is to put together the best possible case and forward it on to the DPP. It's not up to us to be judge and jury as well.'

'I know that, sir. I just thought . . .'

'Thought he didn't do it?'

She shook her head vehemently. 'I never said that.'

'Well, what are you saying then? Is there a problem? Something I don't know about?'

Yes. There is. But to be perfectly honest, I have no idea myself what the problem is. He's guilty as sin, but something's not right. We shouldn't be going ahead with this. Not at the moment.

She sighed. 'I'm just saying that personally, between you and me, I don't like the guy, never have. Can't stand him, in fact. But on the other hand, I'd feel a hell of a lot more comfortable about this all if . . . if . . . if we had something more. A positive blood test from her, the pink tumbler for trace evidence, the other half of that call . . . something . . . anything . . .'

'I know. But we don't, Sonya,' he said, making to leave. 'It's that simple. What we *do* have is a strong circumstantial case and a robust complainant who'll give her evidence well. And hey, sometimes all you can do is rely on your gut. That's what I'm doing and I really mean it when I say I'm not losing any sleep over charging Greaves. I'm certain he did it. So go home, sleep on it and come back with a fresh set of eyes in the morning. I want you to pick up Dan Williams first thing. Will can charge and bail Greaves and do up the press release.'

She mustered a weary half-smile, convinced they were making a mistake but too tired to fight. 'If you say so, sir.'

● ● ●

By the time she pulled into the driveway of the standard New Town red-bricker she was feeling no better about the whole situation. She switched the headlights off and sat in the darkness contemplating the enormity of what would be unfolding back at the station. A copper, and not just some copper, but a distinguished one with an immaculate service record and a promising future before him, was being charged with the worst of crimes. He'd get bail, of course, but it'd make the papers first thing in the morning, courtesy of the stock-standard press release. Any attempt to keep it from the media at this stage would just result in allegations of a cover-up further down the line if and when the vultures did finally get hold of it.

Greaves would be suspended; nothing was surer. After all, they couldn't have him bumping into Lucy in the corridors. Most likely there'd be stringent bail conditions restricting his life, if not a restraint order. He'd probably be shunned by his peers who wouldn't want to get involved in the whole sordid mess. Gone were the good old days when the crew rallied around. These days, if Professional Standards were looking at you, everyone else looked the other way.

At that moment in time, one man's life was in the process of being ruined. She took a deep breath and prayed again, for the millionth time that day, that they were doing the right thing.

As she clicked the car door shut, she decided, for once, that it was futile to stew over it for a second longer. The decision was made even easier given the fact that Kate's car was in the driveway, the lights were on and, judging by the smell in the air, Kate was making her world-famous lasagne. She grinned, felt her shoulders sink and the tension in her neck dissolve. There was no way she was going to drag that crap over the doorstep and into the sanctity of their home if she could help it. Kate didn't deserve it. Hell. *She* didn't deserve it. Besides, there was nothing she could do about it now. Moore knew how she felt. Torino would prepare the file, Lucy would hopefully give the best evidence of her life and . . . well . . . that was it really. Her job was done.

She climbed the stairs and smiled as the sensor light came on. 'Honey, I'm home,' she called facetiously, throwing her bag on the hall stand and stretching her arms out as the tiny ginger-haired child in the pink fairy costume ran towards her. 'Mummy, Mummy, Mummy . . . guess what we're having for dinner.'

She pursed her lips and gave her most serious expression. 'Chocolate mud cake?'

'Nope.'

'Um . . . Hawaiian pizza?'

'Nope.'

'Um . . . strawberry ice-cream?'

'No, no, no. I'll give you a clue. It's your favourite ever.'

'Well, in that case it has to be Kate's lasagna! Am I right, or am I right?'

'Yes!' squealed the little girl, turning in circles and tapping madly back up the hallway towards the kitchen, the heady scent of the rich meaty bolognaise doubling, tripling, over-taking her foul mood with every step.

When she reached the kitchen she couldn't help but smile at the scene that greeted her. It was as expected. Kate, although she made possibly the best lasagna in the entire Southern Hemi-sphere, had a habit of utilising every single dish and utensil in the kitchen during the process. It usually took an hour to clean up afterwards. Not that she could get annoyed when the result was so amazing. On top of that, Kate always managed to look as though she'd done three rounds with a pack of unwieldy, food-fighting gremlins, and today was no exception.

'How was your day?' she asked, stopping to wipe a smear of flour off the younger woman's cheek before giving her a quick peck.

'*Very* eventful. While you were out catching bad guys and changing the world, I finished the chapter I was working on yesterday, totally rearranged three major paragraphs from chapter two, despaired over how many times I've used the word "said" and realised that my murderer doesn't *actually* have a motive for what he's done. So, yeah. Great.'

She threw her hands up and Sonya laughed. She loved hearing about Kate's writing, even though she always had to prise it out of her. Kate was reluctant to talk about it, felt that it didn't really compare to what Sonya did for a living. But still.

'Most eventful then,' Sonya said with a wink.

'Totally. And then I picked Miss Elizabeth up from kindy and we went to the aquatic centre for a paddle.'

'Nice,' Sonya said. 'And the fairy costume?'

'Oh, when we got home it was time for a game of Magic Faraway Tree in the backyard,' she said matter-of-factly, pouring a glass of sav blanc and passing it to Sonya.

'But of course. Ta.'

'And you?'

'Pah, nothing exciting. Just the usual,' she said, taking a long sip of the wine and throwing her jacket across the back of a chair.

'Well, I hope you're hungry. Because Lizzie and I have been busy and the lasagna will be ready in approximately half an hour.'

'Perfect. Time enough to give someone a bath, take a packet of Panadol and wash it down with approximately half that bottle of wine.'

Kate watched as Lizzie disappeared into the lounge and threw Sonya a quizzical look. 'Everything okay?'

'Fine, fine. I'm just tired, that's all. Nothing to worry about.'

'Well, I *do* worry. So I expect to hear the full story.'

Sonya smiled again. So much for trying to keep everything at work. As well as being her soulmate, Kate did a pretty good impression of being the best sounding-board in the world. She was possibly the most sensible person Sonya had ever met and she knew without a doubt that despite her best efforts to separate work from home, by the end of the evening she'd have spilled the lot.

'So?' Kate said, taking the second bottle of white and moving from the now clean kitchen to the plush brown sofa. 'Want to tell me what's going on?'

Sonya followed, curling her feet up underneath her and offering her glass out for another pour. Lizzie was tucked up in bed, the fire had settled from fierce roar to comforting crackle and a stillness had descended on the house. 'Where do I start?'

'At the risk of sounding condescending, I usually find the beginning is a good place.'

'Okay. Well . . . Once upon a time there was a little girl who wanted to join the police force . . .'

Kate giggled and threw a cushion at her. 'Maybe not that far back.'

Sonya paused. Kate had heard enough war stories over the years to get where she was coming from. Hell, she'd even briefly been a copper before chucking it in and deciding it wasn't for her, a decision that had been even easier to make when two months out of the academy she'd gone and fallen hopelessly in love with a woman on her shift, the older married woman with a child to be precise. And the situation wasn't made any easier considering their shift sergeant at the time was the husband in question. Some days, even now, three years down the track, Sonya marvelled that the whole sordid mess had all turned out as well as it had. So while Kate might not have been in the job for long, she was by no means ignorant of the politics.

'Well, while we were devouring that lasagna, let's just say that something fairly major was going on back down at the station.'

'Let me guess . . . the commissioner actually cracked a joke?'

Joking is probably the last thing on his mind at the moment. 'Ha-ha. Not *that* monumental! But seriously, do you remember a copper, Nick Greaves? Tall, dark, total beefcake, SOG?'

Kate shook her head. 'Not really. Those meatheads all kind of blend into one.'

'True. Anyway, this particular meathead is in the process of being charged with rape and,' she stole a quick glance at her watch, 'is probably being bailed as we speak.'

Kate gave a low whistle. 'Pretty major, hey? And that was one of yours?'

'Yes and no. I've been working alongside CIB, but, that said, they ran most of it and I was just the token toecutter. There to dot the i's and cross the t's.'

'Pfft. Don't be so modest. But back to the main question, why is Constable Greaves bugging you more than I've seen anything else bug you in a long time? I mean, it's not like it's your first sexual assault.'

'True.' She nodded, thinking back over the last couple of years. There was the licensing copper up in Launnie who'd touched up the pissed clubber he'd been driving home one night. The Queenstown constable who'd schtoiked his fifteen-year-old stepdaughter. The Bellerive D who'd been rooting one of his informants, only to have her turn around and make a complaint when he'd finally broken it off with her.

She sighed, fingered the tassels on the cushion in her lap and began her admission, an admission she knew wasn't going to sound great when translated from brain to mouth. 'It's the victim.'

'Mmm?'

'A copper.'

Kate's eyes bulged. 'Oh shit, really? Anyone I know?'

'No. She's a junior burger, been out . . . hell, not even a year yet. Lucy. Lucy Howard.'

'Riiight,' Kate said slowly. 'But I still don't get why it's bugging you. What's the problem? Do you think your guy's innocent?'

Sonya snorted. 'Christ, no. I reckon the filthy, underhanded prick was totally capable of doing what he's been accused of.'

210

'So, what's the problem then?'

Sonya smiled. She should have known Kate wouldn't understand. Not that it was Kate's fault. She wasn't explaining it very well. But hell, she wasn't actually sure she understood herself. 'It's Lucy that's the problem, I think.'

'The fact that she's a copper?'

'Nail on the head, baby. And, don't quote me on this because I know it sounds really, *really* awful, but . . . I'm just so fucking pissed off. With *her*.'

There. She'd said it. The thing that was bothering her. And she was right; it did sound crappy out loud.

'Hmm. Let me get this straight. You're pissed off at her for being raped? Not sure I follow, compadre.'

'No, no. Of course not,' she cried. 'It's just that, jeez, I don't know how to say it.' She took a deep breath, tried to order her thoughts, make some sense of them. 'The thing is, I'm pissed off that she's reported it. It's not about the rape itself. It's about the way this whole thing has unfolded. It's about . . . the ramifications. That's it. The ramifications.'

Kate screwed up her face, looked at her as though she was stark raving bonkers. 'Surely the only ramifications that matter are the ones where he's found guilty, she gets some support, gets over it and gets on with her life.'

Sonya hesitated. Maybe Kate *had* been away too long. Or maybe she'd never had the chance to understand the culture the way she herself did. 'Of *course* that's important. And of course I hope that happens. Christ, anything less than that doesn't bear thinking about. But the problem is, there's going to be so much more to it than that.'

'Such as?'

'Such as . . . look at the big picture. A young female cop makes one of the worst allegations possible against a well-respected, well-liked, experienced male cop. *Male*, Kate. I joined up in '95. Back in those days, women were still fighting to be recognised as equal. The ranks were still chockers with old dinosaurs who couldn't accept that we were breaking away from a time when our entire existence consisted of standard-issue high heels and tights, standard-issue handbags instead of a firearm and . . . and . . . and . . . babysitting the children while the men went out and did the real police work!'

She poured another glass of white and rocked forwards on her heels. 'And that was the middle of the fucking 1990s. Not the 1920s. Ever since I joined I've been fighting to be recognised as being not only equal, but valuable, to the service. Me and every other chick out there. It's been like a war zone. A silent, sneaky, covert and devious one, but a war zone all the same. We've had to fight to gain *their* trust at every juncture, fight to convince them that we're worthy of being permitted to do the same job they do, fight to gain their respect time after time after bloody time. The most basic of rights which we should always have had. You know, I've had to do the job twice, no, three times, better than a bloke, to get any acknowledge-ment at all. And hell, not even acknowledgement. Just fucking acceptance, minus the sneers, the innuendo and the jibes. The sad fact is that blokes can afford to rock the boat. We've never had that luxury. And all it takes for that precious equilibrium to come crashing down is one Lucy fucking Howard.'

She fell silent and Kate seized the opening. 'I think I under-stand what you're saying, but . . . don't you think it's a bit harsh, love? I mean, she can't help what happened.'

'I know that,' she said, taking another swig. 'And that's not what I'm saying. I feel for the girl. I really do. Date rape is a crappy, fucked-up thing to go through. And I understand exactly why she's made a complaint. Like she said to me when I first went through her statement with her – she's a bit of an introvert who feels like she's been walked over her whole life. Now it's time to stand up for herself. Also, the fact that what he gave her could've killed her in the right circumstances. That's a pretty strong motivating factor. Not to mention that hypothetically speaking, if he got away with it and did it to someone else and killed *them* . . . well . . . she'd have to live with that for the rest of her life – the fact that she did nothing to stop him. So don't get me wrong; I totally understand where she's coming from. I just wish there was another way of . . . I don't know . . . going about it.'

'But there's not,' Kate said. 'So you need to respect what she's done, even if you don't like it and stand by for the fallout.'

Sonya snorted. 'Fallout? That's the understatement of the year. As of tomorrow, when this comes out, what do you think's going to happen? I'll tell you. Every bloke in TasPol, and probably every other state police service who hears about it, will side with Nick and we'll be back to square one. Once again, female coppers will be untrustworthy, incapable of looking after ourselves, and jeez, if they believe Nick is innocent, then we'll just be labelled little crybabies who make shit up and go running and dobbing for no good reason!

'After everything we fought so hard for, we're going to be back where we started. And it pisses me off.'

Kate frowned. 'Okay, okay. Let me get this straight. You think he probably did assault her?'

'Of course. Why else would she go through all of this shit?'

'Okay. So I guess the question is what else could she have possibly done about it? Just . . . glossed over it and carried on as normal?'

Sonya paused, stared into the bottom of the wineglass. *I don't know.*

'Let me put it this way,' Kate said, 'what would you have done if you were in her position?'

What would I have done?

She paused again, her thoughts catapulting to the novel she was currently reading. She'd chewed through the first half of book one of Larsson's Millenium trilogy, unable to put it down, and had only last night relished the scene where the ballsy heroine Lisbeth Salander enacted her revenge on her rapist. A guardian. A lawyer. A public personality who people assumed they could trust. Not so unlike Greaves.

Propped in bed with Kate snoring gently on one side and the alarm clock humming on the other, she'd read over the section again and again and again savouring every word, every deed, every future implication. Salander's revenge of taser, hand-cuffs, anal rape, tattooing and blackmail was, simply put, perfect. The ramming tear of the unlubricated butt plug, the sting of the whip as it cracked across his genitals, the muted compliance, the astonished fear that flickered in his eyes the moment he realised that their roles had been reversed, that she had taken control.

All perfect.

Salander was her hero. And on reading the section, it had occurred to Sonya for the first time that perhaps she'd chosen the wrong profession. She'd spent the next few sleepless hours turning the thought over, prodding it, poking it, unable to refute it. She'd originally joined the force to clean up society, not realising in her youthful naivety that society itself with its rules, its regulations, its red tape and its burning need to 'give a bloke a fair go' above all else made that task impossible. She'd arrived at the conclusion that perhaps the only people who ever achieved anything even remotely close to the satisfaction of cleaning up were the Salanders of this world. The vigilantes who bypassed the system, giving it a big 'fuck you' as they went.

She reached for the bottle on the coffee table and refilled her glass. Kate had asked what she would have done and she contemplated the question for a moment longer before replying.

'You know what, Kate? As a copper, if I can't play by the rules, then I'm nothing. I'm as bad as the next crook. But some days I feel like I'm the only person in society who plays by the rules. And it makes me tired. Some days, like today, being a stickler for the rules pisses me off to the point that I want to puke. So, to answer your question, if I was Lucy Howard, I would have marched around to Greaves's house, smashed his door in, kneed him in the balls, squashed them into the carpet with the heel of my boot while he was down and told him in no uncertain terms that if I ever found out that he'd so much as looked sideways at another woman, let alone with the intent of drugging and raping her, then I'd be back. And next time, I would tie him down, rip his nuts off with my bare hands, stuff them and mount them on my mantelpiece.'

And I mean every word of that. It may not be as exciting as Salander's form of revenge, but it's something.

Kate cleared her throat, a twinkle of amusement glistening in her eye. 'Hmm. I won't remind you then that as Internals – oops, I mean Professional Standards – you're kind of meant to be squeakier than squeaky clean.'

She gazed into the fireplace and laughed, the sound emanating from her throat colder than a thousand Hobart winters. 'Well, perhaps I've been wrong all along. Perhaps there are some things that shouldn't be done by the book.'

The Mate

7.35 pm Friday 1 July

Dan Williams pulled his Ford Courier into the car park beneath the police academy parade ground, switched off the headlights and waited quietly in the darkness. The cold, grey shadow-filled cavern was practically empty aside from the handful of cadets' cars parked up near the entrance to the accommodation block. He wound down his window, held his breath, watched and listened to see if he'd been followed.

Ten seconds.

Twenty.

Thirty.

Forty.

Fifty.

Sixty seconds passed without another set of headlights bobbing down the driveway. Likewise, there were no footfalls.

No heavy breathing, no clunks, scrapes or bangs that would indicate another presence. It was deathly silent with the exception of a stereo playing some boppy shit and a peal of laughter, both of which drifted from the top floor of the nearby accommodation block.

Fucking cadets.

He looked at his watch, vowing to give it another sixty seconds before declaring himself officially clean. He'd done the advanced surveillance course a few years back, was well aware of how the doggies worked, how they followed, how they rotated vehicles. Most importantly, he was also expertly trained in cleansing manoeuvres and had been employing them since the second he'd left his own house.

Stop, wait.

Stop, wait, pull into a driveway.

Stop, wait, cleanse, pull into a shop.

Stop, wait, cleanse, pull into the academy.

Stop, wait, cleanse.

He stepped out of the car, clicked the door shut carefully and paused in the darkness listening for a sound, any sound – a footfall, a car door, a whisper, the crackle of a radio. But there was nothing. He was clean.

Not that he was entirely sure why he'd been that worried. After all, Nick had been charged and as such, the department, tight-arse bunch of pricks that they were, wouldn't waste another cent on persecuting him. And more importantly, it was after hours. Anyone who knew how the doggies worked knew they'd be tucked away somewhere by now sinking beers and playing darts. Even an A1 info report on a fucking towel-head threatening to blow up the entire government would be hard-pressed to change TasPol's policy on paying out overtime to the dogs.

All in all, he felt safe. But still. When Nick had called him from a payphone the previous night, told him the bad news, he'd known that Internals would probably call him in sooner rather than later. They also agreed that they should no longer talk on the phone and that they needed to meet asap.

Sure enough, he'd been right and Internals had struck first thing that morning. Too late for Dan to know the full story from Nick but he'd managed to bluff his way through the interview, anyway. However, if there was any chance they were thinking of hauling him in again and taking another crack at him, then meeting was even more important. He needed to know *exactly* what Nick had said in his own interview. Needed to be prepared.

But they'd have to be quick and quiet. You never knew who was watching and listening.

He peered over at the weights room and noted that the fluoros were already on. *Fuck.* He was late. But it wasn't his fault, for on top of all the time-consuming cleansing, Ange had insisted on picking a fight just as he was trying to get out the door.

'What are people going to say if they see you with him?'

'Everyone knows Nick's one of my best mates. I'm hardly gonna just fucking ignore him now, am I?'

'Maybe you should. Unless of course you want people to think you condone rape?'

'What about innocent until proven guilty and all that?'

'What about it, Dan? You saw that girl. She was hardly Lindsay Lohan, was she?'

'What the fuck's that supposed to mean?'

'Look at her, for Christ's sake! She's not some sexual tigress. Don't you remember her from that night? Remember the way she dressed, the way she sat, the way she could barely make eye contact with us she was so bloody prissy and shy?'

'And?'

'And . . . I'm saying that the chick we met that night was NOT into Nick. And, what's more, she wasn't pissed. She was sipping her drink like a bloody budgie.'

'So you think he's guilty then, do you?'

'I don't know what to think. All I know is that I don't think you should be hanging out with him until this all blows over.'

'That's just so fucking typical, isn't it, Ange? You have no idea what loyalty means.'

'I don't care about loyalty and I don't give a shit what he wants me to say. I'm not doing anything that'll look like I'm supporting him and in case you've forgotten, you being dragged in by Internals for an interview isn't exactly the best career move . . .'

'Firstly, they're just fishing with me. It was nothing. Secondly, he's my mate, he hasn't done anything wrong and I'm gonna support him. If you don't like it, then that's just tough.'

'What I don't like, Dan, is that you're prepared to get dragged in for an interview and then to talk about giving evidence in court for him. There are limits, you know . . .'

He'd stormed away and driven off before he said something he would have regretted, fuming all the way out to the academy. Normally Ange was rock solid when it came to stuff like this. Normally she supported him in whatever he did and took his word on things. Her show of defiance was out of character and it pissed him off no end. He was beginning to wonder if he could count on her to back Nick up with a statement if and when it came to that.

It was all getting too fucking complicated for his liking and despite his loyalty to Nick and his show of bravado to Ange, he was beginning to feel sick to the stomach about the way things were panning out. His life, before this, was exactly the way he liked it. Good house, great girlfriend, awesome job, solid reputation – all in order, sorted. But by backing Nick, he was risking turning the order into chaos, and he hadn't spent eighteen years of his life working so fucking hard to get where he was, just to chuck it all away.

It wasn't fair.

Then again, he *was* kinda fucked, anyway. He couldn't have walked away if he'd tried. For even though Dan hadn't used the pills, they were his to begin with – passed around to a few of the guys at the gym when his regular dealer came up short on his roids order and gave him *a little something special on the house for a valued client.*

Mind you, it was all supposed to have been a bit of a laugh. He never in a gazillion years thought that anyone would actually have the balls to use them. Even Nick, despite his big talk. He could have sworn Nick was just bluffing, talking it up like they always did.

In fact, Dan'd be fucked if he knew how it'd got to this point.

He'd been seething with silent fury since he'd been interviewed and questioned over his relationship with Nick, his comings and goings at the gym, his knowledge of drugs at the gym and his knowledge of a certain phone call. Judging by the fact that they'd let him go, it wasn't looking completely pear-shaped for him.

But still. While he might have been mildly relieved about not being arrested and charged with being an accessory, he was also pissed off to the max. The whole thing had got him so worked up that after he'd been released from the station he'd gone straight home, stormed out the back of the house and slammed the punching bag so violently and so many times that the fucking thing had ripped out of the ceiling sending a shower of plaster across the back deck. And that pissed him off even more.

He couldn't believe the little slut had gone running to Internals. Coppers, *real* coppers, knew better than anyone in the world that it was pointless to take a rape charge to court, especially one that could be so easily lost on a consent defence. She was a stupid cunt, all right, but he hadn't banked on just *how* stupid she was to think she could go crying like a fucking four-year-old who wasn't allowed to have a chocolate at the supermarket and then expect to keep working with everyone as if nothing had happened.

By her very actions, she was betraying them all, betraying the golden rule: what happened at work, stayed at work. If the bitch had a problem, she should have sorted it out in house instead of going screaming to the brass.

His knuckles cracked and clenched just thinking about it. When he thought about what Nick, Ange, the boys from the gym, not to mention he himself, were going to be put through because of her, he almost screamed with outrage. The rational side of him knew he should really be pissed at Nick for being a dickhead, pissed at himself perhaps for dishing the pills in the first place, but at the end of the day, Nick was his buddy, had been since day one, and buddies stuck together. Backed one another up no matter what. If you learnt anything from being a SOG, it was that loyalty triumphed over all.

No. It was the Howard bitch who deserved the brunt of his anger. *She* was the one dragging them through a sea of shit. He thought how satisfying it'd be to line her up on the range, see her cower in fear, pump her full of JHPs and watch as the tissue in her body ripped and exploded. Just like the rats he shot at the tip.

Vermin.

That's what she was.

And there was another thing. One more emotion pinging through his cells. As well as relief and anger, he was jittery as fuck. He'd spent the twenty-four hours since Nick's arrest stewing over the three other gym buddies who'd shared in his freebies. Stewing on their reliability. Nick would keep his mouth shut. No doubt about it. But the others, well, he wasn't so sure. Luckily he'd been able to contact them all and warn them what was going down, but he still wondered if he could trust them to keep their gobs shut seeing as CIB and Internals had apparently already been up there nosing around and asking questions. Hopefully they'd lie low and avoid the place for the time being, like they'd promised.

He was also on edge about some so-called informant who, according to Internals, reckoned he'd heard Nick and Dan laughing about using date rape drugs at the bar in the gym. An informant who was prepared to give evidence. The toecutters

223

hadn't given much away in the interview, but the knowledge that this prick was out there and gobbing off was enough to make his guts churn, anyway. It was made worse by the fact that this person, whoever he or she was, was an unknown quantity.

So here he was – stewing, agitated, suspicious, playing the waiting game. Waiting it out and hoping to fuck he survived. And if it looked for even a second as though he was going to go down with Nicky, then the Howard bitch wouldn't know what hit her.

With one swoop he grabbed his backpack from the tray and strolled towards the weights room. He hadn't been here for years, preferred Apollos with its superior set-up, not to mention the overabundance of gym bunnies in their tiny, tight Lycra shorts and boob tubes which left very little to the imagination. The academy weights room had fuck-all in both those departments. But it did have one thing that their regular couldn't offer: privacy.

Hopefully.

'Yo,' he called, swinging the door open and spying a morose-looking Nick perched on one of the tatty benches curling free weights.

Cheer up, Daniel. He doesn't need you bringing him down even further.

''Bout time,' Nick said, plonking the weights on the floor beside him and stretching out his arms. 'Thought you were gonna stand me up.'

Dan chuckled. 'As if.'

'All quiet out there?'

'All quiet.'

He threw his bag in a corner and glanced around the sparsely furnished room before turning his nose up in disgust. 'I knew there was a reason we didn't train here. Where's all the fucking equipment? There's even less here than last time we trained.'

'You know what this fucking place is like. Maybe they sold it off to cover some overheads.'

Dan laughed again. It was probably true. For as long as he could remember the academy had struggled to get an even share of the budget pie. And every time he came down for a training course the place had got shabbier and shabbier. When he'd been a cadet, all those years ago, the buildings had been crawling with staff, teeming with extracurricular courses, overflowing with gourmet food and booze and, all in all, it was a fucking good place to spend a week or two on a course.

But now, the previously well-manicured gardens and golf course were dry, patchy and overgrown due to the fact they couldn't afford a gardener anymore, the kitchen ran on a skeleton crew, the bar had been shut down, which was probably more to do with the fact that the cadets got smashed night after night and set off the fire-extinguishers, the quality of the food was pretty fucking average and, worst of all, everywhere you went, you ran into weirdos doing their own training courses in and around the grounds – fucking ambos, firies, SES and driving instructors. The admin staff had figured they could charge a fee and make a few bucks and ever since then, they'd moved in and taken over. Being a copper at the police academy these days was like being a whitey trying to find your way through the fucking seas of Asians in the streets of Melbourne. A rare bird indeed.

He stripped off his navy windcheater, threw it into the corner with his pack and started doing a few warm-up stretches, determined to let Nick talk in his own time.

'You see the fucking Mockery today?' his friend asked not two seconds later, unscrewing the end of his bar and slipping a couple more twenties on it.

'Yeah,' Dan said, thinking of the tiny snippet in the *Mercury* newspaper, *Elite SOG Officer Charged with Rape*, sandwiched way down in the local crime section in between *Politician's Teenage Sex Romp* and *Footballer Extradited on Drugs Charges*. 'At least it wasn't front page, mate.'

'It will be when it actually goes to court though,' Nick said glumly. 'But funnily enough, there was fuck-all in the *Mirror* about it.'

'Ah. That'd be because that fuckhead Tim Roberts is doing something bigger about it, I reckon,' Dan said grimly.

'Whaddaya mean?'

'Badger from the gym rang me a couple of hours ago to say the prick had been phoning up there. Reckoned he knew a heap of SOG blokes went to Apollos, wanted to know who was in the gun for the rape and if so, who he could speak with in relation to getting an inside scoop on them. I mean, seriously!'

Nick fumed. 'Hope Badger told him to fuck off.'

''Course.'

Dan pulled one arm in front of the other and stretched, feeling the muscles in his biceps and shoulders go taut. 'Did you go see the lawyer today?'

'Yeah. Woodsy reckons I've got nothing to worry about. All the background stuff about there being GHB at the gym is just fluff. It doesn't mean shit.'

'That's something then. But what about this alleged informant who's happy to give evidence about us? They wouldn't tell
me who it was in my interview.'

Nick shook his head, this time managing a weak smile.
'Piss and wind, mate. It's fucking Duane Macallister. You
know – that jerk-off who's always hogging the squat cage to
do fucking curls in it.'

Dan nodded. He knew Macallister all right. A few of the
boys'd had run-ins with him over the years about his etiquette.
'Yeah, I know him. The dick who sweats all over the equipment and grunts like a fucking polar bear on heat when he's
curling about three kilos.'

'That's the one,' Nick said.

Dan paused, thought back to the gym a month or so
earlier. To the scene of himself, Nick and three of their mates
laughing over a few power drinks in the upstairs bar after a
work-out. Laughing about the pills. About what it'd be like to
render some bitch unconscious. Trash-talking, but talking all
the same. Sure enough, Macallister had been there. Drinking
on his own like the fucking arse wipe friendless loser he was.
About a metre away from them.

Fuck.

'Anyway,' Nick said, 'when they told me he was gonna give
evidence I *did* shit myself for approximately three seconds,
but then I thought about him. D'you remember that time he
was trying to wheedle his way into our group by crapping
on about the roids he's on? About how he got busted a few
months back with a heap of dodgy gear?'

'Yeah. I remember him big-noting himself about beating
the shit out of his missus too,' Dan said.

'True. Thing is, I went and looked him up at work 'cause he'd been annoying the shit out of me at training, and he's got a list of priors longer than his arm. Drugs, stealing, assault. By the time Woodsy's done with him on the stand, he'll look about as reputable as Ivan fucking Milat. So you don't need to worry. He's not worth losing any sleep over.

'Basically it's gonna come down to consent,' Nick continued. 'My word against hers. Woodsy'll paint her as the silly slag with the nasty boyfriend who's currently serving time for a vicious assault. She screws around, worries he's going to flog her and hey presto, she's come up with her pre-emptory sordid tale. I'll be the hardworking, well-respected, not to mention highly decorated innocent party who's been unwittingly dragged into the middle of their ugly domestic affairs.'

Dan stole a glance at Nick, not sure if he actually believed his mate's bravado. He wasn't sure Nick believed it himself. But he played along, determined to match Nick's brave face. It was, after all, a welcome change from the feeling that'd been eating him up over the past twenty-four hours. 'Sweet. So he reckons it'll be okay then?'

'Better than okay,' Nick said dismissively. 'He says that when we're done crucifying her we'll put together a suit to sue her and the department for loss of income, pain and suffering. He said that payouts are good at the moment. Apparently there was a bloke in Melbourne a couple of years back who got half a mill after appealing his rape conviction and winning. Something to do with the problems they'd had over there with their forensics lab. Lawyer argued there was a chance that the DNA sample *could* have been contaminated and he fucking walked. He did a few months in jail but still . . . can you imagine?'

Dan nodded. 'Fuck me. I'd do a few months inside for half a mill.'

'Wouldn't we all, mate? Wouldn't we all? Set you up for a few years, that sort of cash. Anyway, Woodsy's confident it won't come to jail. He reckons the statements from you and Ange'll be the icing on the cake that'll put me right in the clear.'

'So, what do you want me to say to Woodsy?' Dan asked, his guts spiking again at the thought of it.

'Just keep it simple. You and Ange came around to watch DVDs and have a drink. Lucy was there, she was relaxed, you assumed she was into me just by the fact that she was at my house on a Friday night, you saw her have two drinks only. She made some comment about taking it easy because she had her car. That said, the way she was looking at me, you didn't think she had any intention of driving anywhere that night.'

He shrugged. 'That's pretty much what I said in the interview, anyway. But . . .'

'But what?'

'It's Ange.' He sighed. 'She's not fucking happy about it and I dunno if she'll be too obliging about giving a statement to Woodsy.'

Nick lay back on the bench and reached up for the bar above his head. 'Well, she'd fucking better if she wants this to end well. Don't forget it could be your arse in the sling as well.'

'Not that Ange knows that,' Dan pointed out.

'Well . . . I'd hate for her to find out that I got the pills from her fucking boyfriend,' he grunted in between reps.

His words hung in the air, heavy, almost threatening. Dan stared at him, hardly daring to believe the implied threat. 'What the *fuck* is that supposed to mean?'

Nick placed the bar back in its cradle and sat up, the sweat glistening on his brow. 'Chill out. I didn't mean it like that. I'm just saying that if the roles had been reversed, you know I'd be doing everything I could for you.'

Dan bristled. Nick might have been his best mate, and Ange might have been carrying on like a fucking pork chop, but there were limits, boundaries you didn't cross. Mates did *not* pull that sort of shit with mates. Especially them. Throughout their working lives, they'd been Dan and Nick. Dan, the slightly older, marginally wiser and definitely tougher of the two. And a month earlier Dan would have fucking smashed him for daring to go there. But somehow, this . . . *incident* . . . had knocked him off kilter. It was like a light had been switched, shifting the status quo of their relationship. Nick was now in charge and he was now the kid, trembling in his boots.

But at least I'm loyal, he reminded himself.

They locked eyes across the room, unsure of the next move, when the door opened slowly and a scrawny, pimply-faced youngster in a cadet tracksuit peered around. 'Um . . . will you guys be long? It's just that a few of us had the room booked for a work-out . . .'

'Fuck off!' they yelled in unison, rising from their respective positions and glaring at the cadet who proceeded to do exactly as he was told, slamming the door behind him.

His hasty scurry broke the tension and Dan let out a nervous chuckle. 'Sorry, mate. I'm just fucking stressed out about all this shit. I'll get Ange to make a statement.'

'Thanks, mate. But you reckon you're stressed out?' He smiled wearily, picking up the bar again. 'How the fuck do you think I feel? I've gone over and over it in my mind and I just can't believe what that dumb cunt is doing. It's unbe-*fucking*-lievable.'

Dan hesitated. 'Um . . . I've gotta say, mate, when I heard about it, I couldn't believe that you'd . . . you know . . . actually gone ahead and done it.'

Nick looked at him in surprise. 'Whaddaya mean? You were there. I told you I was gonna do it. You asked me to tell you all the gory details.'

'I know, I know,' he said slowly. 'But I never thought you'd *actually* do it. I thought you were just talking it up. I mean, I knew you'd probably end up doing her, anyway . . .'

'. . . because she's only human.' Nick chuckled.

'Because she's only human.' Dan smirked, amused at his friend's self-confidence. 'But . . . fuck. I dunno. And now, here we are.'

'Here we are indeed. Wherever *here* is. I've been suspended. Bailed to court. To *fucking* court. Just lumped in with every piece of scum in this town. What's more, it could take months to come to hearing. I tell you, mate, I've had an absolute gutful of this fucking town. I'm gonna head off tomorrow.'

'Where?'

'To Melbourne for a week or so to stay with my parents, just till things settle down a bit.'

'What about your bail conditions though?'

'They're fine. Nothing on there says I can't. As long as I turn up for court.'

'Oh. Okay.'

Dan felt a twinge of relief. The longer Nick stayed over there the better as far as he was concerned. At the very least he wouldn't have to have a repeat performance of his fight with Ange, not for a little while anyway. And by the time he came back, things might have changed. Ange might see the light and realise that there was nothing as important as loyalty.

'Fair enough. I'm just sorry you're the one who got pinged, mate.'

'You're not on your lonesome there. Have you had a chance to warn the others yet?'

'Yeah. Everyone's flushed what they had. Only Smitty and Gillsy had a crack with 'em a few weekends ago, but they reckon they're in the clear. They just picked up a couple of chicks from Isobar and gave 'em false names all night and stuff. They're pretty sure there's gonna be nothing to trace them back. So they've just gotta keep a low profile for a while and it'll blow over.'

A shadow crossed Nick's face and Dan felt a nervous flutter in his stomach. 'What is it?'

'Nothing. Well, maybe nothing. Just something Torino said in my interview. Something about another chick having made a complaint. A uni student or something. She'd had tests which showed up positive for GHB but had no idea who the guy was, said he was just some random dude she met at Isobar.'

Dan swallowed. 'Fuck. I'll let the boys know they'd better stay lower than low in that case.'

'Or at least get a fucking haircut and a dye job, eh?'

'Yeah,' Dan said, his mind racing. Contacting them again was going to be a pain in the arse since he didn't want to go into details over the phone. You never knew who was being tapped these days.

232

'I think it'll all be right though,' Nick said thoughtfully.

''Course it will,' Dan said cheerily. Probably too cheerily. 'Everyone'll be behind you, mate. No question. No one's going to give that stupid little bitch the time of day.'

'I know,' he said. 'The phone's been ringing all day. And hey, you'll never guess who called.'

'Nuh?'

'Good old Uncle Costa.'

'Costa Tsiolkas?' Dan asked, his eyes widening in surprise. 'Now there's a name I haven't heard in a while.' The Greek had been the senior connie on their shift way back when. Solid, dependable. An all-round good guy.

'Yeah. Poor bastard's been off on stress leave. It was nice of him to call out of the blue. Said he'd heard what had happened to me. Had a bit of a rant about the department being a bunch of pricks who are more concerned with looking after their image rather than with looking after their troops. How they didn't give a flying fuck about loyalty and long service and that all that mattered was covering their own arses. Gotta be seen to be doing the right thing and all that, even if it's not. He also said not to trust any of them and that at the end of the day the only person you can count on is yourself.'

'Can't argue with that,' Dan said drily.

'True. He also said that I shouldn't let them make me feel as though I'm in it alone. That if I ever need to catch up for a beer and offload then he's a friendly ear.'

'Nice,' said Dan.

'Yeah. A decent bloke, old Uncle Costa.'

'The Greek,' Dan mused.

'The fucking Greek,' Nick said with a smile and a nod.

'Hey, speaking of wogs,' Dan said, 'how was Torino, anyway? D'you reckon he's gonna cut you any slack? He's a bit of a dodgy bastard himself from memory.'

'Funny you should mention that,' Nick said with a chuckle. 'I had a chance to have a quiet word with him about a certain house party I'd witnessed him at a few weeks ago. About how I'm sure the promotion board really wouldn't appreciate the fact that he was attending such nasty little functions.'

'And?'

'And I think I just pissed him off. But hey, hopefully he'll take that home with him and sleep on it and maybe do a less than brilliant file about yours truly.'

Dan picked up a pair of free weights and stood in front of the mirror counting out bicep curls, the veins in his temples throbbing with each rep. An idea had been forming in his mind during the day. An idea spawned chiefly by his overwhelming commitment to the concept of loyalty. And one that might restore the power imbalance between them. Get them back to the way they were. It wasn't an idea that he would relish but was certainly one worth considering.

'I did have another thought along those lines,' he said between breaths.

'Mmm?'

He put the weights down and dropped his voice to a whisper. 'Something a little more proactive. I know *you've* gotta be a bit careful about the direction this all heads in now, but there's nothing to say I can't try and convince our young friend Lucy that she might wanna . . . you know . . . back off.'

'Whaddaya mean?'

'Nothing major. Just let her know that her actions are not, how shall we say . . . *appreciated.*'

Nick whistled. 'Jeez. I dunno. It's one thing for the dumb bitch to have come this far with it, but if you start messing around with threats and stuff . . .'

'I didn't say anything about *threats*. Come on, mate, she must know she's got Buckley's of getting a conviction. If we can just reassure her that that's the case, then maybe she'll drop it altogether.'

'When you say *we . . .*?'

Dan rolled his eyes. 'I mean me, of course. Look, we're in this together. I gave you the stuff. You used the stuff. We're both kind of fucked, so if there's something I can do to rectify it, to stop it dead in its tracks, and save not only your arse, but mine as well, then I'm happy to do it. That's what mates do, right? Look after one another. So leave it to me. You just sit back, relax and enjoy your holiday in Melbourne.'

Three nights later Dan sat quietly in the darkness in the little park on the corner of Warwick and Hill streets analysing the finer points of the first part of 'Operation Nobble'. He was determined to keep it simple but effective with a minimal chance of being caught out. Fuck-all chance, come to think of it.

He glanced down the slope of Warwick Street at the huge red-brick place a few doors down, set well back and high up off the street, like most of the houses surrounding it. He noted the purple Hyundai Excel parked directly in front of the house. It was the right place.

He waited, short white wintery puffs of breath bursting silently from his nose. A set of headlights caught his eye as a car rolled slowly down Hill Street towards the intersection. He tensed, only breathing easy when it cleared the intersection and continued past him. The garish fluoro lights outside the takeaway shop on the corner flicked off and he held his breath again, listening to the sounds of close of business: the rumble of wheelie bins on gravel, the low murmur of a Greek conversation – two voices – and finally, a car door and engine. He watched as the car pulled out of the driveway and rolled down Warwick Street leaving the night perfectly still.

Then he sat. He'd give it another five minutes just to make sure the area was clear. He didn't mind sitting patiently. He'd had plenty of practice over the years. It was one of many things an efficient SOG operative did well. Five hours behind a bush here, three hours in a ditch there. His most memorable wait had been one of his first-ever SOG jobs when, as a rookie, he'd spent two hours silent and shivering in a wet verge with his gun trained firmly on Martin Bryant's head as he roamed from room to room in Seascape Cottage. His finger itched on the trigger, his body was rigid and his gaze steady. He desperately wanted to take the shot, wanted to be the one to put a stop to the madness of that cold, blood-soaked autumn afternoon, but he knew right from the word go he'd never be given the order. Not while it was unfolding in this country – Australia, Land of the Royal Commission, Land of 'but what about his human rights?', Land of 'let's publicly condemn the police for shooting the mental patient even though we have no idea what the fuck actually went down out there'. No. The brass were first and foremost a bunch of arse-covering soft cocks.

In the Land of Litigation, Bryant was always coming in alive. An irritating, yet wholly unsurprising fait accompli.

He sniffed, a dewy drop of snot clinging persistently to the inside of one nostril. When the sniff didn't help it he wiped a black-sleeved forearm underneath it, wondering if the night could possibly get any chillier.

Somewhere off in the tree-lined hills around Mount Knock-lofty a large dog barked once, twice, three times, no doubt ready to come inside after its evening whiz. A low-slung car with a modified exhaust sped north on Harrington, its thumping bass fading into the darkness. In a house not far away, within two blocks max, a couple argued over an intrusive, bullying mother-in-law.

But when the five minutes were up and the immediate area remained cleansed and still, he pulled a black woollen beanie from his pocket, jammed it firmly on his head and crept from shadow to shadow down to the purple Hyundai. Fortunately it wasn't parked under a streetlight. When he was but five metres away, he paused under the cover of a large tree on the neighbour's nature strip, pulled the spray can from his pack and stepped onto the road. He moved gracefully, in one fluid motion towards the rear of the car, hardly able to contain his smirk as he streaked the four letters in bright, fluoro pink paint from rear panel to driver's side door.

LIAR

The audible gush from the can was loud against the silence and he resisted the urge to shake it, knowing the rattling of the ball bearing could prompt a dog bark, or worse still, a hurriedly switched on porch light. He snuck catlike to the nature strip and this time constructed another quick four letters from the front passenger side door to the bumper.

SLUT

There was no time to stand back and admire his handiwork. He placed the pink can back in his pack, froze, listening again to the dark world ticking around him and, still sensing no threat, reached in his pack for a white can, a good colour choice and one that would stand out nicely against the high red-bricked fence. Removing the lid, he shook the can gently within the confines of the backpack and moved silently from one side of the wall to the other, spraying huge white letters, careful to make sure they were well constructed and easily legible.

LUCY HOWARD IS A LYING SLUT

The second the final 'T' was done, he stepped back towards the darkness of the tree, placed the can in his pack and paused. His eyes scoured the ground before him, scanning every bit that he'd stepped on. His size-eleven Blundstones were the most generic shoe available to man so his concern regarding foot-prints was minimal. He searched for anything else that might link him to the scene. But there was nothing. His backpack was clean with the exception of the two cans, all the better to minimise his risk of accidentally dropping something. The cans themselves were also clean and untraceable, having sat in the back of his work shed for the past twelve months.

When he was happy that the scene was clean, he listened again and noted the silence before moving off down Warwick Street, sticking closely to the shadows and taking the first left onto Lochner Street where he'd left his car. He rolled the beanie up as he approached the car, opened the door quietly, clicked it shut even more quietly, started up his engine and drove off into the night. With one final detour to dump the cans in a public bin behind the shopping centre in North Hobart, he tracked back down along the highway and headed over the bridge, home to Bellerive, grinning all the way.

His only regret was that he wouldn't be there to see the bitch's face in the morning.

The following afternoon he popped into the station on the pretext of picking up some paperwork he'd conveniently forgotten all about the day before. His step was light, his ear to the ground, intrigued to know what, if anything, the stupid bitch had done next. Part of him longed to drive past the house in Warwick Street and laugh his arse off at his handiwork, perhaps catching the silly mole out there frantically trying to scrub it off herself, but his sensible side said no way.

To his disappointment there wasn't so much as a whisper in the crib room. He made himself a cup of tea, sat at a table and perused the *Gazette* folder. But after ten minutes there was still no movement, let alone chatter or gossip.

After twenty minutes a flustered-looking Kurt Jones clamoured in, grabbed a new radio battery, nodded a stilted hello and left again. Kurt's sergeant, Stu Walters, an ex-SOG who claimed to have moved on to greener pastures, a notion any self-respecting SOG would scoff at, flitted briefly into the muster room to pen the duty allocations for the day up onto the whiteboard. But he was distracted, far too busy to chat. Not that Dan was going to let that stop him.

'What's up, Stuey?' Dan asked casually, closing the folder in front of him.

Stu rolled his eyes. 'Just the usual. Jobs everywhere and no one to do them.'

'Where's all your shift?'

He sighed. 'Kurt's racing around like a blue-arsed fly and I've got two probies split up and monitoring the mall; we had some trouble down there earlier with a few Glenorchy cretins lobbing into town to start World War Three. Matty French is on a course at the academy, they haven't given me a replacement for Cam Walsh yet – some bullshit about how I'm gonna have to wait until the next cadet course comes out of the academy – and on top of all that Lucy Howard has called in sick. I mean, I know she's got a lot on her plate at the moment with everything going on, but she couldn't have picked a worse day.'

She hasn't reported the paint then. Hmm. Interesting. Might be able to ramp it up a notch or two.

'I didn't know she was one of yours,' Dan said innocently.

'Yeah,' Stu said with a roll of his eyes. 'I take it you heard what's going on? Oh, fuck. Sorry, mate. That's right. You were interviewed too, eh?'

'Yeah, good luck to me,' he said sarcastically.

'Yeah. DI Moore filled me in on the QT the other day once they arrested Greavesy. Puts us all in a prick of a position,' he said with a shake of his head.

'Fuck, yeah. I s'pose you have to tread lightly, eh? Pity. I'd love to give the lying cow what for,' Dan said, pausing to test the waters.

A look of surprise crossed Stu's face. 'You reckon she's making it up then?'

''Course. Nick and I are mates, but even if we weren't I'd take his word over hers any day, and according to him, she

240

was the one putting the hard word on him, coming around to his place, snuggling up to him on the couch. Jesus, I was there myself that night, and I've gotta say, they were practically playing tonsil hockey in front of me. She was well up for it.'

'Christ, I didn't know you were *there*, mate. I just thought you were interviewed 'cause you're mates with Nick,' Stu said, a look of concern passing across his face. His jobs momentarily forgotten, he pulled out a chair, predictably hungry for the gossip. And Dan intended to provide him with everything he needed.

'Yeah. Me and Ange stayed for some telly and a drink. Lucy was all over him. He gives her one and then the next morning she fucking freaks out 'cause she doesn't want her boyfriend to find out she's been screwing around on him. Next thing you know, Nick, the poor cunt, is being fucking arrested and charged.'

He paused, giving the maximum dramatic effect. 'He's pretty fucking cut up about it all. Didn't even want to stay in the state anymore. He hoofed it to Melbourne last week to spend some time with his mum and dad who are pretty old, not to mention pretty fucking devastated as well.'

Stu sighed again and fingered the paperwork in front of him. 'Bloody hell. Thanks for filling me in. I'm just glad we've had five days off after night shift so I haven't had to deal with her since it's broken. And now hearing that, I don't give a rat's if she's off sick. She can take as long as she likes. I'll be buggered if I want to deal with her.'

'Yeah, imagine if it was you she was screaming about,' Dan continued provocatively. He leaned in and dropped his voice to a whisper, once again adding to the drama. 'Mate, I don't want to tell you how to suck eggs, but just a word of advice. If she can do this to poor Nick, just make sure you're looking after your own back, if you know what I mean. I know you're her sergeant and everything, but make sure you're never in the same room alone with her, yeah? Don't give her the chance to cry foul. Imagine getting hauled in and charged. Think what it'd do to your wife and kids.'

He nearly burst out laughing at the look of horror on Stu's face.

'Yeah. You're right, mate. I hadn't thought about that. But I guess that's one thing, eh? At least she's not gonna bust up a marriage or anything with Nick, but still . . . poor bastard . . . to get dragged through this shit.'

Dan pushed the folder away and drained his cup. 'Yeah. Makes you think, eh? But his lawyer's convinced there's fuck-all in it and they'll probably even get it dismissed straight up on a "no case to answer".'

Stu snorted. 'That's something, I guess, but what about in the meantime? Being suspended, having everyone talking about him as though he's some sort of crook, not to mention going through the rigmarole of a whole court case. Christ, it makes me want to spit. What hope has your ordinary bloke got when shit like this can happen to one of us?'

Dan nodded sympathetically and Stuey looked pensive.

'What gets me, though, is if what you say is true, and, mate, I don't doubt you for a second, then why the hell would she do it, knowing what she's getting herself into? I mean, she's gotta be aware of the shit storm she's stirring up, not to mention the fact that people are gonna back Nicky two hundred per cent. Is it really worth it just to get herself off the hook in case Walsh found out she was screwing around?'

Dan leaned in again, glanced around covertly, a move designed to make Stu feel like the most trusted confidant in the entire world. 'Promise me you won't say anything?'

Stu's eyes widened and he nodded frantically.

Hook, line, and sinker.

'The thing is,' Dan continued, 'according to my source up in the Victims of Crime Unit' – *yeah, right, like I'd have a fucking source up there* – 'she marched straight up there before she even made her complaint and asked how much cash she'd get. They told her it'd be quite a tidy little sum. We're talking thousands, if she gets him convicted. But even if she doesn't get a conviction, she can still go via the civil court and sue him there. Apparently you only have to make the accusation down there, not even have to prove it, and they'll start writing out the cheques.'

Stu nodded slowly. 'I hadn't even thought of that.'

I'll bet you didn't. Lucky you've got me to help.

'Yeah. So I'll leave it up to your imagination as to what those twenty or thirty thousand special little motivating factors might be, Stuey.' Dan studied his face, knowing full well that the second he was out the door Stu Walters would be straight on the phone to every other gossip around the state. He tried to suppress his own grin.

Perfect.

'Yeah, mate, just an idea, but it might even be worth having a word with the boss about getting her swapped to another shift – conflict of loyalties and all that. After all, you've worked in SOG with Nick a lot longer than you've known her.'

'Good idea. Might get her moved to shift three with the rest of the front bums, eh?' Stu said with a wink.

Dan smirked. Shift three was the running joke on the Hobart watch. Not only did it have a female sergeant, but four fifths of its connies were front bums as well and its new male probationer was clearly a fucking fag. You only needed to take one look at him and his stupid faggy over-the-top mannerisms, his high-pitched gay laugh and his annoying little mincing walk. The bloke was obviously gagging for cock, a notion that grated on Dan, not to mention the rest of his male colleagues. In fact, just about every single bloke in TasPol agreed that one day, sometime in the not-very-distant future, his tendencies would get him pummelled whilst on duty, and not in a way the little knob gobbler would have enjoyed. He'd be lucky to last six weeks on the job.

'Yeah. Shift three might be the best place for her,' Stu said, rising to leave, no doubt itching to get to a phone. 'She's not gonna find many friends here after pulling a stunt like this. Anyway, I've *really* gotta go, mate. Give my best to Nick. I'll give him a buzz when he gets back, let him know I'm thinking of him. Times like this we need to let him know he's got mates.'

Dan smiled, more than pleased with the way the conversation had unfolded. He gave Stu a swift pat on the back before the sergeant headed back to the privacy of his office to commence the rumour mongering. Things were going to plan. Within the hour the rumour mill would be firmly in motion. And despite his initial trepidation about getting even further involved in the situation, he experienced a tiny chill of pleasure at what he'd begun.

From there he made his way along the corridor, up two flights of stairs and straight into the silent recess that was the Crime Management Unit, the station's intel cell which proudly displayed its motto on the door in the form of a leprechaun straddling a treasure chest proclaiming *We turn your shit into gold*. Not only did they perform magic tricks with half-baked, half-arsed information received from the public, they were also, to Dan's knowledge, one of the most easily accessible sections in the Hobart Police Station where you could find a computer that regularly sent out large group emails.

Humming as he rounded the doorway, safe in the knowledge that he'd already planted a great big fuck-off seed of doubt with one of the most renowned gossips in the whole of TasPol – a title for which there was plenty of stiff competition – he commenced the execution of plan C.

'And how's the most beautiful intel officer alive, love of my life, meaning of my existence?' he said smoothly, pulling a chair up in front of Veronica Pratt who sat alone devouring a supersized Mars bar and a *Woman's Day* with the intensity of a chemistry professor creating a new transuranic element. The awkward, big-boned woman with bad teeth had been stuck in the CMU due to an unnamed medical condition, which Dan, as well as every other man and his dog in TasPol, was well aware amounted to nothing more than an allergy to night shift.

She made a living by sitting on her fat arse and shoving shit into her head all hours of the day and night, two traits that Dan found overwhelmingly offensive in any self-respecting copper. Still, it was hardly surprising that at fifty years of age she'd found herself struggling with the demands of shiftwork, considering she'd joined the job at forty-five as part of the recruitment office's strategies to combat ageism in its hiring policies. But even though she was a fucking hopeless operational copper, she still had her uses.

At the sight of her favourite constable, she threw down her well-thumbed magazine and greeted him with her usual swat, blush and giggle, something he found unpalatable, almost disturbing from a woman of her age. 'Oh . . . you're an old smoothie, Daniel. Or should I say, what do you want?'

He grinned, tried to swallow his distaste and reassessed. Perhaps the silly old bat wasn't so silly after all. 'You caught me out, Ronnie. Actually I *was* after a favour. I was just telling one of my mates about this new online wholesaler I'd found to get hold of some weight training supplements and I couldn't remember the name of it for the life of me. Any chance of logging onto the Net so I can just check it out? I'll only be a sec.'

''Course, darlin',' she said, looking thrilled to have a moment of company in her otherwise uninterrupted day. She pointed a fat finger towards a computer on the other side of the office. 'Just flick that one on. Login is "SCMU" and the password is "password" . . . would you believe?'

But of course.

He gave a little laugh. 'Bloody hell, they keep it simple around here. Anyone could log on and do something nasty.'

She shrugged and took another bite of her Mars bar, a few stray specks of chocolate crumbling onto the blotter before her. 'So long as it's not porn, my darling, I don't mind.'

'Ah . . . is that what you get up to here, locked up in the office all day by yourself?' he teased, the old duck blushing the colour of a freshly polished Red Delicious.

'Wash your mouth out, Daniel. We haven't all led the depraved lifestyle you young ones have these days.'

If only you knew, Veronica. If only you knew.

He laughed again and flashed her a cheeky grin, one she'd probably take home and think about when she was fingering herself later on, given that she was so obviously fucking gagging for it. He shuddered at the thought before making for the computer, logging on and bringing up the CMU generic email lists.

He felt a flutter of nerves at what he was about to do. But only briefly.

For the fact was that the entire police force boasted only one computer specialist. Commissioner Chalmers had spent years plainly declaring to the media that cybercrime in Tasmania was practically non-existent and as such there was no point wasting their precious budget paying a whole team of experts to look into it all. It was a bit like the non-existent Outlaw Motorcycle Gang crime that Chalmers had specifically instructed no longer be monitored. Too many resources being wasted on something so insignificant.

Dan, along with every other copper in the state who'd ever dealt with bikies, regularly rolled on the floor with laughter at Chalmers's idiocy. Nevertheless, for the time being, the distinct lack of focus on cybercrime was pleasantly reassuring. It swept away ninety-nine per cent of the niggles Dan'd had in relation to this op.

It was made even better by his knowledge of the sole super cybercrime fighter himself. Dan had known him for years. Knew that porky, middle-aged, bespectacled Alistair Masters's specialty consisted of sitting in his tiny, darkened office in the Forensics section with his door bolted day and night scrutinising porn and enjoying it altogether more than a professional in his position should.

On the actual work side of things there was only a handful who really knew what he got up to in his own little domain, not to mention how long it really took. This cloak of secrecy, combined with his unbending hatred of the brass dating back to some refusal in the early nineties for them to pay for part of his Computer Science degree, meant that he could receive an official forensic computing request, something that might only take ten minutes, and explain to the officer just how complicated it was and how it'd take at least three weeks before he could have it back. He would then promptly close the door, throw it in his 'to do' tray and return to the lesbian, brunette shower scene he'd been so rudely disturbed from. Those select few in the know were well aware how Alistair operated. And Dan was one of the select few.

A thought that comforted him. Made him *almost* certain of what he was about to do.

But there was a momentary hesitation regardless. And with good reason. TasPol mightn't have given a flying fuck about cybercrime, but when it came to internal matters, the toecutters were like a pack of Tassie devils fighting over a rabbit carcass, making a meal of whichever poor bastard wandered into their sights. They loved to make an example of a copper so they could report back to the public that they were the squeakiest of the squeaky clean. They'd investigate his actions, for sure. So to that end, Dan needed to play carefully, not to mention smartly.

While Veronica nattered on in the background, something about her horses, the farm, her old man who sounded at least a hundred years older than her, some nasty hoof diseases – hopefully the horses and not the old man – he tapped away, expertly searching the address lists for the Southern District group. He shoved his brand-spanking-new, and therefore clean, stick into the thumb drive, hit copy and then quickly pasted the Southern District address book across to it. He would have taken the whole thing, the all-staff list, but it might have caused a spike and the last thing he needed was some snotty-nosed toecutter isolating the computer the spike originated from, storming down to the CMU and quizzing Veronica about who'd been in here using this particular computer. The dumb bitch would probably inadvertently give him up. The Southern list was fine. It was, after all, the one that was accessed on a daily basis.

That was all he was going to do for the moment. Anything else, even just bringing up his Gmail account, risked leaving a trail on the computer, which was far too risky. The less done on work computers, the better.

The remainder of the plan would be carried out at the internet cafe in the mall. The one with no surveillance. The one where he wore his glasses and beanie and paid in cash. The one at which he'd already created his bogus Gmail address. The address from which he'd shortly send out his masterpiece email.

He let out a deep whistling breath between his clenched teeth, as the addresses finished loading onto the stick.

'You all right there, darlin'?' Veronica asked, sucking the last remnants of chocolate off her fat fingers one by one.

'Yeah, I'm a bit slow, Ronnie. Such a computer spaz. I've nearly got it,' he said, pulling out the stick and hurriedly closing the windows. He logged on again, opened Google and searched *weight training supplements Hobart*.

'Ah, there it is,' he cried dramatically.

'Oh, you boys and your weights,' she tutted. 'Back in my day we did so much manual work on the farm that we didn't need all those fancy gyms and protein shakes and whatever else you boys have nowadays. Now my Clem, he used to say . . .'

Oh, for fuck's sake.

'Sorry to cut you off, Ronnie, but I'm now about half an hour late for coffee with Smitty, so I'd better head off.'

'Oh, of course, darlin', don't let me stop you. And you remember, anytime you need anything . . . *anything* at all . . . then you come and see me.' She threw him a big flirty wink, a gesture that left Dan shuddering inwardly as he paused to consider the flabby, wrinkled, mothball-scented wasteland that lay beneath her uniform.

'Thanks, Ronnie,' he said, giving her a quick peck on her old cheek and trying not to gag at the feel of her skin on his lips. 'You're a legend and you know if Ange wasn't on the scene . . .'

I still wouldn't touch you. Not even with Greavesy's dick.

But he let the sentence dangle teasingly. *Nothing wrong with giving the old bat a bit of a thrill.* Her face lit up like a stadium for a night game and he made a quick exit, in case she tried to flirt any more with him. It was well and truly enough for one day. More than enough. In fact, he was even beginning to gross himself out.

He picked up the pace as he left the sanctuary of the Crime Management Unit and headed out the back fire-escape doors, past the smokers, down a couple of flights of stairs, through the garage and out the door onto Argyle Street, humming all the way to the internet cafe.

The Prosecution Clerk
3.45 pm Tuesday 5 July

'Yes, I'm aware of that, Sergeant, but it doesn't make my job any easier. All I'm asking is that you teach your probies the correct procedures regarding the replication of complaints on files. Believe me, capuchin monkeys have mastered this; there's no excuse for your troops not to.'

Chrissy Matterson crossed her slim, Armani-heeled legs beneath her desk, and switched the phone from left to right, sandwiching it between her ear and shoulder while reaching for a nailfile and rattling off a few expert flicks. Rob Brown, a new shift sergeant at the outlying suburban station of Glenorchy, droned along on the other end of the phone with the usual, none-too-creative excuses she was forced to endure when new shift sergeants were informed that their troops' files were not up to scratch. Excuses that, quite frankly, Chrissy

252

was bored with. During her three-year reign as the Hobart Prosecution clerk she'd heard the same monotonous variation on a theme over and over again, and then some.

My troops are overworked and don't have time for paperwork.

The shift is short. They're all out on the road and haven't had time to do up the files properly.

Surely you don't mind filling in those details from your end?

That's the way they were taught at the academy.

She rolled her eyes, and wished that just once, someone would come up with an imaginative excuse. Regretfully, she'd put money on the fact that it wouldn't be today.

'They're just doing it the way they've been taught at the academy, Chrissy, and personally, I don't see anything wrong with that.'

Bingo.

'Of course you don't, Rob,' she huffed, pausing to dig back an impenetrable cuticle with the end of the file. *Because let's face it, Sergeant, you yourself are lazier than a Centrelink full of Bridgewater bogans with fists full of freshly signed baby bonus cheques.* She smiled at her own wit, before swivelling around on her chair, extending one leg and admiring the length of her stockinged calf, trim and toned after a gruelling hour-long regime of calf raises and squats at Apollos the night before.

'It's a short cut for them,' she continued, crossing her legs again and swivelling back around to carry on with her long-winded, well-rehearsed explanation to the aggrieved sergeant. 'It might save them time, Rob, but it adds a whole lot more time and effort onto my day. Now I don't mean to be rude, but do you have any idea how many files cross my desk each day?'

'That's really not my pro –'

She ignored him. 'See, if the complaints are done up according to the manual with full details inserted into the correct fields, then I can get through them on time – barely. If not, then I don't get through them. I fall behind with my workload, the files take too long getting to the prosecutor and the prosecutor then gets his butt kicked by the mean-spirited and not-terribly-understanding magistrate. This, as you know, can result in the magistrate dismissing the case because of police incompetence. Now I know you wouldn't want to be responsible for that, would you?'

'All right, all right,' he grumbled. 'Although I think you're being a bit dramatic about the whole thing, Chrissy.'

Dramatic? Moi?

'Yes, well, you have to be dramatic to accomplish anything around this place,' she said in her sweetest voice. 'But regardless, I look forward to seeing their new and greatly improved files.'

'Point taken. See you, Chrissy.'

'Bye, Rob,' she said in her singsong, girly voice. She hung up the phone and placed the nailfile to one side of her desk, happy to have sorted out at least one problem prior to close of business. Newly promoted Rob might have been the golden-haired child as far as the hierarchy was concerned, but he was essentially lazy and she'd be damned if she was going to sit by quietly and watch his predilection for short cuts rub off onto a whole new batch of probies.

She probably should have brought it up with her boss first, had him do the official intervention bit, but Inspector Craig Sherwood, commonly referred to around the traps as Inspector ,Lunch-a-Lot, was worse than lackadaisical when it came to such matters. It would have taken him a year to raise the matter with Rob, with all those long morning teas, long lunches, long afternoon teas and even longer after-work drinkies taking up all the hours in his working day.

On second thoughts, sod him.

If anything, Lunch-a-Lot should be thankful he had her; the office would come to a dirty great big grinding halt if it wasn't for her and her hard work. There was no point changing things now. She would of course continue to let him *think* he ran the joint, but that would be as far as it went.

Her email pinged. She swung around and peered at the screen, puzzled at the name in the 'From' box. She clicked on The Truth Teller's email, entitled 'Allegation', her mouth falling open as she read down.

As many of you are aware there has been a foul, unjust and completely unsubstantiated allegation made against one of our finest. This in itself is bad enough. More worrying even still is the fact that the allegation has come from a person who CLAIMS to be one of us. It is truly disturbing to think that Lucy Howard has been so motivated not only by the fear of being caught out by her boyfriend for engaging in a consensual affair, but also by a compensation payout (that she was over-heard bragging about) that she will go to these lengths to destroy a fellow officer's career.

*I call upon all officers of TasPol to beware of the
likes of Constable Howard and her disgusting, money-
grubbing ways. Be alert – ensure you are never alone
when working with her. Do not give her the opportunity to do this to some other good officer, for once
her flimsy, pathetic case against this officer falls apart,
which it will, she will be on the hunt for a new victim to
leech. And it could be you.*

Any of you.

*Don't think you're safe, ladies. What about a sexual
harassment suit against another female? I'm just saying
. . .*

*We cannot give her the chance. We must rally around
our maligned fellow officer in this matter and provide
him with the support he deserves as he is subjected to
the long, drawn-out, degrading case brought about by
her devious, sneaky, underhanded lies.*

*Remember, she could have chosen any one of us as
the unsuspecting victim in her grab for riches. This is
a betrayal, not only of Nick Greaves, but of each and
every sworn and unsworn officer in Tasmania Police.*

Before she'd reached the last line her phone started ringing.
She snatched it up, forgetting her usual polite greeting in the
excitement of the moment.

'Have you checked your emails?' asked the caller in a
frantic whisper.

Chrissy giggled at her housemate's excited, hushed tones.
'I was just about to call you, Jillian. Can you believe it?'

'It's pretty funny, eh? Who do you think did it?'

'No idea,' she said, frowning, wondering who on earth would have had the balls to write and then forward such a letter through the internal system. The departmental email policy was pretty clear when it came to what was acceptable and unacceptable use and even if it was done on an outside Gmail address, The Truth Teller's email was clearly from a copper. It breached the rules in just about every possible way and was without doubt, a sackable offence.

'You don't think it was Nick?' Jillian hissed.

'God, no. I was talking to him last night. He's still up at his parents' in Melbourne and is staying well away from the whole thing.'

'Ooooh. Well, whoever it is obviously has it in for what's-her-name.'

Chrissy giggled. 'And rightly so. Uptight little bitch. She should be bloody ashamed of herself. I could name a dozen women who'd eat their own knickers just to have the chance to fuck our friend Nicholas.'

Jillian laughed. 'You're evil, Chrissy . . . Ooh, wait a second, phone's ringing.'

Chrissy reached for the nailfile again as the piano sonata tinkled in her ear.

'You there?' Jillian said ten seconds later.

'Yeah.'

'It was Assistant Commissioner Hemmingway, wanted to talk to the boss as a matter of urgency. I'm guessing he's just read his emails too.'

Chrissy laughed. 'That should be amusing. Be sure to watch the Prince's face closely. I want all the details later. You coming to the pub?'

'Yep. I'll just finish up here. See you up there in an hour or so.'

'Rightio,' she said, placing the phone down and giving an excited giggle. She loved hearing about Chalmers's day firsthand. He thought he was so untouchable, his comings and goings *so* confidential. He would have screamed blue murder if he knew that only two degrees of separation made him a regular talking point over a few glasses of white in the share house most nights of the week.

She scanned the email again, searching for clues about the author. But there was bugger-all to go on. Someone who was pro-Nick – that was about as much as she could tell – not that that narrowed it down. Hell, she couldn't think of a single person at the station or beyond who actually supported Lucy's tattle-tale. Just about everyone she'd run into over the last few days had slagged her off and told her to pass on their best to Nick.

Which reminded her.

She pulled her mobile from her handbag and tapped out a quick message.

Need to see you tonight. 7 pm, your office?

She searched the contacts list, arrived at D and hit the 'send' button, before crossing her legs again, leaning back in the chair and waiting for the reply. Her mind drifted back to The Truth Teller.

Who would have had the balls to generate something like that? It was a huge call. The author had placed themselves in a dangerous position. One thing was for sure: their identity wouldn't stay a secret for long. Nothing ever did around this place. And she'd be the first one to give him or her the big congratulations they deserved.

Nick was a good man, and her closest male friend. He would have done anything for her and vice versa. The stuff they knew about each other . . .

He'd technically been her fuck buddy for a couple of years now and everything about his performance in the sack was unparalleled. Big hands, tight abs, smooth skin, a big, thick cock and her favourite bit, the rock-solid thighs which she'd had the pleasure of straddling and riding to screaming clitoral orgasm more than once over the years. Not to mention the fact that he always smelt nice – a combination of clean, healthy man with just a splash of spicy aftershave. Her men had to smell nice. It was the deal-breaker that determined whether or not they'd be granted a repeat performance. And Nick never let her down in that respect.

In fact, if she'd been that way inclined, she would almost have settled down with him. But she wasn't and had no intention of ever being so. They fucked occasionally, when they felt like it, when there was no one else, and were buddies in between times. Drinking buddies. Advice on the opposite sex buddies. Falling asleep on the couch in front of the telly buddies. There was no jealousy. It was the perfect relationship. Balanced and fulfilling. They both agreed that permanent, stable, committed were just polite ways of saying *boring, boring, boring*.

Permanent, stable and committed were the three things she'd vowed never to be again.

Her heart, once healthy, whole and normal, had been destroyed by a sexy English tour guide on a five-week Contiki trip around Europe only months before she took on the Prosecution job. She'd returned from the whirlwind tour with giddy plans of uprooting her entire life and starting fresh. He would throw in his touring job, get a nine-to-fiver, they'd get an apartment in London and spend every night and weekend under the sheets recreating their experiences from Paris, Florence, Venice, Nice, Barcelona . . . especially *Barcelona*. At least, that was the theory.

His idea had been more along the lines of kissing her goodbye as the bus pulled into Contiki headquarters, and climbing on board a new bus, and probably a new chick, the following day. Not that he'd bothered voicing that until she'd been home for two weeks, planning – *sublet house, find job, sort out accommodation, apply for work visa, purchase one-way plane ticket* – ready to embark on her new life.

His three-line email had destroyed her in a way she'd never thought possible. Heartbreak was one thing. The holistic, seemingly carefree annihilation of her past, present and future was a whole other ball game. And during the worst moment, the one where she lay curled up in the foetal position after collapsing on the cold, wooden floor in the dead of night, vomiting, as she had no tears left to purge from her body and had to get rid of the hurt somehow, she wasn't convinced she would ever recover. But sure enough, a few months on, the sun began to shine again, softly, fractured at first, almost as though it was beaming through a dirty, mud-splattered window. But it was there. She knew she'd survive.

And when she'd finally picked herself up, cancelled her meticulously planned future, cleaned the empty bottles away, wiped the last tear from her pale, sunken cheek, she vowed she would never get serious again. She would never put herself in that pathetic, dependent state, childishly hovering over the computer waiting for the next email, racing to the mailbox searching frantically through bills for a postcard and waiting at home night after night for calls that never came. No. Chrissy had waltzed back into her own life and taken charge of her affairs, supremely confident that she would never be hurt by a man again.

At twenty-seven she was the envy of every plain, bitchy female constable in the station and beyond. And instead of hiding herself behind the dowdy, ill-fitting blue uniforms and mandatory hair and make-up clauses, her proudly toned gym body, gleaming natural honey-blonde hair – *no dyes needed here, thank you very much* – and perfect pout were without fail showcased in the latest flattering fashions from Yeltuor, the most expensive French lipstick, and the best of haircuts from her flamboyantly camp hairdresser, the most outrageously overpriced in the state, of course. She turned heads. Literally. And sometimes not only men's. She'd copped 'the look' from a few of the hardcore dykes in the ranks, something she found faintly amusing.

And that in itself was power personified.

She made a conscious decision never to relinquish that power. Flirting was mostly her thing. The tilt of her head, the pointed, cross-legged tapping of a toe, the secret smile, the accidental brush in the hallway, the light, seemingly thoughtless touch on an arm during a conversation. It was all pure, unadulterated power. Married, single, bi, commissioned, uncommissioned, they were all fair game and all equally as pathetic, predictable and slobbery when it came to her practised seductions. And despite their phone calls, their pleas, their filthy, whispered suggestions, she rarely ended up fucking them. That wasn't what it was about. It was more fun to just get into their heads, not to mention their spank banks, show them who was boss and then get on with her life. Unless it fell in line with her plans and her own desires, it was far more potent to be unattainable. And on the occasions when she *did* make herself attainable, it was all the more powerful to then walk away and leave them wanting more.

Sex equalled power. The simplest of equations.

And image was all part of it. She went to great lengths not to come across as a complete slut. There was nothing worse, in her opinion, than looking like a cheap whore. She'd found, in her travels, that men loved the way she dressed, leaving something to the imagination. Her signature work look: light make-up, a waft of Givenchy Amarige on both wrists, fitted business shirts with a button or two casually undone, pencil skirts cut just below the knee and killer heels to emphasise her calves. Suggestive, without being slutty.

She might have looked perfectly ordinary if dropped up the top end of Collins Street in Melbourne rush hour, but in Tassie, she was anything but ordinary. Not to mention, a total contrast to dowdy little Lucy Howard who resembled an ugly old spinster librarian who lived in brown cardigans and smelled of mothballs. Chrissy truly believed, and had done so from the second this had all come out, that Lucy would have enjoyed her romp with Nick. Because no woman in their right mind would have turned down a chance at tapping Nick Greaves.

Especially a stupid, nerdy, ugly one like Lucy.

Sure, Chrissy had heard the rumours about drugs at their gym. They'd done the rounds for years. And she wasn't stupid. She could tell who was on the juice and who wasn't. Her favourite was a couple who frequented the gym most nights. There was nothing natural-looking about either party and she and Nick shared a running joke about them.

'I dunno what they do for a sex life. The roids would have given him a tiny dick and dried her box up so she couldn't take him even if she wanted to!'

They laughed all right. But despite the whispers of drugs, there'd never been even a hint that Nick was involved in them. He was as natural as they came. Dan was a different matter. But she always figured that if he wanted to be on the juice, then that was his business. Not her problem. So as for the story of Nick having drugs, well, she just didn't buy it. And when he'd come to her, looking pale and dishevelled only hours after he'd been interviewed by Internals and CIB, she'd had to ask. Couldn't help herself.

'Look, if it was just, like, a bit of a joke that's gone wrong, you know you can tell me. I won't say anything,' she'd said simply.

But he'd looked completely horrified. 'Jesus, Chrissy. You know me better than anyone. Do you *honestly* reckon I'd need to spike someone's drink in order to get them to sleep with me? I mean, seriously.'

She'd immediately felt bad for even asking. Nick was, after all, one of the most fuckable guys she knew. It made no sense for him to have to resort to that.

And last night on the phone, when he'd sounded so damned dejected, she'd put it straight on him.

'Why are you worried if you haven't done anything? If they've only got her word for it, then surely the DPP won't even be bothered running it? It'll come to nothing, Nick. Just chill out.'

'It's not just that,' he'd finally admitted. 'As well as a bunch of information reports about drugs doing the rounds at Apollos, they've gone and got a statement from that fuckhead Duane Macallister saying he overheard me and Dan talking about using GHB.'

Chrissy had paused, a ripple of unease trickling through her belly. 'That loser? But he doesn't even know you. Why would he say that?'

'Two big fuck-off reasons,' he'd spat. 'He's been hanging around trying to get in with the in-crowd at the gym for months and we've told him to fuck off, so he's pissed at us. Plus, I've done a bit of digging. He's got some drug charges coming up. Got sprung with a shitload of dope. No doubt he's looking to do a deal. Like, I give you info on your bloke and you either drop a few of the charges or do me a decent sentence.'

She sighed, the unease vanishing. It made perfect sense. Crooks were always doing deals, especially before their matters went to court. It was as natural as breathing. Why wouldn't a disgruntled druggie make a false statement in order to cut himself some slack?

And the more she mulled it over, the angrier Nick's revelation made her. Clearly poor Nick was being made the scapegoat in this whole mess. He'd end up in jail because, according to station gossip, some stupid lying slut was chasing a cheque and some faceless, aggrieved druggie was protecting his own arse.

It was spectacularly unfair. So unfair that it made her want to march straight up to Richard Moore's office and demand to know how he could be so blind. How he could let a good man go down to satisfy the whims of a couple of liars.

But as the hours had passed and the anger about the injustice mounted, a thought had come to her. One that would enable her to nip this whole ridiculous mess in the bud once and for all.

It would be effective, no doubt about it, and it required at most, an hour of her time. It wouldn't exactly be pleasant, but it was a small sacrifice to make, nonetheless. One she'd gladly make for the most important man in her life. More important to her, she was coming to realise, than she had previously cared to admit to herself.

And to hell with it. If everyone else wanted to abuse the system for their own personal gratification, then perhaps it was a case of not beating them, but joining them.

The mobile buzzed before her.

See you at 7 pm.

She grinned. 'Ha. Gotcha.'

Knowing she wasn't going to get anything else done that afternoon, Chrissy shut off her computer, checked to make sure Inspector Lunch-a-Lot wasn't in his office, as she knew he wouldn't be – something about lunch with 'a friend' – grabbed her handbag and headed out the door fifteen minutes before knock-off, smiling as she went at the thought of the email.

As she made her way through the corridors she rounded a corner and bumped headlong into Sergeant Stu Walters who clearly wasn't looking where he was going.

'Sergeant,' she said, fluttering her eyelids and untangling herself from him. 'We have to stop meeting like this.'

'Why? It's the highlight of my day.'

She gave a lingering glance down towards his crotch area and raised an amused eyebrow. 'I'm sure I don't know what you mean, Sergeant.'

'I'm sure you do. You going to the OC tonight?'

'Maybe. If I don't get a better offer.'

'How about I make you an offer you won't be able to resist once we get there?'

She laughed and flicked her hair back over her shoulder. 'Well, I'm *always* open to suggestions.'

They locked eyes for a moment, before she flashed him a flirty grin, turned on her heel and headed off down the corridor, the sound of his laughter following her as it bounced off the walls.

After dropping off her dry-cleaning and popping into the little lingerie shop in the mall to buy a red bra and matching knickers, she lingered for a moment, salivating over the latest neon pink Jimmy Choo platforms in the window of the tiny, funky boutique at the top of Liverpool Street. After glumly admitting that they'd set her back more than her entire fortnightly salary, she headed towards the OC, making her grand entrance through the familiar swinging wooden door at five on the dot. She immediately spotted Jillian who had just thrown her bag and a monstrous bunch of long-stemmed red roses down in one of the corner booths.

'Nice flowers. What'd you do to deserve them?' Chrissy asked with a wink. But Jill pulled a face. 'Don't ask. They were sent to work anonymously, but then just as I was walking up here, that smarmy journo from the *Mirror*, Tim Roberts, used them as a pretext to try to chat me up. They're probably from him. Well, I'm guessing they're from him, although God knows why. Unless he knows I'm Chalmers's PA and wants to milk me for info about something.'

Chrissy shuddered. 'Ugh. Creepazoid. You're probably right. He wants an in. As usual. Isn't that what journos always want? Trying to butter you up 'cause he's run out of coppers to harass. Anyway, you're here now,' she said, sweeping forwards and air kissing her housemate, a gesture that was relatively foreign to Hobartians. It was one she'd picked up on after spending time with friends in Sydney, one which suggested that she was in touch with big-city etiquette and worldly experience, one which made her stand out even further from the local rabble.

Jillian, long used to her little quirks, returned the greeting. 'What are you drinking?'

'Ooooh . . . a sav blanc, I think.' She didn't really go much on the drink itself but fancied a wine. Chardonnay, which she would have preferred, was just so unfortunately noughties. Sav blanc, on the other hand, was yet another indication of her sophistication. Not that Jill was falling for it.

'Wanker,' she said, disguising it with a loud, fake cough.

'You know it, darling.' Chrissy grinned.

'Ugh, too much information,' Jillian said with a mock shudder before making her way to the bar.

Chrissy laughed and slipped into the booth, noting a pair of tall footy types by the window who stopped mid-conversation to stare at the spot where her skirt rode up above her knees. She flashed them a winning smile – *Yes, I see you, boys* – before taking out her mobile and casually checking her messages. Six in all.

Did u see that email? Tell Nick we love him. Money-grubbing bitch will b feeling sorry 4 herself!

Nice email. Good on whoever 4 having the guts to say it!

Loving the email. Was it u?

Burn, Lucy Howard, burn!!! He he he . . .

Go, Truth Teller!!!!!!!!!

Glad 2 see someone saying it like it is. Give Nick our best. Hope the silly cow rots in hell xxx

'You look pleased with yourself.'

She looked up to see her other housemate, the tiny, compact pocket rocket that was Constable Sara Burt. She was based in the otherwise all-male Traffic Liaison Office, her dream job and one that had taken eight years of uniform policing to get into. She kicked her backpack under the table, unzipped her Windstopper and rubbed her chapped, white hands together. 'God, it's bloody freezing out there. What's the latest, Chrissy, my love?'

'Don't tell me you haven't heard?'

'What? Oh, let me guess, you're referring to the anonymous and incredibly articulate Truth Teller?' she said, pulling up a pew.

'The very same. I've just had half-a-dozen texts about it.'

'I'm not surprised,' Sara said bluntly. 'The Traffic office was full of it before I left. The boys are all saying that whoever wrote it is a fucking legend. And get this. Hayesy – yes, *the* Hayesy – even publicly declared that if he can find out who it is, he'll buy them a carton for their good work. And that's saying something.'

Chrissy raised an eyebrow. Everyone in TasPol knew that crusty old Senior Connie Joe Hayes, who'd spent most of his thirty-year career in Traffic, was notorious for never putting his hand in his pocket. He was literally tighter than a novice nun's nasty. He brought his own packed lunch to work every day, refused to join the social club because he reckoned that ten dollars a month for all the tea and coffee you could drink was a rip-off and preferred to bring his own tea bags and reuse them at least four times each. He was also, without fail, the first one out the back door at the merest mention of a whip-around for a farewell gift, or get well soon pressie.

Joe proposing to lash out for a carton was news indeed.

'That's *if* the infamous Truth Teller reveals their identity, of course,' Chrissy pointed out. 'And let's face it, it's hardly likely considering the ramifications.'

'S'pose,' Sara shrugged. 'But good on them anyway. They're only saying what the rest of us are thinking. And you know the thing that pisses me off more than anything?'

'I have a feeling you're about to tell me.'

'Damn right I am. It's the fact that by doing what she's done, Lucy's making us *all* look suss in their eyes now. I swear to God the boys reckon I'll be the next one to jump on the bandwagon, just 'cause I'm a chick. I mean, fuck me, did she not *think* about what this would mean for every single female cop out there who works hard, keeps their mouth shut and gets on with the job? Not to mention every female probie who sets foot out of the academy? It'll take twice as long to earn trust once you start on the watch now.'

'Ooh . . . someone's in a good mood then,' Jillian remarked, setting a tray with three white wines in the middle of the table and promptly unloading them.

'Ah, you read my mind, Jill,' Sara said, taking a long sip before continuing. 'And for your information, I'm in a perfectly good mood. At least I was until you got me onto the topic of Lucy "let's cry wolf" Howard.'

Jillian rolled her eyes and sat down. 'Mmm. How long's she been out of the academy . . . five minutes?'

'If that. But still, she's got no excuse. That's long enough to know the rules,' Sara spat, a look of disgust crossing her pixie face. 'I can't believe she's gone and done this. What's more, I can't believe Internals actually took it seriously. From what the boys were saying there's bugger-all evidence.'

'There's none,' Chrissy reiterated, deciding they didn't need to know about Duane Macallister. The fewer people who knew the better. 'And believe me, ladies, I would know. They shagged. He wanted it, she wanted it – what woman wouldn't want it? – end of story. And despite the fact that we all know, and everyone else knows, that he didn't do anything wrong, his reputation is going to be absolutely trashed once he gets dragged through court. And don't even get me started on what the papers are going to do with it.'

'Well, one thing's for sure,' Sara said, 'it'll never stand up in court, especially when the judge hears that she's been mouthing off about getting a great big compo payout. If she's pulling those sorts of stunts, she's digging her own grave. What's the first thing Nick's lawyer's gonna be bringing up in court?'

'Motive,' Chrissy said smugly.

'Precisely. Hayesy reckons she's already got a lawyer onto it.'

Chrissy tutted. 'The things people will do for money, eh?'

Before Sara could respond, Kurt Jones, who was on his way past balancing a drink tray in one hand, startled them

270

by leaning into their conversation. 'You should be ashamed of yourselves. Whatever happened to female solidarity and all that?'

Chrissy looked up, vexed at his intrusion. Her eyes narrowed. She knew Kurt. Not intimately, of course; there was no way in hell she would have lowered herself to touch him with a barge pole, but she knew enough about him. Knew that he and Lucy were on the same shift, that he was besties with her jailhouse boyfriend and, worst of all, that he was one of the few coppers in TasPol who said it like it was, an interesting quirk in a workplace where telling the truth could cost you dearly in terms of promotion, courses and transfers. But he didn't seem to care who he insulted. Some people might have admired his forthrightness, but personally, she thought he was a vulgar cretin with no social graces and she'd be damned if she was going to give him more than two seconds of her precious time. She leaned forwards, running a finger and thumb seductively up and down the stem of her wineglass.

'Not that it's actually any of your business, Kurt, but at this table we're more concerned with that quaint little mantra of innocent until proven guilty. You may be familiar with it? Nick's done nothing wrong. And female solidarity goes out the window when it comes to supporting our friend.'

Kurt snorted. 'Is *that* what you call him?'

'That's right, Squirt, oh, I mean Kurt, or should I call you Germaine Greer?' Sara said, her eyes flashing. 'Nick's been our friend for a whole lot longer than What's-Her-Face Howard has been on the scene and he's a damned good copper. One of *us*. And personally, I consider loyalty to my colleagues to be far more important than some washed-out seventies notion of female solidarity at whatever the cost. And not only that, but there's the whole little matter of what *she's* doing to the concept of female solidarity by going ahead with her lies. Every bloke in TasPol is going to be suspicious of working with a female now – *any female* – because of the precedent this is setting. So, if you wanna talk female solidarity, Kurt, I suggest you go and have a quiet word to *her* about it. Your little friend has gone and set women in policing back about thirty years.'

'Not to mention *legitimate* victims of rape,' Chrissy said with a nod.

'Yeah,' Sara sneered. 'She cries wolf and makes everyone sceptical about the real cases that cross CIB's desk. The *genuine* rapes. She's no better than those scrags who scream rape about footy players. All they want is their fifteen fucking minutes of fame. If you ask me, and ninety-nine per cent of the population, if you're on the piss, you're slutted up and you traipse back to a hotel room with a guy, you *know* what's gonna happen.'

Nods all round the table.

Kurt took a step back, surprise etched across his face. 'You guys can't be serious? You're about one step away from telling me that unless you're sitting at home in a turtleneck sipping a mug of tea and reading a magazine, then you're gagging for it.'

Sara shrugged. 'Make of it what you will. All I'm saying is that your little friend went to his house, on a Friday night, got on the gas and stayed after his mates had left. You do the maths, Squirt.'

Kurt flushed red with anger. 'Lucy's a really good chick. And, just in case you hadn't noticed, Sara, she's also one of us, not to mention the fact that she has absolutely no reason to say that it happened if it didn't.'

'Apart from the compo,' Chrissy said pointedly.

'What compo?'

'Oh, come off it, Kurt, read the email. This is all about the cash. Victims of Crime and all that. She'll rake in thousands if she wins. Plus, there's that little matter of covering her tracks so her boyfriend wouldn't think she'd cheated on him.'

'You don't really believe that, do you?' he cried, gobsmacked.

'Of course. It makes perfect sense,' Chrissy said, growing rapidly more annoyed at his intrusion. 'I know Nick better than anyone else and I know that he doesn't need to drug women in order to get them to sleep with him. Unlike some.'

She gave Kurt a sly sidelong glance which prompted a shriek of laughter from Sara and a muffled giggle from Jillian.

'Oh, well, I'm glad you all find it so bloody amusing.' Kurt glowered. 'But just for once, ladies, maybe you should sit back and think, what if she's not making this up? What if it really happened like she says? What if he got away with it because she wasn't strong enough or confident enough to pursue it – and then he went and did it to somebody else? Wouldn't that worry you in the slightest? Can't you see exactly why she's doing this?'

Sara shook her head. 'Oh, piss off and pester someone else with your sanctimonious crap, Squirt. She won't find any sympathy here and judging from the responses to the email, I suspect you'll be the only one on her cheer squad in the whole of TasPol. So run along and dust off your pompoms. There's a good boy.'

'Fine. At least she'll know she's got one true friend. Which is more than I can say for you lot of backstabbing bitches.' He stormed off, not even bothering to glance back at the group of women as they burst into another round of laughter.

'Mmm. Someone needs to get themselves laid,' Chrissy remarked, taking a delicate sip of her sav blanc.

'Chance'd be a fine thing. He's got a head on him like a bucket of smashed crabs,' Sara mused.

'That, my friend . . . is an insult to smashed crabs,' Chrissy said solemnly.

They laughed again before Chrissy turned to Jill. 'Hey, you never did tell me how the Prince reacted to The Truth Teller.'

'Well, it was really funny. I expected the usual swearing, cursing, throwing of furniture that I've come to know and love.'

Chrissy grinned, well acquainted with Jill's unusual and rather amusing work environment.

'But there was *nothing*.'

'Nothing? I find that hard to believe. That man goes off like a mini-van full of fertiliser if someone so much as sneezes.'

'Usually, but not this time. After I got off the phone to you, he strode out of the office and actually . . . get this . . . *smiled* at me!'

'No way,' Sara exclaimed. 'The Prince? Smile? Did someone die?'

Jill laughed. 'Nope. I'd put money on it, it was The Truth Teller's email. He didn't even try to hide it. He asked if I'd received it, then asked me to pull it up, stood over my shoulder and read it and just . . . smiled and made some comment about it being nice that Nick had support.'

Chrissy nearly dropped her drink. 'No way! Wish you'd told old sad sack Kurt. I wonder what he'd think if he knew the boss was siding with Nick?'

'Oh, God no. Please don't say anything. You know I'd be in the poo if it got out.'

'Of course I wouldn't, Jill. Although it is bloody amusing. I always knew the Prince was a bit of a man's man.'

'You're not wrong,' Sara chimed in. 'You should see his face whenever he does a swearing-in ceremony at the academy and a female steps up to the podium. He goes all grey and pasty, his lips get even thinner than usual and I swear to God he looks like he's about to choke on a fucking fur ball!'

At that point Chrissy almost spat a mouthful of wine across the table. But she recovered quickly, drained the glass and took a quick look at her watch.

'Hey. What's with the time check?' Jill asked. 'You don't perchance have a date I don't know about?'

'Of course I do,' she said, smiling secretly, wondering for a split second what her friends would think if they knew the truth of the matter.

'Sluuuuut,' Sara said.

'Mmm. Let me see . . . no, wait . . . I can't deny it. I *am* a total slut.'

Jill laughed. 'In that case, you can buy one more round before you bugger off and leave us all alone.'

'Done,' Chrissy said, sliding across the bench, picking up her handbag and making for the bar. One more sounded good. In fact, she wished she could have made it two. And big ones at that. God knew she was going to need to be as anaesthetised as possible.

• • •

By twenty to seven she'd slipped into her new lingerie in the cramped toilet cubicle of the pub, touched up her lippy, placed a fresh dab of Givenchy on her wrists, neck, elbows, knees and inner thighs and brushed her hair out until it gleamed. Most importantly, she'd uncapped the tiny tube of KY she'd popped in her bag that morning and squirted a glob on her finger. She pulled her panties aside and expertly coated her lips. She then took another dollop, squatted elegantly and inserted it deep inside her, smiling and taking perhaps a moment longer than was absolutely necessary. She closed her eyes, an image of the sexy French chef off *My Kitchen Rules* floating through her mind. But seconds later, realising that she was on the verge of running late, she adjusted her knickers, washed her hands and left with a renewed sense of confidence.

By ten to seven she'd left the pub to a final round of air kisses, walked back to the station, grabbed her car and driven to the ugly tan, multistorey executive building on Murray Street.

Taking a final deep breath, she walked towards the building entrance and nodded cursorily at the rotund security guard propped up behind the front desk before stepping into the lift and pressing the button for level eight. The ding of the lift announced her arrival and she stepped into the corridor. It was eerily silent and dimly lit. The clang of the elevator doors echoed the length of the main corridor and she couldn't help but marvel at how transformed the space was from day to night.

During business hours when she stepped out of the lift with an urgent file, or some last-minute file amendment, the space was a flurry of phones, freshly brewed coffee, heated arguments, the sweat of panic, laughter and fist thumping on desks. But night-time brought calm. A solitary light under a door at the far end of the corridor, heavy footsteps, the sound of coins jangling in a pocket.

She looked up as the portly fifty-something man made his way down the corridor towards her. He was an ugly man, possibly the most unattractive she knew. When she'd met him some three years earlier she'd tried not to giggle, consumed with the thought that if the old adage about dog owners looking like their dogs was true, and he owned a dog, then he would undoubtedly own a bulldog.

And he hadn't improved much over the years.

One covert glance at his crotch confirmed that he was indeed pleased to see her. And that was what mattered. She swallowed her revulsion, flicked her hair back and offered him her flirtiest grin.

'David. How are you?'

'All the better for seeing you, Chrissy,' he said, unashamedly running his eyes from her hair to her toes, lingering momentarily on her breasts. She half expected him to lick his lips, he was so obviously hot for her. She tried not to laugh out loud at his transparency.

You silly, ugly little man.

'Now what can I do for you at this hour? I must admit I was intrigued when you texted earlier.'

'A little business, a little pleasure . . . if that's all right with you?'

'For you, anything. Follow me,' he said, turning and heading back towards his office.

'It's very quiet here this time of night,' she remarked.

'Mmm. That's normal. Everyone else is out the door five minutes before knock-off. I'm the only daft sod ever here this late.'

Perfect.

When they reached his office he closed the door behind her and proffered her a seat on the plush brown leather couch.

'Drink? I was having a Scotch.'

'Make it two then,' she said, thinking that a few mouthfuls of the thick amber liquid were exactly what she needed flowing through her veins.

As he poured her a Johnnie Walker Blue she moved gracefully to his window, unbuttoning her heavy winter coat while she admired the view out across the water. The lights from the array of yachts, fishing boats and restaurants in and around the harbour glimmered, creating a starry canvas against the blackness of the Derwent.

He handed her a crystal tumbler and she shuddered briefly at the sight of the fat, hairy sausage fingers enclosing the glasses.

Suck it up, Chrissy. All for a good cause. Nick is your best friend. He'd do it for you if the roles were reversed.

'So, what first? Business or pleasure?' he asked, settling himself into his leather recliner.

She gulped a mouthful of the Scotch, closing her eyes and relishing the warmth as it slid down her throat. 'A little of both,' she said, taking another sip and placing the glass on the table next to his.

'Shoot.'

'I require a certain . . . shall we say . . . favour. A tiny, insignificant favour regarding a friend of mine which, in the big scheme of things, will mean nothing to you. Less than nothing in fact, but everything to me.'

He raised an eyebrow, intrigued. 'Ask away.'

'Ah. Before I ask away though, I need to make sure that you're fully aware, David, that I will be most happy to . . . shall we say . . . *compensate* you for your assistance. If you'll allow me to show you a little token of my gratitude, that is.'

As she spoke, she brought her fingers to the top button of her silk blouse and gently undid it, watching his lips fall open. His eyes were riveted to her hands as they moved to the next button.

'Go on,' he said hoarsely.

She continued unbuttoning the blouse before sliding it off her shoulders and exposing the pale, perfectly proportioned breasts that lurked beneath the lacy red bra.

You are an actress in a porn movie. Give the audience a show to remember. Give him what he wants. It's not about you tonight.

She paused before teasing him. 'Are you absolutely sure you want me to show you how grateful I'm prepared to be in return for my tiny favour? I wouldn't want to do anything that makes you uncomfortable, David.'

He cleared his throat, fixed his eyes on her chest. 'No, no, I'm completely comfortable with anything you want to show me.'

She smiled and leaned in to whisper, making sure he caught a whiff of her scent. 'I thought you'd be okay with it. You are, after all, the smartest man I know.' She reached down her left-hand side and deftly opened the slimline zip on her skirt, letting it fall to her feet before stepping out of it delicately.

Naked but for her slingback heels and sexy new lingerie, she took a step towards him, pushing his chair out from the desk, settling her arse on the cold desk blotter and pulling him back towards her so she was effectively straddling him. She leaned forwards, her hair caressing his face and slid his tie off with expert hands.

With one manicured hand she teasingly pulled back the inner cup of the bra exposing a perfect pink nipple. She paused, let him take it all in before placing her other hand on the back of his head and guiding his mouth towards it, smiling with cold amusement at the look of excitement on his face. But as his mouth came within mere centimetres of the nipple, she grasped a handful of grey, dandruffy hair, holding his head steadily before it so he could almost touch it with his tongue.

Almost. My, my. The most powerful man in the entire legal fraternity. The head of the bloody DPP. The final port of call in terms of deciding what goes to court and what falls by the wayside. And here you are at my utter mercy. Hilarious. The ultimate power trip. Why, that's almost a turn-on itself.

'I take it I can count on your help with my little problem then, David?' she asked sweetly.

He nodded, his erection straining against his trousers. 'Anything, Chrissy. Anything for you.'

'You promise?'

'As God is my witness.'

'Thank you, David. I know you're a man of your word, so . . . perhaps we'll do pleasure before business, shall we, and . . . who knows . . . once the business is taken care of . . . there might even be time for . . . a little more pleasure,' she whispered, before guiding his mouth against her nipple and closing her eyes.

Don't think. Just get it over and done with. It's no worse than copping a bad draw at one of Roger's parties. And it is, after all, the most effective way to nip the bloody file in the bud now. Before it gets any further. Before it goes to trial. Before it does any lasting damage to Nick's career and reputation. 'Cause that's what mates are for . . . right?

And with that thought, she cut herself loose from reality, another image of the sexy brown-eyed French chef flowing through her mind as the ugly but incredibly powerful little man sucked like a baby, his rough, fat sausage fingers falling onto her skin with glee.

The Prisoner

8.17 am Friday 8 July

Cam Walsh stepped out into the daylight, blinking like an emaciated, disorientated bear waking from the longest hibernation of his life. He rubbed at his eyes with clenched knuckles, trying to adjust to the light again. The day was grey. Winter grey. Depressing, Hobart, winter grey, but nevertheless it burned the back of his retinas forcing him to squint.

The front door to the otherwise inconspicuous remand centre clicked shut behind him and he looked out onto Liverpool Street. It was slick, black and dismal from an early-morning downpour. A heavy residual mist hung in the air, threatening an encore at any moment. The steady stream of peak-hour traffic meandered towards the heart of the city stopping and starting at every ill-timed set of traffic lights along the way, passing him by without so much as a second glance, the morning no doubt being given over to fogged-up windshields, squeaking wiper blades, noisy back-seat children and morning radio chatter. Not to lost souls.

Glum, rain-soaked pedestrians on all four corners of the busy intersection at Liverpool and Argyle likewise ignored him, anxious to escape into their cosy, artificially lit offices before another downpour battered the streets. He was just another stranger caught out in the weather. But if passers-by had taken a second look, they might have found him something of an oddity up that end of town. He was too clean and well dressed to have been a crook from the court building. He wasn't bandaged or choofing on the obligatory cigarette which may have connected him to the outpatient section of the Royal, and he was far too thin, morose and faded for the police station. He was now a stranger in this part of town and as such, he didn't intend to spend another second there.

As he took his first tentative step away from the door, he realised with a sigh that he was free. His time was done. Not easily, but done all the same. It was a small blessing that, being a copper, he'd been permitted to serve his time at the remand centre rather than at the infinitely more hardcore Risdon. But that didn't change the fact that for eight weeks, he'd been his own worst nightmare. Eight weeks' worth of incessant internal chatter had almost driven him mental and he'd wondered silently, at least once a minute, every minute of every hour of every day, how an intelligent, thoughtful, rational person serving a longer sentence – twelve months, two years, six, ten – could survive without eventually stringing themselves up.

His gaze strayed across the road to the Royal Hobart Hospital. Speaking of nightmares, Darren Rowley, the filthy, rotten, cop-killing piece of scum, would probably still be in there following the flogging he'd received months back, still comatose, still hooked up to an array of beeping machines, still as guilty as hell but never likely to face the consequences of his actions. Still bleeding the taxpayer dry, albeit in a different manner than before. Still probably laughing on the inside.

A spot of rain landed on his nose, luring him back to reality. He wiped it off calmly, stuck his hands in his pockets and began walking, the image of Rowley branded across his mind.

Between the moment his sergeant had been murdered in January and the moment he'd set foot in the remand centre, Cam had spent every waking minute consumed by a destructive cocktail of rage and revulsion for Rowley. It was simple cause and effect. If Rowley hadn't killed John, then Cam would never have smashed the living daylights out of the fat mouthy prick at the pub who'd added his two cents' worth about police deserving everything they got. He wouldn't have ended up in court, wouldn't have lost his job and wouldn't have spent the last eight weeks contemplating just how fucked up the world was.

But now, staring out in the gloomy morning chill, thinner, paler and decidedly calmer than when he'd gone in, he felt nothing. Less than nothing. The anger, the blame, the burning hatred had all dissolved into nothingness. He walked, collar up to avoid raindrops on the back of his bare neck, and tried to analyse where it had all gone. A futile exercise, but then, there wasn't much else to think about.

John White was dead and wasn't coming back. A fact he couldn't remedy. Darren Rowley, courtesy of God knows who – someone who was smart enough not to get caught –

would by all accounts be a vegetable for the rest of his life and wouldn't be hurting anyone else. A result, albeit not ideal. But a result nonetheless. Cam himself was now unemployed, not to mention in possession of a criminal record.

Oh, how the mighty fall.

He pushed the 'walk' button on the corner, waiting three seconds before the green man appeared. He crossed, head down, taking a brief peek up towards the Capita Building on his right. Somewhere up on the ninth floor, the commissioner would be starting his day soon, plotting the downfall of some other upcoming, promising young copper, no doubt. He shook his head and kept walking.

Yes.

He was best off out of it.

No regrets.

The serious thinking time in jail had left him with the indelible impression that policing itself had been the weapon of his destruction. It had filled him with blackness, negativity, hatred, and had strung him along to the point where he could no longer enjoy the sights, smells, sounds and pastimes that the rest of the population took for granted. A simple stroll down by the waterfront had him scanning for drunks, tramps and nutters who had the potential to ruin his peace; grabbing a milkshake at his favourite cafe in Salamanca meant finding the seat at the back so he could study patrons, their dress, make-up, conversation and manners in order to anticipate troublemakers; pubs and nightclubs were impossible, with fellow clubbers being too loud, too drunk, too obnoxious, too ready to swing a punch over an accidental brush past.

Even the seemingly uncomplicated act of sitting in a patch of morning sunlight, sipping on a latte and picking up a newspaper was no longer a joy. Papers were loaded with drunken, violent incidents in town that attracted mere suspended sentences: men who let animals starve to death, hired mainland QCs and walked out of court laughing about the beauty of legal technicalities; scumbags who bashed, terrorised and even killed innocent overseas students and blamed it on drinks, drugs and bad upbringings; paedophiles who applied for overnight custody visits with their young daughters, despite the fact the daughters were terrified of them, and got their way. Because everyone deserved a fair go.

Then there was Grant Nesbitt, lawyer, columnist and prison advocate, bleating on about how prisoners only went on violence-fuelled rampages at the newly built Risdon prison, causing three million dollars' worth of damage and hospitalising four guards because they were 'bored'. Society and the system had let them down in terms of stimulating activities. A crock of shit, of course. He was qualified to say that now, and despite his own challenging eight weeks, he still truly believed that it didn't matter how bad things got, there was no excuse for behaving like a pack of rabid animals.

Pffft.

No. Newspapers weren't for relaxing, and hadn't been for a very long time. They were for scowling, frowning, clenching, bitching, sermonising and being outraged about. And quite frankly, Cam was tired of being outraged. Tired of automatically seeing the worst in everything.

Eight weeks in jail had shown him that he no longer wanted to be bitter. He couldn't stand it a second longer. He didn't want to hate the world anymore, whinge about its injustices and moan about the fact that the glass was not only half empty, but as dry as a Northern Territory desert in its tenth consecutive drought year. And it was odd; in one way he felt utterly defeated, in another, real, whole and ready to live life for the first time since he'd pulled on the blue uniform all those years ago.

Defeated, but hopeful.

He looked over his shoulder up Liverpool Street and smiled sadly at the line of police cars parked out the front of the Hobart headquarters. Only a couple of months earlier he would have waltzed into the station and asked the duty shift for a blue-light taxi home. But that was over now. He was no longer one of them. Everything was different.

He pulled his grey beanie snugly down over his ears, crossed the street, the icy-cold wind whipping at his cheeks, and headed through the back alleys towards the bus mall. Despite the bitterly cold weather, the usual suspects lurked in and around the doorways. A pair of boys no more than twelve rolled handmade cigarettes and spat simultaneously on the footpath. Back out in the Elizabeth Street mall, a fifteen-year-old girl screamed into a mobile, threatening her mother that if she didn't come and pick her the *fuck* up, she was never coming home. Ever. Three boys, slightly older, sprinted in front of him in long strides chasing a panic-stricken child in a school uniform. A solitary pock-faced guy in black lurked in a takeaway shop doorway, unashamedly eyeing up the pockets, laptop bags and handbags of passers-by. A cluster of teenage girls staked their territory outside Target, two of them flicking small silver pocketknives, sneering at shoppers and turning back to laugh raucously at their dazed, fearful expressions.

The whole thing was a test. And as he walked past them all, watching as the individual scenes rolled into one grim montage of bleakness, he lowered his gaze and focused instead on the cracks in the footpath, the globs of chewing gum, a collection of cigarette butts, half a bus ticket, a urine splatter and a Snickers wrapper crawling along the gutter lip in the breeze; and he felt . . . *nothing*. No worry. No responsibility. No burning need to help, change, save.

Not my problem anymore.

Thank God.

A freezing-cold blast of wind slapped him across the cheek and he grinned at the simple beauty of the epiphany.

It's over.

As the 632 rolled to a stop beside him, he climbed the stairs and threw the weary, defeated-looking bus driver a warm smile and nod, knowing that the poor bastard would spend his day dealing with the usual rudeness, graffiti and occasional assault while he, Cam, would never be bothered by it again.

The bus pulled out of the mall just as he had settled himself up the back, rows away from the only other traveller who was perched up near the driver for safety, no doubt. He peered pensively out of the fogged-up glass as the heart of the city melded into greyness behind him. He sighed and settled back into the seat. It was only at that point that she crossed his mind.

Lucy.

He sniffed, mildly irritated at the thought. He *should* give her a call. It'd been eight weeks since they'd spoken. She'd looked gutted when he announced in court that he didn't want her visiting him inside, but as the days had passed, he'd had no regrets about the decision. He didn't want any witnesses to his shame. The last thing he needed was stilted conversation, awkward hand holding, teary reassurances. He just wanted to do his time, move on and make a fresh start. For the first week or so she'd meandered through his mind a lot. And at the time he'd assumed that his fresh start would be with her.

In fact, on that first night, when the cell door banged shut and he tossed and turned on his mattress, the relentless whirring of the evaporative fan in the airless building humming through his ears, he'd cried just thinking about her. After relying on her so heavily for so long, he wasn't sure he could survive without seeing her cheery face, hearing her nervous giggle or feeling the touch of the hand he'd come to know so well.

He liked her. Suspected he might have been a little in love with her even. But by the end of week two, the day Darryl the security guard had come by on the evening mail round, everything had changed.

'Interesting news for you, Walsh,' he said with a grin, slipping the already opened pale blue airmail envelope through the door.

He'd scurried off the bed and grabbed it up, hungry for a break in routine, elated to have something different to think about for the next few minutes, no matter how mundane it might actually turn out to be. He sat back down on his bed, holding the envelope aloft. The stamps were international: British. The handwriting, unarguably female. He closed his eyes, one name on the tip of his tongue, silently begging, pleading for it to be from her.

He fumbled with the seal and pulled out the two-page letter on the cheery mauve paper, a cluster of suns, moons and stars dotting the top right-hand corner. As he read, the two-week-old knots in the pit of his stomach began to slowly untwist.

Dear Cam,

I hope you don't mind me writing to you. It seems a very old-fashioned thing to do these days, but then again, there's not really much choice given the current circumstances. I keep in touch with a few people from the old days and found out what happened. I cried when I heard the news, thinking of you in there. More tears on top of what I'd already cried for John. I'm so sorry for everything you went through that day and for the way it turned out. I'm more than sorry for the fact that this is the first time I've felt up to contacting you since it all happened. It was all too much for me to take in and I guess part of me hoped that if I didn't think about it, then maybe it wouldn't be real. I tried to pretend that you and Kurt and John were all still there, working away, laughing your butts off like we used to in the good old days. But it didn't work. Things clearly weren't right, and no amount of avoiding the issue was going to change that.

But apart from that, trust me when I say I've been thinking about you and hoping that you're doing okay.

I've been sitting back wondering what you will do with your life once this is over and done with. Mel told me it was the end of your policing career. In one way, I'm sorry. But in another, I'm actually pleased for you.

Don't despair, Cam. Despite the naysayers (and you know who I mean – the hardcore, wouldn't do anything else if you paid me a million buck types), there IS life after policing, Cam. And a GOOD life at that. Every time I rock up to work at the British Library (OMG) I pinch myself and thank my lucky stars I managed to get out when I did. If I'd stayed another day, I might not have made it.

It takes a bit of getting used to, but once you do, you'll be amazed at the changes real life brings. You start to see the good again, Cam. You'll notice the swans gliding across the Derwent, the yachts bobbing down by Mures, the rainbow of fruit and veg at Salamanca on a Saturday morning, the smell of a freshly brewed latte wafting through North Hobart and the way that the bridge sparkles against the water in the late-afternoon sun. It's not all doom and gloom; it just seems that way when you've spent years dealing only with the black side of society – the depraved, the devious, the hurtful, the dishonest, the manipulators, the evil. When you focus on that, you end up forgetting that there's good out there.

And honestly, there's plenty of good. It's there. You just have to remove the blinkers and take a deep breath.

And if you need a change of scenery – and hey, I can totally understand that, after all, it's easier NOT to be reminded of policing if you go somewhere completely new – then come and visit. London is the most amazing city on earth. You can't come here and feel down – there's always something to see, do, taste, smell, walk on, marvel at.

I'm not with Simon anymore (don't even go there – massively long story, makes War and Peace *look like a novella!) and have moved back into a share house with some old uni mates in Archway, a lovely Georgian three-storey place with a spare room should you feel tempted.*

Remember the laughs we used to have? Well, you'll have them again, Cam. That much, I guarantee you.

Email me when you're out and we'll catch up one way or another.

Thinking of you.

Love Jo

xxx

He sat, the letter in his lap, mulling over every word, every phrase, searching for meaning. She'd been the only one for him since the day he'd walked into the Hobart Police Station to begin his first-ever shift. She was slightly older, a heck of a lot wiser and, despite being on the same shift, not to mention the fact that she was senior to him, he'd always known they were destined to end up together. It was just a matter of time. He'd been devastated when he found out she was actually sleeping with their sergeant, annihilated when she'd just upped and disappeared to London without so much as a goodbye. But perhaps, just perhaps . . .

The letter ushered in a rush of untapped emotions and all of his pre-Lucy yearning came bubbling back to the surface. *Why* was Jo letting him know that she was single? More to the point, why was she single? What had happened to the swanky

London fiancé? What had changed so drastically? Was it possible that she'd realised that they had unfinished business? Did he dare hope? The invitation seemed to confirm it. And after reading the letter one more time, he knew that the second he left the remand centre he was going to pack up, sublet his flat and head to the UK – to Jo. The timing was right. There was nothing left in Tassie for him, apart from Lucy. She was great, but compared to Jo – or at least the hope of being with Jo – she wasn't . . . *enough*.

Lucy had been a mate, of course. She'd sat with him, laughed with him, cheered him up during his time of need. He'd relied on her and together they'd fumbled their way through John's death, using each other as emotional crutches. That was all it had been. They'd fallen into bed because they were lonely and . . . and . . . it seemed like the right thing at the time.

She *must* have understood that.

She'd feel the same way.

Wouldn't she?

But as the green and white bus belched and groaned up and over the Tasman Bridge, he was rattled by a sickening lurch. Who was he kidding? He *would* need to call Lucy. That afternoon. She knew his release date. She'd be waiting. She would have been waiting since the second he'd been led away by the court staff. And he'd just bet she was still pinning her hopes on a happily-ever-after.

But there was no chance. Jo was the future.

Lucy was unfortunately part of the past he needed to sweep clean.

• • •

293

He shook his jacket out on the front doorstep, stuck the key in the lock and switched on the light. He sniffed, a faint hint of mustiness hanging in the air, but otherwise, the Lauderdale flat was exactly as he'd left it. Neat, tidy, sparsely furnished. It might have been a one-bedroom granny flat with seventies carpet and God-awful dado walls, but it was home. He sagged with relief.

Closing the door behind him, he threw his jacket on the back of a kitchen chair and opened the blind above the sink to let some light in, before pausing and snapping it shut again. The view, which consisted of the neighbour's garden shed, a rusted-out dog pen and a concrete wall, all dripping with rain, was hardly inspiring. On top of that he wasn't quite ready for the outside world yet. The walk and bus trip had been enough for one day.

He turned the fan heater onto high and collapsed on the couch grimacing as the fleeting smell of burning dust filled the room. He reached for the mobile in his pocket and switched it on for the first time in two months, his face blank as message after message pinged into the inbox. There were half-a-dozen well-wishers, mostly people he'd worked with outside the force who'd read about him in the paper. Then there was the sister in Perth who he usually spoke with twice a year, wondering where he was, obviously not having read the paper. There was the landlady thanking him for his up-front rent payment and assuring him the flat was fine, Telstra wanting him to upgrade his contract and an unknown number, urging someone called Bobby to contact them as soon as possible. Another half-a-dozen missed calls from journo Tim Roberts who he'd managed to avoid ever since the arsehole had screwed him over big-time by using his information to write up a shitty article defending Darren Rowley for killing Sergeant John White. Tim, who'd even had the nerve to ring the bloody remand centre trying to book an appointment to see him while he was inside. Not that he'd seen him though.

He shook his head and deleted the calls and messages one by one.

Boring, boring, boring, weird. Fucking annoying.

By the time he reached the last message he felt even flatter and more dejected than when he'd stood in front of the judge and listened to his sentence being read out. Almost everyone in the world – *the policing world, the one that mattered* – had abandoned him. The loyal years of service, the friendships, the professional respect had all but vanished. While he'd been away, the brotherhood had closed ranks and he'd clearly been left outside banging on the gates.

He'd half expected it, and had likewise expected to feel disappointed about it. What he hadn't expected was the over-whelming ache of sadness that consumed him. His earlier feelings of satisfaction at his new-found lack of responsibility flickered and faded at this new discovery. He might not have been responsible anymore, but his utter abandonment was a high price to pay.

He sighed with self-pity again, hit '121' and listened to the final message – the one Kurt had left only the day before.

'Mate. Jonesy here. Checking in to see how you're travel-ling. I'm guessing you're out tomorrow. Let me know if there's anything I can do. Oh. And, by the way . . . um . . . look after Lucy, eh? She's had a pretty rough trot since you . . . you know . . . Anyway, give me a call when you're up to it.'

Despite his bleak mood, Cam stared at the phone and laughed. *Look after Lucy? Are you kidding me? I've just spent eight weeks in solitary, with one hour a day to socialise with the handful of paedophiles in the segregation block alongside me. I'm unemployed, a social leper, and you think Lucy's had a rough trot? Good one, Kurt.*

But after the laughter died down, her name stuck in his throat. Rough trot or not, it was time to take care of the situation once and for all. It was the first step in trimming the fat. And, he cheered himself, when he was done with that, he could jump on the computer, email Jo and find himself a decent one-way ticket to London.

After another twenty minutes of agonising over how he was going to explain that he was leaving and that she wasn't invited, he pulled his shoulders back, manned up and admitted to himself that it should be done in person. It was the least he could do.

I'm back. Swing on by if you're not working.

He hit 'send', and started a fresh round of agonising over how she'd interpret the message. She was bloody over-analytical at the best of times. He'd aimed for casual, then kicked himself thinking he should have kept it more formal, prepared her a little for the blow.

And suddenly, a thought. *Maybe she's already moved on.* A little glimmer of hope pulsed through his veins. *Maybe she met someone new.* He kicked himself, wondering why he hadn't thought about it before. *How arrogant of him to think she'd been out there holding her torch for him. Perhaps it would be*

*fine, after all. They'd hug, laugh and go their separate ways
. . .* and just as he'd managed to convince himself that there
was nothing to worry about, the phone buzzed in his hand.

See you in half an hour xxx

He closed his eyes, a heavy stone sinking in his gut.

Kisses.

It was going to be bad.

By the time he heard her car pulling up outside, he'd worn a
track in the already threadbare carpet with his pacing. The
insides of his cheeks felt like sandpaper and his hands dripped
with sweat, so much so that they slipped off the doorknob as
he pulled it tentatively open.

The second he saw her face, his stomach heaved. Again.
The kisses on the text were a warning; her broad grin, newly
bobbed haircut, make-up, dress, boots and outstretched arms,
the death knell. She'd come to impress, oblivious to the fact
that he was about to stomp on her heart.

'Hi, come in,' he stuttered, letting her wrap her arms around
him and forcing himself to give her a light hug in return.

Dear God, let this be over with quickly.

'When did you get home?' she asked, her face beaming.

'Uh . . . an hour or so ago. I just wanted to get settled in
before I . . . before I rang you.'

She stepped back and examined him, a look of concern
flitting across her face. 'You lost weight.'

'Well, the remand centre isn't exactly known for its fine
cuisine.'

'I suppose not. But you look pale too.'

Yes. Solitary will do that to you.

But she missed his flicker of annoyance. 'I guess we'll have to feed you up. What do you say to lunch at the Ball and Chain? My treat. A nice thick juicy T-bone will do you the world of good.'

I'd rather spend a winter's night naked on top of Mount Wellington. Complete with gale-force winds. And a foot of snow. And a spaceship full of anal-probing aliens.

He grimaced, tried to take a step back, but she embraced him again. Now it was just getting plain awkward. He tried to untangle himself.

'Jeez, Luce, I'm pretty tired . . . um . . . maybe another day?'

She smiled brightly, missing the hint again. 'Sure. I understand. How about we just get in some takeaway then? I know they've been missing you down at the Thai restaurant . . .'

He squirmed, thinking it best to avoid the lunch question altogether. 'Um . . . how about we decide later?'

'Okay,' she said.

Silence.

She hovered by the door.

'Um . . . can I get you a cuppa?'

He kicked himself again, this time for falling for the old trap of filling in the silence. *Idiot. That means she'll stay even longer. But on the other hand, it's a better way to break it to her. Sitting down. Mature responsible adults having a cup of tea.*

She brightened at the suggestion, nodded and followed him into the kitchen where she dragged out one of the chairs and made herself at home, like she'd done so many times before.

He reached in the cupboard for the box of tea bags, the silence now becoming intolerable. So while he filled and boiled the kettle he chattered nervously.

'Hey, I got a message from Kurt on my phone. He said you'd had a bit of a rough time while I was gone. What's with that?'

He looked up and was startled to see her face drop.

'Shit, ah . . . is everything all right?'

She hesitated before composing herself and giving a pained half-smile. 'Sure. It is now.'

'Oh?'

'Yes. Now that you're out.'

'Oh.'

More silence.

This time she was the one to fill it. 'Um . . . yeah. Look, I was going to wait before I told you, Cam. After all, today is about you, not me.'

Oh, dear God, maybe she's breaking up with me, after all. Yes, yes, yes.

'What's going on?' he said, plonking the mug of tea before her, his hand shaking so badly he nearly sloshed it all over her.

'Look, it's a bit difficult to talk about. Come to think of it – and trust me, I've been thinking about it, ooh, pretty much since you went inside – there's no easy way of saying it.'

His heart leapt. *Thank God. She's going to do it. All I have to do is sit back, look surprised, and a little crushed, hug her, tell her it's okay. She can move on. Yes, yes, yes.*

'Just spit it out, Luce. Sometimes it's easier that way,' he said, leaning forwards.

She took a deep breath. 'Okay. The thing is, while you were away, I got friendly with one of the guys on the CIB course.'

Yes, yes, yes, yes.

Keep it cool.

'Oh right. Who was that?'

'Nick Greaves.'

'Oh yeah. I know Nick. Good guy.'

Her face fell again. 'Not a good guy, Cam. Not a good guy at all.'

'Uh . . . what do you mean?' he asked, now thoroughly puzzled.

'The thing is, I went over to his place for drinks and movies one night and . . . he slipped something in my drink and . . . and . . . raped me.'

He practically spat the mouthful of hot tea out onto the table in front of them. 'What?'

'I said, he raped me. You know, had sex without my consent,' she said calmly.

He stared at her, open-mouthed. Not only was it the last thing he'd been expecting to hear, but, well, it was the last thing he'd expected to hear. She wasn't dumping him. *Shit. That sucked. He'd been so sure . . .* But on the other hand, *what the fuck?*

He blinked.

Digested her words.

Raped by Nick Greaves?

It had to be some sort of mistake. Nick was a decent guy. Bit of a gym nut, bit too macho and definitely a player, but a decent enough guy all the same. They'd briefly worked on the same shift a few years earlier when Nick was having a break

from SOG due to some injury. He was always up for a laugh.
A bit of a funny bastard actually . . .

Surely not.

'Um . . . are you sure, Luce? I mean, Nick always struck
me as . . .'

'A good bloke? Yeah. I've been hearing a bit of that.'

'Sorry. But I mean, spiking your drink? That's pretty full-on.
How do you know?'

'I just know. Okay?'

'Shit. Sorry, Luce.' *Tread carefully.* 'I don't mean to come
across as a total arsehole but . . . you didn't just have a few too
many and . . . well . . . you know? 'Cause it's fine if that's what
happened, Luce. I won't hold it against you or anything.'

She stared at the mug between her hands. 'Wow. And here
I was thinking that even if no one else believed me, you'd be
the one person in the world who would.'

Sensing her hurt, he backpedalled. *Tell her what she wants
to hear.* 'I believe you, Lucy.' But it sounded hollow to his own
ears.

Placated, she heaved a sigh, put a hand out and brushed his
sleeve. 'Thanks. I know that must have been hard to hear and
I'm sorry I just put it out there, but you were going to find out
before long anyway and the main thing is that it's being dealt
with. Everything'll be fine. I'm okay. I'm seeing the police
psych who's *really*, really good by the way, a nice lady . . .'

'Lucy, stop! You don't just get raped and then everything's
fine.'

'Well, not fine, fine, but like I said, Cam, it's all being dealt
with.'

'How?'

She sighed. 'I went and saw Sergeant Torino. He looked after us so well after John died and . . .'

As she spoke his heart dropped again.

Sergeant Torino? In CIB? Please, God, don't let her say she's lodged a complaint against Nick. Surely she wouldn't be that silly?

'. . . and we talked about it . . . *a lot* . . . and in the end I decided to go ahead and make a formal complaint. Sergeant Torino and DI Moore were awesome. They worked out a strategy and investigated and a couple of weeks later . . .'

Oh shit, don't say it. Don't tell me he's been charged . . .

'. . . they charged him.'

She saw the look of horror on his face and stopped. 'It's going to be all right, Cam.'

You can't be serious.

He cleared his throat. 'Wait. I'm not sure I've understood. You're telling me you've had Nick Greaves, Constable Nick Greaves from the SOG, charged with rape?'

A look of defiance and hurt crossed her face. 'Yes, I have. And there's no need to look so surprised.'

'Well, I *am* surprised. I'm bloody horrified actually. What the hell were you thinking, Luce?'

'I was thinking, *Cam*, that I'm a grown-up, I'm a victim of a crime and . . . oh, by the way, I get paid to make sure victims of crimes have a voice and have their day in court, so I kind of thought it might be appropriate to follow that route. I thought you'd be proud of me for making a stand . . .'

Oh shit. Now she's gonna cry.

Fuck.

'Look, Lucy. I know it might make you feel better *now*

taking this option, but seriously, wasn't there any other way you could have worked this out without resorting to having him charged?'

He heard the hysteria rising in his own voice and tried to temper it. He knew what the blokes in the job would be like with something like this, knew how they resented having women in the ranks at the best of times – felt that they were creatures who were to be viewed with suspicion, no matter how well they did the job. This would only confirm those beliefs. People would naturally rally to Nick. That's just the way things worked.

'Listen, I weighed everything up, like DI Moore and Sergeant Torino told me. They both told me right from the start that it wouldn't be easy. They said if they couldn't get anything else on him, then it might come down to my word against his. But at the end of the day, as the complainant, it's my choice. I thought about all the pros and cons. Sure, there are more cons than pros – I'm not stupid – but the thing is, I *have* to go through with this. I'm compelled, as in, I have absolutely no choice. Besides, it's actually shaping up well. They've got some really strong evidence to corroborate my statement.'

And then it clicked. *This must be what the fucking journo has been chasing me for. Fuck.*

'Luce . . . please . . . you really need to think about how this is going to . . .' he said weakly.

She cut him off dead. 'No, Cam! I don't need to think about anything! I've done all my thinking! I've been walked over my entire life. I've spent the last twenty-two years apologising for . . . for . . . *everything*. I apologise when I don't have the right change at the shop. I apologise for working late and waking my parents when I creep into the house. I apologise for taking up the whole washing machine so I can do a separate wash of just my work shirts. I apologise on a daily basis for not having done enough to have saved Sergeant White. Some days I've even caught myself apologising simply for existing. And you know what, there comes a time when you have to make a stand. And this is my time. It's time to quit with the apologies, to start believing in myself, to acknowledge that I have as much right as anyone else on this planet to have a life and to take control of that life. And who knows? Maybe I'll win, maybe I won't, but at least I can say that I tried, rather than just sweeping it under the carpet and hoping to forget that it happened. And quite frankly, I can't understand why you're not just supporting me on this.'

He took another deep calming breath. *Try not to offend her*. 'All I'm saying, Luce, is that by having him charged, it means that people feel the need to take sides. He's been around for a lot longer than you . . .'

'I know; they've already started. But it's nothing I can't handle, Cam. I know I'm doing the right thing and if people choose to be small-minded about it . . .'

'Oh shit, what's happened?'

'I told you it was nothing I couldn't handle,' she said, nostrils flaring again in anger.

'All right, all right, just calm down. I'm just trying to play devil's advocate here.'

'Well, I don't need a devil's advocate. What I *need* is your support.'

She stopped and looked squarely across the table, her eyes boring through him, challenging him.

'I just don't want to see you get hurt,' he said placatingly, knowing they'd make a meal out of her.

'Well, I *have* been. But by taking charge of it and making sure Nick understands the ramifications of his behaviour, I feel better. More empowered. And I won't let anyone take that away from me. All I'm asking is that you support my decision, Cam, and be there if I need a shoulder to cry on. That's not too much to ask, is it?'

He dropped his gaze to the mug in front of him and flushed with embarrassment. After all she'd done for him during the months leading up to his imprisonment. All the meals she'd cooked, the movies they'd watched, the times she'd been there on the end of the phone and in person when his world was crumbling before him, to listen, encourage, cheer and hug him. He could never thank her enough, but it was impossible to live up to.

'Luce, you know I can barely support *myself* at the moment, with everything that's happened,' he pleaded.

Her face drained of colour as his words sank in. 'What exactly are you saying, Cam? That you *won't* be there for me? Because if that's the case, then . . . then . . . we really should get it out there on the table now before the trial starts. If you can't face the idea of being my support person, as the psych calls it, then you'd better tell me now. I don't want this whole thing to begin, only to have you jump ship halfway through.'

He bowed his head again, overcome with shame at what he was about to do, but unable to stop himself from trashing her hopes. A lump welled in his throat and he closed his eyes. *Just say it.* 'Luce, I'm sorry. I've been thinking about *us* while I was . . . away . . . and . . . and . . . the thing is . . . I value your . . . your . . . *friendship*, more than anything I've ever had. You were there for me when I needed you, when everyone else had pretty much walked away. But the thing is, I'm pretty weirded out after the whole prison experience and . . . and . . . I don't think I'd be much good for anyone else at the moment.'

A noise – a cross between a cry, a sob and a choking burst of laughter – escaped from her lips and she covered her mouth with one hand. 'Oh my God, did you just do the whole "it's not you, it's me" routine? Are you, Cameron Walsh, actually sitting in front of me delivering the greatest cliché of all time?'

He looked away, the shame burning his face. 'I'm so sorry, Luce.'

By the time he looked back the tears were forming in her eyes and he fought the urge to spring from his seat, run from the kitchen and throw up. He'd never felt like such a complete prick in his entire life. It was like taking a lollypop off a kid. No. More like kicking a defenceless puppy who'd just curled up in your lap and looked up with big, adoring eyes.

He swallowed. 'I'm sorry, Luce.'

'Yes. You keep saying that.'

He bit his lower lip, stared at the mug again. 'It's just that I need to be alone for a while, take some time out, get away from Tassie . . . you know?'

She nodded, a single tear rolling down her cheek and landing on the tablecloth. She swept a hand across the moist track it'd left. 'I guess I understand. Maybe it was selfish of me to expect you just to come out the other side and be good old Cam again. But hey, you do what you need to do, have a few weeks away, whatever it takes, and maybe when things are back to normal . . .'

'It might be more than a few weeks, Luce,' he said quickly. *Silence.*

'So. You're telling me it's over then?'

He bowed his head.

Coward. You're an absolute coward.

She nodded, pushed her chair back and placed her cup gently in the sink without wasting further emotion. 'No worries. I guess deep down I knew it'd end like this. What can I say, apart from I hope you find whatever it is you're looking for, Cam.'

He stared, resisted the urge to scream. How could she be so fucking calm? Where was the sobbing, the pleading, the threats, the anger? All the usual stuff that accompanied a break-up? It didn't make sense. He'd just let her down completely and yet, here she was, still wishing him well. It was almost beyond belief. He *deserved* to be yelled at. At the very least. He was going to be free and she was so fucking calm. He took a deep breath. 'But what about you? What are you going to do about Nick?'

She shrugged and gave him a tight, emotionless smile. 'I'll be fine. We'll have our day in court, and maybe, just maybe, judging by the way it's shaping up, I'll win. In fact, I'm quietly confident that I'll win. But whatever happens, win or lose, I'll move on, knowing that I was the better person for standing up for myself for once and refusing to be a doormat.'

She turned and before he could speak again, tell her how much he admired her, how strong and healthy she seemed, how *together* she was, she walked out the front door and disappeared into the grey late-morning mist.

• • •

In the end, it was mostly easy. It had taken less than a week to sort out his life. The plane ticket was booked, the lease on his flat, courtesy of his extremely understanding landlady, had been torn up and his meagre belongings had been either tossed, sent to the Salvos or placed in packing boxes and deposited in the landlady's garage. And by the middle of the following week he was left with a suitcase full of clothes and every hope in the world that his future would involve a bright new beginning in one of the most exciting cities in the world, not to mention the company of the woman he had always truly loved.

But it hadn't all been easy. The week had been punctuated with more than the odd, queasy pang of guilt over Lucy. He'd let her down. Worse than let her down, actually. And he had done it at one of the worst possible times in her life. But there was no way around it and he justified it by constantly reminding himself that he'd at least had the guts to be relatively honest with her. A more dishonest man would have stuck around, held her hand when he didn't mean it and then later walked out when she was at her lowest. And besides, she seemed really together about the whole thing. A lot stronger than he ever would have thought. Of course, she'd need to be.

For things would get worse. No doubt about it. From the little he'd heard about the case, he knew she hadn't hit rock bottom. Yet. When he'd finally found the courage to call Kurt, he got the full run-down on the ongoing campaign of torment she was being subjected to at work.

'She's doing it tough, man. Full-on cold glares in the corridors, most of them on the watch talking pretty openly about their fear of working with her, our own sergeant recommending that she go to another shift so as to avoid a "conflict of interest". She's had hate mail poked through her locker, there's a really shitty email about her doing the rounds and I even heard that someone had been around to her place and trashed her car.'

He fell silent. Didn't know what to say.

Kurt rambled on. 'And word is that it was fully consensual, that she's just after compo and that a jury is gonna wipe the floor with her. She's trying to put on a brave face, but, jeez, I dunno . . .'

Cam sighed, thinking about the trial itself. About how she'd cope in the witness box. Rape victims were generally torn to shreds in the box. The defence would play their usual hand; they'd bring up past boyfriends, past rumoured boyfriends, any male she happened to have spoken to more than once in her life and suggest that as a female copper she was probably sleeping with all of her colleagues. She'd become the slut who led Nick on. They'd pick at any tiny inconsistency in her state-ment, highlighting the fact that as a copper, there shouldn't be *any* inconsistencies. Because of course, coppers were coppers, not human beings.

When he could take Kurt's downer no longer, he stopped him mid-sentence, gave an excuse – *Gotta go, the landlady's here* – and hung up. And as he continued packing, his thoughts drifted back to previous rape cases he'd sat in on, watching in agony as the defence wore the victim down.

'Well, Miss Smith, were your trousers below your knees or above your knees when he was supposedly holding you down and anally penetrating you?'

'Your statement says they were above and now you say you can't clearly recall?' (Turns to the floor and raises one amused eyebrow towards the prosecutor.)

'The fact that it was eighteen months ago really is irrel-
evant. I ask you again. Were the jeans above or below your
knees at the time of penetration?'

'You can't recall?

'Well, you should be able to recall.

'I put it to you that you can't recall because you're making
it up.

'You can't recall because it simply didn't happen, did it,
Miss Smith?

'You made it up, just like you've been making up this entire
allegation. Isn't that right, Miss Smith?'

He shuddered, knowing exactly how Lucy's case would
pan out. It would pan out as most rape cases panned out. And
she would hit rock bottom.

In a way he was glad he wasn't going to be around.
He couldn't bear the thought of watching on as she was
dissected and destroyed by the system they were supposed to
champion.

And every time the thought crossed his mind, he packed,
lifted, cleaned a little harder, pushing it all to the back of his
mind. It was too hard. Way too much to deal with.

As he left the airport security section first thing the following
Thursday morning, grabbing his carry-on pack and pulling his
cap back down across his face, his mobile rang. He fumbled,
fished it out and groaned at the number on the screen.

It was her.

Maybe she'd heard on the grapevine that he was leaving.
He closed his eyes, his thumb hovering over the 'end call'

button. There was no point doing goodbyes. It was best to leave quietly. He couldn't face prolonged explanations about his state of mind and his future plans. Without thinking any further on it, he pressed the 'end call' button, slotted the phone back into the pack and wandered off towards the coffee stand to grab a quick latte before the flight left for Melbourne.

While sitting in the waiting area, cap pulled down lest anyone should recognise him and try to engage in conversation, he reached for the phone, meaning to switch it off as his flight had just been called. He looked at the screen, saw the voicemail message icon and out of sheer curiosity dialled '121'. He took another sip of the latte, eyes scanning the waiting area, as the message played in his ear.

'Cam, it's Lucy. I just wanted to let you know that . . . that . . . um . . . I know I have no right to ask you, but the DPP has called DI Moore and me into a meeting tomorrow. It's all kicking off and I just wanted to ask you one more time if you'd consider being my support person? I really need you, Cam. I know I said I was fine the other day and I've tried to put on a brave face, but underneath I'm . . . not so good. It's all become a bit real, I'm copping some serious flak now and, to be honest, I'm terrified about how it's all going to play out. I know you don't want to be with me – hey, I guess I knew deep down that I was always going to lose you over this – but . . . I was wondering if there's any way you'd just be here to support me? If you'd please come to the meeting with me? Just as a friend. I just thought . . . oh, look . . . it'd just be great if you could come. Um . . . okay. Hope this finds you well. See you.'

He stared at the phone for a moment before pressing the 'delete' button, switching it off and slipping it back into his pack. He sculled the last of the lukewarm coffee, hurled the cup into the bin, pulled his cap down even further and headed towards the gate.

It was too hard.

It was just too, too hard.

And as the final call boomed across the lounge, he got up and walked, studying the swirling patterns on the brightly coloured carpet as he went: a blob of gum, a trail of dusty footprints, the black rubber matting leading out towards the doorway, the light crack in the tarmac and the orange barrier flags fluttering in the icy breeze.

She was no longer his responsibility.

The Director of Public Prosecutions

3.50 pm Friday 15 July

'Come in, come in,' he said, rising from behind his desk and reaching a hand out in greeting.

'Sorry we're a bit early,' DI Moore said.

'That's fine. Grab a seat. And you must be Lucy,' he said as the girl behind Moore stuck out her hand. She nodded. Her hand was warm and clammy but her grip was firm and she looked him squarely in the eye.

'Nice to meet you, Mr Short,' she said crisply.

'Please. Call me David. No point getting all formal when it's just us three in the comfort of my office.'

She nodded and he looked her up and down one more time before returning to his chair. She wasn't what he'd

313

been expecting. Having read the file, he'd had some vague notion that she'd be childlike, unsure of herself, probably self-consciously studying her toes throughout their meeting. But instead, rather pleasingly, she had an aura of confidence. She was together. Businesslike almost. And would no doubt be a pleasure to deal with after the usual teary, nervous-wreck rape victims.

He opened the file on his desk, adjusted his glasses and pretended to peruse it while they sat in silence before him. He squirmed, remembered for a split second that he hadn't brushed off the ever-present lamington shake of dandruff from his shoulders before they arrived. But there was nothing he could do now. They were both staring intently and any move to dust it off, casually or otherwise, would be embarrassing. He sighed, willing himself to relax.

Perhaps they won't notice anyway.

Surely they'll have more important things on their minds.

Okay. Down to business.

One more deep breath, then . . . just say it.

David Short detested dishing out bad news, but as the Director of Public Prosecutions the buck stopped with him and there was no point putting it off for a moment longer. The longer he stalled, the longer they'd be sitting in his office. And there was his four-thirty appointment to consider.

He looked up and snapped the file shut, studying Moore's face. He liked the detective inspector. He was a genuinely pleasant sort of bloke. He'd often thought about including him in their weekend golf rounds, but something told him Moore would politely decline. And David wasn't into rejection. Moore was young for a DI, but a damn fine operator all

314

the same. And David admired his professionalism. Respected it, even. If a file with Moore's name attached to it crossed his desk, he could be guaranteed it'd be completed to the highest standard possible.

Not that that would assist him today.

'I've been over Lucy's file, Inspector,' he said, pushing it to one side. 'And the thing is . . .

'The thing is . . .' He faltered, stopped again. An image of Chrissy Matterson flooded his thoughts. She was naked, gloriously bare-arse naked, kneeling before him as he sat in this very chair, running her lips around the rim of his cock and putting her deal on the table, in between the licks, the sucks, the soft breathy blows and long firm tongue strokes.

'The thing is, David, it would make me very happy if you would have a quick flick through that file on Nick Greaves and come to the same conclusion that the rest of the service has come to. Namely,' she paused, ducked her head, ran the tip of her tongue lightly up and down his balls, and waited until he had stopped groaning, 'that it's meritless, that there's not enough evidence and that consequently, the Crown won't be taking it to trial.'

He'd opened his eyes in a panic, realised what she was saying and tried to back his chair away, his dick shrivelling instantly at the enormity of the request. He'd promised her a favour, sure, but perverting the course of justice was a little more significant than a favour.

'Uh . . . Chrissy, I really don't think . . .'

But she stopped him dead, took his balls deftly in one hand, clamped her fingers around the base of his dick and took the rest of it, the shrivelled, floppy few centimetres of it that remained, in her mouth where she began a long, rhythmic sucking motion that sent him hurtling backwards in the chair, unable to utter another word. The protest died on his lips. He closed his eyes again as she sucked, banishing the file to the far reaches of his mind and concentrating on the soft, wet sucking of her mouth. He felt himself growing longer, stronger, harder. Harder than he'd been in years. He gasped, the first tingles of a screaming orgasm setting his skin on fire. But before he could come, she pulled away, took him by the shoulders and draped him across the table. She climbed elegantly up on him, slipped his cock effortlessly inside of her and smiled as he groaned again. Louder this time.

'I promise . . . you won't . . . regret it . . . David. If you do this one little thing for me, then I can guarantee that I'll be in your debt . . . if you know what I mean . . .'

And as she rode him faster and faster, the hard, plastic edge of the blotter digging into his back, her nails digging into his shoulders, the file digging into his subconscious, he decided that for once in his uptight, perpetually by-the-book little life, he didn't give a shit.

'Yes.

'Oh yes.

'Oh, Chrissy, yeeesssss . . .'

And it'd been that easy. Made even easier by the fact that once he'd perused the said file in the cold, hard, unaroused light of day, he noted with a pang of glee that it wasn't *such* an unreasonable conclusion to draw. The girl's statement was good and with her knowledge of police procedures she'd know exactly what to say and do in the box, but pretty much everything else could be explained away by a decent lawyer, thereby relegating the case to a lower priority. Maybe not so low as to not be heard at all, but it certainly wasn't out of the question.

The phone call between Greaves and Williams could well have been nothing. The rumours of drugs in the gym were just that – rumours. Another rape connected with GHB at that same gym? Pah. It was so long ago the relevance was negligible. The independent witness who'd reported on their conversation had a list of priors a mile long and, to make matters worse, it could reasonably be construed that he was volunteering information in order to cut himself a plea deal on his latest drug bust. He'd be discredited by a lawyer within thirty seconds.

There was no medical evidence of drugs in her system, no evidence of physical injuries. There was nothing from the search, even less from the interview and nothing from the follow-up listening devices.

And to add fuel to his fire of destruction, a quick phone call to the defendant's brief, Andy Woods, confirmed that it would be a not guilty plea, an argument for consent corroborated by a handful of witnesses who'd already made statements attesting to the fact that the complainant had been encouraging the defendant, had wanted him right from day one of the CIB course.

What looked like a strong circumstantial case on paper could certainly be painted as a borderline one if push came to shove.

In an ideal world he would have let the Howard girl have her day in court, and who knew? She may well have given good evidence, had a sympathetic jury and had a win. But as it stood, it was perfectly justifiable to state that they'd be pushing shit uphill. If what's-his-name had raped her, then he'd done it well enough to beat the system.

You're not doing anything wrong, David.

Well . . .

Maybe.

But then there's Chrissy and her repeat performance to consider . . .

Stop it.

He cleared his throat, banished Chrissy from his mind and started again.

'The thing is, Lucy, Inspector . . . I've looked at it every which way and I'm sorry to say, but there's simply not enough evidence for the Crown to file an indictment.'

Moore rocked forwards in his chair, clearly stunned. 'Ah . . . are you sure, sir? I mean, there's a good, solid prima facie case . . .'

'Yes, there's a prima facie case. But you and I both know that according to the guidelines, while it's certainly necessary, a prima facie case alone is not always sufficient for launching a prosecution, Inspector. There has to be more to it.'

Richard shook his head. 'But Lucy's statement . . .'

'Won't mean a thing on its own.'

'She'll give evidence on oath,' he appealed. '*Good* evidence. And she made her initial disclosure only a fortnight after it happened to her. In accordance with res gestae . . .'

'Yes. That gives her allegation more weight. I do know how these things work, Detective,' he said solemnly.

'I'm sorry. No disrespect. Of course you do, sir. It's just that . . .'

He placed a hand up to silence the man before him. 'Inspector, I'm not sure you understand me. I'm not opening this up for debate. The thing is, and my apologies to Constable Howard, but the case is purely circumstantial and . . . well . . . weak.'

He swallowed, another image of Chrissy popping into his subconscious. But Moore was determined not to be placated.

'But there's a history of GHB moving through the gym.'

David shrugged. 'Meaningless.'

'What about the independent witness then, Duane Macallister? He's corroborated the story! He tells you what Nick was talking about and planning! You can't just . . . gloss over that,' he exclaimed, throwing his hands in the air.

David sighed. 'Inspector, Macallister has extensive priors. That alone gives Greaves's lawyer, Andy Woods, licence to rip him to pieces on the stand and make him out to be a total liar. You know how it works. Plus, there's the fact that he's also got his own charges pending. The defence will just argue that he's cut a deal, told you what you want to hear, in exchange for getting a lighter sentence on his own matters. Any half-decent defence lawyer – and unfortunately Woodsy's better than most – will make a meal out of him. It'll just be embarrassing. Not only for him, but for you for having him up there in the first place.'

He paused, tried to look contrite. 'Inspector, I'm afraid the case simply isn't strong enough. There are too many opportunities for it to fall to pieces. You know better than anyone else that the Crown's case needs to be watertight before we even set foot in a courtroom. And even then, even when it's absolutely rock-solid impenetrable, we can still lose.'

'I know, sir, but . . .'

He put up a hand, stopped Moore from interrupting. 'You yourself have seen us lose the most unlosable cases in history. You know the system. Juries are mostly ordinary, everyday yobbos who would rather give a bloke a "fair go" than see justice meted out accordingly. And they're so intent on giving a bloke a fair go, that unless a case unfolds like an episode of *CSI*, *Law and Order*, or bloody *Bones* – that is to say, unless we have a semitrailer full of DNA – then modern-day jurors are increasingly sceptical that a crime has been committed. And this is especially problematic when it comes to sexual assault trials.'

'I know that, sir. I've read quite a few articles on the *CSI* Effect. And I agree that it's frustrating,' Moore said. 'But shouldn't Lucy at least be given the chance to tell her own side of the story, just like any other victim?'

David looked at the girl. She still hadn't contributed a word to the conversation. Her face remained impassive. She sat rigid in the chair, her eyes unblinking. No indication of distress or bewilderment, apart from the barely noticeable tightening of her lips and the tiny drop in her shoulders. If anything, Moore himself appeared more shocked and distraught than she did. Regardless, David refused to be bullied or guilted into changing his mind. Especially when he was this close to securing another naked romp with Chrissy.

'I'm sorry, Inspector. The final decision rests in my hands and the decision has been made. Unless the investigation turns up anything new, anything concrete, then it stands.'

Lucy nodded curtly, just the once, and broke her silence. 'I understand, sir. Thank you for your time.' She rose to leave and extended a hand over the table.

'Thank you for being not only professional, but under-standing, Constable. My job is all about making difficult decisions. I'm not always comfortable with them, but some-times my hands are tied.'

Like they will be literally when I get my return visit from Miss Matterson. This time at a five-star hotel, on my terms.

He shivered at the thought, remembering the only time he'd gathered up the courage to pay a visit to a prostitute while on a conference in Melbourne. It'd taken him forty years of life to find out that he, one of the most powerful men in the state, enjoyed nothing more than being tied up, spanked until he was raw and told just how bad he'd been.

Oh yes. His hands would be tied all right.

Lucy gave a final nod before heading straight for the door and he was swamped with a sense of relief. It was over. And she'd proved easy to handle. If she was going to burst into tears, he'd really rather she didn't do it in front of him. He hated it when they did that.

'Detective Inspector Moore, a moment more of your time if you don't mind?' he said, sitting back down.

'I'll meet you down in the foyer, Lucy,' Moore said, turning to her. She nodded again, bit her lip and left without uttering another word. David waited until the door had shut quietly behind her. He studied the man before him. Moore was clearly furious but fortunately knew better than to argue.

'Again, I'm sorry, Richard,' he said, somewhat more sweetly. 'The thing is – not that I was at liberty to go into details with Lucy sitting here – I just don't have the money to take a case to trial for two, three, four weeks which is going to end up in an acquittal. As a manager yourself, you understand about

321

budgets and prioritisation. I've got too many other cases that have a better chance.'

Moore remained tight-lipped, obviously wanting to say more than he was going to. 'I understand that, sir. I'm just a bit disappointed that budgets take precedence over justice.'

A fleeting ripple of annoyance ran through him.

Don't play semantics with me, sunshine.

'Oh, come on, Richard. We both know how it works. Rapes are harder to prove than arsons or . . . or . . . attempted murder,' he said, settling back into his chair and thinking over a couple of the more recent cases he'd seen come and go on the mainland. 'Did you see that rape in Melbourne last week, where the woman had just moved into the neighbourhood, invited her new, friendly, chatty neighbour over for a cuppa only to then find herself assaulted from one end of her house to the other?'

Richard nodded. 'Vaguely.'

'The defendant argued consent. *Consent*, Richard, despite the fact that the woman was a prominent lesbian who'd last had sex with a man some thirty years earlier. The jury in all their infinite wisdom let the defendant walk right out the front door. They agreed that because she hadn't picked up the phone and dialled triple-O immediately, then it probably *was* consensual and that, oh, by the way, she most likely harboured a deep-seated desire to have sex with a man and was just worried that her lezzie friends would find out.'

Moore twitched. 'I know what you're saying, but that's one case, sir. *One*.'

David gritted his teeth, teetering on the verge of losing his patience with the DI. It was *more* than one case as they both well knew. *Far* more. He scratched at his beard and thought back over the past few months alone. On his own watch he'd had cases that didn't get any further than the initial report at the police station. Like the one where the alleged victim, who happened to be a prostitute, had walked in the front door and was subsequently turned away some ten minutes later by a crusty fifty-something sergeant who was of the opinion that pros couldn't be raped. The forensic evidence had walked out the door with her and when a well-meaning constable managed to track her down two weeks later, the forensics, along with the victim's faith in the system, had disappeared.

He'd seen trials aborted before they even began, such as the one in Burnie several weeks back. The victim in that case, a retarded twelve-year-old girl who'd been systematically sexually assaulted by a carer at her respite home, had been, as per the defence's opening statement, formally declared unfit to give evidence by the judge on day one, thus ending before it started. This, despite the fact that an extremely dedicated policewoman had spent three days tirelessly coaxing every word of the girl's horror story out of her and committing it to paper in a logical, intelligible form which would have been perfectly adequate for the hearing.

And it wasn't just on *his* watch. Every time he picked up a damned paper he read about a rapist walking out the revolving court door. Only that morning over his fry-up at the cafe down the road, he'd raised one tired, defeated eyebrow about a Sydney trial, where a couple of jurors, a forty-eight-year-old mechanic and a sixty-three-year-old retired salesman, had concluded that because the victim had been wearing skinny jeans at the time of her assault, she must have been consenting.

For it would be impossible to remove skinny jeans without the consent of the wearer. The jurors proudly proclaimed that they'd researched the fact, had read about similar cases on the Net – in Italy, in Korea, in Sweden, where skinny jeans were being hailed as the latest in chastity belts.

They wouldn't entertain the prosecution's assertion that the offender had struck such fear into the forty-two kilogram, eighteen-year-old victim that she had lain motionless on the bed, unable to put up a struggle lest he punch her, or worse, and that the jeans hadn't been that difficult to rip down.

The skinny jeans theory. Possibly one of the most absurd notions David had ever encountered, but a notion nonetheless that was being accepted by the great ignorant unwashed. Those who knew no better. Just another weapon to be used against victims in the long, impossible uphill struggle to convict their rapists.

It was a losing battle – more accurately, a losing war – because no matter how much of a fight they put up, the justice system was rigged so far against them that quite frankly, David had stopped getting upset about it. That was just the way it was. It didn't work. It wasn't a matter of being broken, it was a matter of it never having worked in the first place. You could throw amendments at it until you were blue in the face, but the sad fact was that things were never going to change. Not as long as you had human beings on the planet. There were the powerful and the weak and Mother Nature dictated that one would always exploit the other.

If it was his wife, son, daughter or family friend, there was no way in hell he'd recommend them dragging it through court and after having that exact same conversation with a number of coppers he socialised with, he knew he wasn't alone.

And in a way, in a small way, it was this thought that comforted him regarding his decision about Lucy. For he was actually sparing the girl, carting her off the battlefield with a minor leg wound before the bayonet ripped through her heart and left her for dead on the courtroom floor.

Moore might have been pissed, but he'd get over it.

'So . . . that's it?' Moore asked.

He shrugged, tried to muster his best apologetic face. 'I'm sorry, Richard, but we've both spent enough time in and out of courtrooms to know how the system works. I've said it before and I'll say it again. Unless a complainant presents two seconds after the event with her head caved in, semen dripping from head to toe, her vagina ripped in two, clutching a DVD containing footage of the entire incident, followed by a full and frank confession by the guilty party, we're not . . . going . . . to get . . . a conviction.'

Moore ran a hand through his hair, evidently exasperated. 'But . . . we had more evidence for this case than we can ever get for them most of the time and I just feel for Lucy. She's credible, articulate and probably the most conscientious copper I've ever met in my entire life and I truly believe it happened like she said.'

David clenched his teeth. *Okay. Now you're pissing me off.*

'I'm not questioning her credibility, Richard. But your defendant would be just as credible in the box. More so. He's got ten years on her. That's ten years of experience in giving evidence in the box. The burden of proof is "beyond reasonable doubt". Even presented in its best light, we won't be able to prove that. We can't run it. I'm sorry, but it's literally, case closed.'

Let it go, Richard.

Moore shook his head again but slumped in his chair, finally conceding defeat.

'But moving on,' David said crisply, glancing up at the clock on the wall, 'the Chalmers case. I've reviewed the file and it's looking good. You've done a fantastic job on it. When are you going to begin the interviews?'

Moore hesitated. 'Late next week. We've got rolling searches and interviews planned for the pollies – Gresham, Gilroy and Martinez, the Premier and his wife – and finally, the commissioner. If everything pans out, we'll interview and charge him on Thursday, maybe early Friday.'

David smiled. It was the best news he'd heard all day. In a way he was irritated at having to let the Howard rape slide. After all, it would have been the perfect vehicle for making Ron Chalmers squirm, but *this* would more than make up for it. He'd see that smarmy old prick marched out on his ear and dripping with humiliation if it was the last thing he did. With any luck they'd even be able to snatch his pension off him. The Premier and a few pollies were nothing more than collateral damage.

'Excellent. So how are the charges shaping up then?'

'At the moment we've got a mixed bag. A couple of code of conduct breaches for his yabbering on to the Premier about all and sundry, so not that serious in the big scheme of things.'

'But?'

'But by the time we're through with the pollies' interviews we'll have more than enough to charge him with about ten counts of perverting the course of justice: for the infringement notices, the Myers case and his interference in tipping them off in their own sordid matters. The Premier made the fateful mistake, after his initial conversation with the commissioner, of taking it upon himself to do a spot of housecleaning, in the form of phone calls to Gresham, Gilroy and Martinez. We've got him on TIs telling them that you're sniffing around and that they're not to land him in it for passing on the info from the commissioner. Once they know we've reopened their investigations they'll cooperate. We'll make it clear that it's Chalmers we want, not them, and that it'll be in their best interests to cooperate.'

'Lovely. Good work,' David replied. And he meant it. He wouldn't mind being the proverbial fly on the wall watching them squirm when the long-forgotten matters were outlined to them, the matters that had been swept under the carpet because of a lack of evidence at the time. The journo's article at the basis of the Myers matter made it clear that Chalmers had been the leak, tipping the pollies off time after time and enabling them to save their butts before the shit hit the fan.

Why, if it wasn't for Ron Chalmers and his big mouth, the fat, smug local member, Dick Gresham, would have been sitting in a cell weeping about being sprung in the very centre of a well-orchestrated Hobart-based amphetamine ring. Nicola Gilroy would be sweating it out at the women's prison for her role in assisting forestry officials cover up their systematic assaults upon conservationists in the Upper Florentine Valley and Guy Martinez would have been sweeping out the yards at Risdon wondering why he'd let himself get tangled up with that international kiddie porn ring. But instead, calls had been made, threats issued, paper trails shredded and hard drives wiped. Chalmers had passed on the investigation details that had allowed them to clean up after themselves, and it made David want to spit.

He felt his fists clenching just thinking about the arsehole.

'Keep me updated then, won't you?'

'Of course, sir.'

'Right. If there's nothing else then, Richard?'

The DI paused, half stood and hovered, before shaking hands and leaving the room, obviously thinking it better to keep his mouth firmly shut. David sank back into his chair, letting the results of the meeting wash over him. Moore was clearly disappointed about the rape matter, but he'd get over it. And besides, he'd be so busy with what was going to begin unfolding next week, that he wouldn't have time to scratch himself, let alone worry about something that had never stood a chance in the first place.

Thanks to Chrissy's intervention.

Remembering the dandruff, he swept a hand across both shoulders and frowned as the light dusting of snow bounced off and fell to the floor. It'd been worse than he'd thought.

Ugh.

Hopefully they hadn't noticed.

The phone buzzed in front of him.

'Yes?'

'Your four-thirty is here, sir.'

He smiled and reached for the bottom drawer of his desk.

'Send him in.'

He had the usual Friday night drinkies glasses out and the bottle ready for pouring by the time Magistrate Alex Hudson strolled through the door. The man radiated presence and one glance was enough to indicate to even the strangest of strangers that he was a man of authority. His tailored navy suit, funky Italian-made frames and the hint of salt and pepper sprinkled throughout his otherwise full dark head of hair singled him out of a crowd. Alex Hudson got second looks even before he opened his mouth and on top of that, his breezy manner and graceful, effortless long-limbed moves made even the trendiest of the try-hards who moved in court circles green with envy. He would have inspired a bitter jealousy in most, had he not been as interesting, as down to earth and as truly self-deprecating as he was.

Truth be told, Alex inspired equal parts bitterness and camaraderie in him. Most days David worshipped his longtime friend. Some days, like today for instance, he was consumed with inadequacy and self-doubt the second Alex entered the room. He was squat to Alex's tall; dowdy, sweaty and ill-fitted compared to Alex's immaculately maintained and constantly evolving wardrobe; faltering and awkward compared to Alex's aura of natural confidence. To make matters worse, David had also developed a full-blown case of follicle envy as the years had passed them both by, his beard and moustache never quite compensating for the sad, thinning patch that crept closer to his forehead whenever he looked in the mirror – a thinning patch that he knew, with dismay, would eventually leave him resembling a tonsured monk. They might both have been forty-five, but Alex would have passed for late thirties while David himself was constantly mistaken for fifty-five.

In fact, every time he looked at Alex he was reminded of how he'd come runner-up, second to Alex's first in every single subject throughout their five-year Law degree. Second at school, and now, second in life.

He subconsciously dusted his left shoulder as Alex lay his overcoat across the back of the chair.

'Long day?' he asked, pouring out a couple of Scotches.

Alex pulled a face. 'The usual. The morning was taken up by about a million formal matters followed by a defendant who decided it'd be a good idea to represent himself on a drink-driving matter.'

'Sounds like fun?'

'You wouldn't read about it. He was an old farmer. Down from Jericho. Seriously, Dave. You should have seen him. All dressed up in his Sunday best, looking like he'd just stepped out of the 1950s. Anyway, first, he tells me the whole sordid story, which went on for at least an hour, and *then*, just as I was about to doze off, he up and volunteers his entire driving history to me. You should have seen the prosecutor's face,' he said with a grin.

'Oh?' David said, fully aware that the defendant's history was never raised in the courtroom until after he'd been found guilty.

'Yeah. He starts rambling on about how it might *look* like he's had a stack of speeding charges in his history, but that only two of them were really his own.'

'What?'

'Yeah. He goes – get this – "The other six or seven were ones I took for my boys. They paid the fines and I just said it was me driving, but it wasn't really. I just signed them stat dec thingies to say it was me so me boys wouldn't lose their licences through points."'

David burst out laughing, as much at the man's idiocy as at Alex's amusing country bumpkin impersonation.

'I *know*,' Alex said, chiming in with his own laugh. 'Something about perverting the course of justice. Poor old bastard. He had no idea what he'd said.'

'What did you do?'

'Ah, just let it slide. I did have a little word about what that actually meant and he looked suitably embarrassed when it clicked but it was bloody funny, after all.'

David continued laughing, wiped a small tear from the corner of each eye. It was funny. But still. He didn't miss the courts at all. Was much happier driving his desk, well away from the great unwashed.

'Ah . . . it's the little gems like that that make the day worthwhile,' he said.

'Agreed,' Alex laughed. 'Anyway, how was your week? Any more exciting news?'

David settled back in his chair, wiped his eyes again. 'As a matter of fact, yes. I just had Richard Moore in here. He reckons they'll be arresting and charging Chalmers next week. Friday most likely.'

Alex let out a long, low whistle. 'Interesting. Glad I'm on next week.'

'Tell me about it.'

'What about the others? Mr Martinez and friends?'

'Depends on how they play their interviews. If they cooperate, we'll downgrade their charges and put in a good word for them with whoever ends up on the bench. At the end of the day, they're not important. It's Chalmers's scalp I'm after. The others are small fish.'

'What about the Premier?'

David sighed. Christopher annoyed him with his constant melodrama, his inability to make a decision when it counted, his countless backflips on publicly made promises and his embarrassing gaffes, but he didn't conjure up the same level of disgust in him that Ron Chalmers did. In fact, he didn't really care one way or the other. Chalmers was what mattered, not the dimwit Premier.

'If he puts himself right in it, especially about the spilling of secrets and the traffic infringement notices, then we might have no choice but to charge him. But . . .'

'If he plays smart?'

'If he plays smart, argues that he didn't know what happened to the missing infringement notices, that he hadn't thought any more on it when he didn't receive summonses for non-payment, he'll probably be able to sweep it under the carpet. The leaking of info might be a bit trickier. But if he manages to talk his way out of that, then he'll no doubt convene the usual parliamentary committee, who'll spend a few weeks "reviewing" the case. They'll call in a couple of select media-friendly witnesses and push around a few bits of paper before declaring that all is well in the state of Tasmania. They'll quietly disband and go about their business. Just the usual.'

Alex laughed again and poured himself another Scotch. 'And it'll all be forgotten by the time the next election comes around.'

'But of course.'

'Bloody hell, I don't know how Christopher does it. The amount of scandals he's survived . . . that man has more lives than a cage full of feral cats.'

'He'll need them over the next few weeks if he wants to weather the storm,' David said drily.

'Mmm. So who'll be representing Chalmers then? Any idea yet?'

'Probably Andy Woods.'

'Oh right. I heard a rumour he was turning to the dark side. He's looking after another copper, isn't he? . . . The one charged with rape. That should be interesting, eh?'

David cleared his throat. 'Ah. *That* one won't be going any further. There's not enough in it. We'll be putting forward a motion to drop it next week. Just giving you the heads-up.'

Alex downed his drink and looked thoughtful. 'Fair enough. Pity though. Sounds like it would have been interesting. I was kind of looking forward to hearing the preliminaries. Something different from the usual rubbish. I'm afraid it's all spectacularly boring at the moment. Just the regulars up on the same old, same old. It's all I can do to stop myself from falling asleep on the bench some days and it's only got worse since Christopher's laid down the law that Risdon is chockers and I'm not to give out custodial sentences unless it's practically a bloody murder. If I have to give out another suspended sentence or community work order to someone with a hundred priors, I'm going to go postal!'

David smiled wearily. Personally he didn't know how Alex did it. It'd drive anyone insane to have the same old crooks traipsing in and out of the revolving courtroom doors with the same tired old excuses. But nothing was going to change in a hurry. There were too many of them, committing too many crimes and not nearly enough resources to deal with it properly. *Never* enough resources. And while the government continued paying them to breed, the situation was only going to get worse. 'Another wee dram?'

'Why not?' he smiled, proffering the glass as David swung the bottle back into action. 'I'll get off my soapbox for the minute. What else is new? How's Gina?'

David's brow furrowed at the mention of his wife of twenty-four years. How *was* Gina? Honestly, he had no idea. She could be dying of cancer and he probably wouldn't know. They didn't talk about such things anymore. Hadn't done for years. Instead, their conversations consisted of 'What time will you be home for tea?', 'Martin's performing in the uni revue next Wednesday – do you think you'll make it?' and 'The neighbours at number three are getting their driveway done. Perhaps we should think about getting ours done as well?' Gina's world had shrunk dramatically in recent years and if it didn't involve meal planning, their children's amateur dramatics or the latest street gossip, chances were she wasn't very interested.

She hadn't been very interested in anything else since the kids had left home. Especially in him. In fact, the second their younger one, Martin, had followed his older sister Miriam to go and live in his uni share house, so he could quote unquote 'fully appreciate the student life', Gina had moved into the spare room of their huge and now rather empty Battery Point house, announcing perfunctorily that they both got a much better night's sleep by themselves anyway. There was no need to keep up the pretence any longer. Not that there had ever been much of a pretence to keep up.

She hadn't so much as let him touch her, with the exception of a morning peck on the cheek, for three and a half years. His last touch, the final time his fingertips had graced her skin, had been a stolen grab of her breast in the shower one morning before work, which he'd paid for dearly ever since with her frostiness. She reminded him of Annette Bening's character in *American Beauty*, only minus the physical attributes.

In fact, the last time they'd had sex, albeit begrudging on Gina's part, was before Martin had left high school some five years before. And right up until and including that point, it had been lights-off, partially-clothed, missionary-position, over-in-minutes sex. Masturbation was, in her eyes, appalling, and the one time he'd tried it with her lying beside him, she'd rolled away in haste, unable to overcome her disgust for days. And if he did it in his spare time, then she wasn't the least bit interested in knowing about it. Touching oneself was primitive, animal-like, something to be left to the lower classes.

He sighed. He loved his wife. She was, after all, the mother of his children and she put on a reasonable show when doing her duty at the odd public function. And divorce was . . . well . . . unthinkable for the Director of Public Prosecutions. So they muddled on blithely with their own lives, each hoping the other would never raise the topic. There was no point in confronting a whole host of uncomfortable truths.

How was Gina? He certainly didn't know. Alive and well and as different from Chrissy Matterson as that sex bomb pop music star, the blonde thing who wore the silly wigs and stupid clothes, was from the middle-aged Scottish singer from that talent show.

Ah. Chrissy Matterson.

On that particular score, he would dearly have loved to share the juicy details of his Chrissy tryst with Alex. He trusted him entirely, but Chrissy was something he wanted to keep to himself. Alex would never have disapproved or, God forbid, passed it on in a million years, but part of him wanted the satisfaction of being able to smile quietly in the knowledge that there were only two people in the world who knew about it. Chrissy was *his* dirty little secret.

'Good, mate. Gina's as busy as ever. And Jackie?'

Alex smiled. 'Yeah. Busy too. She's just taken on this new client who . . .'

And as Alex launched into the latest annoying spiel regarding his model-like wife and her scandalously successful, high-powered accounting company, David felt his mind drifting to Chrissy, to the soft, pale flawless skin of her inner thigh brushing against his cheek, the wetness of her cunt, a sure sign of just how much she wanted him. And he toyed with an idea. If he worded it right and if it involved enough jewellery, cars and maybe one of those swanky two-bedroom apartments down by the waterfront, then perhaps, just perhaps, she could be his on a more permanent basis. If not, then he certainly had one over her. A *big* one. One that could come in handy in the future if she decided she wasn't so keen on a return visit.

Ah yes. Either way, he'd see Chrissy Matterson again.

He smiled and tuned back in to Alex.

The Journo

'You've got first pick of the dailies,' Artie Myers announced as he strode past Tim's desk and tossed a circular highlighting the run-down of local events next to his laptop. Tim stopped his typing, picked up the folder and flicked through it without the slightest hint of enthusiasm.

Dollhouse and Miniatures Extravaganza at Botanical Gardens

Managing director of Sustainable Timbers Tas. Ltd. (accompanied by wife) to make announcement regarding allegations of affair with underage stripper; press conference 11 am

Tasmanian Writers' Centre book launch

Cupcake day for RSPCA; interview with local vet Fiona O'Reilly

National Tree Day; planting on Domain at midday

337

'Hmm. It's all *very* exciting, Artie, and don't get me wrong – I'd give both nuts to see that smug arsehole from STT finally chow down on his long overdue share of humble pie, so that one's extremely tempting – however . . . put me down for the vet interview.' He snapped the file shut and returned to his laptop, squinting through weary eyes at the text that unfolded before him.

'The vet?' Artie cried, a look of surprise crossing his face. 'My star investigative reporter wants to interview the bloody vet? I was just being polite by giving you first choice, Tim. Surely you want the STT story? It's gonna be huge.'

Tim paused and cracked his neck, touching left shoulder then right. What he wanted was to be left alone to get on with it. He wanted, no, *needed*, Artie and his painful, pointless list of dailies to get the hell out of his office so he could recover from his hangover and work on his current piece.

Instead, he took a deep breath and reminded himself not to yell. Artie might have been a fat, whiny halfwit and a front runner for the 'Micromanager of the Year' award, but still. He'd stood by Tim earlier in the year when the world turned to shit and hence, he didn't deserve to be yelled at.

'Artie,' he said calmly, 'I said I'll do Fiona O'Reilly, who, incidentally, is a tiny, blonde thing with an enormous rack. And more importantly, I *also* happen to like dogs. How many more reasons do you need?'

He shook his head. 'Jesus, Tim. What the hell has happened to my chief ball-buster?'

Oh fuck off already.

'Artie? We've had this conversation.'

'Yeah, yeah. Some shit about you losing your mojo

338

after your Darren Rowley article. But we're done with that. I thought you were getting back up on the horse? And STT is gonna be big . . .'

Tim frowned and scratched mindlessly at the three-day growth he'd unwittingly accumulated during the week. He *was* getting back up on the horse. And the story he was working on was a fucking doozy that would drag him out of obscurity, make all the doubters do a double take and put him firmly back on the front page. But until he was absolutely, one hundred per cent sure that it was ready to go to print – a long bloody way down the track at the rate he was going – he wasn't interested in being distracted by anything else. He'd do the vet with the big tits if it helped Artie out, but that was it.

'Artie, I'm happy to help out with the dailies if you're stuck for staff, but I'm kind of in the middle of something right now and I really don't want to be tied down to anything major. I just want to spend the morning focusing on my police rape piece. It's going really well,' *liar*, 'and I've got an appointment to see someone in an hour who might be able to help me take it to a whole other plane.' *Double liar.* 'So. If I spend the morning on that, I can tee up a time to do the vet later this afternoon.'

Artie scratched his head. 'Oh shit. I forgot you were still working on that. I knew there was something else I had to tell you. I had a drink with a contact of mine whose wife works in the DPP. She told him that apparently the head honcho has binned the case. Reckons there's not enough evidence to prosecute.'

Tim stared slack-jawed, his long-awaited journalistic resurrection, accompanied by a pay rise, new flat, national recognition and barrage of lucrative, big-end job offers, crumbling before his eyes. 'Tell me you're kidding?'

'Sorry. She just found out that Shorty's looked it over, reckoned that there's no reasonable prospect of a conviction and canned it pretty much straightaway. Apparently the girl and Richard Moore had a meeting with him last week and it ended with Moore storming out of the office, steam pouring out of his ears, face like a thundercloud. So, it'll be officially dropped when your man comes up on his first appearance.'

'Today then. His first appearance is this afternoon. And you're telling me it's not even going to make it past the first hurdle?' he cried. 'And more to the point, why the hell am I only just finding this out now?'

'Sorry,' Artie said with a shrug. 'I thought I told you yesterday. I'm getting forgetful in my old age. So. You wanna bin the article or tie it off with that before you go out and do me some real work on the STT story?'

Son of a bitch. No way. No way in hell.

'Just whoa up, Artie. Things like that don't just get binned. It all sounds a bit suss to me. Maybe there's more to it.'

Artie rolled his eyes. 'Or maybe there really just wasn't enough evidence.'

'Bullshit.'

'Why? You got a whiff of something else?'

Yeah. A whole load of horseshit. And it's drifting up from the direction of the DPP.

'I just might have something, Arthur. Leave it with me. I need a moment to stew.'

Artie hovered in the doorway, hands on hips, watching as Tim digested the info.

Tim racked his brain, sifting through every shred of evidence he'd compiled thus far, searching desperately for the angle. There'd be one for sure. There always was. The mother of his child, now firmly ex-girlfriend – 'Fuck Features' as he lovingly referred to her – had spent three years bagging him out for assuming there was a dirty great big conspiracy theory underpinning every single aspect of life. She thought it was a joke. But she didn't know shit. She didn't know humans like he knew humans. Nothing was simple. No one ever said what they meant. And it paid to be a bit paranoid. In fact, paranoia could be a lifesaver at times. And he'd found in his experience that most of the time, *most* of the time, he was right.

This time would be no exception.

Okay. Start at the beginning, Tim. What do you know?

Moore.

DI Richard Moore would have put in a decent file. He was, after all, the best in the business, not to mention thoroughly incorruptible – something Tim knew from firsthand experience. He might have been a bit of a prick at times, but he was incapable of doing up a crap file. Plus, according to Artie, Moore was spewing about the decision. So, the question remained. How the fuck could DI Moore piece together a file and confidently forward it to the DPP for prosecution, only to have Short-Guts himself turn around and say there wasn't enough in it?

He pushed the laptop away and stared mindlessly at the filthy, chipped, brown-ringed coffee cup before him.

Think, Tim, think.

Had Moore just been pandering to the female copper . . . what was her name again . . . Lucy Howard? Had he expected all along that there wasn't enough evidence and had just been placating her? Had he done his best and left it up to someone else to stomp on it and give her the bad news?

No.

Moore had always played it straight down the line. He would have tried to talk her out of it if he knew it was going to get cut off at the knees that early.

So.

Was there something more sinister at play, as tended to be the case when police and pollies were thrown together in this filthy, stinking corrupt little state? Did it by chance – *oh, please, God, make it true* – have something to do with Ron Chalmers? After all, the commish himself had to be satisfied with internal files that related to his members before they crossed the DPP's desk.

A number of tantalising half-formed theories danced through Tim's mind. But in the end, the train of thought petered out. The file *had* made it to the DPP, after all. So it must have crossed Chalmers's desk and kept travelling. It couldn't have been Chalmers interfering. If he hadn't wanted it to go ahead, he would have put a stop to the investigation long before Greaves was ever arrested and charged. And besides, Chalmers never flinched when it came to having coppers charged. Tim remembered his ex-informant Cam Walsh. Recalled him snidely remarking on more than one occasion that Chalmers's favourite motto was 'Let's test it in court.'

Which left one person. The DPP himself. Short-Guts. *David Short.* The repulsive, smarmy turd had made the final call, so ultimately the decision rested with him. And ultimately he had no reason *not* to give it a run in court. *Unless* . . . perhaps the rape case was the latest in the power struggle between him and the commissioner who, by all accounts, hated each other's guts? Chalmers wanted Greaves prosecuted and Short-Guts was sending him the big fuck-offski by not obliging?

Possibly.

Regardless, the only logical conclusion was that the buck stopped with Short-Guts.

It had to be Shorty.

But that felt all wrong. Would he really sabotage something as serious as a rape case just to piss Chalmers off? There had to be more to it. *Dammit.* He closed his eyes and rested his forehead in his hands. Normally Shorty was the first in line to lynch a copper if the opportunity arose. The DPP wasn't jokingly referred to as the Department for Prosecuting Police for nothing.

More to it.

More to it.

More to it.

Blackmail?

No.

What the hell else could it be?

What's the link?

Think logically, Tim.

What if Shorty knew Greaves and had, say, done him a little favour by tossing the file before it hit court? It was a distinct possibility. Tim didn't have much on Greaves. Couldn't even get his hands on a bloody photo, given the nature of the guy's work. But from the digging he *had* done, it was obvious that Greaves moved in some interesting circles. He was a Soggy. A *Son of God* as the wankers called themselves. And that in itself, as far as Tim was concerned, stank to high heaven. There were the old rumours about the traps – unsubstantiated, of course, but always floating out there nonetheless – that members of the SOG had over the years indulged in some rather unsavoury behaviour after hours; hence, why his gut instinct told him that the Greaves rape article had the potential to develop into something huge.

Roids at the gym, all-night eccy binges, swingers' parties. Not such a big deal for Joe Citizen, but a pretty big fucking deal when it came to *Constable* Joe Citizen. And not only *Constable* Joe Citizen, but Constable 'Black Pyjamas, Covert Ops and Tactical Response' Citizen.

There has to be a link.

SOG.

Drugs.

Parties.

Whores.

The strip club.

Ha. Gotcha.

He'd only heard the other day that Shorty's daughter was doing a spot of stripping at the Men's Gallery in order to prop up her PhD studies. He rubbed at his temples again.

God, this fucking state is small.

Now, if he could just link Shorty back to Greaves via his daughter, then . . .

Artie, still lounging by the doorframe, cleared his throat. 'So, what's it to be? You scrapping the article or what?'

He drummed his fingers on the desk and paid court to the distinct feeling of unease that rumbled through his gut like a steam train. 'Nope. Not at all. There's more to this than meets the eye.'

Artie rolled his eyes and threw his hands in the air. 'Put the coffins and the candles away, ladies and gentlemen, my star investigative journalist is back from the dead. Hallelujah, it's a miracle.'

Tim grinned. 'Enough with the sarcasm, old boy. But yes, I *do* have a feeling about this one. Any chance of me skipping the vet so I can spend the day on it?'

'Sure. If her cans are as good as you say they are, then Roddy'll be champing at the bit for the scoop. So long as you dig me up something worthwhile.'

'Thanks, Artie,' he said, watching with a grin as the fat, trusting man toddled off towards his office.

He closed the depressingly skeletal article he'd been working on and clicked back to his research notes, scrolling up to the top of the thirty-odd pages. The article itself, only half a page at this stage, was unimpressive compared to his usual thorough spreads. And it was pissing him off. He had rumours galore and had been working his backside off since the day Greaves had been arrested and charged. The problem was, he'd been stonewalled every time he attempted verification. Even on the tiniest details. Hardly surprising, but fucking infuriating nevertheless.

It'd been like that ever since his Darren Rowley article had broken. His masterpiece. The one he'd used to defend the kid and attack the system that had created him. The one that had publicly cast doubt on his alleged guilt regarding the killing of the cop. He'd been stonewalled and ostracised for the past six months. *Six fucking months.* Oh, every man and his dog was initially kissing his arse when he was the first one to put two and two together and give the tip about the Rowley boys being in custody for killing the copper, but sure enough, they'd all turned on him. Each in their own way, for their own petty, selfish reasons. His best informant, Cam Walsh, who hadn't appreciated the way he'd used his info, the police themselves who blamed Tim's article for influencing a magistrate into granting Darren bail, thereby being in a position to get flogged, thereby never facing the consequences of his actions. Now instead of helpful tip-offs and access to crime scenes, he was met with silences, blank faces and turned backs wherever he went. Even bloody Judy Rowley herself had turned on him. If he hadn't written the stupid article in the first place, then her boy would still be locked up safe and sound in a cell. He'd be out of harm's way. He wouldn't have been flogged and turned into a vegie. And with her powerful Aboriginal friends in high places, there'd also been mention of suing him and the paper at one stage.

Even the bloggers on the *Mirror* website had turned on him, labelling him a 'coon-loving cunt who ought to fuck off out to the bush and live with his new mates'.

No. The Rowley article had brought his brilliant career to a dirty great big screeching halt and the flow-on effects had been annoying at best, disastrously obstructive at worst.

In fact, it was game, set and fucking match. He'd been well and truly nobbled by an entire town that'd closed its doors on him. And as he'd downed beer after beer after beer alone, in his cold, miserable flat, unable to face the pubs, he realised that he was an investigative journo with fuck-all sources and a month-long hangover to boot.

A lesser man would have curled up and admitted defeat, but once he sobered up and returned to work after his Artie-enforced 'holiday' he decided that he wasn't a lesser man. And eventually, after much consideration, he'd formulated a plan of attack.

It was simple. He'd lie low, avoid the crime stories, ride out the hate, stick with the mind-numbing dailies and in a few months, when everything had blown over, he'd get back into real investigative journalism. Like a savvy celebrity who gets sprung with a nose full of blow, a hooker on his knob or his fist in his missus's face, he, Tim Roberts, would keep his mouth shut, his head down and quietly await his comeback.

And for a few months, it'd been looking good. He'd success-fully faded into the obscurity of agriculture shows, local food festivals, regional cricket finals and family reunions.

But then things changed. The rape scoop had come a-knocking. And he could hardly ignore it.

The second he heard about it he trembled with that long-forgotten wave of exhilaration. It was his ticket back into the game. Regretfully, it was a smidge too soon – as was made evident by the fact that even though he'd been working his backside off night and day, he'd made bugger-all headway. Thirty pages of research for half a substantiated page of article.

Ron Chalmers was making no comment, Richard Moore refused to return his calls and even Jack Peters, the official police media liaison officer refused to give anything more than the stock-standard half a sentence. An officer had made a complaint and another officer, one of the SOG, had been charged and was bailed to a court date a few weeks down the track. That was it.

Despite begging for some off-the-record snippets – anything would have done – Peters had dismissed him, not coldly, like all the others, but dismissed him all the same. And despite hitting up another usually trusty old contact who was rumoured to be representing the copper, he'd been completely blown off by a single-line, fuck-off text from Andy Woods.

Client–solicitor privilege.

Not even a fucking 'sorry, buddy'.

Before the day was done, he'd given up entirely on official sources. It was only then that slowly, excruciatingly slowly, a couple of inconsequential pieces of the puzzle manoeuvred themselves into position.

He'd rung the Glenorchy gym where he knew a few of the SOG meatheads worked out. *Apollos.* But had been given a very swift 'fuck off' by whoever it was who had picked up the phone.

Not to be deterred though, he'd then contacted a mate's cousin who happened to have a friend in the Drug Squad, and that time he'd struck gold. He'd managed to find out the names of those involved, the fact that the chick, none other than the poor unlucky cow who'd been on duty the very day the copper was killed, was alleging rape and the possibility that there were drugs involved. From Terry, the longstanding security guy at the courthouse, a man who was always happy to oblige if the deal involved a fudge brownie from the local cafe, he'd learned that the chick was shagging his ex-informant Cameron Walsh, it was some sort of threesome gone wrong well before he went to jail and that they were all stoned at the time. But the story trail stopped cold after that. And his mind turned to Walsh. Angry, screaming Walsh. Walsh who'd torn him a new arsehole for allegedly misusing the info he'd leaked him about Rowley.

Perhaps he hadn't meant it when he'd told him to sod off and never contact him again. It was definitely worth a try.

The second he'd got off the phone to Terry he rang the Hobart remand centre, only to be politely rebuffed. Mr Walsh did not wish to speak with him or see him.

He slammed down the phone, knowing it was pointless to argue. He picked up a photo from the file and stared at it, meditating. It was a snap of *her*. The chick. Published in the *Mercury* the day the copper was killed. She was being led away from the scene, pale, dishevelled and zombie-like, but it gave him a rough likeness nonetheless. He needed to know more about her. Her personal life.

Within the next twenty-four hours he'd got hold of her uni records, knew she'd graduated third in her police recruit course and surmised, rather frustratingly, that she wasn't into any form of social networking, judging from the complete lack of an electronic fingerprint on the Net.

The big breakthrough came when he tracked down her parents' house in West Hobart, courtesy of old Con Sorotos. Con, the subject of one of his earlier family reunion pieces, had a brother Dimitri who happened to run the West Hobart Deli and felt sure that the girl's family lived just around the corner on Warwick Street. What's more, according to his wife, there was a daughter living with them.

But when he'd banged on the door of the red-brick bungalow he was disappointed to be greeted by a prim, tight-mouthed carbon copy of Quentin Bryce in canary yellow.

The mother.

It has to be.

'Hello, my name is Tim Roberts and I'm from the *Mirror*. Is Lucy in, please?' he'd asked, flashing his ID quickly in her face.

She paused, not bothering to hide her tight-lipped disapproval as she gave him the once-over. 'May I ask what it's about?'

'I'd really rather speak with her directly . . . Mrs Howard, I presume?'

'I make a point of never presuming anything, Mr Roberts. And no, she's not in. Perhaps if you leave a card . . .'

'I'd rather not,' he said hurriedly. There was no way on earth she'd call him back if he left a card. 'If she's not in, then perhaps I could come in and ask you some questions in relation to a matter I'm investigating at the mo –'

'I'm sorry, Mr Roberts. But the only people I speak with in relation to investigations are the police. As I said, if you'd be so kind as to leave a card, I will make sure that Lucy receives it. Now, if there's nothing else . . .'

Bitch.

'Well actually, Mrs Howard, there is. That graffiti on your front wall . . .'

'Random vandals, Mr Roberts. Nothing more.'

'But they specifically name your daughter. Don't you think it's a bit . . .?'

'As I said, vandals. Considering your profession, Mr Roberts, you are no doubt well aware that my daughter is a police officer. Police officers incur the wrath of the lower classes who are generally unable to express themselves in what you and I would consider a polite, civilised manner. Hence, the graffiti.'

'But . . .'

'But nothing. I'm sorry if that answer isn't to your liking, but I really think you should leave now,' she said firmly.

Snooty bitch. Time to play the cards.

'So it has nothing to do with the rape allegation your daughter has made?'

She bristled visibly beneath her perfect grey coif and he hid his grin. He'd rattled her. But before he had time to capitalise on her surprise, she kicked his foot out of the way in a most undignified, un-Quentin Bryce-ish manner and slammed the door in his face.

Conniving, rude, snooty bitch.

He knocked and begged for a few minutes but was met with silence. *Lucy has to be in there.* Scheming, he sat on the front doorstep and lit a smoke in the hope of luring the stuck-up old bat out with annoyance. She'd be sure to go apeshit over something as 'lower class' as smoking. But no such luck. Not even a twitch of the curtains.

When he got to the butt he stamped it out, raked a hand through his wild hair and considered his options. He scoped the windows and the back door but was met at every turn with fully drawn curtains and blinds. At one of the side windows – *a bedroom perhaps* – there was the vaguest of movements from inside, the shuffle of shoes on wooden floorboards, hushed, unintelligible conversation, but no more sign of life for the day. Clearly, the Howards didn't want to chat.

And after spending a while hunched in his car sucking down smoke after smoke and tossing the butts out the window, he'd come up with a big fat fuck-all. There was no sign of the purple Hyundai Excel that the Transport Department reported as being registered in Lucy's name.

And it continued to drive him nuts.

He'd snapped a handful of pictures of the front fence with the graffiti scrawled across it, a couple of the mother and presumably the father coming and going but he still hadn't managed to catch sight of the chick herself. So he was reduced to her workplace.

A place he dreaded. A place that made his stomach churn at the mere thought of it. And when he'd rung on the pretence of being a complainant in a stealing matter, he'd been politely informed that she was on duty that afternoon and that he should ring back or pop in.

His stomach flip-flopped at the thought of finally meeting her in person.

But when he strolled through the front doors of the police station, cap down over his face – *just to be sure* – and requested to see Constable Lucy Howard regarding a theft matter she was investigating for him, the constable at the front counter hesitated before calling in a fat, grey-haired senior connie who recognised him immediately.

'Better bugger-off quick smart, sunshine, unless you want to be charged with trespassing. Oh. And if you set foot back in here again, I can't guarantee we'll be as polite.'

He'd sighed, stuck his hands in his pockets and left.

Thwarted again.

But if anything, it made him more determined.

After a bit more thought and a few beers, he reconsidered his angle of attack. Following his run-in at the police station, he thought it might be prudent to have another crack at the gym. This time in person. Not as a journo, but undercover, in an attempt to glean the gossip around the traps. Thus, with renewed confidence, he'd traipsed up the front stairs of the gym, took a deep breath and pushed the door open.

An unlikely surge of trepidation fluttered in his gut. It was unfamiliar territory. The old Tim, the pre-Rowley article Tim, didn't give a rat's arse about unfamiliar spaces, but the new Tim, the hypervigilant, anticipate-trouble-at-all-costs Tim, shuddered. The front area was quiet. In the distance he heard the steady thumping bass of work-out music, the clanging of weight bars against stands and a referee's whistle. He closed his eyes and breathed through his nose. It smelled like sweat, cleaning agents and the fear of ageing. He hesitated, knowing he stood out like dog's nuts. He looked just plain daggy in his ratty green T-shirt, left over from his university days, and old pair of footy shorts, so excruciatingly tight they squashed his balls and nearly cut him in half. But there was no going back now.

Suck it up, buddy.

He adjusted his sack, berated himself for being a total pussy and took a step towards the front desk.

'I'd like to apply for a membership, please,' he asked, flashing a smile at the hulking, heavy-set grunt with the shaved head who bore more than a passing resemblance to full-forward legend Barry Hall.

The giant stared at him and frowned. 'You're that journalist.'

Fuck me.

'Um . . . look, I really don't think that has anything to do with . . .'

'We don't take your kind here,' the giant growled before pulling up his seat and returning to the body building magazine he'd been studying when Tim had first strolled through the door.

'Um . . . there's obviously been some sort of misunder-standing. I just want to apply for . . .'

The giant casually shut the magazine and rose from his seat.

'Maybe you didn't hear me right.'

Tim swallowed. 'Look. I haven't done anything wrong. I just wanted . . .'

The protest died in his throat as a pair of chrome-domed doppelgangers emerged from the weights room and perched beside their mate at the counter. Tim fixed his gaze on their biceps – freshly ripped, glistening with sweat and fucking monstrous.

Been in there bench pressing a mini-van, fellas?

'Problem, Harry?' one of them asked the front desk guy.

'No problem, boys. Our journo friend was just leaving.'

Goon number one chuckled and cracked a knuckle. 'Yeah. We were warned you'd be sniffing around.'

Tim's legs trembled in his silly little shorts. He imagined how it might feel if their fists connected with his nose. It would hurt, all right. There'd be a sudden, sickening splat, followed by immeasurable pain and the warm ooze of his own blood as it dripped down his chin. He trembled again.

Goon number two leaned in close and Tim recoiled at the stench of sweat, halitosis and hint of stale garlic. Somewhere in the mix was the unpalatable odour of his own raw fear. 'Best to do as Harry says then. And consider it a friendly warning, but if we ever catch you sniffing around here again, we'll bench press your scrawny arse all the way to Timbuktu. Got it?'

He nodded, unable to form an intelligible syllable, and fled out the front door and down the bright blue front stairs before they changed their minds and decided to take a less friendly approach.

Once safely halfway down the block he composed himself and blinked with astonishment at what had just passed, wondering if he'd somehow inadvertently walked onto the set of a Guy Ritchie movie, complete with a thug named Harry.

They'd known he was coming.

Apparently the campaign against him was more widespread and prolonged than he could have imagined.

Fuck.

No one was budging and unless something changed quickly and drastically, he wasn't going to have a story. All those wasted hours for nothing.

After a few more beers, a load more scheming and a number of discreet inquiries – *discreet enough to ensure he didn't end up a smooshed pulp on the end of a roided-up giant's fist* – about the whereabouts of the defendant Nick Greaves himself, his mate's cousin's friend reported back that he'd been suspended from work and had buggered off to the mainland.

Another dead end.

In a final, desperate attempt to penetrate the inner sanctum Tim sent a dozen red roses to the commissioner's PA with an anonymous love note attached. Whoever she was, she'd be a civilian – one step removed from coppers, one step removed from their arrogant, unabiding hostility. She would know stuff. Perhaps, like most civvies in the police building, she'd be a gossip.

Hopefully.

He hovered out on Liverpool Street at knock-off time, watching as the peak-hour traffic bumped and ground its way up Argyle Street, the afternoon already gloomy courtesy of winter. It didn't take long to spot her: short red bob, tight arse and arm full of red roses. She stepped out onto Liverpool Street, waved goodbye to a colleague and turned left onto Argyle. He grinned to himself and followed, catching up to her and pausing beside her as she stopped at the lights on the corner of Bathurst.

'Beautiful flowers. You must have done something right to get those,' he said, flashing her his flirtiest smile. The one he'd practised in the mirror as a teenager. It accentuated his dimples, made him appear a bit boyish, cute and a little vulnerable even – or so Fuck Features had told him once.

The PA was even prettier close up. But she looked him up and down coolly, and he knew it was over before the words even escaped her lips.

'You're that journalist, aren't you?'

Before he could protest, the pedestrian light turned green and she stalked off. Her high heels clacked up the road leaving him dumbstruck on the corner. A fast-flowing sea of commuters grumbled as they stepped around him and trudged across the street towards their cars, homes and hearty winter dinners.

It was no good. He was persona non grata in good old Hobart town and there was fuck-all he could do about it.

He'd made his way home, shoulders slumped, and over yet another few lonely beers, had conceded that perhaps it was time to admit defeat.

Over the following two weeks he'd realised that the story was pretty much rooted. There was no other source to hit up, contrary to the lie he'd told Artie. He had no way in. Judging from the amount of doors that had been slammed in his face from one side of the Derwent to the other, his career as an investigative journo was fucked and he was faced with the ultimate cold, hard, sobering reality. Perhaps he wasn't going to be able to write his way out of the state and on to bigger and better things. Perhaps he was destined to remain in his shitty flat with his crappy, badly paid job, exorbitant maintenance payments, and nothing to look forward to except the prospect of drinking himself into a coma every night. And with that thought, he had reached for the bottle of Scotch up the top of the kitchen cupboard, the one he kept for emergencies.

And that had been yesterday. By the next morning, after four Scotches and two Stilnox tablets, or white dreams as he lovingly referred to them, it had come time to face one more cold hard reality. He was consumed by the mother of all hangovers, which was accompanied by the tired, dry, numbing fog of the sleeping tablets. A car door shutting three blocks away felt like his head was being slammed between two metal garbage lids. His mouth tasted like a piece of carpet covered in ten years' worth of dust mites and dog hair and despite the double-shot espresso, his eyelids were like a pair of fishing weights.

Not only was he monumentally depressed about his future prospects, but he was depressed and hung-over. A delightful combination. Two more espressos, a splash of cold water and a shitload of codeine later, he was feeling marginally more professional. He was resolved to sit at his desk, spend the next couple of days finishing the rape piece to the best of his ability, submit it to Artie and move on to something else.

Which is where he found himself when Artie dropped the perfect clanger fair in his lap and fired him up all over again.

The case had been dumped – something that was bound to create new leads. Somebody would want to talk. It was just a matter of finding out who. It was time to regroup, reassess and go grab the story – *the real story* – by the nuts.

As he filled his coffee mug again with the cheap nasty instant shit from the kitchen, he paced the hallway back to his desk.

Who to hit up?

Who to hit up?

Of all the arseholes up at police HQ, Richard Moore was most likely to give him something. It was, after all, his case and he might, at the very least, talk about how disappointed he was about it being pulled.

Time for round two. Ding, ding, ding. He's back, ladies and gentlemen.

Feeling marginally more cheerful, he took another sip of his coffee, scrolled down his contacts list and dialled the CIB front desk number.

'Hobart CIB, Lexie speaking, how may I help you?'

He cleared his throat. 'Oh, hi, Lexie. It's . . . ah . . . Stan Johns here. I'm a . . . a . . . friend of Detective Inspector Moore's and I was wondering if I could talk to him, please?'

'I'm sorry, Mr Johns, but he's busy at the moment.'

'Look. If I could just talk to him, it's really impor –'

'Um, I mean it, Mr Johns. He's *really* busy. It's been a heck of a couple of days here,' she said with a breathy sigh.

'If you could just give me his mobile then . . .'

'I'm sorry, Mr Johns. I can't do that. And as much as I hate to point out the obvious, if you're a friend of his, as you say, shouldn't you already have his mobile?'

Bitch.

'Of course I had it, but silly me, I've gone and lost it, haven't I?' he said with a self-deprecating laugh.

'Oh well, I'll let him know that you, his *friend*, called and have him call you back then, shall I?'

He sighed. Richard Moore would never return his call. Not only was he busy, but he would probably chuck the number in the bin thinking it was just some psycho who claimed to be a friend. But seeing no other way around it he gave the girl his mobile number and slammed the phone down in frustration.

What to do?

What to do?

Perhaps if he spoke with Ron Chalmers himself, then he could persuade the grumpy old fuck that he'd like to do an article on it with a positive spin, something about Tasmania Police having a squeaky-clean reputation and how the DPP had made the correct decision. The old man might just be insane enough to listen to reason and spill some inadvertent beans in the process. Chalmers hated his guts – nothing was more sure – but he was always grasping at ways to get a bit of positive PR. The more he thought about it, the more he liked the idea and hey, worst-case scenario, Ron could always tell him to fuck off, a suggestion he was getting well and truly used to by now.

So scrolling through his numbers again he hit 'commissioner's office' and stared out the window while it rang. He tapped his feet as he counted the calls. One. Two. Three. Four. Five. Six. Seven. Eight.

Just as he was convinced it was about to go to message bank, a slightly breathless female picked it up.

'Commissioner Chalmers's office, Jillian speaking.'

Ah. So your name is Jillian then.

Thinking once more of her tight arse, he adopted his most ingratiating voice. 'Hi, Jillian. It's Tim Roberts here. Please can you just hear me out before you hang up? I need to talk to . . .'

'No, you can't! Jack Peters will be issuing a statement later on today if you're interested. So please don't ring back here again,' she snapped, hanging up and leaving him scratching his head.

What the fuck? Was it that big a deal that they were finally going to release something a bit more substantial?

Puzzled, he took another sip of coffee, removed the phone from his ear one more time and scrolled down to Peters's number. If nothing else, he could get the scoop and might even con Jack into giving away a few more juicy details over the phone.

This time the phone rang six times before an extremely harassed-sounding Jack answered.

'Yes?' he said curtly.

'Jack. Maaaate. How are you? Tim Roberts here.'

'Oh fucking hell, mate, not already?'

Tim frowned. *Already? What the?* Something in Jack's tone told him to play along rather than launching straight into him about the unsuccessful rape case.

He gave a casual, friendly laugh. 'Sorry, old boy, but you know what we're like when we get a whiff of something.'

'What I want to know is how the hell you even get your whiffs?'

'Ah, can't go giving away my sources now, Jacky boy, can I?'

'I've gotta say, Tim, I'm abso-fucking-lutely amazed. They haven't even finished processing him yet and already there's a leak. This place . . . fuck me. You know the saying "leaks like a sieve"? Well, this place leaks like . . . like . . . oh fuck. I don't know what I'm talking about. I need sleep and a coffee.'

Finished processing him?

What the fuck?

This wasn't about the rape.

This was something completely different and, judging by the tone of his voice, not to mention Jillian's, this is something big.

His stomach gave the familiar lurch of excitement.

Play along.

Keep it casual.

Processing. He strained his memory of police lingo. That meant fingerprinting, photographing and DNA swabbing – the processes that took place following an arrest.

Play along.

361

'Sorry, Jack. I wanted to jump in quickly though. Just to make sure the info is correct and that they're not putting shit about. He's been arrested then?' Tim asked innocently.

'Yeah. He has. Yeah. They picked him up before dawn.'

'Oh,' he said, racking his brain to come up with something else that wouldn't give away the fact that he had no idea what they were talking about.

'Um . . . any word on the exact charges yet?'

Jack sighed on the other end of the line, obviously hesitant to give anything away.

'Look, Jack, it's all going to be out today anyway, so all I'm asking for is a tiny scoop, yeah?'

'Okay, okay. Something to do with breaches of the code of conduct for divulging information, perverting the course of justice and possibly blackmail. But that didn't come from me, all right?'

Tim ran an agitated hand through his hair. Whatever was going on *was* huge. It was obviously a copper, but who?

'Of course not, Jack. Um . . . how's he taking it? Off the record, of course.'

Jack laughed wearily. 'Of course. Well, you know our delightful commissioner – swearing, screaming, cursing and threatening till you can see the steam pouring from his ears. Refused to do an interview, so he'll be charged with that as well. Coppers don't have the same rights as your normal run-of-the-mill scumbag. I don't envy Richard Moore one little bit at the moment, but hey, they had a job to do and looks like they've done it well. As usual.'

Tim almost dropped his mobile in shock. *Ron Chalmers arrested? Jesus H. Christ!* He pushed his chair back from the desk and hightailed it towards Artie's office.

362

'So what's next for the old goat then?' he asked, trying not to betray the tremble of excitement in his voice.

'He's due in court around 2.30, 2.45ish. He'll get bail, of course – there's not going to be any opposition to it – but it'll be fairly embarrassing all the same. Look, Tim, we're trying to keep it as low key as possible, yeah? Can you just do me a favour and wait till I've got this press release organised before you do your usual bull-at-a-gate thing? Just give me an hour or so,' he pleaded.

'Of course, mate,' Tim said, his mind working overtime, wondering if he had time to grab a bite to eat before hitting the courts to see if they had any of the paperwork yet.

'Oh, and by the way, just to save me another phone call, let your boss know that it'll all be okay as far as he's concerned. I believe they're going to add something to his bail document about not approaching him directly or indirectly, not that Ron would anyway. But, you know, just to be sure.'

'Ah, yeah. No worries, mate,' he said, puzzled. 'Absolutely. Leave it with me.'

'Thanks, Tim, I'll chat to you later.'

'See you, Jack,' he said, hanging up the phone and barging straight into Artie's office.

'Since when did knocking on a door go out of fashion?' Artie growled, looking up over his glasses.

'Oh, trust me, boss, you're not going to give a fat rat's arse about knocking when you hear what I just found out,' he said.

'All right, all right, you got my attention, so spill.'

He gave a lengthy dramatic pause, watching Artie's face for his reaction.

'Ron Chalmers has been arrested.'

Artie pushed his glasses back up with his middle finger and returned to his paperwork. 'Oh. Already? I got the impression it'd be a few more days yet.'

Tim felt like a balloon that'd had a gigantic pin stuck in it.

'You *knew* this was going to happen and didn't tell me?' he stuttered.

'Sure.'

'But . . . but . . . *why*? And more to the point, what the hell does it have to do with you?'

Artie sighed and laid his pen down. 'Look. It was an ongoing investigation, to do partially with that government corruption article of yours that I couldn't print. Remember when I told you there was a good reason why I couldn't print it and that you'd just have to trust me?'

Oh yes. The government corruption article.

The one you shelved months ago for no good reason.

The one that could have opened doors for me.

'Yeah?' he said with a twinge of irritation.

'Well, Chalmers was blackmailing me. Told me to can it or else he'd expose certain information that he had on me.'

Tim dragged out a chair and slumped into it, trying to take it all in. 'You serious?'

'No. I'm fucking with you, Tim. Whadda you reckon? Of course I'm serious. Your article was right, Tim. You were onto him. You'd brought to light his connections with the Premier and a handful of other dirty pollies for that matter. But you'd only touched the tip of the proverbial iceberg. Looks like our friend the commissioner was in it up to his neck – looking

364

after his mates, passing on classified information, making things disappear . . . You get the picture?'

'But, but . . . how do you know all this?'

'I happened to let it slip to Shorty a while ago. You know how he feels about Chalmers. Well, he couldn't wait to launch an investigation into it, to see the grin wiped off our friend's face once and for all. Your article gave him the initial ammo he needed and he took it from there, set up a covert task force and, well, sounds like they finally had enough to pick him up on,' he said with a shrug.

'So every time I gave you the shits about why you weren't running with the article . . . ?'

'I was working on a way to do it proper justice.'

Well, fuck me. The fat man did good. And here I was doubting him.

'And now?'

'And now, you'd better go out and get the details so you can make the front of the paper with it tomorrow.' He smiled.

'You're gonna use it?'

'Sure. We'll need to be careful though. I don't want a repeat of the Rowley saga. We can't be seen to even be remotely doing anything that might prejudice the hearing.'

'Wouldn't dream of it. The chance to see Ron Chalmers finally caught with his trousers around his ankles is too good an incentive.'

'Good to hear. And if we can't use it all tomorrow, then we'll look at it for sometime down the track – as a supplement, a feature, something to follow up your piece on him tomorrow.'

Tim beamed. Finally. *Finally.* He was going to get his chance to shine.

'*You* . . . are a *fucking* legend, Artie. I won't let you down.'

'I know you won't. Now piss off out of here. Haven't you got a date up at court?'

'Sure do, boss. Sure do,' he said, whirling back towards the door, his only thought, to race up to the court building and secure prime position in the press gallery.

At 2.30 pm on the dot, Tim was politely turfed out of the hearing room along with every other interested member of the public, as the magistrate had directed a closed court. He'd half expected it, given it was, after all, the biggest event in the recent history of Tasmania Police. So it was time to instigate plan B. He fled from the corridor down the escalator and out onto the front stairs where he proceeded to secure the prime position. Jack had assured him that Ron wouldn't piss off out the back entrance once he was done. The big cheese was keen to make a statement.

As he waited, the minutes stretched out into eternity. He glanced at his watch at least once every minute, his mind ticking over at the thought of what was going on behind the closed doors of courtroom one. He smoked cigarette after cigarette, holding each one between his lips while he rubbed his hands together to stop them from freezing as the wind cut through Liverpool Street sending discarded cigarette butts and a lone polystyrene cup sailing along in the gutters. His frustration grew as the precious minutes rolled by.

Every two seconds a different news crew set up below him. *Pricks*. The secret was out. Huey the cameraman from

WIN TV was scoffing down a steaming-hot pie and whinge-ing about the fact that his latest privately made exposé on the forestry industry was being ignored because of various powerful magnates lurking within all the stations he'd tried to pitch it to; Wendy from TTT FM fought with her offsider about whose turn it was to do a coffee run; Danny Minchin, his nemesis from the *Mercury*, made his fifteenth comment about how this felt like the coldest winter on record and Deidra Hollingsworth from Southern Cross had a loud conversation on her mobile with her best friend about what a jerk her most recent and unfortunately still married boyfriend was turning out to be.

Every few minutes Tim flinched, prepared to move into action as the doors swung around and someone new scurried past the waiting throng.

A tall, good-looking guy in an expensive suit, distinctly out of the ordinary in that environment, followed by a taller, muscly blond guy and an attractive chick in stilettos.

Not your usual magistrates court customer, he thought, eyeing them up and down.

A morbidly obese twenty-something woman in Uggs and a flannie, giving the finger to the media.

A scruffy, fifty-something in a lumberjack beanie and coffee-stained windcheater clutching something that looked like a bail notice.

A scowling teenager in rugby top and scuffed sneakers.

A pasty-faced, druggie-thin chick, baby clutched over her shoulder, lighting up a smoke as she took her first step outside.

Pissed off at the constant chatter of the ever-growing pack around him, Tim lit up his fourth and peered through the thick glass of the revolving doors again, the pattern now becoming monotonous. Glance at watch, peer through glass doors, drag on cigarette.

Where are you, you nasty old goat?

Changed your mind?

Going through the back door, after all?

As he took another drag, wrapped his jacket tighter and glared at the rival crews on the steps, he frowned, thinking it more and more unlikely that Chalmers would show. He was bound to be humiliated. It was far more likely that he'd slink out unnoticed and get Jack to do up the obligatory palaver later on in the day to be sent out to the press en masse. He shook his head, pissed off at the thought and looked down the stairs at the waiting media once more.

Pack of fucking vultures.

At the bottom of the stairs, however, on the footpath, he paused, his gaze falling on a young woman in a red coat. She'd stopped to watch the circus that had gathered on the stairs, an odd look crossing her face. *Concern? Bewilderment? Anxiety?* He couldn't pinpoint the exact expression. But there was something familiar about her. Her dark ponytail and wide-set eyes were vaguely familiar. If she'd been about ten kilos heavier, he could have sworn . . .

But before the thought had finished crossing his mind, the revolving door opened and the collective throng of a dozen chatting, laughing, bitching local media turned and burst into a chaotic kerfuffle around him. Food and drink was hurriedly discarded, mobiles were unglued from ears and the throng pushed forwards as the cry went up.

'He's coming out!'

Tim snapped his mind back into work mode and switched on his DAT as Ron Chalmers, flanked by his red-headed PA, Jack Peters and lawyer Andy Woods – *the unreliable, back-stabbing prick himself* – strode through the door and out onto the top landing. Woods placed a hand on Chalmers's arm and whispered something in his ear before turning and heading back into court.

Instead of appearing flustered, disconcerted and terrified as Tim had hoped he might, the commissioner was as un-fucking-readable as a Dickens novel. He assumed his well-rehearsed press conference poker face and waited until a hush settled over the crowd before commencing.

'Ladies and gentlemen, I'll keep it brief. As you may or may not be aware, this morning at approximately 5 am I was arrested by members of the Hobart Criminal Investi-gation Branch in relation to an inquiry regarding allegations of improper conduct involving members of the Tasmanian government. I have been interviewed and charged and a short time ago I received bail. I would like to make clear from the outset that I will be vigorously defending these charges. I am guilty of nothing other than doing my job as the police commis-sioner of Tasmania. One of the most important aspects of that job is liaising with government officials. I have at all times acted within the confines of the law and with the best interests of the people of Tasmania in mind. That said, I understand that my members have a job to do and I plan on cooperating fully with the investigation.

'Further to that, on advice from the Governor himself, I have decided that it is in the best interests of justice if I temporarily abrogate my responsibilities as commissioner of police by standing aside until such a time as the matter is concluded. I will say nothing more on the matter today.

'Thank you.'

The crowd exploded in a burst of questions and camera clicks.

'Commissioner Chalmers,' Tim yelled, shoving his DAT almost directly in Ron's face. 'You talk about improper conduct; what about the blackmail charge involving Arthur Myers?'

Ron ignored him and jostled his way down the stairs towards a waiting black Statesman. But there was no way in hell Tim was giving up that easily.

'Commissioner, is it true you've been doing favours for the Premier?'

He pushed through the crowd, following hot on Chalmers's heels but Ron kept his head down, his face grim and his lips closed.

'Commissioner, is it true you made threats against the officers investigating you? Have you been charged with blackmail? Do you intend to keep all your perks while you stand down . . .?'

But it was a losing battle. Chalmers cracked the door open, slid himself into the comfy leather seat of the waiting car and, despite the surge of media, slammed the door shut and drove off along Liverpool Street at speed, leaving them all shaking their heads.

Arsehole.

I will get your story if it kills me.

He grabbed for the mobile in his pocket and hastily dialled Artie's number.

'Myers?'

'It's me. Do you still have that contact inside the Premier's office, the one who gave me the original inside goss for my corruption scoop?'

'Yeah. Why?'

'Ring him. Find out where the Premier is. I want to offer him the exclusive on this. Give him a chance to tell his side of the story and distance himself publicly from Chalmers.'

Artie laughed. 'Leave it with me. I'll call you back asap.'

Tim slammed the phone shut and paced frantically as he contemplated his next move.

The DPP.

It had to be the DPP who was behind the Chalmers investigation.

He needed to talk with Shorty himself.

Now.

The phone rang and Artie's name flashed on his screen. He answered and began quickly laying out the game plan, the blow-by-blow strategy that would give him the exclusive of the year. As he spoke, oblivious to the rest of the world turning around him, he looked up and noted, then immediately forgot the girl who he'd seen at the bottom of the court building stairs only minutes before. But as he ran another hand through his hair and cursed Artie for the delay in getting his interview – *no, it has to be tonight for fuck's sake, tomorrow is no good* – she turned away, stuck her hands in her pockets and walked down Liverpool Street, the winter shadows growing longer, the wind whipping at her red winter coat.

The Soggy
Courtroom Two: Hobart Magistrates Court
2.10 pm Friday 22 July

He inhaled, wiped his sweaty palms down his well-cut suit trousers and tried to look composed. He knew what was coming, that it was only good, but it was unsettling nevertheless. Just sitting in the front row, waiting for your name to be called, *like some filthy rotten bogan piece of shit*, was enough to make any self-respecting copper want to puke. Beside him, sensing his unease, Chrissy gave him a reassuring little pat on one hand. On the other side Dan glanced around the room disinterestedly and fished in his top pocket for another Tic Tac.

'Good crowd,' he whispered, offering the box.

And he was right. Nick had already scanned the benches and noted his loyal band of supporters. Half-a-dozen blokes from the watch, in uniform – Chalmers would have a shit fit about that, no doubt – Gillsy, Tex, Coops and Rosco from SOG, a couple of brass who'd given him a nod and a wink on the way in, a handful of Traffic guys and even Costa Tsiolkas. The poor bastard might have been on stress leave but even he'd made the effort to come along, take him aside and whisper his best wishes before they'd headed in. It was enough to make anyone feel warm and fuzzy.

Compared to him, the Howard bitch had no one. She hadn't even fucking bothered to turn up. Hardly bloody surprising considering what was about to happen. Shorty, the fat fuck, was at the bar table and Wheeler, the fucking dyke bitch from Internals, sat in the back row snarling.

Whatever.

Moore and Torino had been late, only crashing through the door a few minutes earlier, but they'd made straight for the dyke – *oh, how predictable* – and took up positions nearby. His lawyer, Andy Woods, had been similarly late and out of breath by the time he'd arrived, thrown his gear on the table and cracked the file open.

Nick twitched, looked at his watch and listened to the low rumble of chatter around him. Magistrate Hudson was the only one left to arrive. Then all the players would be assembled and they could get on with this farce. The one that should never have come to this. The one that had taken over his entire fucking life and almost, *almost* resulted in him losing everything. And there was only one person to blame.

Lucy Howard.

Lucy crybaby fucking Howard.

He closed his eyes, let the hum of chatter fade into oblivion and cast his mind back to the moment it had all begun.

373

The police academy. The two-week Detective Training Course. May.

He'd singled her out on day one of the course. The second he set foot in the room and dumped his gear on the desk bearing his name tag. It was, conveniently, the desk beside hers. And from that very moment he'd scrutinised her every move. He studied her the way a leopard, crouched on a tree branch ten metres in the air, studies a tiny, lone springbok wandering aimlessly below the canopy, blissfully unaware of the danger above. Two weeks. Just biding his time. After all, there was no hurry. And during the two weeks, he noted and methodically filed every facial expression, every twitch, every sigh, every lost stare off into space, every stuttered answer to a question and every clumsy stumble.

The lack of laughter, the hunched shoulders, the silent, lonely meals and the look of agony that crossed her face every time the lecturer suggested a group activity, had given him plenty of ins. He'd jumped at every chance to hold a door open for her, direct his jokes towards her, always with a smile and a wink. Most importantly, he'd seized upon every available opportunity to 'norm' her. And when it came to norming, Nick Greaves considered himself a champion. It was a passion, a hobby, an amusing pastime. He'd needed no pointers or reminders and had sat back lazily in his chair, smirking as the lecturer coincidentally raised the topic during the second week.

'Study your suspect with the aim of becoming their best friend prior to the interview,' DI Richard Moore had said, pacing the length of the stuffy wood-panelled classroom. 'They are more likely to provide you with information if they get the impression you're their best friend. Metaphorically speaking, if you smack a crook in the head, they're not going to want to be your friend. If you're a prick to them, they'll be a prick back. And yes, ladies and gentlemen, I know they're mostly pricks anyway, even without any provocation, but the thing is, if you at least *try* to norm them, then you might just get a result. I'm sorry if this is teaching you how to suck eggs, but from time to time we forget to employ this most important, basic skill. And as important as it is to practise it in everyday policing, it's even more important when it comes to CIB. There's more at stake. Bigger fish.'

He paused, eyes washing over the class.

'If they smoke, give them a cigarette. Do they like Macca's? Send a connie down to grab some burgers. Find out their favourite band, engage them in conversation about it, ask them questions, nod, make *them* feel like the expert. Do they hate their wife at the moment? Funny that, you're also going through woman troubles with your bitch ex-wife from hell. Money problems? I know. Banks are all corrupt. Those bastards getting the dirty great big fat golden handshakes need a bullet.

'What else? Is he a breast man?' *A titter ran through the class.* 'Alert him to the finest pair on the street. And don't forget, it's not just about hobbies. Norming also relates to language and body language. If he's clearly ill at ease around you, look at how you're presenting yourself. Assess the tone of your voice. Adapt in order to put him at ease. Uncross your arms. Take a step back, get out of his face. If his every second word is fuck, then your every second word is . . .?'

'Fuck,' Nick said, nodding at the chorus of giggles that ricocheted around the room.

'Correct, Constable Greaves. Mirror his language, make him feel at ease. And by the way, remember, it's not just crooks. Norming is for everyone you run into, every single person you meet during your day. What about the old lady who's called police convinced her neighbours are trying to break into her house and steal her hundred-year-old china teapot?'

Nick raised a hand, another smile on his lips. 'Tell her it's just a fucking teapot, for fuck's sake?'

Laughter. He rode it, revelling in the attention. He was the funny man, the class clown. The world was as it should be. He stole a glance out of his peripherals, the hunched shoulders beside him shaking. Awesome. *She* thought he was funny. And that was all that mattered.

'Yes, yes, very good, Nick,' the DI said, gesturing at the rest of the class to calm down. 'But I was hoping for something more along the lines of, "Oh yes, it's a beautiful teapot, Mrs Bloggs. So exquisitely crafted. Where did you get it from? Was it handed down from your family? Et cetera, et cetera." Make her feel comfortable; reassure her. Somehow I doubt if little old Mrs Bloggs's every second word would be fuck.'

'You haven't met my granny, Inspector,' Nick quipped, rocking on the back legs of his chair, catching the wave and riding it.

Moore gave the class a wink. 'Now *that* would explain a lot, Greaves.'

'Anyway, Nick's foul-mouthed granny aside, this, ladies and gentlemen, is what is commonly referred to as "norming" your suspect, a skill which, as experienced police officers, you should already possess, but one upon which we're going to build in order to turn you into the finest detectives in the state. Now . . .'

As Moore prattled on, Nick slouched again, his cold blue gaze seemingly following Moore's every move, his mind, light years away.

Norming. He'd been practising all right, right from day one of the course. The object of his rehearsals: the girl sitting beside him, his new little friend.

Her boyfriend was in prison? It'd be okay; the two-month sentence would pass in the blink of an eye. The boyfriend didn't want her visiting him in there? It was probably for the best, he wouldn't want her seeing him in that state. She needed to put his wishes first; after all, it was difficult enough without challenging him over everything. She was worried about the so-called boyfriend's future job prospects? Nick himself had contacts in a few different industries; he'd help sort it out. She was sad? He told jokes. She was lonely? He understood loneliness, pointed out the silver linings. She liked dogs? He lovingly described his parents' black and tan bitzers, related stories of their bed-hopping, bone-digging, postman-chasing mischief and flashed photos, much to her delight.

By the middle of week one he'd elicited a smile.

The end of week one, her life story.

The middle of week two, a laugh. Strained, distant, but a laugh nevertheless.

And by the second and final Friday of the course, he was quietly confident – keeping in mind Nick had never been accused of lacking confidence in his entire life – that the groundwork had been firmly and expertly laid. He had normed the fuck out of her and she, *she* who was supposed to be some crack up-and-coming D – *what a joke* – was none the wiser. He almost pissed himself laughing at the thought.

If anyone had asked him why he was spending the time grooming her, he would have assessed it clinically and arrived at three interlinked and overriding factors. Boredom was the biggie. Boredom, followed by the challenge and lastly, the amusement factor. Because when you'd reached his age and tasted more hot, wet, willing pussy than was considered accept- able in polite society, you needed a challenge. And someone like *her*, someone who wasn't the least bit interested in you or what you had on offer, was a challenge, and an amusing one at that.

By lunchtime on the second and final Friday he was moving in for the kill. He trailed behind her at a discreet distance – out of the classroom, past the dark echoing stairwell which slowly filled with yabbering, overexcited cadets, through the double wooden doors and into the food hall. The heavy aroma of deep-fried food, coupled with a somewhat less fortunate scent, something slightly more acrid, more charred, invaded his nose and he rolled his eyes. The deep-fried monstrosity would be fish and chips. Friday lunch was *always* fish and chips. The menu hadn't changed in the decade since he'd been a cadet. The burnt stench was less familiar, more challeng- ing to identify, probably worth avoiding. He sighed. Plastic, frozen fish and half-cooked chips it was then. Boring, but rela- tively safe compared with some of the other dishes he'd seen plated up over the years.

He continued across the polished, parquet floor towards the little hole-in-the-wall servery, glancing out at the windows on his left. Beyond the tired filmy curtains and dirty glass lay the sprawling bitumen of the parade ground, the jumbled grey concrete of the accommodation block, a hint of partially thawed green lawn and, finally, the icy, shadowy waters of Ralphs Bay.

As he neared the serving line he stepped up the pace, catching up and casually taking his place directly behind *her*. It was only twelve-thirty, but already more and more people were arriving. In another five minutes the line would snake out and along the carpet back towards the door. Three cadet courses, two in-service courses, a handful of instructors, guests and miscellaneous uniform hangers-on who, like annoying neighbours and rellies, seemed to miraculously appear in the vicinity at mealtimes.

The low hum of chatter was punctuated by a rainbow of sounds: spurious laughter, a girly shriek, the scrape of chair legs on the floor and the clatter of cutlery against crockery. A serving trolley rumbled past with a squeak and a groan, the old kitchen duck beginning her mind-numbing routine of back and forth, back and forth, collecting soiled plates from the early sitters and placing fresh ones out for the next lucky lot of lunchtime punters.

He ignored the old blue rinse and focused on the short, dark, neatly bunned head thirty centimetres in front of him. Time to execute phase three of his four-part mission.

'Oi!' he said, tapping her softly on the shoulder. 'Come round to my place tonight.' He made it a statement. There was no room for questions in phase three. She jumped and turned, her eyes far away, cheeks flushed, tray clutched across her chest.

'Oh, hi, Nick. Um . . . thanks but I don't really think . . .'

'Look. It'll be nothing major. We'll get a few DVDs, a bottle of . . . what do you drink again?'

'Uh, Bundy. Bundy and Coke.' She turned back to the blue rinse behind the counter. 'Fish, please.'

'Bundy, of course. My favourite too. A bottle of Bundy and Coke and we can . . . you know . . . just hang out. Chicken parma, thanks,' he nodded, peering towards the bain-marie, finally identifying the scent and deciding to take the gamble. The expressionless serving lady slid one of the less burnt ones onto a plate and hovered suggestively over the vegies. He passed and followed Lucy to the salad bar.

'So, I'll see you around seven-thirty then,' he chirped, heaping the tired Friday greens onto the plate beside the parma.

He stole an upwards glance, tried to judge her reaction as she made for the pasta salad. She was definitely hesitating, but it was hardly unexpected. She was after all a bit of a goody-two-shoes. As he'd predicted, she was by this stage on the defensive, assumed he was finally hitting on her.

It called for reassurance. And he was well prepared. He made for the bread basket, keeping it casual.

'Look. I just want to be a *friend*, Luce. That's all. I know you're having a bit of a rough time of it . . . with Cam going to jail and all. But think about it. He wouldn't want you moping around on a Friday night, now would he? You said yourself he wants you to keep chugging along as per normal, not to worry about him.'

380

'I suppose so, but you know, I still don't think . . .'

He held up a hand. In his op order, protestations were given the same weighting as questions. 'And I feel it's my duty, as your friend, to make sure that doesn't happen. Plus, if it makes you feel better, one of my mates from SOG and his girl-friend were going to drop around anyway. They've been on at me for ages about catching up.'

She bit her bottom lip, the trace of reluctance lingering.

'Come *on*, Luce. Please. Don't make me beg. Look. The thing is, I've just bought the place and I haven't had anyone over yet. Consider it a mini house-warming as well as an end-of-course celebration. I'm formally prescribing a night of frivolity to cheer you up. Come on.'

He noted the subconscious dip of her shoulders, the subtle smoothing of the furrowed brow and the lukewarm half-smile that crossed her face, a face that for the past fortnight had reflected little but tear-filled, sleepless nights.

'Well, I guess I don't have anything else planned,' she said reluctantly.

'Good. It's a date then. Not a *date* date, just a date, yeah?' She nodded.

'Beauty. Grab a bite before you head up and I'll see you around seven-thirty. I'll text you the address.'

'Do you want me to bring anything?'

'Nope. Just yourself. I'll grab the DVDs and some nibblies and we'll just switch off, yeah?'

'Um . . . okay,' she agreed, throwing a slice of the usual three-day-old bread on her plate. 'Um . . . I'm just going to go and sit with Renae. We're talking strategies for this after-noon's video interview prac. But I'll see you at seven-thirty.'

He grinned and watched as she walked off. A metre away she turned, her gaze grateful. 'And Nick?'

'Yup?'

'Um . . . thanks. I could do with a laugh right now.'

'Lucky for you, Luce, that's my area of expertise.'

That and my superior cocksmanship, of course.

She turned and left. He paused for a moment by the condiment trolley, scooped a dollop of mayo beside his parma and watched under lowered lids as she ambled across the food hall and joined the chick table. Her movements were slow, awkward, completely lacking in self-confidence. Like she was perpetually afraid of tripping over herself or running into something.

The thought made him smile.

She was the one all right. He'd known it from the second he'd met her two weeks earlier. She might have been going out with that lightweight soft cock Cameron Walsh, but with him safely out of the picture, karma was calling. And not only calling, but calling *his* name.

He felt a laugh rise in his throat, but cut it off dead. Squirting a squiggle of tomato sauce across his parma, he bit the inside of his cheeks and breathed steadily through his nose, just in case someone was watching. There was *always* someone watching him.

As if he just wanted to be friends.

Him. Nick Greaves.

Nick 'I can have any woman I choose' Greaves.

Nick 'you should be so fucking lucky for me to choose you' Greaves.

A faint snigger escaped and he turned quickly away.

Oh no. He wanted much, much more of Lucy Howard.

Now utterly composed, he pulled his huge shoulders back, puffed his pecs out and strolled past the chick table. He approached, *two, three, four steps*, monitored the break in their pointless conversation and slowed his pace, giving them maximum viewing pleasure of his retreating arse. The second he passed, the whispers began again, whispers punctuated by a girly giggle. Understandable, of course. For it didn't matter which neck of the woods they were from, what their viewing preference – arse, legs, smile, hair, eyes; all the usual shit chicks loved – he had something for everyone. The uniform might have done fuck-all for the front bum form, but on him, people sat up and paid attention, everyone except the pair of newbie dykes at the end, that is, whose heads remained bowed in whispered, secretive dyke chatter.

Whatever.

He scoffed inwardly, ambled by. Fucking dykes. There were more and more of the fucktards joining the job, an anomaly that pissed him off no end. With their stupid cropped hair cuts, their stupid walks, like they had balls – *ha, they wish* – their fucking loud mouths and their need to try and outdo the real men all the time, always failing dismally, of course. No. His old man might have been a drunken waste of space most of his life, but he got one thing right: dykes only licked the carpet 'cause they were too fucking ugly to get a man.

End of story.

Nevertheless it paid to be polite. You never knew when you might have to cross paths next. He summoned a quick smile for the dog-ugly bitches before continuing gracefully down to the long white table full of blokes at the far end of the room. Dan Williams sat at one end, an empty seat beside him. *Perfect.*

Nick nodded to the clutch of instructors and dragged out a chair. Dan stopped chewing long enough to give him an upwards nod.

'S'up, homo?' he said.

'Fuck-all. Just gotta get through these interview pracs this arvo and then I'm done.'

'Beats me why you're doing the poxy course in the first place,' Dan scoffed. 'CIB's for pussies. You know, you might as well just stand up on the table and announce that you fuck guys in the arse.'

Nick punched him, his fist glancing off the granite beneath the short-sleeved shirt. 'Scared I'm gonna hit on you, Danielle?'

'Fuck off, you little arse bandit,' he snorted. 'I'd fucking kill you first.'

'Yeah, yeah, before or after you wipe my cum out of your eyes?' Nick grinned.

'Fuck you.'

'You wish. But seriously, there is a point to doing this fucking course. I've gotta have a plan B,' he said, ripping off a huge chunk of the dry old parma that now, upon closer inspec-tion, resembled the sole of a boot.

'What the fuck for? Nothing even comes close to SOG. Fucking CIB and their homolicious suits. Man, you couldn't pay me enough to do that crap.'

'Yeah, I know, dickhead, but in case you hadn't noticed I've had a bung knee, bung ankle and a fucking dislocated shoulder already this year. I'm not getting any younger and there's gonna come a time when I can't do this shit anymore. It might not be tomorrow or the day after, but I've gotta have a backup plan.'

Dan scoffed again. 'Oh, Nichol-arse, Nichol-arse. You, my little princess, need to wipe your tears and go drink a nice big mug of harden-the-fuck-up. But then again, if you'd prefer to ponce around in a skirt, pushing a desk rather than wearing the black jamies and kicking doors in, then that's fine. Leave the *real* work to us *real* men.'

Resisting the urge to punch him again, this time harder and in the region of the nuts, Nick ripped off another piece of the chicken, exposing a pink chunk of gristle and a blood clot the size of a twenty-cent piece. He pushed the plate aside in disgust and munched on his bread roll instead.

'Take the piss all you like, Williams, but when you've done your knee in and get dragged kicking and screaming back to the watch to issue fucking traffic infringement notices and lock up drunks for pissing on the footpath, then we'll see who's laughing.'

'In case you hadn't noticed, my friend, some of us treat our bodies like temples and will still be wearing the black jamies when we're fifty-five.'

Nick laughed. 'Yeah, I suppose that's why you've just polished off your second helping of trifle.'

'And about to head back for round three. You want some?' he said, pushing his chair away from the table.

'Nah. I've gotta go get ready for pracs. What about you? Back on the range this arvo?'

Dan rolled his eyes and lowered his voice. 'Yeah. Lucky fucking me. Spending a whole afternoon trying to teach cadets how to shoot. Most of 'em don't know a barrel from a trigger and wouldn't be able to hit an African elephant standing three metres in front of them with a great big fuck-off target pasted on its huge grey arse.'

Nick chuckled. Dan was a funny fuck for sure.

'Anyway. As much as I think you're a total pussy . . . good luck with the pracs, man. You heading out tonight?'

'Nope.'

'Soft cock.'

'Ah . . . I might be staying in, but I didn't say I was staying in *alone* . . .' he said with a grin.

'Chrissy coming round?'

'Nope.'

'Who then?'

'No one you need to worry your pretty little head about, Williams.'

'Huh. What's with all the secrets?'

'Nothing. Just drop it all right,' Nick said, taking a quick glance back at the chick table. The last thing he needed was Lucy hearing him lining her up. But Dan wasn't going to give up that easily, or quietly.

'Fuck off. You can't say that and then not follow through.'

'Oh, fuck me. Look,' he said in a whisper, 'I *have* got something special in mind, involving a certain young lady. All right? Thought I might introduce her to our *new friend* . . . if you get my drift.'

Dan paused. 'Holy fuck, you're really gonna have a crack?'

'Sure. No one else has had the balls yet. But here's the thing.

Is there any chance of you and Ange popping around tonight for a drink about seven? She's a bit skittish and I need another starter to help break the ice.'

'Anything to be of assistance to you, my brother.'

'Excellent.'

'On the proviso, of course, that you give me a full run-down on all the action.'

Nick laughed. 'Have I ever let you down in that department?'

'Hmm. Come to think of it, I know the ins and outs of *your* dick better than I know my own.'

'Which is saying something considering mine sees fifty times as much action as yours.'

'Fuck you,' Dan said good-naturedly, giving him a dismissive wave and wandering back towards the dessert line. Nick watched as the big guy shouldered his way through the sea of grey-clad cadets. He chuckled at the scene before pushing his chair back and striding out through the double doors towards the classrooms. First things first. Interview. Home. Fourth and final phase.

The afternoon drifted by in a haze. The CIB classroom on the second floor of the training block was stifling, due to some unidentified thermostat problem which maintenance had promised to fix on day one but never got around to. The oppressive aroma was one of stale cigarette smoke lingering on woollen jumpers, sweaty armpits, last-minute cramming and, above all, fear, a stench which had only increased during the day as the mostly seasoned coppers were marched out one by one for their practical video interview exams down the hall.

When his number came up he'd been relieved to escape, even if the alternative consisted of a tiny office under the stairwell where he nervously shuffled his notes of prompts and tried to sound authoritative while grilling Scott Murray Traynor, burglar extraordinaire, aka DI Moore, complete with flannie, dirty jeans and bitch diva attitude from hell.

But by three-thirty, the closing pro forma interview bullshit finally uttered – *Do you wish to make any complaints about the manner in which you've been treated today?* – Nick was quietly confident he'd nailed it. Moore hadn't exactly fallen apart, wept or confessed to being even remotely involved in the make-believe burglary he was accused of but he *had* sought him out afterwards and patted him on the back.

'Good job, Nick. You had me on the run there for a few minutes.'

Ha.

He grinned, adopted his suitably modest look and launched into full on arse-kissing mode, determined to make sure the legendary DI remembered him.

'Thanks, Inspector. It's a bit of a new direction for me, having been in SOG so long, but hopefully it's the start of a new career. Um . . . before I go, do you have any handy hints for me? I know there'll be a written report, but it's always nice to get some immediate feedback from someone as experienced as yourself.'

'Sure. And it's good that you ask. Lets me know that you're keen. Let's see. Just watch it a bit with the leading questions and remember to take your time. I know it's just a prac scenario, but in the real world there's no rush. I've done interviews that have lasted for two days. If that's what it takes to get a result, then that's what it takes. And perhaps most importantly, if you can avoid it, never ask a question that you don't already know the answer to.'

Nick nodded, tried to look thoughtful. 'Thanks, Inspector. That's great. I'll make sure I practise that and look forward to working with you one day, hopefully. There wouldn't be any secondments coming up, would there?'

'Ah . . . actually, yes. There'll be one towards the end of the year. Make sure your name crosses my desk, okay?'

After another suckhole handshake, just to make sure, he shut the door behind him, grinned and swaggered back along the silent corridor eyeballing the evenly spaced hallway mirrors that never usually saw the light of day, thanks to the hordes of pesky cadets who fluttered, straightened, smoothed and preened before them. Outside the CIB classroom he made the most of the silent corridor and looked himself up and down, digging the view.

Piece of piss, my son. Piece of piss.

Pleased with the afternoon's work, he strode back in and took his seat beside Lucy. She turned away from her revision notes, cheeks pale, eyes brimming with last-minute jitters. 'Well?'

'Piece of cake,' he whispered reassuringly. 'You'll be fine.'

She grimaced. 'Easy for you to say.'

But before he could reply their course commander Tania Peterson, aka Vinegar Tits, stalked in on her issue high heels and cut him down with a glare. He flashed her an apologetic smile and settled back in his seat watching her fossick about with what appeared to be a list of names on her lectern. Vinegar Tits inspired only contempt, especially in her students. The tiny birdlike creature with the icy, don't fuck with me eyes and tight cat's arse lips had never done a real day's policing in her life. She knew it. The class knew it. Her colleagues knew it. She'd been promoted after coincidentally spending six months fucking the head of the promotion board, a crusty, dried-up arsehole of an excuse for a bloke. It was a price, upon reflection, that Nick thought was way too high – on both their behalves. To make matters worse, if being a talentless halfwit promoted way beyond her capabilities wasn't bad enough, she made up for her own pathetic insecurities by being a bitch to anyone below the rank of sergeant who happened to cross her path, gender notwithstanding. And the hatred was returned tenfold.

Indeed, Vinegar Tits would have wet her panties had she had any inkling of the conversations that bounced off the accommodation block walls at night invoking her name, mostly involving the one remedy they prescribed for her perpetual grouchiness.

Needs a good root.

He threw his hands behind his head and yawned. Vinegar Tits finished perusing her list and zeroed in on Lucy.

'You're next, Howard. And hurry up. Inspector Moore doesn't have all day.'

Lucy sighed, shuffled her chair backwards and steadied herself with one hand on the desk looking as though she might keel over at any given moment.

'See you tonight. Break a leg,' he whispered, stifling another laugh as she tripped over one of her chair legs, dropped her notes, gathered them up again hurriedly and stumbled out of the room as though she was headed to the guillotine.

He was home by five, relieved to finally be the hell away from the academy. The neat ground-level two-bedroom flat on Augusta Road, the main drag of Lenah Valley, was his first venture into the real estate game. The location was good. It mightn't have been Sandy Bay, Battery Point or Tranmere, but it sure as hell wasn't fucking Gagebrook, Claremont or Bridge-water. There was an acceptable strip of shops, a tiny stretch of mud, tanbark and patches of African feather grass doing its best impression of a park, an RSL, a hospital, but best of all, the distinct absence of housing commission scummers. It might have been a little too far north, a smidgeon too close to Glenorchy, but as far as he was concerned, it was firmly south of the Flannelette Curtain. And therefore satisfactory.

He'd picked it up at auction, moved in at the beginning of May and chucked the last of the flattened packing boxes into a handy skip the weekend before. The kitchen was stocked and the lounge fully functional – gigantic plasma, pine coffee table and overstuffed couches being all he needed. The boudoir was similarly sorted, the work bench inviting with its freshly washed sheets and doona. By seven he'd had a leisurely trip to the supermarket, a fleeting stop at the bottlo, a hasty spring clean and a shower. It was all systems go.

He took one last look around the bedroom and nodded in satisfaction before focusing back on the image reflected in the full-length mirror before him, one of three in the flat.

He tucked his shirt into his jeans, frowned, pulled it out again, turned, paused and tucked it back in, loosening it so it rested casually over his low-slung belt.

Perfect.

A few months earlier it had crossed his mind to put in for the next season of *Make Me a Supermodel*; after all, he was way hotter than most of the fucking wieners on the current series. But luckily for the next batch of contestants he'd run out of time. For when he wasn't working, he was training. And when he wasn't training, he was fucking. And such was his life. Work. Train. Fuck. Not necessarily in that order. But regardless, he'd missed the application date.

He turned for another admiring gaze. At one-ninety-three centimetres, it was as though clothes were designed especially for him. Smaller guys, shorter guys, looked like pipsqueaks trying to pull off the latest fashions, but *he* looked awesome. And it wasn't just his height. The years of training had paid off too. His baggy Levi's were appropriately snug while accentuating his arse. His fitted blue, short-sleeved shirt mirrored his eyes and made his biceps look massive. Which left his feet. At the last minute he'd chucked off his brown loafers, deciding on a more casual, round-the-house look with a pair of navy socks.

All the better to make Lucy feel comfortable.

He swept a hand through his closely cropped dark hair and practised his warmest, most welcoming smile, congratulating himself on money well spent for the teeth whitening he'd endured a couple of weeks back. A quick mist of Versace's Black Jeans and he was in business, just in time for the knock at the door.

Irresistible.

He paused, flashed a final winning smile at the hallway mirror and sashayed to the front door.

'Dan, Ange, come in, guys. Glad you could make it,' he said with a mischievous wink which went totally over Ange's airhead. He didn't mind Dan's chick, as far as women went, but the bottle-blonde hairdresser with the crow's feet, Spak-fillaed make-up and the demeanour of a doped-out golden retriever wasn't even remotely his type. In fact, it remained a constant source of amazement to him that old Dan had managed to keep his dick in his pants during their eight- or nine-year history; well, apart from the barmaid with the big tits at the Brooke Street Grill. But that had only been a couple of times so it didn't really count.

Dan and Ange had been 'Dan and Ange' for as long as he could remember.

She leaned in for her usual air kisses and he played along with the wanky *mwah, mwah*.

'Hi, Nicky, you're looking delicious as usual. How've you been?'

'Good, Ange. It's been too long.'

'Mmm. The salon's been flat out over the last few months. I haven't had time for anything much lately. Speaking of which . . .'

She took a step back and examined him, a frown crossing her plastic features. 'Has someone else been cutting your hair, you naughty boy? Why didn't you come back and see me?'

'Cause you spend the whole appointment talking at me. Not to mention the fact that you can't cut hair for shit.

Dan scoffed, herding her inside with a light tap on the

bottom. 'Enough, woman. We didn't come here to give the man the third degree. Can't stay long, mate. We're meeting a group of Ange's workmates out at the Caz at tennish. You wanna come?'

Nick winked again. 'Nah. I'm gonna have a quiet one in. But come in and make yourselves at home.'

Nick headed for the kitchen, cracked a couple of Cascades while Ange threw herself onto one of the couches, switched on the telly and made herself immediately at home.

'Beer, Ange?' he yelled.

'Yes, please. Ooooh. *Find My Family*. I just looooove this show.'

Dan trailed after Nick, perched in the alcove between the kitchen and the lounge and rolled his eyes. 'That fucking show. Classic. Can you imagine; you spend a lifetime searching for your biological father and when you track 'em down, they're some filthy, toothless alcoholic or at best a brain-dead, fucked-up retard ex-con who lives in some shitbox in Gagebrook, has thirteen other kids, a wife on a disability pension and fifty warrants out for his arrest. Fuck me. Personally, I'd rather be bent over and fucked up the arse with a flaming witch's hat than admit I shared the same DNA as any of the losers they manage to dredge up on that show. No doubt about it.'

Nick chuckled, handed him a beer.

'Don't be so mean, Dan,' Ange tutted, turning up the volume.

'Truth hurts.'

'Not that you'd know,' she said, swivelling back to the telly. Right on cue, a shrivelled bogan with a hunch and pasty skin pulled taut over his protruding cheekbones flashed up on screen. He smiled, a solitary brown tooth peering from between his lips as he dragged deeply on a ciggie, gave a thick phlegmy cough and explained how he couldn't wait to introduce his new 'daughter' to her five other half-siblings. Luke, who was closest in age to her, had just been released from Goulburn, for a crime he didn't commit, of course, and was just hangin' to meet her.

'Ah. Fuck it's hard being right all the time,' Dan smirked.

But Ange wasn't conceding. 'They're not *all* retarded.'

'All right. You're glued to this shit every week. Tell me, when was the last time you saw a long-lost rello who runs their own business, wears clean clothes, speaks instead of grunts . . . seriously, Ange . . .'

Nick ignored their bickering. From the corner of his eye he saw a vehicle pull up outside the flat.

A purple Hyundai Excel.

Brilliant.

He grinned, made for the door and stepped out onto the porch. Gave her a wave.

Here we go.

'Hey, hey, hey, glad you could come.'

She slammed the car door, shoved the last of her KFC burger into her mouth and balled the wrapper in her other hand. He gave her the once-over. Out of uniform, the girl was a looker. Not model stunning, but far from plain. Black three-quarter-length pants and a shimmery pink top that clung nicely to her tits. He did a quick visual stocktake.

Waist? Small enough to get my hands around in one go.

Tits? Firm. Even. The perfect handful.

Arse? Tight, round. Would look perfectly at home bouncing

up and down on my cock . . . if the circumstances were different.

Perrrfect.

The arse was super important. There was nothing worse than a hot chick with a flat, droopy mummy's arse. No such problem with young Miss Howard though.

The thick chestnut-brown hair that hung down past her shoulderblades finished off the portrait nicely and he wondered for a moment what it would look like cascading down her naked back.

Oh yeah. You are on the money, Nicholas.

As she inched nervously towards the front door, he couldn't help but think how terribly young she looked. Or perhaps it was just her nerves making her look like a scared little kid. Twenty-two might have been young compared to the other occupants in the house, but it wasn't *that* young.

And anyway, as the old saying goes, if there's grass on the wicket it's time to play cricket.

He grinned as she paused for a moment on the front porch and held up the burger wrapper. 'Sorry, I should have asked if you wanted me to grab you one.'

'Nah, I ate earlier. Anyway, come in, come in. You made it through the prac okay then?' he asked, ushering her in, his fingertips grazing the small of her back.

'Uh, yeah. It was fine.' She turned, flushed, stepped hurriedly away from his touch. His eyes lingered on her arse, and as he closed the door behind them, locking the world out, he wondered what lay beneath the black pants. She didn't seem like the Brazilian type – a little too old-fashioned, way too much of a goody-two-shoes. She'd be au naturel no doubt. The thought amused him. He couldn't recall the last unplucked, unshaved, unsculpted, undyed twat he'd laid eyes on. *Hmm.* It'd be a pleasant change to have something different on the menu.

In the lounge, the tearful melodrama continued, complete with cheesy, heart-rending soundtrack and carefully measured solemn, monotone male voice-over. *But Paddy has been living with a secret. He's been anxiously waiting to hear from his daughter Kylie for twenty-three years, ever since she was born. Since the day he was forced to walk out on her mother and was subsequently sentenced to six months' jail for having underage sex with her . . .*

Dan, now perched on the couch beside Ange, howled in victory, then made a quip about Jack Thompson having gone to the same voice-over school as Bernard Curry, Damian Walsh-Howling and Grant fucking Bowler. Ange continued her vigorous defence. Lucy hovered uncertainly.

'Oi, guys, this is Lucy Howard; we've been on the CIB course together. Lucy, this is Dan and Ange.'

She gave a nervous wave. 'Nice to meet you.'

Ange merely nodded, still engrossed in the show. Dan leaned forwards to shake Lucy's hand. 'You're on the watch then?'

'Yeah, shift two.'

'Ah . . . but not for long, Dan. Rumour has it that Lucy will be climbing the ladder to CIB within the next twelve months,' Nick interrupted.

'Oh, I don't know about that,' she said with a shy smile.

'Well, I hear CIB's great. The best place to be if you want to get ahead in the job,' Dan said, throwing a wink in Nick's direction and watching him roll his eyes behind Lucy's back.

'Now. Drinkies. Bundy Red and Coke, Luce?' Nick asked, heading for the kitchen at her hesitant nod. He grabbed the ice container from the freezer, paused and listened to the conversation unfolding in the lounge. Hopefully Dan wouldn't be too much of a smart-arse about the whole CIB thing. It was one thing to take the piss out of *him*, but another entirely to start in on Lucy about it.

'So, you're in the SOG with Nick then?'

'Sure am. And aside from CIB, I have to say there's no better job in the whole of TasPol. I've been doing it for most of my career now. Tried out for the squad the second I got shot of my cadet course. It took a couple of goes to get in as they reckoned I was too junior, but . . .'

Nick relaxed, set about mixing the drinks for Lucy and himself. Dan could brag about work for years and not get bored. Throwing a handful of ice cubes in both plastic tumblers – *pink for girls, blue for boys* – he poured a generous nip of the thick honey-gold liquid into each, added another nip to the pink for luck and topped them both with Coke before heading back to the lounge.

'Sorry about the crystal ware,' he joked. 'I still haven't unpacked all of my boxes.'

'*How* long have you been here?' Dan asked.

'Not quite a month.'

Lucy took a sip of the smooth liquor, closed her eyes, stifled a cough. 'Whoa. That's got some kick.'

'The perfect end to an exhausting two weeks,' Nick said, thrusting a bowl of barbecue Samboys onto the coffee table before plonking next to Lucy and smiling. 'Kick your shoes off and make yourself at home.'

'Um ... okay,' she said, taking another long sip of the Bundy. Black sandals were removed and kicked to one side. A quick glance from his peripherals confirmed that she was relaxing; the colour returned to the knuckles that were clenched around the drink and her shoulders dropped.

Perfect.

Once long-lost father Paddy had been firmly reunited with daughter Kylie, the product of his statutory rape, the final credits rolled and the entire cast burst into tears. Dan insisted loudly that the chick was only crying because she realised she should have left the past in the past. Ange stuck to her guns and eventually told him to get fucked. *Find My Family* then morphed into one of the many reality cop shows that inspired tears, this time of mirth, in the small audience gathered before it.

'*RBT*. You're kidding me, right?' Dan said indignantly. 'That's what they called this show?'

'Why not?' Nick quipped. 'It conjures up such an . . . *exciting* image.'

'Yeah. Let me think. Rain. Frozen hands. Frozen face. Hours full of attitude from smart-arse drivers and if you're lucky, a blower at the end of it all so you get to spend the next fifty million hours doing a court file. You're telling me that's exciting? Jesus Christ. What's next? A reality show about watching fucking grass grow?'

'No offence, Dan,' Nick said, turning to Lucy and winking. 'But . . . when *exactly* did you last stand at an RBT site?'

Ange sniggered. 'Good one, Nicky.'

'Oi. Whose side are you on?'

Their squabbling took off again, gathered pace. But Nick's mind was elsewhere. He'd been watching Lucy's tumbler, growing fidgety and irritated by the fact that she was sipping her second drink for the night in tiny, slow, half-mouthfuls.

That won't do.

He leaned over and cut through the banter. 'I'm going to the kitchen. Can I top that up for you, Luce?'

'Oh. No, thanks. I'd better take it easy. I don't want to get put on the breatho on the way home. Wouldn't want to find myself on one of these shows,' she smiled. 'Two's enough for tonight.'

'No worries,' he said, draining his own tumbler and making for the kitchen where he paused, emptied another bag of chips into a bowl and composed himself before heading back out.

Dan and Ange made their polite exit shortly before nine-thirty, still bickering about the pros and cons of reality TV all the way out the door and down the front path. 'Thanks for coming, old boy,' Nick said, smacking Dan on the back. 'See you Monday, yeah?'

'Yeah,' he said, his eyes following Ange as she made her way to the truck and clicked the lock open. 'All going according to plan then?'

Nick tapped his nose with one finger. 'I hope so.'

Dan laughed, headed for the car. 'In that case, don't do anything I wouldn't do. Not that I imagine you will for a second, because I'm pretty sure you're a total pussy.'

'Yeah, yeah,' Nick said, giving him the finger.

'All right. See you then, buddy.'

'Bye.'

He clicked the door shut. In the semi-darkness Lucy was perched on the edge of the couch, eyes like a possum in the headlights, clearly uncomfortable at being left alone with him.

'Um . . . I'd really better think about going too, Nick . . .'

Not a chance.

'Come on, Luce. The night is young. Just one more drink and half an hour of the DVD. If you're still yawning by ten, then I'll give up on you.'

He handed her the DVD and the remote control, picked up the pink and blue tumblers and headed for the kitchen again, cutting off all further opportunities for protest. She was too polite to insist. Just as he'd thought.

'Just make mine a half,' she called after him. 'That was pretty strong before.'

'Done!' He popped the two tumblers onto the counter and tiptoed back to the archway, watching silently. The back of her head. The crack of the *Top Gun* DVD case. The rattle of disc into player. A barely audible sigh of resignation. Cheesy, synthesised eighties melody with high-pitched, tinny bass. The roar of an F-14 Tomcat filling all six speakers and drowning the lounge. And another. Louder than the first. Voices over a loudspeaker. A heavy, repetitive, bass guitar riff pulling him back to his childhood. Kenny Loggins. 'Danger Zone'.

The silhouette sank back into the couch.

Turning back and humming, he pulled the ice from the freezer and rattled a few pieces into each cup. His heartbeat quickened, pulsing in time to the music, his hands trembled as he reached for the Bundy and unscrewed the top, pouring a serious full nip into both tumblers. As another F-14 roared overhead he dug into the space at the back of the pantry, underneath the box of tea bags and fished out the small white pill he'd stashed in there earlier. It seemed tiny, harmless, as it rolled between his fingertips. A pressie from Dan who'd inadvertently scored a whole bloody bag of the things, courtesy of his roid dealer who'd come up short on his regular order. *A little something special on the house for a valued client.* Sure, Dan'd dished them out to a few of their trusted mates up at Apollos, but as far as Nick knew, no one else had had the balls to use them yet.

In the lounge, Maverick and Goose were notified of an inbound intruder approaching. Status unknown.

He topped both drinks with Coke and slipped the little white dream into the pink tumbler. He watched, a cold smile spreading across his face as it slipped under the black surface and fizzed into nothingness. Undetectable.

Invisible.

Odourless.

Tasteless.

Perfect.

And after a quick stir and a prod around with the spoon brought nothing to the surface, he finally managed to breathe.

From the lounge, Cougar panicked about the baddie having a missile lock on them.

Nick flicked off the range hood light, thought better of it, flicked it on again, picked up the tumblers and joined her on the couch, thrusting the pink one into her outstretched hand.

'Cheers,' he yelled over the roar of the MiG on Cougar's tail. He grabbed a handful of chips and settled back. Waiting and watching. Waiting and watching. She took a couple of long sips of her drink before placing the tumbler on the coffee table and leaning back as Cougar now panicked about running out of fuel.

The actor's agitated dialogue spiked and bubbled on Nick's lips, the words memorised to perfection during child-hood, only to be miraculously conjured up out of thin air and regurgitated some twenty years on. While Cougar panicked and Maverick soothed, Nick's eyes dropped from the screen to the still full pink tumbler, his fingers tapping impatiently on the back of the couch.

He reached casually forwards for the bowl of chips and swung it in her direction. She obliged and he bit his lip when not ten seconds later she reached for the pink tumbler, taking a couple of big quenching gulps. Right on cue.

On the screen, Maverick yelled. They were coming in too low.

The vision blurred, an aircraft carrier hazily out of reach, the music pounding a steady, insistent rhythm through the speakers.

Wheels touched down and a stellar career ended with an arse reaming from the boss and a badge thrown across the table. The drama peaked. Nick reached for the chip bowl again, swung it before her. She refused with an open palm. He insisted.

'Come on, I don't want any leftovers. I'll only eat them for breakfast which is bad for my waistline. Eat up.'

She grinned, grabbed another fistful and washed it down seconds later with another couple of gulps of her drink. He focused on the screen and vowed to count to sixty before looking again.

Maverick and Goose earned themselves a trip to Top Gun.

The guitar riff again. 'Danger Zone'.

Fifty-eight, fifty-nine, sixty. A stolen peripheral glance. He swallowed, struggling to keep a straight face at her bowed head and droopy eyelids.

Holy fuck. It's actually working.

Better test the waters.

'Come on now, Luce, I know you're tired, but you're not gonna go nodding off mid-movie, are you?' he joked, sitting forwards.

Her eyes flicked open, but were unmistakably glazed in the darkness of the lounge. 'Sorry,' she murmured. 'Must have been a longer week than I thought. I'm just so tired all of a sudden . . .'

He smiled. 'That's okay. It's been a hell of a fortnight. Hey, it's been a hell of a month for you with Cam and court and everything. You're welcome to crash on the couch if you want. I understand totally.'

She shook her head drowsily, attempting a half-hearted protest. 'I should really be going . . .'

Before them, Maverick encountered his nemesis for the very first time and Nick, briefly distracted, marvelled at how Val Kilmer, a young, slick montage of pearly whites, blond tips and cockiness had grown paunchy, middle-aged and depressingly obscure in the years that had passed. But then again, Tom Cruise had turned out to be a couch-jumping weirdo and Kelly McGillis, a fucking dyke, so maybe Val got off lightly. Nick chuckled as Iceman lit up the screen with his rapid-fire sarcasm.

He looked back to Lucy and had to smother a giggle at her nods. He bit his lip, adopted his sternest father-figure voice. 'Lucy, you're not driving anywhere if you're this tired. I'm not going to be responsible for you drifting off behind the wheel. Now just relax, finish your drink and we'll sort it out at the end of the movie.'

She nodded, eyes still half closed, and he turned back to the screen.

Three minutes and you're mine, Lucy Howard.

He counted silently while Maverick and Iceman faced off in the bar. An array of eighties-looking chicks with eighties hair and eighties make-up shimmied and flirted, the jukebox pumped a generic eighties synth.

Goose challenges Mav.

Kelly McGillis rolls into shot on cue.

'You've Lost That Lovin' Feeling' fills the bar.

Maverick smirks, the mike is seized and the seduction began.

Nick grinned and pointed as the bar joined in the chorus. 'This is my favourite bit. Used to watch it about twenty times a day on video as a kid.'

When she didn't reply, he looked over. Her eyes were now fully closed and her chin had sunk to her chest. He quivered with excitement and leaned over to check her cup. It was almost empty.

Holy fuck. It's working. The fucking thing is working.

He leaned towards her and listened to the steady, regular breathing, waving one hand daringly before her eyes as though she was blind.

'Lucy? Can you hear me?'

A groan rumbled in her throat and she sank back into the couch, her head lolling and coming to rest on the thick blue arm.

He gave her a little shake on one shoulder. Better to be safe than sorry.

'Lucy?'

This time there was no response. He sat back, his eyes wide. Up until now it had just been an amusing idea, but all of a sudden, here she was slumped before him. The movie played on, the familiar scenes now long forgotten. Completely irrelevant. He wanted to clap his hands, ring Dan to laugh out loud, take a photo, anything. Well, actually, not a photo. Only the stupidest of bastards would get caught with a fucking photo. But still. It was fucking awesome whichever way you looked at it.

But first he had to check, see how far he could go with it. He reached for the remote and flicked the telly off. In the light of the eerie glow casting from the range hood in the kitchen he leaned over, picked her bare feet up from the floor and pulled them onto the couch, stretching her out. He stopped, drank in the perfection of the scene he'd created, before reaching across and lightly kissing her. Bundy and chips danced from her slack lips to his.

He pulled back, tried to gauge her reaction but . . . there was nothing. Satisfied, he ran a fingertip lightly across her left breast, feeling the nipple rise to his touch.

'Lucy?'

'Mmmmmmmm?'

He jumped back, the soft hiss almost knocking him sideways in surprise. He hadn't been expecting that.

What to do, what to do?

Does that mean she's not completely out of it?

Should I wait a little longer?

Or . . . is the fact that she can mumble but isn't protesting an even better outcome? At least, if the world turned to shit and she decided to kick up a stink, saying he'd got her drunk and seduced her – for she'd never in a million years guess about the pill – her talking now added to his defences.

Not that she would kick up a stink.

After all, he'd chosen the perfect specimen to begin with. Shy, self-conscious, a bit of a loner. Plus, thanks to his meticulous planning, Dan and Ange could vouch for the fact that she'd been boozing and could well have seduced *him* once they left.

No. Mumbling is fine.

Refuelled with confidence, he leaned in again and monitored her deep, rhythmic breathing before taking the next step.

'Lucy,' he said calmly. 'You're out of it. You've had too much to drink so I'm going to insist you stay over, all right?'

She managed a faint sigh, softer than the last. He stood up and looked over the sleeping form for an instant before bending down and scooping her up. Her neck hung from the crook of his elbow, her head rolled back and forth and her mouth fell slightly, comically, open as he took the first step. An arm dangled, the thin wrist leading the way through the kitchen and hall towards his bedroom. He placed her gently on the black and red doona and took a step back, flicking on the bedside lamp, pushing a strand of hair off her cheek and studying her face for any sign of waking. Satisfied, he smiled once more before taking the hem of her pink top in both hands and peeling it over her head like he was skinning a rabbit. The material was soft, warm to his fingertips. He folded it neatly in half, placed it on the floor.

Slowly.

It has to be done slowly.

You don't know when you'll get another opportunity like this.

Savour it.

At the sight of the naked shoulders, the black bra and the firm breasts, his cock hardened and pressed against the denim of his jeans. He closed his eyes, his mind swimming, and wondered if he'd ever been this turned on in his entire fucking life.

He exhaled, opened his eyes, licked his lips and moved to unzip her pants, his fingers still shaking. He lifted her hips and peeled them down to reveal a pair of off-white Bonds undies that had seen better days. He continued, pulling them down her thighs, calves and over the ankles before folding and adding them to the pile.

Oh yeah. Now we're in business.

A low, mirthless chuckle rumbled in his throat. He stopped again, savouring the sight of the unconscious, near-naked copper before him. According to Dan he had a window of at least three hours to play with. There was no way in hell he was going to rush this experience.

He lowered his head, pressed his face against her warm, silent flesh, closed his eyes and drank in her scent . . .

'All rise!'

The call from the court clerk snapped him out of his

reverie and he struggled to his feet. Woodsy beckoned for him to approach the bench as Hudson strode in and assumed his position.

Woodsy, as senior counsel, leapt in, giving no one else the chance to take over the afternoon with their second-rate formal matters.

'Your Honour in terms of formal matters today, I represent the defendant in the matter of the Crown versus Greaves. We have been informed by the Crown that the matter can be resolved this afternoon.'

'Is that correct, Mr Short?' Hudson asked briskly, shuffling through the papers on his desk.

'Correct, Your Honour.' Shorty rose to his feet. 'After much consultation, the Crown will not be seeking to indict Mr Greaves on the charge before you. We request that the matter be adjourned sine die and that Mr Greaves be free to leave.'

Hudson peered over the top of his glasses and scribbled on the paperwork before him. Nick held his breath.

'In that case, I'm left with no alternative but to agree to the prosecution's submission. The matter will be adjourned sine die, that is, permanently stayed. Mr Greaves, you are free to leave.'

Free to leave.

The words washed over him like warm summer rain.

Free to leave.

It was over. He'd won. There'd be no hearing, no giving evidence, no ramifications. He exhaled slowly, feeling the weight of the past few weeks melt from his bones.

'Well done, hun,' Chrissy whispered, flinging her arms around him and planting a quick peck on his cheek. From the other side, a relieved-looking Dan clapped him on the back.

'Good work, brother.'

And he grinned, really grinned, for the first time in weeks.

It was over. The tension swept away, making way to a surge of bravado. Howard, Moore, Torino, dyke bitch and Shorty could kiss his arse.

Fuckers.

Fucking losers.

A hushed ripple ran through the spectators while the magistrate called for the next case. Unable to resist, Nick swivelled around to look at the bitch's cheer squad. He locked eyes with a clearly furious Torino, grinned and tapped the side of his nose. Torino rose, hatred burning in his features, but was pulled back down by Moore who whispered in his ear. Nick grinned again, thrilled to know he'd got under his skin.

That's right, wog. Two up on you now, buddy. Not only did I fuck your wife, but I fucked you and your little mates as well.

Nick rose, smoothed down the creases in his suit and gave Woodsy a big thumbs up. The lawyer nodded back before shuffling his papers together, closing his briefcase and springing to his feet. He gave Nick a hasty pat on the back before he hightailed it towards the door. 'Well done, mate. Sorry I've got to run. Got an urgent one next door. But we'll be in touch, yeah?' And with that he was gone.

Not wanting to wait around for a second longer than he was required, Nick leaned over to Chrissy and Dan and whispered, 'Come on then, soft cocks. What are you waiting for?'

He gave Torino a final wink and headed straight for the door charging through it to freedom, grinning all the way. First stop – spread the good news that he'd wiped the floor with the bitch. Second stop – tell the boss he'd be back at work first thing Monday. Third stop – gather the supporters. Final stop – pub.

He let out a long, steady breath and without waiting for the hangers-on, walked down the stairs, out the door and into the cold, dwindling sunshine.

Epilogue

3.15 pm Friday 22 July

Lucy trudged along Liverpool Street towards the police station, shoulders hunched, eyes to the footpath, stomach churning at the thought of her four o'clock start. But at the bottom of the courthouse stairs she stopped and shivered in the late-afternoon sunlight. Something was happening up by the front door. Something that would enable her to put off the inevitable for a few more seconds. She wrapped her red woollen coat tighter in an attempt to block out the bitter wind that whipped down the street and watched as the commotion unfolded. The commissioner, tall, serious and commanding, made his defiant statement and her eyes widened with each word that fell from his lips.

Interviewed.

Charged.

413

Standing aside.

The scene was almost surreal and it took her a moment to digest his words. But almost before she could do so, he indicated that the brief statement was over and the media descended on him like a pack of footy players in a scrum. They jostled, microphones thrust in his face, cameras held high, questions shouted. Somewhere off in the distance, against the backdrop of their excited crescendo, Lucy was vaguely conscious of the faint wail of a police car against the howl of the raw winter wind.

She loitered in disbelief at the bottom of the stairs as Chalmers's words melded into the wind. Seconds later he emerged from the pack and pushed his way down the stairs, leaving the media machine buzzing and humming with obvious disappointment at his failure to answer their questions.

As the full meaning of the scene sank in, she felt a mild flush of warmth against the iciness of the day and almost smiled. It seemed as though finding the silver lining was becoming easier as the days went on. And God knew she'd been given plenty of opportunities to search for it.

To begin with, her case against Nick was being formally dismissed that very day. He would not be held accountable for his actions and would perhaps grow stronger, even more manipulative, moving on to another victim. But there was nothing more she could have done. And in a way, the thought comforted her.

Cam was gone from her life. It had indeed been too good to be true. Too wonderful to last. But then again she'd predicted as much the moment she left Nick's unit that Saturday morning in May. A phone call to Kurt the day after her meeting with the DPP had revealed, much to Kurt's discomfort, that Cam had done a runner in all senses of the word. Fled to London to be with some long-lost girlfriend. Although Lucy was devastated, she was realistic enough to know that she'd survive. She'd never trust anyone with her heart again, but she'd pull on her big-girl panties, plaster a fake grin to her face and get on with it, vowing to follow in the footsteps of her mother – never to do emotion again.

It was far too painful.

Cam, even more so than Nick, had taught her a valuable lesson: not only could you not trust anyone, but you couldn't rely on anyone, no matter how much you wanted to.

Then there was the added issue of her mother. The woman who, according to all the theories in the world, should have been the one person to believe in her, support her and love her in her time of need, when, in reality, she had engaged in a protracted campaign of ignoring both Lucy and her plight – hoping that if the so-called 'unpleasant situation' wasn't acknowledged, then it couldn't possibly be real.

But much like the situation with Cam, Lucy had spent the week mulling over her mother's reaction, trying valiantly to take something positive from it. And at last it had come to her. It was time to break free from twenty-two years of maternal disapproval. Time to grow up. To leave the family home and to find her own place. Somewhere she could finally be herself without living in fear of judgement every second of the day. With that thought, the long-term future no longer seemed quite so bleak.

And her new-found, albeit tentative, sense of liberation and bravado, was readily applicable to the whole work situation as well. Her colleagues might have been revelling in finding new and creative ways to prolong her agony, to let her know that she was the station leper, but she was able to remind herself daily that their torment would eventually end. They couldn't keep it up forever. She'd show them that she wasn't going anywhere and that it'd take more than their current campaign of threats, whispers and bullying to bring her unstuck.

And as she stood in front of the courthouse, she realised that there was now one final, surprising consolation. The brightest thought amid the darkness, the uncertainty, the bitter chill of reality.

The commissioner.

His story would be big. Bigger than big. Front page. And that was something indeed.

She, Lucy Howard, was clearly yesterday's news and the quicker the rumour mill cranked up around the station, as it would, the quicker her own sorry story would hopefully fade into obscurity.

More than a little comforted by the thought, she sighed, stuck her hands in the pockets of her coat, pulled her shoulders back and walked slowly towards the station – alone, defeated, but not entirely without hope.

Acknowledgements

Many thanks to my sister-in-law Liz Erskine for reading the earliest version of this manuscript and contributing such thoughtful, valuable feedback. Thanks also in this respect to my wonderful husband Sam for reading, discussing, clarifying and encouraging.

Continued thanks to my awesome agent Sophie Hamley for her constant support and enthusiasm for this project . . . and for answering all of my annoying questions about ebooks!

To my publisher Beverley Cousins from Random House – it has been delightful working with you on this manuscript. Your suggestions, advice and support throughout the entire process have been invaluable.

To the extremely talented team at Random House – in particular, my fantastic editors Roberta Ivers and Virginia Grant. I don't know how you do it, but like the sign on the CMU door, you do indeed 'turn my shit into gold'.

To my amazing publicist Shannon Lane who has worked tirelessly over the past twelve months promoting both books. You do such an incredible job behind the scenes and I'm so thankful to have you.

Finally, back to Sam. I recently read Lionel Shriver's *So Much for That* and was surprised by her comment in the acknowledgements that 'novelists thanking spouses for their amazing patience during the agony of artistic creation gets pretty tired'. Well, sorry, Lionel, but I'm going to respectfully disagree and go there anyway. I've said it before and I'm going to say it again. Not only has my husband been the epitome of patience, but he has been my greatest advocate, my greatest defender, my greatest supporter – emotionally and financially. Without him, I would not have had the opportunity to pursue my dream to become a published author and for that, there is nothing I can ever say or do that will enable me to thank him enough. I'm truly blessed to have him in my life.

About the Author

Yvette Erskine spent eleven years in the Tasmania Police Service. She was active in front-line policing and served as a detective in the CIB. She is also an historian with an honours degree in Early Modern History. Yvette lives in Melbourne and is happily married with two dogs.

Photo: Blush Photography, South Yarra

The Brotherhood

Y.A. ERSKINE

One dead cop . . . One small island . . .
An impact that will last a lifetime . . .

When Sergeant John White, mentor, saviour and
all-round good guy, is murdered during a routine
call-out, the tight-knit world of Tasmania Police is rocked
to the core.

An already difficult investigation into the death of one of
their own becomes steeped in political complexities when the
main suspect is identified as Aboriginal and the case, courtesy
of the ever-hostile local media, looks set to make Palm Island
resemble a Sunday afternoon picnic in comparison. And as
the investigation unfolds through the eyes of the sergeant's
colleagues, friends, family, enemies and the suspect himself, it
becomes clear that there was a great deal more to John White
– and the squeaky-clean reputation of the nation's smallest
state police service – than ever met the eye.

The Brotherhood is a novel about violence, preconceptions,
loyalties, corruption, betrayal and the question a copper
should never need to ask: just who can you trust?

'A compelling tale . . . One not to be missed' *Canberra Times*

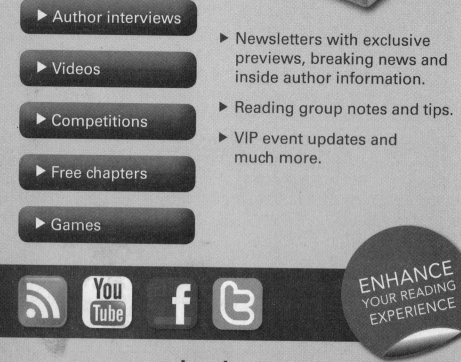